KT-407-665

The Things
I should
have told
You

Harrington lives with her husband, Roger, and
, Amelia and Nate, in a small coastal village in
. She credits the idyllic setting as a constant source
piration to her. She has won several international
s including Kindle Book of the Year and Romantic
of the Year at the Festival of Romance in 2013.
age-turning novels are published worldwide and
been translated into eight languages so far.

el is a regular on Irish TV as one of the panelists
3's *Midday* show and writes feauture articles for
sh Independent. She is also a popular motivational
at events in Ireland, UK and US.

is the chairperson of the Wexford Literary Festival,
she co-founded.

To find out more about Carmel, go to
www.carmelharrington.com

X400 000003 8336

Also by Carmel Harrington

Beyond Grace's Rainbow
The Life You Left
Every Time a Bell Rings

CARMEL HARRINGTON

The Things
I should
have told
You

HARPER

Wolverhampton City Council	
X400 000003 8336	
Askews & Holts	06-Feb-2017
	£7.99
	TR

Copyright © Carmel Harrington 2017

Carmel Harrington asserts the moral right to
be identified as the author of this work

A catalogue record for this book
is available from the British Library

ISBN: 978-0-00-815010-5

This novel is entirely a work of fiction.
The names, characters and incidents portrayed in it are
the work of the author's imagination. Any resemblance to
actual persons, living or dead, events or localities is
entirely coincidental.

Set in Sabon LT by Palimpsest Book Production Limited,
Falkirk, Stirlingshire

Printed and bound in Great Britain by
Clays Ltd, St Ives plc

All rights reserved. No part of this publication may be
reproduced, stored in a retrieval system, or transmitted,
in any form or by any means, electronic, mechanical,
photocopying, recording or otherwise, without the prior
permission of the publishers.

MIX
Paper from
responsible sources
FSC C007454

FSC™ is a non-profit international organisation established to promote
the responsible management of the world's forests. Products carrying the
FSC label are independently certified to assure consumers that they come
from forests that are managed to meet the social, economic and
ecological needs of present and future generations,
and other controlled sources.

Find out more about HarperCollins and the environment at
www.harpercollins.co.uk/green

For my siblings, Fiona Gainfort, John O'Grady
and Michelle Mernagh.

Every childhood memory I have includes these three.
We know each other as we were, as we are and as who
we are yet to be. In just one glance, with a single word,
we can share family jokes, remember feuds, keep
secrets, laugh, cry, love.

My childhood co-conspirators and collaborators.

My friends.

This one is for you guys.

(Now go tell all your friends to buy my book. You
know it makes sense.)

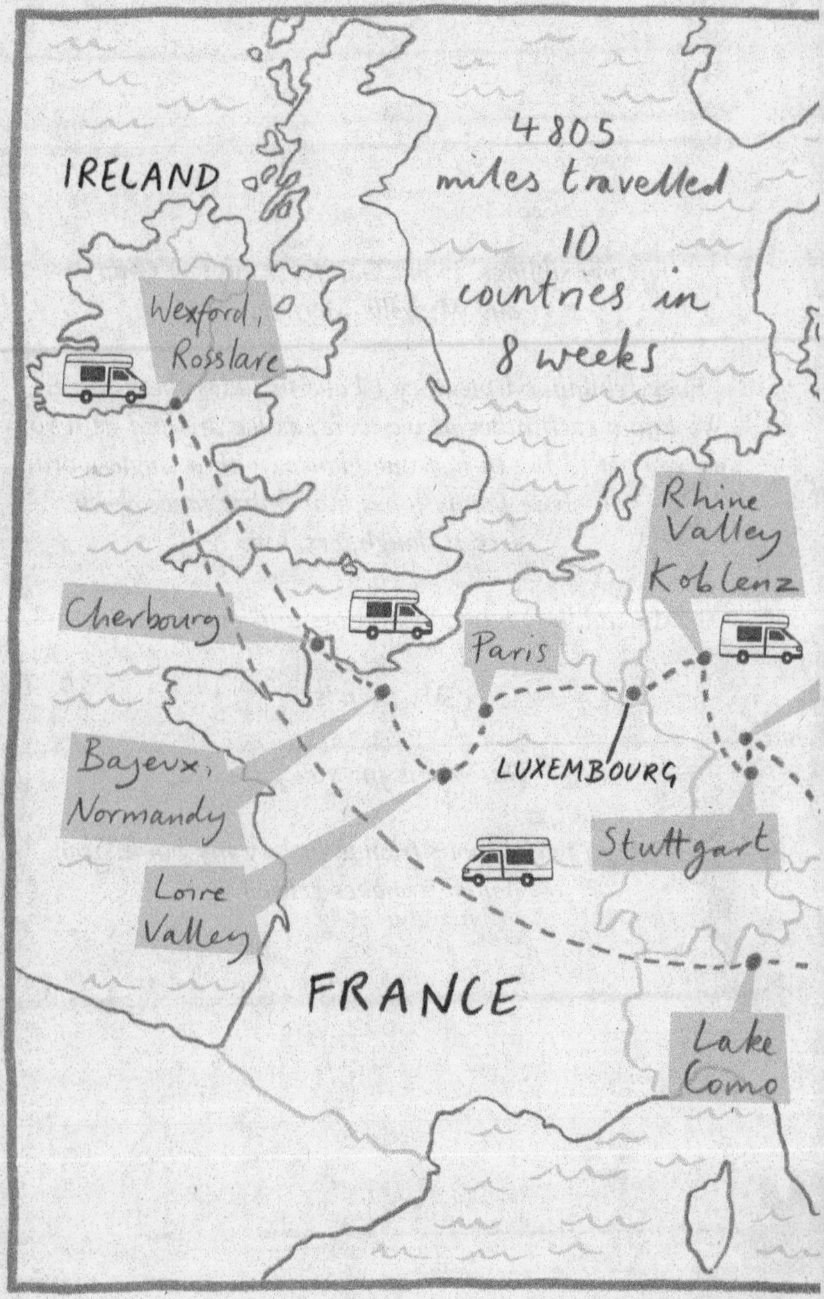
4805
miles travelled
10
countries in
8 weeks
IRELAND
Wexford,
Rosslare
Cherbourg
Bayeux,
Normandy
Loire
Valley
Paris
LUXEMBOURG
Rhine
Valley
Koblenz
Stuttgart
FRANCE
Lake
Como

The Guinness Family's European Adventure

GERMANY

Cleebronn

Salzburg

Innsbruck   Vienna   Budapest

                                        ROMANIA

AUSTRIA   HUNGARY   Bucharest

        CROATIA   SERBIA

Pula

                        Belgrade

ITALY

Prologue

OLLY

Our lives are just a series of moments. From the small, mundane occasions that we let pass us by without notice, to the big showstoppers that make us pause and take note. Then, when you least expect it, a moment so powerful and defining happens that changes everything in a split second.

The thing about change is, it's not always good.

Today was a day of insignificant moments, until Jamie's scream bounced off the walls in our house and time slowed down. Relief at seeing him in one piece was fleeting as I followed his eyes and saw what he saw. Evie, my thirteen-year-old daughter, lying unmoving, vomit splattered on her face and chest, dripping into a noxious puddle on the dark floorboards.

Time then sped up as we made our frantic dash to the hospital. And now we are in no-man's-land as we wait for more news on Evie.

A kind nurse has just left our cramped hospital waiting

room and the musky, woody scent of her fragrance lingers in the air. Vanilla, apples, sandalwood. It's Burberry perfume, I'd recognise it anywhere.

I look to my right and am unsurprised that the smell has sent Pops right back to 1981 too. A time when it was the norm in the Guinness house to spray that scent into the air every morning, in an effort to bring someone back. Until one day the bottle was empty and Pops said, 'That's enough now lad.' I watch him as his grey eyes water up and he turns to hold my gaze, nodding. A silent acknowledgement of mutual pain triggered by the scent of a nurse's perfume. For maybe the one-millionth time in my life, and I daresay in my father's, I yearn for my mother.

MAE

How long have we been sitting in this room now? It feels intolerable and I long to see my daughter. I seek out the clock on the wall and realise that it's almost nine p.m. Three hours' sitting in this small room waiting for news on Evie. Meagre updates from harassed but kind nurses and we cling to the fact that at least she's alive. Panic overtakes me once again at the thought of any scenario that doesn't include . . . I can't complete the sentence. I continue bargaining with God.

My mantra, my prayer, is simple – don't let my baby die. I'll do anything if you grant me this one thing. I'll be a better mother, I'll be a better wife, I'll be a better person. Please keep my baby alive.

Is this my punishment? Perhaps divine intervention from a higher level, stopping me from making a huge mistake. The thing is, it didn't feel like a mistake earlier. It felt good.

I look at my husband and wonder what would he think if he knew that when he called me this evening, I was in a bar with another man. And that five minutes before that, I had made my mind up that I wasn't coming home tonight.

OLLY

Evie. I catch a sob in my throat before it escapes. Even so, Jamie hears it and looks at me, his little nose scrunched up in worry. I smile to cover it up. He's scared enough without worrying about me as well. I glance at Mae, but she's looking out of the small window, lost in her own worry and pain. Should I go over to her? I chicken out and decide maybe later.

MAE

My mind races. I cannot understand how Evie could end up in such a state. I peek up at Olly again, as that same irrationality that won't stop plaguing me jumps up and hits me in the face. Shouldn't my perfect house-husband have known that something was wrong? I want to scream at him again, 'Why didn't you see this coming, Olly?'

I know his answer to that baseless accusation would be, 'What about you, Mae, where were you? Why didn't you see this?' And the weight of my shame makes me hang my head low. The blame sits on both of our shoulders. Somehow or other we've let our daughter down.

OLLY

That bloody perfume cloys at me now and memories batter me, determined to be heard. Mam was only thirty-three when she died, younger than I am now. I look at Mae and contemplate a world where my wife dies. As my chest tightens in panic, I look back at Pops and wonder how he ever managed to smile after he lost my mam, his love.

Evie and Jamie. I have my answer. My children. Of course Pops smiled for me, his son. He had no choice but to keep trucking on. We don't have a choice, as parents. We keep going no matter what curve ball kicks us in the bollocks.

I resist the urge to grab my father to hug him and cry for our loss. Instead I reach over and pat his knee. I am alarmed at how bony and frail it feels. The cancer is eating him up and I know that he must be in pain sitting here in this room for hours on end. But he won't go home, he won't rest in bed, so I know that there is no point in asking him to leave. He's stubborn, but I suppose I am too. I glance at Jamie. Like grandfather, like father, like son.

MAE

'You need to get that sorted,' Pops says. He misses nothing and has noticed me wincing from back pain again. I nod and refrain from biting back, when on earth would I have time? My life is a blur of early mornings and late nights at school. If I'm not at work doing my principal duties, I'm at home marking papers or setting assignments. Whilst simultaneously trying hard to fit in some quality time with a family who don't seem to need me any more. Self-pity, now there's an ugly trait that has joined forces with irrational jealousy. What have I become this past year? I used to be a happy, self-assured woman.

My mind keeps going back to that brief flash I caught of Evie when I arrived at the hospital. Her complexion the colour of unspoilt snow. Perfect, unblemished. Still. Too still.

I can feel Olly's eyes boring into me, but I avoid making eye contact with him.

'Do you need anything?' I fuss over Pops instead, noticing he is very pale. 'A hot drink?'

'I'm good. Don't be worrying about me. It won't be long now, I'm sure. They'll be in soon to confirm she'll be fine. She's a strong one, our Evie.'

I hope he's right. I know that I must find a way to make this better. Please, give me the chance to make this better. Don't let her die. A sob escapes again, so I lower my head, allowing my hair to hide my face. I think I hear Olly whisper my name, but I'm not sure. The realisation that I yearn to feel his strong arms around me confounds me. Most of the time I want to stab him with a fork, slap him, shout at him – anything to get a reaction, get noticed. But right now, I want him to murmur reassurances that everything will be alright.

Yet, I don't look up or move towards my husband. I stay on my own, back aching, sitting on a cold, bloody plastic chair. It's most likely one of the most uncomfortable chairs in the room. I realise that there's a whole month of therapy in that choice right there.

OLLY

I look around the small family room we're camped in, typical of the kind of waiting room that you find scattered around hospitals all over Ireland. Shades of magnolia with faded pictures of landscape scenes framed on the nondescript walls. Despite their best efforts, they fail to brighten up the tired room. There's a small cream-leather sofa that has seen better days pressed against the back wall. A potpourri of tears and coffee stains embedded into the fabric.

Jamie is sitting upon it, cross-legged, with his iPad Mini. But, for once, the usual tip-tap of his hand, as he battles his way towards the next level of *Candy Crush,* is still. He looks scared.

Mae is still at last. Since her arrival, she's paced the room like a caged lion. She's cried, she's shouted at me once or twice, then she's paced the room some more. Pops sighs loudly with dissatisfaction and then throws in a loud 'arra' for good measure. He's letting us know that he can see what we're doing to each other and he doesn't approve one bit. I decide to ignore that for now and move over to the couch so that I can pull Jamie in tight to me. At seven he's almost at that age where he doesn't need cuddles any more. Not in public, anyhow – but today is an extreme circumstance and he relaxes into my arms.

I can hear his heart hammering away through his shirt. He catches his breath in jagged succession as he tries to stem the tears that are threatening to escape.

'It's going to be okay, dude,' I whisper. He looks up at me, doubt making his eyes dark and I reiterate the statement with authority. Somehow or other I need to make my words come true.

MAE

Olly is rocking Jamie back and forth in his arms. His little eyes are heavy with fatigue, flickering as they always do when he puts up one last defiant fight to stay awake. I smile at my baby, my youngest child, and wish that I could just walk over and snatch him from Olly into my arms. I want to feel his soft breath on the nape of my neck as he snuggles in close to me. I want to be the one to give him comfort. He loves that spot under my chin to rest his head. Or at least he used to.

As hurtful as it is, I know that while I need Jamie right now, he needs Olly more. He's gotten used to having him at home at his beck and call these past few months. He's forgotten that it used to be me that he ran to when he scuffed his knees or banged his head. I haven't, though. I ache to hold him, but I know that it would be selfish of me to do anything about it.

This position I find myself in, I feel powerless to change. I do not have the luxury of slowing down in work. We need my salary as my husband seems to have given up on ever finding a job again. His sole focus these days is being the perfect house-husband. The only problem with that is, he also seems to have given up on me. On *us*. I simply don't know what to do.

I sigh and turn away from them. I know it's not fair to blame Olly for the relationship he has with Jamie, after all he's earned that closeness, their bond. But watching our son relax in his arms right now, in a way that he hasn't done with me for a long time, makes me want to run over to my husband and slap him hard across his saintly face.

The violence I've been feeling towards my husband these days startles me. I love him. Or at least I think I do. I just don't like him very much. I know I sound like a prize bitch. I'm well aware that every thought is irrational. In fact, I can feel something oozing out of my skin, like a septic pus. What I'm feeling is jealousy in all its ugly and green glory, the cause of all my irritations. But acknowledging something and being able to stop it are two different things.

I take a long, deep breath and look at my son. I remind myself that Jamie has not stopped loving me. But the balance of power has shifted in our house since Olly became a stay-at-home dad. I wish I was a nicer person who could find it in her psyche to be happier for the new-found father-and-son bond that they have going on. But I'm not. I suppose, in my defence, I would cheer with abandon for them both, except for one thing. The stronger they seem to become, the weaker my relationship with the children becomes. I sigh in frustration at the stupidity of this.

OLLY

I can feel my father's eyes upon me once again, worry emanating from his every fibre. He looks like he wants to say something to me, but keeps changing his mind and he finally settles on holding his counsel. I smile at him, tell him that I'm fine.

Pops, my allegiant. I'm not sure I can remember a time when he wasn't here by my side, when I needed him. Before and after that apocalyptic day in 1981. Many men would have faltered and lost their way, I reckon, doing the whole single-father gig, but not my father.

He's strong and I wish I were more like him. It always makes me laugh when my friends worry that the older they get, the more they are turning into their fathers. I worry that I'm not.

I close my eyes and think of Mam once more. What would she make of this if she were here? Would she feel disappointment in her son, with the mess he's making of his life? I hazard a guess that she would, because I'm pretty pissed with myself too. Somehow or other, I've taken my eye off the ball. Now things have gotten all screwed up and my thirteen-year-old daughter is lying in a room hooked up to tubes.

I've felt shame a few times in my life. When I lost my job a year ago that was a kick-you-in-the-balls day for sure. A close second is the first time that I had to ask Mae for money because my personal bank account was depleted of funds. My debit card had become as much use as a chocolate teapot. And don't get me started on the endless pit of desolation as rejection letters began to pile up high on our study table. But none of these are even close to the shame I feel now, as I sit in this waiting room.

My beautiful Evie, fighting for her life down the corridor.

I'm bewildered. I don't know how this has happened. And then, with surprise, I acknowledge another emotion bubbling up inside – I feel angry. I know that rage is only counterproductive and I need to fight it, to stay calm.

The door opens and a doctor walks in, his face unreadable, and we all jump to attention.

Chapter One

POPS

Tick tock. I can hear the grandfather clock that stands in the corridor outside my bedroom march on towards the start of a new hour. I fancy that the sound of the clock moving time along gets louder every day as I, in turn, get weaker.

Tick tock, time is moving on, but running out for me.

I feel it in my bones. I don't mean the cancer, which has now spread throughout my body. I mean, I can feel it in my bones that it's my turn to go. I've not asked Doctor Lawlor for a timeframe on how many weeks or months he thinks I've got, because I don't need to. It's close. He knows it too, because I can see it in his ever-more sympathetic eyes when he comes for his weekly visit.

I'm at peace with my fate and that's a good job because there's not a blind thing I can do to stop it anyhow. When death has you in its gnarly vice-like grip, you're buggered. Beth knew that at the end and I know it now.

'Beth,' I whisper her name, savouring how it sounds. I miss saying her name out loud. I miss her.

The sicker I get, the closer I feel to my wife. And that, right there, gives me comfort. As sure as I know that the sun will rise every morning, I know that she's waiting for me, with great patience. I can feel her. And I don't intend to keep her waiting much longer. She's been on her own long enough.

'Hold on, my love, I'm on my way. I've to sort out one or two things here first with our Olly, then I'll be right with you.'

Olly strides into my bedroom, as if he can hear me taking his name in vain. 'Who you talking to?' Concern etched on his tired face, looking around the room for signs of my non-existent company.

'Your mam,' I answer, more flippantly than I should. Olly now looks more worried than usual. He's enough on his plate without thinking I'm losing my marbles too.

I throw in a feeble joke to lighten the moment and change the subject. 'She says to say hello and don't forget that the bins go out tonight.' It works, a smile breaks out on his face.

'You don't smile enough any more.' I worry about that. A life without laughter isn't worth living at all.

Olly just shrugs in response. He doesn't answer me, but I've a fair idea I know what he's thinking right now.

What have I got to smile about?

'You've more than most,' I reply to his thought and he looks startled.

'How do you do that?' he asks me, starting to laugh. And as it is with laughter, it's contagious, so I join in.

'I always know what you're thinking, lad,' I tell him when we calm down. And it's true. It doesn't hurt that his face has always been like an open book. He wears his heart on his sleeve, always has done, just like his mother. Mae, now she's a different kettle of fish. She's harder to read. She keeps it all bottled up inside. But it's obvious that she's as unhappy as Olly is right now, and that worries me.

'How are you feeling?' he asks.

I think about lying, but he's not a boy any more, he's a grown man with a family of his own, so I do a thumbs-down sign. A pain shoots up from my left thumb all the way to my neck, making me regret my gesture.

But the pain was worth it, because Olly smiles in recognition, as I knew he would. When he was a boy he used his thumbs to depict how he was feeling all the time.

'That bad?' he says, the creases of worry on his face deepening.

'It's near time for painkillers and then I'll be all . . . ' I hold up two thumbs and smile, encouraging Olly to do the same.

'I wonder what your mam will make of me when she sees me,' I say, as I look down at the paper-thin skin on my arms, blotched with age spots and wrinkles.

I've never been a vain man, but I've always taken care of my appearance. I shave every morning as soon as I get up and while I don't have the energy for a shower every day, I'll always wash my hair. But even so, I know I look a bit . . . unkempt. My skin sags wearily on pointy bones and there's a greyness to my complexion that wasn't there a few weeks ago. Last time I saw Beth I was young, vibrant, full of vigour. Would she even recognise me now?

'How can you be so sure that you'll see her when you die?'

'I've faith, lad.'

Scepticism fills Olly's face. That, right there, is part of his problem. 'What makes you not believe?' I'm curious.

Olly shrugs, but he has no answer for me. I've had time to think about my own faith. Goodness knows, it's been tested many times, not least of all when Beth died. But it was faith that I'd see her again one day that has got me through the past thirty-odd years. Had I not believed that, I don't think I would have managed to smile and laugh and enjoy my family and life as much as I have. And that would have been a crying shame, because I've had a good life with Olly, Mae and the children.

I look at him and wish that I could find words that might explain to him how I feel. I scan my bedroom and my eyes rest on the battered brown briefcase propped against my dresser. I carried that to work every day for nigh-on thirty-eight years, right up until I retired. Now it contains a shiny silver laptop that Olly and Mae bought me a few years back. I thought I'd never get the hang of it. Googling seemed like a ridiculous word, that made me giggle like a silly teenager whenever I thought of it. But now, well, I love it. I think it's the fact that I can travel anywhere in the world courtesy of that silver box. It's amazing what you can find on the internet.

Then I have one of those light-bulb moments.

'Think of Wi-Fi, lad. You can't see that, right? Faith is just like Wi-Fi, with the power to connect you to so much, to places all over the world.'

Olly seems amused at the direction my train of thought has gone. I dive in with my analogy.

'Think about it. I have faith that your mother is waiting for me. I can feel that more and more every day. I'm sure of it, lad, in the same way I know that I'll be waiting for you, when it's your turn to go too.'

'Not for a few more decades though, please, Pops!' and we both laugh together at that. 'You've a great way of looking at things. It's a nice thought, either ways.'

'Well, you remember what I said about the Wi-Fi when I'm gone. I'll connect with you again one day, lad. Somehow or other, we'll find each other. You mark my words.'

Olly squeezes my hand, pain etched all over his face. I feel his love for me and know that he is already mourning my inevitable absence in his life. I hate that I'm adding to his worry right now.

'Are you honest to God worried about how you look?'

When I nod in response, he looks at me with a critical eye, 'I suppose you could do with a hair-cut. You're looking a bit Spandau Ballet-like there, Pops.'

Ha! He's funny, my son. How many times did I nag him when he was a teenager and into all that New Romantic nonsense? He grew his hair long and started to wear white floppy shirts. Eejit.

'I'll book the hairdresser,' Olly assures me. He bends in towards me, so close we're almost nose to nose. 'Mam loved you. She won't care what you look like. She wasn't like that, worried about stupid superficial stuff.'

I daresay he's right.

'Sure, maybe you'll become young again when you die,' he adds.

'Aye, maybe I will that.' I like that thought. This body of mine is gone all worn out, like a set of brake pads past their sell-by date. I'd happily swap it for a younger version. 'Would you get my good suit dry-cleaned for me, the one I got last year in Neon's?' I've gotten my suits in that shop in Talbot Street for over thirty years now. Mind you, when I bought it, I had no idea that it would be the last time I'd ever buy a suit. Had I known, I might have splurged and bought two!

I watch Olly's face go through several emotions. From shock, to anger, to sadness and then finally it settles on acceptance of a kind. While I know that it's time that I start working through all the finer details of what I want, I hate seeing the effect that it has on him.

'That's what you want to wear . . . when . . . you know?' He stammers out and his face has gone a funny grey colour.

'I do,' I reply. 'But make sure you put me in my shiny shoes. The ones I usually wear for a black-tie do. And I want my white dress shirt too with the cufflinks that I wore for your wedding. I always feel dapper when I wear those. Oh, and I want the blue tie that Evie bought me last Christmas to finish the look off. She'll like that.'

Olly blinks, then nods, leaning in to grasp my hand and squeeze it tight.

'I want to look smart,' I tell him, but damn it, my voice catches. I blink fast. I need him to understand that this is important for me.

'I won't forget, Pops. I'll make sure you look perfect,' Olly promises, and I know I'm in safe hands. When Olly promises to do something, he never lets you down. He's solid. A good man. But with the weight of the world on his shoulders these days.

Since he was made redundant, it's like he's lost his spark. At first he was all bluster, full of anger, I suppose. That kept him buoyant as he started looking for a new job. But each 'Dear John' chipped away at his confidence. He's given up even trying to find work now. I've got to find a way to bring back the old Olly. Reignite that spark of his.

'Will you tell Mam that I'm sorry,' Olly whispers. His voice is so quiet that I almost miss it.

'Not that nonsense again. Aarra! You've nothing to be sorry about, lad.' He always blames himself for her accident and he is no more to blame than I am.

'Even so, will you tell her?' he says and I nod as I can see how important it is for him.

We sit in silence for a few minutes, each lost in our own thoughts. I close my eyes to rest for a moment. It feels peaceful and I think, this wouldn't be a bad time to go.

After a while, something changes and a tension seems to hover in the air like large ice particles, ready to drop and pierce our heads any minute.

I open my eyes half expecting to see the grim reaper standing over me. But the room is empty except for Olly. His whole demeanour has changed, his shoulders hunched and his fists are clenched by his side.

'Lad? What is it?' I ask.

'Life just seems too fucking complicated right now,' he says.

I look at my son and think for the first time that I can

remember, he looks every bit of his forty years. I hear the clock tick tocking in the background, reminding me of my limited time left. Not now. I need more time, damn it.

I want to say something that will proffer some change, melt those blasted ice particles before they do any damage.

This is my big opportunity to dispense some father-like advice and make a difference. Here goes. 'Life can be as complicated or as simple as you want it to be.'

Olly snorts. That went well.

'You need to take control of your life.' I wince inwardly as I realise that I sound a bit like one of those cagey inspirational speakers.

'How am I supposed to do that?' Olly says with irritation and I don't blame him. My advice is falling short. I need to come up with something better than soundbites, no matter how true they are. How can he take control back? That is the million-dollar question, lad, no doubt about it.

'What do you want from life? That's as good a place as any to start with,' I say.

'I'm losing my family. I want them back. I want my family back.' His sincerity strikes me dumb.

I wait for him to continue. I can see him grappling with whether he should talk, whether it is fair to burden me or not. He knows I'm in pain.

And as soon as I think the word 'pain', the dull ache that has been nagging me for the past hour begins ramping up and demands more of my attention. I sit up straighter, try to find a more comfortable position, so I can continue. I smile at Olly as I do so, to urge him to keep talking.

'Look at me, Pops. Washed up at forty years old with no job. Evie is lucky to be alive and we've not even scratched the surface on that problem. She's still not telling us what really happened. I don't buy that bullshit, that she was experimenting with alcohol to celebrate the start of her school holidays. It's too out of character. Jamie is back to pissing in his bed. He's not done that since he was three years old. Don't tell me that's not related to the trauma of finding his sister half dead in her bedroom. And then there's Mae. Pops, she can barely look at me any more. Who can blame her? She can do far better than me. And that's not even the worst of it. What about . . . what about you? I'm not ready to say goodbye to you yet, Pops.'

'Yes, lad. Your life is, without doubt, complicated right now. No one could disagree with that.'

I know that I've got to somehow find a way to make a difference, before I'm gone and it's too late. I grapple to find the right words, feeling ill equipped to give my son something to help assuage his obvious pain. Unlike the cancerous pain I'm enduring, there's not a pill he can take to ease away his aches. He has to work through them, sort them out as best he can himself, without any numbing narcotics.

I'm not sure that there are any words that will help prepare him for my soon-to-be fate. Are we ever ready for a loved one to die? No. And even though there will be no surprise when it's my time to go, I know that he's not ready for me to leave.

I need more time, but I know that's one thing I don't have any more. Tick tock.

'I can't sleep at night worrying about the what-ifs. How did I not see that something was going on with Evie? I'm supposed to take care of her. I'm supposed to be her hero, to save her,' Olly says. 'I let her down.'

'Sure, that's the greatest load of bullshit I've ever heard. You're good parents, good people. But even the best can't get it all right all the time.' I point my finger at him to illustrate how emphatic I am about this point.

There it is in all its glory – self-doubt – one of the ugliest of our inner turmoils, glaring out of my son's eyes.

'I. Should. Have. Seen. It. Coming,' Olly spits out, his voice rising with every word he says.

'You can raise your voice all you like, but that doesn't make your bullshit any truer,' I say.

He stops at my words and half-laughs, saluting me with the tip of his hand. 'It's a while since you've used that line on me.'

'It's a statement I've used to good effect in many a battle of wills. You were a stubborn little fecker as a kid.'

'You used to say it to me all the time. Must remember it for the next time Mae shouts at me,' Olly laughs.

'Don't you be using my good lines to score points with your wife,' I say. But I'm smiling too. Olly starts to fidget and I think that he's about to leave. But I don't want this conversation to end. What if it's one of our last ones? I haven't said everything that I need to.

'Was I a good father to you?' I ask him. 'Don't lie, lad. Speak the truth, now.'

I hold my breath, waiting for his answer. I want the truth, of course I do, but in the name of God, please don't let him tell me I was a crap father.

'The best,' I exhale in relief.

'But did I make mistakes?' I say again. 'Were there times that you thought, fuck you, Pops, and the horse you rode into town on!'

Olly looks shocked at this and begins to shake his head in denial of the statement.

'Liar! You know there were times when I got it wrong. But that's okay, because in the main I got it right and you always knew I loved you, even when I messed up. Right?' I demand.

Olly smiles at me and says, 'I always knew that you loved me. And you didn't get it wrong often, Pops.'

I'm grateful for his words.

'Thanks, lad. But I'm not fishing for compliments from you, although I'm not sorry to hear them. I just want to illustrate that it's okay to have the odd bad day, as long as in the main you get it right. You can't be Evie's hero every day of the week, can you? Even Spiderman gets the odd day off. The girl needs to live her own life, make her own mistakes, learn from them and she can't do that if she's under her parents' coat tails.'

'But every time she goes into her bedroom, I'm worried sick about what she could be doing in there. I tell you, Pops, it's crossed my mind to put in cameras so I can be sure she's not downing another bottle of fecking vodka!'

'Would you whist, lad. Let the girl have her privacy. Sure, God knows, when you were that age you spent half your life in your bedroom and you're still alive. Don't tell me you didn't have a sneaky drink back then.'

'I never ended up in hospital with alcoholic poisoning, though, Pops,' Olly states.

'No, you didn't. But you had my heart broken more than once. Evie messed up. What you need to do is find out why. She's been withdrawn for months now. I know she's not talking yet, but she'll tell you in her own good time what's going on. She's a strong girl, she just needs to remember that.'

I think I'm beginning to get through to Olly because he's stopped stooping and is now sitting up straighter in the chair. He has a look on his face that I've not seen in a long time – determination.

We sit without speaking for a while and I think about Mae and wonder if I dare bring up their marriage. It's a dangerous thing talking about the inner sanctum of a couple's life. In fact, it's true that I have no business snooping around there. But I realise that I have to speak up. Someone has to, because they seem hell-bent on destroying themselves.

'You and Mae. You need to watch that,' I decide to take the bull by the horns and get straight to it. No time to dilly-dally around the issue.

'You don't think I don't know that?' Olly responds. 'I can feel her slipping away from me, every day one little bit further. But I'm powerless to stop her. I don't know who she is any more. She's changed, Pops.'

'Arra, nobody stays the same, lad. We all change as we go through life and that's good, 'cos it would be pretty boring otherwise. You're not the same man you used to be, either. Did you ever think of that?'

Olly looks startled at this piece of information.

'I've seen a change in you these past months, since you stopped working. I daresay that Mae has noticed it too.'

'I'm still the same person,' Olly's petulant and irritated, reminding me of his teenage self. I hope he listens more to me now than he did back then.

'No you're not, son. You're different. I know losing your job has been tough. But maybe it's time to look at your redundancy with different eyes.'

'What do you mean?' he asks.

'Well, you didn't even like that job. Don't lie. You were just punching the clock every day.'

'I hated it,' he admits. 'How did I even end up as an accountant?'

'You always wanted to be an astronaut,' I say. 'Walk on the moon.'

'Think NASA might have an age limit on new recruits, Pops,' he says, laughing.

'Never say never,' I tell him. 'You might not get to the moon, but who says that this can't be the catalyst for you to make a change. Instead of feeling sorry for yourself, why not take this opportunity to look for a new direction? You can't hide out at home forever.'

He looks doubtful. I can almost hear his mind working through excuses.

'That's what life is about, lad – change. You need to talk to Mae. She can't read minds, you know. Tell her what's going on in your head. If you stopped blaming each other for every damn set-back that's happened to you both, you might remember that you love each other. You're being too careless with her.'

'What if it's too late? What if I've lost her, Pops?' Olly asks, shoulders down low again.

'No!' I shout. 'No, God damn it, Olly, no! Stop being

so damn defeatist about the woman you love. I'd have given anything to have the time you have with Mae, with my wife. I didn't get that chance. You need to start paying more attention to her. And I don't care how many times Mae tells you that she's okay or pushes you away, don't believe her. Because she's obviously not! You walk over to your wife and you hold her in your arms. Do you hear me, son?'

I start to cough and know that I'm done for now. Between the wheezing and racking cough and the pain that is now taking control of me, I cannot speak another word.

I hold my hand up, reassuring Olly that I'm not about to die, and he leans in close, clutching my hand once again between his own. I point to the water and my meds and he helps me take a sip to swallow the chalky tabs down. I close my eyes and somehow or other, despite the pain, I manage to drift off to sleep.

When I wake up, it's dark outside. I must have been out cold for several hours. I can smell dinner wafting towards me, but regrettably my appetite has been absent for weeks. I say 'regrettable' because, at a guess, from the beautiful aroma that is snaking its way around my room, Olly has made fish pie. That's one of my favourites. He's a good lad.

Rather, it used to be a favourite. I make a vow to try to eat a mouthful to please him, but just the thought of even taking one bite makes me feel tired.

I've no time to rest because I know what I can do to help my family before I die. Beth and I have come up with a plan. Despite what most would think, I'm not losing my marbles. While I slept, Beth came to me in my dreams and told me what I should do.

Wi-Fi sure is powerful stuff, I chuckle. I knew it would connect me to her when I needed it. I smile as I think of all their faces when they find out what we've planned. Mae won't be happy, I know that. But don't ask me why. I know it will be the best gift I can ever give them. I've got a lot of planning to do to pull it off though. Tick tock. Feck OFF!

'There's life in the old dog yet, Beth,' I say out loud. 'I've one more trick up my sleeve before I say goodbye to this world.'

I think about something that she used to say to me when Olly was a baby, 'I just want to make sure that he gets a happy ending.'

She was a bit of a romantic, my Beth. Well, I'm pretty sure that the only way to give a happy ending to Olly and his family is to give them all a new beginning. So that's what I'm going to do.

Chapter Two

OLLY

Today is my father's funeral.

I knew that this day was coming. We all did. The grim reaper has been hovering at our door for weeks and with every passing day we saw Pops slip further away from us, closer to that bugger. I find it incredible that an event that I knew was inevitable still has the power to wound me, spear me, surprise me. I want to run away from today and all its responsibilities. I'm not sure I have the strength to say goodbye.

I've often lamented my only-child status, but none more so than today. The weight of being his only child feels intolerable. So I'll stay, I'll help carry his coffin and I'll watch them send his body to be burned. And somehow or other I'll get through it.

I was with Pops when he exhaled his last long breath. I'm grateful for that. I was determined that I would be the last person he saw, before . . .

I hope he knew I was there. At the end, it was fucking

crazy. We'd been warned that his breathing would get shallow in those last moments. Erratic. At first his exhalation was longer than his inhalation and, as morbid as this sounds, it was fascinating to witness. The gaps between each breath started to get longer and longer. There were periods of no breathing and this part freaked us all out many times. Almost comical. That's awful, isn't it? His family laughing, with more than a hint of hysteria when we'd think he was dead, then suddenly he'd bellow out another breath and we'd all jump sky high. Pops would have approved of our laughter, though. I fancied I saw a glimmer of a smile on his lips at one point when we tried to stifle our guffaws.

Evie, our resident encyclopaedia, told us that scriptures state that you must always ensure the individual is on his right, like Buddha was at his death, and this will give them a happy, peaceful mind. So we propped Pops up, telling him what we were doing and why. It made Evie happy, so Mae and I went along with it.

We took turns sitting with him, making a pact never to leave him on his own in his last days. Even Jamie joined in our unofficial, unspoken rota when he wasn't in school. Although he was never alone with Pops. Evie on the other hand got to spend a lot of time solo with him, at her own request. She told us that she wasn't scared, so we respected her wishes and let her do her turn.

In the end, it was on my watch when that last breath was exhaled and Pops left us. And you know the weird thing? I was as unprepared for that moment as I had been for my mother's untimely demise. I'd thought about the difference between their deaths a lot over the past few months. Wondered which would be easier. With Mam there was no warning whatsoever, but of course we all knew what was headed our way with Pops. Well, now that both my parents are dead and I've experienced each option, I still don't have an answer to that. There is something I do know for sure, though. Both options suck, both hurt like hell and both I wouldn't wish on my worst enemies.

On one hand, the last few months before Mam died were pretty perfect. There were no shadows on our time together, we just got on about the business of living. And loving. And, boy, did we have a lot of love!

And I suppose in that alone I'm lucky, or at least luckier than most. Although she was taken so abruptly, I have no regrets about anything. Because nothing was left unsaid before she was snatched away from us. In our family, when I was a kid, 'I love you's were abundant and spoken every day. And that's how we roll in my own family now too. I tell the children often how much I love them. My parents taught me well.

I push aside the fact that I can't remember the last time I whispered any endearments to Mae. Or her to me.

While the last few months were tortuous in so many ways, watching Pops fight his illness, at least I got to say goodbye to him. I got to hold his hand and kiss his head fifty times a day, whenever I felt the need to do so. And towards the end, I won't lie, that need was pretty much always there. When I wasn't in the room with him, I fretted and missed him, so I would find myself making excuses to go back.

Another wave of grief assaults me as I ponder a life without kisses to Pop's forehead.

The silence in the room mocks me. I expect to hear Pops say something smart. He always had this knack of knowing what I'm thinking.

I miss his voice. I'd do anything to hear it one more time. He's not been gone more than forty-eight hours and already it feels like forever.

At least he died at home, surrounded by the people he loved most in the world, exactly as he wanted to, and for that I'm grateful. He had a smile on his face in those last moments. Maybe his faith hooked him up with Mam again as he said it would. I close my eyes and picture her in her blue dress, pulling him into her open embrace. Then, holding hands, leading him away from us to wherever their next adventure was about to begin. Tears blur my eyes.

I need to right the emptiness in the house. No matter which room I walk into, his absence is palpable from the silence therein. Even here, in our bedroom for goodness sake, where he had no business being, feels wrong. Mae said to me yesterday that she couldn't remember a time when he wasn't in the house with us. And she's right. We'd go off on our own sometimes, but when we got back, he'd be at the front door waiting, the sound of the kettle in the background whistling, ready to wet the tea.

The thought of being just the four of us scares me. I've never been here without him. I'm forty years old, but I feel like a child again, when Mam died and left me.

The urge to run is back. Fuck responsibility. I can't do this.

The crushing reality is that I am just a fool standing in an empty room, looking for a man that is no longer here. And he's not coming back. I collapse onto the edge of our bed and take several steadying breaths.

'Come on, lad, pull yourself together.' His voice whispers through the air towards me.

I close my eyes and lie back onto the soft pillows. I'm so fucking tired – bone fucking weary, truth be told. The last year, with the constant hospital visits, the chemotherapy, the cleaning up of sick and piss – it's all taken its toll. And I won't be sorry to say goodbye to that. Goodbye to the never-ending cancerous groundhog day, which had only one inevitable outcome for Pops.

And here's the thing. I feel relief. And shame that I feel relieved of the burden of his illness. So many emotions mixed up amongst my all-consuming pain. It's just . . . the man I long for is the healthy, vibrant Pops of last year. Not the shadow of a man he became in these past few cancerous-ridden months. Fuck me! The pain he was in! Nobody should have to live like that.

So yes, damn it! I'm glad he's gone, if living like that was the only choice. A blessed release, that's what Father Kelly said. And he's right, it is a blessed release for him. For me too. It's not just my heart that is in half today, it's my whole body. What I'd give to climb under the heavy duvet and allow myself to sleep through this day.

'How are you doing?' Mae's voice pulls my eyes open and I watch her walk into our bedroom. I sit up and lie, saying that of course I'm fine.

'Do you need some help with that?' She points to the tie that is hanging loose around my neck, waiting. She doesn't wait for an answer, but walks over to me and places it under its collar. Over and around, under and over and she's done, the perfect knot.

'You look tired, Olly,' Mae says, looking up at me. Her hand hovers beside my face, but she doesn't touch me. I look at her and see the pain that I feel, mirrored in her too.

'I just want to get today over and done with,' I say. 'I can't get my head around this whole cremation choice. I was sure he'd want to be buried with Mam.'

'Had he never mentioned it before to you?' Mae asks.

'No. He told me what he wanted to wear. He also told me to call Larkin's, the funeral directors, when it was time. I just assumed it would be a burial. It never crossed my mind he'd chosen cremation.'

Larkin said everything was under control when I rang them. Pops had even paid for everything up front and arranged every last detail himself. I'm not surprised by that. Pops always did everything in his power to make things easy for me. Even down to arranging his own funeral service.

'You know, it's weird, but I thought he was getting better, you know,' Mae remarks. 'This past week or so, have you noticed that he seemed, more energetic or something?'

I had noticed it. He'd seemed stronger to me too.

'He was on his laptop a lot. I thought that was a good sign. I should have copped on that he was up to something. He was organising today. Getting it all in order.'

'It's going be so quiet without him,' Mae said.

'Did you mind him being here all the time?' I ask her.

31

'I know you always said you didn't, but it must have been difficult at times to have a father-in-law living with us.'

Mae shook her head vehemently. 'I loved Pops. I always knew that you and he were a package. Pops and his mini-me. I'm going to miss him so much.'

A tear slips from Mae's left eye and travels inch by inch down her cheek, leaving a white trail through her makeup. She wipes it away with the back of her hand and closes her eyes, to stop any further tears following.

She looks vulnerable and soft and before I allow myself to think and stop, I walk over to her and take her in my arms. I can feel her resistance, the tension that always appears in her body whenever I get close to her lately. But I remember Pops' advice and don't let her go. I hold her tight and stay silent. And then, at once, I feel her body relax and she moulds into my arms. Her soft breasts press in close to my own chest and our hearts seem to beat in unison. I hear her breath quicken or maybe it's mine?

'I miss you,' I whisper into her hair.

'What?' Mae asks.

'Mam, Dad, the car's here,' Jamie's voice bellows out and Mae pulls apart from me. The moment, whatever it was, is gone. But her eyes meet mine and I recognise in them something that I haven't seen for a long time.

Love? Or at least a recognition of the memory of a happier time. A spark of hope gives my grief blessed relief for a moment. All is not lost. I then feel crap that I'm even thinking about myself on the day of my father's funeral.

'Thank you,' I say to her. I want to say so much more, but I don't. I just put on my jacket.

'For what?'

'For being here. As long as I have you by my side, I can get through this.'

She looks away from me and murmurs, 'It's time to say our goodbyes. Come on.'

Damn it.

'That was way cool,' Jamie declares for the third time since we left the crematorium. 'The way the coffin just disappeared behind the curtain. Pops would have loved that.'

'It was creepy. If I die, please bury me,' Mae replies, shuddering.

We are driving home to Wexford. To say it's been a rough few hours is an understatement, but somehow or other we've gotten through two services. The first one was the funeral mass in Wexford. It was a packed church of family and friends, who were all there to say goodbye to a good man, who lived a good life. Then the second service in the crematorium was for just us family. Exactly as Pops requested.

I watched Mae and the children go through so many emotions during those two different ceremonies. I saw sorrow, heartache, desolation, anger and loneliness. I recognised each of them because it is how I felt too. But now, in our car, driving home, the energy has changed. Now there is an air of frivolity amongst us. I recognise it for what it is. It's often the way when things are this serious, giddiness sets in at some point because the mind cannot take any more. It happened at Mam's funeral. Pops and I had said goodbye to the last well-wisher and then Pops farted. A loud, rasping, wet fart. I giggled. And then I felt horrendous. I expected to get a clout across my ear from him for that. But he giggled too. Soon the two of us were making wet, loud, fart noises under our arms, through our mouths, any way we could. We put on a good old comedy act for twenty minutes or so, till we cried with laughter.

I realise now that it would not take much to set us all off. We all need a few hours respite before we face going home to a house that doesn't have our beloved Pops in it any more. So we begin bantering away about death as if we hadn't a care in the world. We could have been discussing the weather, such is our ease.

'If I die, you can burn me,' Jamie states. 'And I want a super-cool urn for my ashes.'

'You know, the largest urn in the world is in Tustin, USA,' Evie says.

'How big?' Jamie asks.

'It's sixteen feet tall,' Evie tells him.

'Cool. Was it for a giant? Or a troll? I bet it was a giant,' Jamie says in wonder.

'Oh, without doubt a giant,' Mae says with a smile.

'You can get urns made in the likeness of people's heads you know,' Evie adds.

'What?' Mae shrieks. 'That's macabre.'

'It's true, Mam. I saw one of Barack Obama once on Facebook,' Evie says.

'Who the hell would want their ashes stored in a president's head?' Mae responds, looking mystified.

'There's a lot of crazy in this world,' I chip in.

'When I die, can I have an urn made into a spaceship?' Jamie asks. 'Or maybe one like Darth Vader? Pops would love that, you know. He loves *Star Wars*.'

'He was more of an Obi-Wan Kenobi fan than Darth Vader,' I murmur. 'But, yes, he loved *Stars Wars*.'

And for a moment I allow myself a daydream where Pops can come back and talk to me in spirit like Obi-Wan could in the movies.

'That would be cool,' I whisper.

'Less of the talk of dying please,' Mae remarks.

'Okay, but Mam, I'm not joking here. I will die if we don't get some food into my body. I'm starving,' Jamie complains and then, with perfect timing, his stomach lets a loud grumble out.

I look in the rear-view mirror and seeing the children smile makes my throat tighten. It's been a tough few days. Damn it, a tough few months. Smiles have been few and far between. I shake my head to stop further tears coming.

'I could eat something too,' Mae says. 'What do you think, Olly? Can we stop or do you want to get home? It's been a rough day, so don't worry if you want to just keep going.'

I peek in the rear-view mirror and Jamie is pretending to faint. Evie throws her eyes up to heaven, but I can see a hint of a smile on her face. Then I spy the golden archway ahead and a decision is easily made for us. We are an unlikely looking bunch queuing for our fast-food fix. Mae in her black trouser suit, Evie and Jamie wearing a mixture of dull greys and black and me in my good suit, with a black mourning tie. I loosen the knot and pull it off, stuffing it into my inside jacket pocket.

'That makes all the difference,' Mae teases.

With our food piled high on red trays, we sit down.

Evie and Mae with their McChicken Sandwich meals, me with my Big Mac and Jamie with his Happy Meal.

Jamie pulls open his cardboard box of happiness and rummages for the plastic bag, eager to find out what the toy is this time. Mid-slurp of my strawberry shake, I pause. I feel a hand on my knee and look down to see that Mae has clasped it.

Time freezes again when I look up and see that Jamie is holding up in his hand a figurine of Obi-Wan Kenobi.

'That's freaky,' Evie says, her eyes wide with surprise. 'We were just talking about him.'

'It's cool,' Jamie replies. 'Look what he can do.' He demonstrates his nodding head.

'Just a weird coincidence, that's all,' Mae says, but her voice is trembling.

Not ten minutes ago I likened Pops to Obi-Wan Kenobi, wishing he could come back and talk to me. And now Jamie is sitting here with his figurine held in front of my face.

I look around and, I swear to God, I expect Pops to be standing there wearing a long brown hooded robe. 'Fooled you,' he'd say and laugh. Oh, how we'd laugh.

I look at the Wi-Fi symbol flashing on my iPhone. That invisible thing that connects us all, no matter where we are. Was this Pops' way of reminding me to have faith? He said he'd find a way to find me.

'It's just a coincidence,' I tell my family, feeling stupid for even contemplating such nonsense. 'Eat up, it's getting late.'

I don't feel hungry any more. I play with my food a bit and wait for the others to finish up, then we continue our journey home. The mood has changed in the car again and we are all back in our own grief-stricken worlds. The welcome reprieve from our desolation, forgotten with the appearance of a small plastic toy from McDonald's.

As the distance to our home gets shorter, the greater my anxiety grows. So I slow down. I'm aware of the irony that an hour ago I thought I'd never get home so I could take my God-awful suit off. Now I am doing everything possible to delay that first entrance through our front door. I look down at my suit and make an impromptu decision about its fate.

'I'm going to burn this tomorrow.'

Mae nods. 'That's one option. Or you could give it to charity.'

'Maybe,' I say, but really, I want to be extreme. I feel justified planning a dramatic end to it, a symbolic burning of the pain I've endured today. Or something like that.

'I burned a suit once before,' I say.

'When?' Mae asks.

'When I was a kid. My communion suit.'

All at once I'm seven years old again and I see Mam's face and remember watching her discuss at length with Pops about what my communion suit should look like. Pops would nod and tell her that she knew best. He'd then chance a conspiratorial wink with me and I'd wink back, delighted with myself.

'Was it awful?' Mae asks me.

'A three-piece ensemble, kind of a biscuity pale brown in colour. But it had a contrasting chocolate-brown trim on the lapel and the pockets. Pops joked I looked like a chocolate hobnob. Mam didn't like that one bit. She wanted me to look perfect and no slagging of the suit was allowed.'

'Sounds lovely,' Mae laughs.

'I know it sounds brutal and, in truth, it was, but at the time I thought I was the dog's bollocks in it.' I glance in the rear-view mirror, checking the kids aren't listening to my cursing. Unsurprisingly, both have their earphones on.

'I can remember begging Mam to let me try it on at least once a day. But she would shake her head no and it remained in a plastic cover in her wardrobe,' I say.

'She wanted it to be in pristine condition for your special day. I get that. I was the same for Evie,' Mae says.

A pain so acute it makes me start hits me under my ribs. 'In the end, I got my wish and wore it before the communion.'

'When?' Mae asks, smiling.

'Her funeral.'

'Oh, Olly,' Mae says, and her smile freezes. I look away. If I see sympathy or pity, I'll start to cry again. I chance a joke.

'I don't mind telling you, I didn't feel in the slightest bit like the dog's bollocks then. Took the shine off wearing it on my communion, too.'

Neither of us laugh at my lame attempt to lighten the mood. She reaches over and places a hand lightly over mine for a moment. 'I'll help you burn it.' Then we drive in silence once more.

'If you go any slower we'll be in reverse,' Mae remarks after a while, but she's smiling as she speaks, so I know she's not having a go at me.

I look at her and wonder if she has guessed why I am so reluctant to go home. These past couple of days, we've been kinder to each other than we have been for the past six months. It's disconcerting and welcome all at once.

'I watched Mam and Pops both die from that house. There's a lot of ghosts at home for me,' I tell her.

'There's a lot of great memories there too. It will be okay, you wait and see,' she murmurs. 'And remember, alongside the ghosts, you have us too. We're right beside you.'

I look at her again and smile, but wonder if she means that. I'm not so sure.

Finally, we turn the bend and our house is in view before me. The house of my childhood that is both the same and also unrecognisable now, with the addition of our modern extension and conservatory at the gable end.

'Holy cow!'

'What the . . . ?'

'Wow!'

The exclamations from my family come in fast unison as we all see it at the same time.

'Olly?' Mae says. 'What on earth is that camper van doing parked outside our house?'

Chapter Three

OLLY

I pull into our driveway with caution. For the life of me, I can't work out why a thirty-foot camper van is sitting right in the spot where I usually park. That irks me, it feels like an affront, especially today of all days.

I pull over to the side of the house and sit for a moment, taking in the spectacle.

'That's so cool,' Jamie enthuses and already he has his seat belt off, eager to go explore. 'It looks like a spaceship, Dad!'

It's funny how one word can send your memories shooting back in time. At once, I'm sitting beside Pops eating popcorn and slurping Coke, as we watch *Close Encounters of the Third Kind*. I try to remember what age I was then. Mam was dead, so I reckon it was around 1983 or 1984. I had to sleep with Pops for two nights afterwards, such was my fear that little green men were going to pay me a visit.

I look up into the sky and half expect to see a spaceship

hovering, ready to beam us all up. My imagination is on fire today. Between Obi-Wan and now this, I reckon I'm losing it. I start to hum the iconic five-note melody from that movie and Mae smiles as she recognises it and joins in.

It's only a small thing but that small act of camaraderie gives me further hope that Mae and I might be okay, when all of this is over. We are still on the same wavelength, at least some of the time. That has to be a good sign. I turn to the kids and tell them, 'Stay where you are, till I see who this is.'

The camper van looks quite modern, as they go. Not that I know much about the world of Winnebagos and motor homes. I once again rack my brains trying to work out who the hell I know owns one of these or would be most likely to drive one. But I come up blank.

It's quite big and has a curved canopy over the driver's cab, which I know is quite common in a lot of the models. I can remember years ago when I was a kid, before Mam died, a cousin of hers and his wife called in to see us driving a huge camper van. They slept in a kind of bunk bed over the driver's cab. I can't even remember this cousin's name now and I'm pretty sure they must be dead, because they seemed ancient back then. God, the smell in that thing! Toiletry odours covered up by headache-inducing air fresheners, that made me want to gag. Surely it can't be those two again?

I check out the van a little closer. It's white in the main, but has blocks of silvery grey across the cabin. It also has a bright-red stripe splashed across both sides, in an attempt at frivolity almost.

For fuck's sake! I'm not sure why I'm so put out by its presence, but I am. It feels like the straw that is about to break my back. As I walk towards the driver's door, I shout out, 'Hello?' but nobody answers me. My heart rate speeds up as adrenalin begins to pump into my blood. I can hear my heart begin to drum in my ears, getting louder and louder as I approach the cab. I'm not sure what I'm expecting to see sitting behind the driver's wheel. But when I see it's empty I'm both relieved and disappointed all at once.

Confused, I turn around to wave to Mae and the kids. I want to signal them that there seems to be no one here, but the side door to the camper van opens with a clang, making me jump back, almost tripping over my own feet. In a pathetic non-hero-like manner, I squeak out a hiss of surprise.

I'm grateful that Mae and the kids are not by my side to witness it. Not my finest moment. I stand up tall in an attempt at redemption and face a middle-aged man. He has neat mousy brown hair parted to the side, wearing a brown pullover and beige slacks. He doesn't look in the slightest bit like an alien. Or dangerous.

'Alright,' his voice calls out to me. I can't work out the accent, but it's not Irish, that I know for sure. Scottish maybe? He steps down from the doorway and smiles at me brightly, like it's the most normal thing in the world for him to be here.

I nod back at him and try to work out if I've ever met him before. Nope, I'm pretty certain this is the first time I've clapped eyes on him.

He holds his hand out and introduces himself, 'Aled

Davies.' He then does this thing where he bows, almost Chinese-like. The lilting voice, singsong, along with the name, alerts me to where he's from – he's Welsh.

'Nice to meet you,' I say, lying. 'I'm Olly Guinness. But you've got the advantage on me, Mr Davies, because I'm not sure why you are parked in my driveway.'

'I'll tell you for why,' he replies with a smile. 'I've come to deliver Nomad to you.'

'Nomad?' I repeat, feeling stupid, like I'm missing the obvious. 'Who's Nomad?'

'Not who, what!' he laughs and with glee points to his camper van.

I'm baffled now and figure that this Welshman must have been smoking something, because he's not making any sense to me. I look him up and down and he appears to be sober, lucid and harmless enough, but so was Keyser Söze and look how that worked out for Gabriel Byrne.

I gesture to Mae and the kids to join me as I'm pretty certain that the brown-jumper-clad man before me poses no threat. I introduce each of them to Aled and his smile gets brighter and bigger with every passing name.

'I've heard lots about you two!' Aled tells Evie and Jamie when they stand beside me.

'You sound funny,' Jamie tells him, looking at him warily.

'Don't be rude,' Mae scolds Jamie, but Aled just laughs.

'Not the first time I've heard that, truth be told. Right, I know you must be wondering why I'm here, but one minute. Where did I put it?'

He starts patting down his jumper and trousers and

then exclaims as he pulls out a white envelope, 'Ah, here it is. I've a letter to give to you, Olly.'

It has my name on the front and I recognise the handwriting immediately.

Pops.

My heartbeat starts to do its loud hammer dance in my ears again. I can feel a line of sweat break out on my forehead. I'm cold, hot, clammy and can't breathe.

I feel a hand steady me – Mae – and realise that I must have faltered for a moment. I look at the figurine of Obi-Wan Kenobi clasped in Jamie's hand and then at the letter in Aled's hand. Wi-Fi. Fucking Wi-Fi.

'I think we should go inside,' Mae says, and she leads me towards the front door, gesturing Aled to follow us. 'It's been a long day.

'Evie, can you make some tea for our guest, please,' Mae instructs, sounding posh and proper and nothing like her usual self. Evie throws her a dirty look and for a moment I think she's going to refuse. But then she glances at me and sighs loudly, scuffing her feet as she walks out of the room. Mae then motions Jamie to go into the den to watch TV. I realise that she is also thrown by the letter and trying hard to hold it together.

'When did he give you this?' I demand as soon as I find my voice again. The envelope feels heavy in my hand and a faint line of moisture from clammy fingers appears on the top right-hand corner.

'Your father sent it to me last week, Olly. He gave me specific instructions that I was to be here on the day of his funeral. He arranged with the funeral director – Mr

Larkin, I believe – to call me when he died, so I could get here on time.'

I hold my breath as he explains the events of the past few days and start to sweat again. What the hell had Pops been up to?

'I'm so sorry for your loss,' Aled said to me. 'Your father was a proper gentleman. But he wanted to do this. He was quite adamant that I should be here today.'

'I'm not sure I've ever heard Pops mention you before,' Mae says, the kids hovering behind her. There's no way they are missing out on whatever this is.

'I'm sorry to say that I didn't meet him in person. But we've spoken on the phone a few times. As I said, he was a proper gent and I would have liked to have spent time with him, if things were different. I think we would have got along pretty well. Maybe it's best you read the letter. I'm sure it will all become a bit clearer when your father explains what he has done. I'll go wait in Nomad while you do. Give you some privacy.'

Mae begins to make noises that he should stay where he is, but I usher him to the door saying, 'Feel free to take your tea with you.'

I don't want to be a complete dick.

Aled stands up and walks out, saying as he leaves, 'Take your time. I'm quite comfortable out here.' He gives me a look of sympathy and I nod back, but my attention is one hundred percent on Pop's letter and I don't want a stranger watching me as I read it.

Part of me wants to rip the envelope open, but there's another part of me that's chicken. What if this message from the grave – or urn, I suppose – has something bad in it? I shiver. Jamie and Evie have joined Mae on the couch and the three of them watch me, waiting for me to get on with the task at hand. I feel fortified by having them by my side. My family.

So steadied by that sight, with fumbling thumbs, I slowly open the envelope. The sound of paper tearing slices through the thundering silence.

I look inside the envelope and enclosed are two sheets of paper. For a moment, my vision blurs as tears sting my already tired eyes. I blink twice, then once more to focus on the words below.

Chapter Four

Dearest Olly and Mae

If you are reading this, it means that I'm gone. Ah, I'm sorry. I know you must have been through the ringer. There was only one thing worse for me than losing your mother, Olly, and that was watching you grieve and then grow up without her in your life. But grief is inevitable. So I'll not tell you to stop crying.

This letter . . . I've found it the most difficult to write. Over the summer you'll get to see all of the letters I've penned. Some were easier than others, but this first one, well, I'm struggling . . .

I can imagine you all sitting in the living room as you read this. Or maybe you are already in Nomad? Well, the main thing is, don't be worrying, this is a GOOD letter. No nasty surprises, I promise you.

So was it a good turnout today in the end? Charlie Doyle had almost a thousand at his mass and I can remember thinking that it must have made his family happy, seeing how loved he was. He was a good man, in fairness, even if he had a neck like a jockey's you-know-what. It's over ten years since he borrowed my drill. Not that any of that matters a blind bit now, of course.

I hope you don't mind that I organised my own funeral. I didn't want any of you to have the burden and, if I'm honest, partly I wanted to control how I leave this world. Beth never got that chance. I always regret that we'd not discussed what she wanted. Did I do right by her? That's weighed on my mind a lot lately. Arra, sure there's no point worrying about that now.

Olly, all this talk about funerals sparked a forgotten memory. 'Are you quite alright?' Do you remember that day at your great aunt Celeste's funeral? I cried with laughter all over again today when I thought about it. Tell the kids, they'll like that story.

Bet you have lots of questions right now. What's with the letters? What's with Nomad? I'm coming to that.

All I've ever wanted in life was to see you happy, lad. And watching you and Mae fall in love and start your own family, well it's been a privilege to be part of. I want to thank Mae, in particular, for letting an old fool like me live with you.

I know that these past six months have been hard. My cancer, along with sucking the life out of me, seems to have sucked the joy out of our family, hasn't it? Don't try denying it, I know it's true. We used to laugh a lot in this house, but the laughs seem far and few between lately.

I can't change the past, but I can help change what happens next. I've decided it's time to inject some fun into the Guinness family.

That brings me to Aled and Nomad. Does he look like Sir Tom Jones? He sounds just like him, at least he did on the phone. Decent bloke.

Nomad is my gift to you all. Isn't she a beauty? I've only seen pictures, mind you, and a video clip, but even so, I can tell she's perfect. She's all paid for, so don't fret about money. And there's a few bob extra for expenses. Aled has promised to show you all how she works before he goes. Now I can imagine that you are wondering what on earth possessed me to buy Nomad. Well, it's simple. And the word simple is key.

Olly, do you remember when I asked you recently what did you want from life and you said to me that it had all gotten complicated lately? Well, I couldn't stop thinking about that. I decided that I'd find a way to uncomplicate things for you.

At first I wasn't sure how to accomplish that, but then I dreamt of the answer. Do you remember our atlas? You, your mam and I would spend hours poring over it, wondering where we'd go to next in our travels. Well, I know how to make things simple again for you all. A holiday! A long one, where you can forget about the past year and just relax. Eliminate all the stresses and complications.

Drum roll please Jamie. You are going on a trip around Europe – in Nomad – for eight weeks. You can all forget about work, school, sickness and death and just focus on being a family again.

Isn't it great? Are you as excited as I am? It won't be all fun, mind you! You see, Evie and Jamie need to realise that the world is not limited to Wexford. There's a lot more out there than Facebook, Netflix or Candy Crush. I want them to see different cultures, taste new foods, watch the sunset from a new vantage point.

I need to talk to you too about my ashes. Some of them I'd like to have buried in the flowers around Beth's grave. But the rest, bring with you and I'll let you know where you must scatter them, in due course.

I'm going to say goodbye for now, because I'm getting tired and I'm sure you are all dying to go outside to check out Nomad. Is Jamie out the door already? Ha!

You need to get my briefcase. I've left everything you need in there. You'll find a letter for each stage of your journey, with full instructions. Time to get packing Guinness Family! You leave on Friday 27th June. I wish I could go with you. But I suppose, in part, I am, or at least my ashes are! That makes me smile.

Before I go, there's just one more thing you need to all remember. Life is short. So don't spend it regretting what you should have said, to those you care about. If you love someone, say so! Not just with words mind, but in your actions too.

Leave nothing unsaid, you hear me?

I love you,

Pops

Chapter Five

MAE

There is a stunned silence in the room, as Olly finishes reading the letter aloud. He lets it fall from his hand and the sheaves of paper float to the floor in front of him. Evie stands up and walks out, wordlessly. I contemplate going after her, but she's back less than a moment later, placing Pops' briefcase in front of her father's feet. She takes a seat by his side and leans in close to him. Jamie walks over and sits on his other side and still none of us speak. They're good kids. United, flanking their father, supporting him.

I lean down and pick up the pages and put them in their rightful order. A large tear lands on the spidery script and the ink smudges. I panic and blot it dry and then fold the letter carefully in two, placing it on the coffee table in front of us. None of us take our eyes off it. And still the room is silent, save for the distant hum of traffic on the road outside and the twitter of the sparrows that nest in the eaves of our roof.

'Olly,' I say. Someone has to break the silence. He looks up at me, his eyes lost and unbelieving.

'He said he'd find a way,' Olly replies.

I nod and my heart breaks for my husband.

'I just didn't expect to hear from him so quickly.'

I know Olly wasn't trying to be funny, but this makes me smile. 'He was always full of surprises.'

'You know, there were gazillions at the funeral,' Jamie states with his usual flair for drama, throwing his arms up in the air to further elaborate his point.

We all grin at that gross exaggeration and Olly says, 'I'm not sure it was quite that much, but he got a decent turnout – more than most get.'

'He was loved,' I state. 'That was evident by the huge crowd gathered. So many people from his job too. And I don't think a single person from the village didn't come out either. All his years on various committees . . . ' I add.

Olly looks down to the brown briefcase and takes a deep breath. He opens it and pulls out an atlas, staring at it, his face scrunched up, perplexed. He runs his fingers over the cover and then, with great care, opens it up, flicking through the pages one by one.

'What is that, Dad?' Jamie demands. 'Let me see.' His hands try to pull the book and Olly swats him away.

'You know, back in the eighties, when I was a kid, there was a recession on. Much like there is now. And it had the country on its knees. But we were doing okay, thanks to Pops' job. I mean we weren't rich or anything, but we had a house, a car and enough money to go on a foreign holiday every year.'

'Where did you go?' Evie asks.

'A lot of Europe, the US once, furthest we got to was Thailand. Mam and Dad loved to travel and explore new places. They would spend months planning where our next adventure would take us. This very atlas here, oh boy, we could spend hours looking through it. Always on the lookout for inspiration on where we could travel to next. My suggestions to go to Timbuktu were always taken into consideration. I always fancied a trip there, for no other reason than I liked the sound of it as it rolled over my tongue.'

'Timbuktu,' Jamie says. 'Can we go there?'

Olly smiles and ruffles his hair. 'Maybe.'

I look at the children and imagine if one of us were to die now, what it would be like for them. Olly was so young to lose his mum. I realise he's spoken more about her death these past few days than he's done in all of our marriage. He often tells us – understatement of the year – about how amazing a mother she was – but he rarely gets into the nitty gritty about what it was like when she died.

'I thought this atlas was binned long ago. It just disappeared one day and I think the furthest we travelled after Mam died was West Cork. I suppose Pops and I didn't feel much like going anywhere without her,' Olly says.

'If he kept it all these years, it meant a lot to him too,' I say.

Olly closes the book and then reaches into the briefcase again. A bundle of letters are tied together, parcel-like, with brown string. A Post-it note is placed on the top and Olly reads it out loud, '*Remember, each letter must be opened ONLY on the date stated on the envelope. No cheating.'*

Olly's hands shake as he tries to untie the string, so I take it from him. We huddle in close to see what it says.

'Open me on Friday 27th June.' scribbled on the first envelope.

'That's Jamie's last day of school,' I realise.

'Will we open it now?' Jamie asks, true to form, my little impatient man.

Olly looks at me for guidance and part of me wants to say, hell yes, we're opening them all now. I want to know what Pops has in store for us. This is way too big to just sit and wait. I want to be forewarned, because off the bat, one thing I know for sure is this – I'm not going camping for eight weeks in that yoke out there.

'We can't open them,' Evie interrupts, the voice of reason. 'We have to honour Pops' dying wishes.'

Damn it. You can't argue with that sentiment.

Olly takes the letters from me and reties the string, placing it back in the briefcase along with the atlas.

'We'll do as you ask, Pops', he murmurs as he closes the latch on the bag. Feck that! I reckon I can steam the envelopes open with a kettle. What the others don't know won't harm them. I look up, feeling Evie's glare and I swear she knows what I'm thinking. Her face is full of reproach and I feel like a naughty kid, caught with her hand in the cookie jar. Okay, maybe no steaming so.

'Hey, Dad, what was the funeral Pops was talking about in his letter?' Jamie asks.

'You know, I'd forgotten all about that day, until he mentioned it,' Olly whispers.

'What happened?' Evie asks.

'Yeah, tell us what happened,' Jamie demands.

'I remember it was a miserable day, the rain pelting down. The kind of rain that makes it near-impossible to see where you are going. At one point Pops had to pull over and park up for a bit. It took us a lot longer to drive to the church than Pops anticipated, so we didn't have time to get something to eat first, as he'd promised me. When the mass was over my grumbles about being starving matched the grumbling noises from my tummy! Pops reckoned if we were "super-fast" we could drive to the chipper. We could then grab something to eat and beat the funeral cortege back to the grave-side.'

The children were all smiles, enjoying Olly's tale. He always had a way with words; people listen when he talks.

'Pops was resourceful,' I say.

He nods and continues, 'Luck was on our side, there was no queue in the chipper and we were back in the car within ten minutes, munching on the best chips I'd ever eaten before. I can still smell the vinegary, salty mix that filled our little car.'

'I could eat some chips now,' Jamie sighs. 'My stomach is grumbling too!'

'You're always hungry,' Evie interjects. 'It's gross.'

'Go on,' I urge Olly and shush the kids to be quiet.

'Well, we rushed to the graveyard and parked up. We could see the funeral car inching its way towards a grave at the back of the graveyard. So we ran, Pops using his hand to wipe the salt from around my mouth as we went.

I can still remember him winking at me as we got to the graveside. We were delighted with ourselves, our bellies warm and full, no one the wiser.'

I watch grief hit my husband's face again, as if the memory of that conspiratorial wink is too much for him to bear.

'So you got away with it!' Evie says. 'Nicely played, Dad.'

'Oh that's only half the story. We joined the mourners around the grave. But the priest kept referring to a "he" not a "she" that had died. We both giggled at first, Pops threw his eyes up in the air. But then his face went all serious, the laughter gone. He shushed me and he gestured around the grave and I saw that there wasn't a single person there that had been at the church earlier.'

We all gasp once more and look expectantly at Olly.

'We were only at the wrong grave! You couldn't make it up, but at that exact same moment, as the penny dropped, we turned around – it felt like in slow motion – and there was another funeral procession entering the main gate. Aunty Celeste's funeral cortege, heading to the other side of the graveyard.'

'What did you do?' I ask.

Olly starts to laugh. 'We started to back away from the graveside. Both of us in long strides, trying to slip away unnoticed. But then Pops tripped over a kerb and fell on his backside, legs up in the air. I started to laugh, couldn't stop myself and everyone turned and looked at us. The priest said loudly, "Are you quite alright?" Pops looked at me and repeated it, and sure we were goners then. We both doubled over in laughter. I could hardly pull him to his feet. The mourners were all – quite rightly – annoyed with us.'

We all join in Olly's laughter, picturing the scene that he has painted for us.

'How could I have forgotten that? You know, for years afterwards one of us would only have to say, "Are you quite alright?" and then we'd be on the floor, laughing again,' Olly says, shaking his head.

'I think Pops wanted us to laugh today,' Evie says. I look at her and marvel at her perception. Of course Pops mentioned that story in his letter for that very reason.

'He wanted us to laugh,' I repeat and lean in to pick up his letter. I scan through it again, soaking up his words, trying to picture him writing this.

'He need never have thanked me,' I say to Olly. 'Where else would he be, but here with his family?'

Olly smiles at me and nods. He is silent again and gestures for me to give him the letter. We all watch him as he reads it to himself.

'He bought us a camper van,' Olly states and we all look to our sitting-room window and take in the vehicle parked outside.

'So cool,' Jamie says. I'm not sure what Evie is thinking. She's holding her cards close to her chest.

'What do you make of it all?' I ask my husband.

He shrugs. 'I'm not sure how I feel myself. I'm still a bit shocked that he had been so sneaky and planned all this without me knowing. What do you think?'

I stand up and walk to the window and thumb towards Nomad. 'Truthfully? I just don't get what Pops was thinking. Eight weeks stuck in that small space. We'd kill each other.'

And when disappointment fills Olly's face. I know I'm trouble. He wants to go.

Shite.

Chapter Six

MAE

Olly ignores my statement. I've no idea what he is thinking because he's gone quiet again. On a normal day he never shuts up, but then again, there's nothing normal about a day when you bury your father.

Jamie is bouncing around the room, jumping and down with excitement. He has already been begging us to let him ring his friends to boast about the forthcoming adventure. Evie isn't saying a lot, but then again it's hard to tell when she's enthusiastic or not these days. We can't get her to talk – not just about the drinking, which she swears was a one-off – but about anything. I know that there is more to this than she's letting on.

It's not just 'hormones' making her moody. She's changed. And there's something in her eyes, fear maybe? I don't know. I can't put my finger on it. We had to put a pause on our questioning, because Pops got so ill. At least she's already on school holidays, so at home, where we can watch her. When I rang her teacher and her principal they swore that there's nothing going on that I should be aware of. But it doesn't add up. I just don't buy the story that Evie wanted to experiment. It's too out of character. I'm missing something. At least now the funeral is done, I can focus on Evie and get to the bottom of it all. And that bloody van out there is not going to get in the way of that.

Damn it, Pops, why did you have to go and leave us, right when we needed you most? If anyone could have gotten Evie to talk, it would have been you.

I cannot for the life of me work out what he was thinking. I mean, fair enough, send us on a holiday. I could handle two weeks in Portugal; we all could. That would have been bliss. But to think that we would even consider heading off on some madcap adventure in a camper van for eight weeks is preposterous.

Of course I like the idea of teaching the children about the big world out there. It's a noble aspiration, but surely we can do that without having to sleep in a metal box on wheels!

'We better go outside to Aled and take a look at the van,' Olly says, walking towards the door. Jamie is out the door before I've even had a chance to stand up.

'Come in, come in,' Aled declares when we knock on the door. I prepare myself for the worst, but as I enter the van I'm surprised. It's larger inside than I anticipated and quite modern. Even so, we keep bumping shoulders with each other, almost tripping ourselves up as we try to fit into it. I give Olly a knowing look that's meant to convey, Yeah, right, we'd live in this for eight weeks? Not a hope! Him giving me the thumbs-up sign doesn't reassure me that he got my look.

We all follow Aled in single file to the left. It's the main living area, I suppose. A sea of walnut-wood cabinets with cream-leather upholstery greets us. A bit sterile looking, really. Not a single feminine touch, but no surprise there, either, looking at him. It's spotless and smells clean, I'll give Aled that much.

'It smells nice,' Olly pipes in, as if taking the thought from my head.

'This here is the kitchen galley. You have all the mod cons, Mae,' Aled says, pointing out the cabinets. This irritates me no end. I mean why automatically assume that the kitchen is my domain? He's wrong, as it happens, it's all Olly in the kitchen these days. Fair enough, I've never been Rachel Allen but I always enjoyed cooking. But since Olly lost his job, he's taken over all domestic duties and won't hear of me doing a thing. When I think about all those times I used to complain about how little he did to help around home, I want to kick myself. Those were the good old days.

'There's not an inch of space not utilised for storage,' Aled continues and I murmur something that I hope sounds encouraging. My back is playing up and I wonder: would it be bad if I left them to do the tour without me?

Aled then directs his attention to the living area in front of him. A table sits between an L-shaped sofa bench in cream leather with a second sofa along the other wall. There are several more cupboards in walnut suspended above this.

'Sit, sit,' Aled tells us all. 'It's proper comfortable.' He beams as he tells us this, like he's showing off a prized poodle or something.

And like obedient children, we all sit as directed and Olly compliments Aled on his soft seating. I try hard not to giggle at how wrong that sounds. When Olly glares at me I only want to laugh harder.

He then points up to the right-hand-side corner, 'You'll be happy to see that I've satellite TV too. Now then, Jamie and Evie, you'll enjoy that, won't you? It has all the channels. Now here's my top tip for you. Get yourself one of those Apple TV thingamajigs. That way you can watch Netflix anywhere you go. Right now I'm on series three of *Orange Is the New Black*. Oh, it's addictive that one!'

Evie does perk up a bit at this news and Jamie starts searching for the remote control so he can switch on the TV to try it out.

'I have to tell you, Aled, this has a lot more mod cons than the caravans I used to holiday in as a lad with Pops,' Olly says. 'Don't you think, Mae?'

I shrug, but I have to concede this much. 'It does appear to be well equipped.'

'Oh, we've come a long way, for sure,' Aled nods in agreement. 'I have friends who live all year round in their camper vans. Proper little homes on wheels they have set up. Truth be told, I'm happiest myself when I'm in Nomad here.'

'Why did you sell it then?' I ask, and I try to hide the smirk that appears on my face. 'If you love Nomad so much, why not keep it?' I think that's a fair question. Go on, get out of that one, Aled.

He leans in close to us, all conspiratorial and says, 'I'm getting married! Me. Fifty-four years old, a confirmed bachelor, I thought, forever. Sure, who'd have me?'

His face crinkles up in joy. 'I've met a woman. Proper lady she is, called Edith. And wait till you hear how we met! Only on the "I love the open road" online forum. Oh that's a cracking website. You'll all be needing to join that I'm sure. Lots of like-minded folk, all happy to share tips, a life-saver, I can tell you, on more than one occasion when I've been on my travels. Well, anyhow, you see I was having some problems with my water pump here on Nomad. It was scalding the water. I couldn't shower without putting my life in my hands. And would you believe that Edith was having the same problem? So we got chatting online about what could be wrong and between us we sorted it out. Wasn't it a problem with the pump for both of us in the end? Would you credit that?'

Olly and I both nod along in unison like a pair of nodding dogs. Despite myself, though, I find myself enraptured with Aled's tale of love amongst the camper vans.

'So we've spent the past few months chatting and then we decided to meet up. Truth be told, I was a nervous wreck. I never thought I'd ever meet a woman who would show any interest in me. I know I'm a little odd. I don't mind telling you I was shaking when I parked up Nomad next door to Almost Home.'

'Almost home?' I ask.

'Edith's camper van. Oh, it's a beauty. Same model as this, but a newer version and it's got the woman's touch. Cracking job it is.'

Aled looks wistful, as if he is thinking about his fiancée. And, despite myself, I'm touched. He may well be a stranger, a man who I only met an hour ago, but even so, I'm happy for him. There's someone for everyone out there, it seems.

'We proper hit it off, the second we met. Before I knew it, I was proposing and she only said yes. So we're getting married next week. And then we are off on our honeymoon in Almost Home.'

I can feel my mouth drop open as I listen to Aled's romantic tale and tears spring to my eyes before I can stop them. My teeth feel watery – you know the way they go when you are about to cry. It's as if the water springs up in every orifice in our bodies, isn't it? Why I feel so upset at such an upbeat tale of love I don't know, but it has thrown me off balance. I glance at Olly and time falls away like the autumn leaves on a tree.

'I've never been so cold in my life!' I shiver as we walk into the warm pub. A long walk on the beach seemed like a good idea until the wind whipped up so strong that it nearly pushed me into the ocean.

'Go over to the fire, darling, and I'll get the drinks.'

As I stand in front of the crackling fire, I watch my boyfriend and feel like the luckiest girl in the world. He comes back with Irish coffees and we sit in front of the fire on two bar stools, hip to hip, our hands clasped around the glasses.

'You've got cream on your nose!' Olly laughs and I dip my finger into his cream and put a dollop on his nose too.

We're being silly and the look from the barman, who clearly thinks we've lost our minds, only makes us laugh more. We're giddy from love. The world is a small place and only includes us two. I love this man so much that I can't bear to be apart from him.

'Marry me,' Olly says, cream still on the tip of his nose.

'What?' I shriek.

'I said, marry me. I love you Mae, I can't live one more moment not knowing that we're going to be together forever. Marry me? Please?'

'Congratulations!' Olly enthuses and starts to pump Aled's hand up and down, bringing me back to the present. I blink away tears quickly before anyone notices. When did Olly stop calling me 'darling'? I can't remember the moment and that feels wrong. I just know he doesn't any more. And the grief at the loss of a simple endearment that used to make my insides sing makes me want to weep. Instead, I turn to Aled, 'I'm happy for you. And Edith too. Congratulations.'

'She's waiting for me in the hotel. We're going back on the ferry tomorrow morning. Tonight, I think we'll just have a nice meal and a walk along the quay. It's a cracking town, Wexford is. I've had many a happy time visiting over the years.'

He then walks over to the driver and passenger seats and tells us that we won't want to miss this. He swivels the seats around, so that they are now part of the living area.

'Ta da!' he exclaims, clearly thrilled with this specification.

'Very handy,' Olly tells him and sits in the driver's seat to try it out for size. 'Comfortable too.'

Oh dear. Olly is angling the mirror to suit him and has begun flicking switches on the dashboard. Jamie jumps into the passenger seat and starts swivelling it around, over and over, squeals of delight with each turn.

'Safety belts here and here,' Aled tells me, pointing to the seating in the lounge. 'Don't worry about the children travelling at the back. It's all taken care of. Safe as houses back here they will be.'

I am beginning to feel quite overwhelmed by it all again. Now that Aled is back doing his sales pitch, he begins to sound like one of those pushy time-share reps. Olly and I had the misfortune to spend time with one on a holiday years ago.

'I want to go up there!' Jamie shouts, pointing to the canopy bed over the driver's cab.

Aled chuckles and pulls down a ladder from it. 'This is one of the double beds on board. I sometimes like to sleep here just for the hell of it. To mix things up, if you like. Although I usually sleep in the master bedroom at the back of the cabin.'

Jamie clamours up and lies down, exclaiming, 'Wow! This is so cool. Come up here, Evie!'

Evie looks at Jamie in horror. 'Over my dead body.' She then turns her back on him, making sure he is under no illusion that the subject is closed.

I hide my smile, but am jubilant that I have at least one ally in my anti-Nomad camp.

'There's also two single beds here,' Aled tells Evie, pointing to the sofas. 'You can have one of those if you don't fancy sharing with your brother. It sleeps six people, you know. Follow me and I'll show you the master bedroom and the bathroom.'

'Sleep in the kitchen?' Evie says, horror all over her face.

'Don't worry, you won't have to,' I whisper to her. She doesn't answer me, but I think I see a flicker of gratitude in her face.

Olly and I walk after him and I notice with a frown that my husband seems more animated than I've seen him in years. He cannot possibly be considering keeping this?

Aled opens a door and we peer inside a small bathroom with a toilet, sink and a minuscule shower. It's spotless and smells of lemons.

'The water and heating system is fantastic. You'll not be worrying about cold showers in Nomad. But here's a top tip for you all. It's easier to shower in the facilities that most campsites offer.' He winks at Olly and me.

'Oh and don't worry about being cold. I've camped out in the iciest of weathers and been warm and toasty inside Nomad.' He tells us this with utmost sincerity.

'Right! This here is the master bedroom.' Aled opens a small door that appears to be floating in the wall. He then pulls down a hatch below it to reveal a little step-ladder. He ushers us to climb up into the master bedroom, which in fact is a closet with a double bed in it. Over the bed are – yes, you guessed right – cupboards right up to the ceiling.

'Lots of storage here too,' Aled tells me and I stifle a groan.

'I don't see any wardrobes?' I say. I mean where are you supposed to hang your dresses?

Aled lets out a belly laugh and wipes at his eyes theatrically. 'Wardrobes! You are funny!'

Olly starts to laugh too, followed by Jamie, who both seem to think that the Welshman is a stand-up comic. I cannot for the life of me see what is so funny about there being no wardrobes in a camper van. I mean it appears to have cupboards in every possible spare inch, why not a bloody wardrobe?

I feel like the outsider in our family once again, out of sync with the rest of them. I never seem to quite get the same jokes as them these days. I should be used to that feeling by now, but I'm not. Only a few hours ago, when we were driving home, it felt like the old days – us four against the world. But with every peal of laughter that they are all now emitting, I feel more alone.

Damn you, Pops, what the hell were you thinking? Have you any idea of the trouble you are going to cause with this stupid trip you've planned?

'Now the beauty of this model is the large garage you have on board. Come with me and prepare to be amazed.' Aled walks quickly out of the cabin outside and we all follow. He's practically skipping with excitement as he disembarks from the van.

Jamie rushes to get out the door first, so that he doesn't miss any of the excitement.

'Cracking,' I say and Evie sniggers. Olly throws a look of irritation my way and shushes me.

Aled opens a door at the back of the van and I realise that what I would refer to as a large boot, he is in fact calling a garage.

'Proper tidy,' he boasts. 'Not all campers have one this size, you know.'

I'm a bit embarrassed when he catches me throwing my eyes up to the heavens.

'I like to say that there's room for a lot of junk in your

trunk on my Nomad!' he tells us. He starts to laugh at his own joke again and everyone laughs heartily with him. My smile feels false, who am I trying to kid?

But then Evie walks over to me and whispers, 'It's lush,' with a mischievous glint in her eye. I could hug her. I wonder, will Olly shush her too? But he just smiles at her. Right, it's just me who is not allowed to make any jokes.

I shiver, despite the warm evening. I have this weird sensation, as if I'm looking at my life from a distance. I see Olly and Jamie, with big grins on their excited faces, as they listen to Aled wax lyrical about Nomad. I see Evie, watching me, worried, because she can see that I'm not enjoying myself. And then, there's me, standing to the left of everyone else. I'm a sorrowful sight with a frown that makes me look twenty years older. And once again I don't recognise myself. Do I even fit in this family any more? I'll never leave my children, I couldn't live without them, but maybe, to be the kind of mother they deserve, I need to leave Olly. Maybe, we've come to the end of our road and we should just accept that. Split custody of the kids. Others make that work, we're reasonable adults, we can too.

I touch my phone in my jacket pocket, knowing that there are several unanswered text messages from Philip. I haven't been in touch with him since Evie's hospitalisation. I swore back then that I'd never talk to him again, that I'd draw a line under the flirtation. Because that's all it was in fairness. A flirtation that nearly tipped over into dangerous territory.

But why, then, haven't I deleted him from my phone? Now there's million euro question.

'Isn't this so cool?' Olly says. No, it's not one little bit cool, Olly, and if you bothered to look at me, to give me more than a cursory glance, you'd know that. But you don't care how I feel. You are going to do exactly what you want.

'And you will be delighted to hear that you have a bike rack, too, so no need to use up the garage for that,' Aled says.

'That's handy,' Olly nods with approval at the news.

'We're not a biking kind of family,' I say at the exact same time.

'Not yet anyhow,' Olly jokes at me and the realisation that we are in trouble here solidifies. There's no doubt about it, he's totally carried away with the whole farce of us heading off in this van.

'You know, I've toured with a two-man canoe, a marquee and a folding table and chairs all in this garage here. You'll not get a better van for storage than my Nomad,' Aled tells us.

'Our Nomad, don't you mean?' Jamie says and everyone laughs again. We are quite the jolly group.

I'm about to tell him that we're not the canoeing type of family, either. But he's gone before I get the chance and at the other side of the van talking about water tanks and sewage and electrics. I switch off because I have no intention of ever getting my hands dirty with any of that nonsense.

'Is it diesel or petrol?' Olly asks. Oh boy! He's taking this way too seriously.

'Diesel. 2.8L turbo. Proper nippy when you get on the open road, let me tell you.'

Olly nods at him with a goofy grin plastered on his face. He's picturing himself driving on an open road right now, I can tell.

I resist the urge to give him a thump.

Aled then stands up straight and tells us to close our eyes. Seriously, he actually tells us to close our eyes for a big surprise, like we are kids again waiting for a bag of buttons. Olly, Evie and Jamie all do as they are bid, much to my amazement, and I feel I have no choice but to join in the madness. That or once again be the party pooper.

Maybe I am behaving like a child, but I can't help myself. I have to take a peek. What on earth is he up to? It takes me a moment to work out what it is, but then I get it and to be fair to Aled, it is quite cool. He's pulled down an awning from the roof and it transforms the van – doubling its width.

'Ta da!' He smiles triumphantly at us all. 'This is the best thing I ever got installed. If it's raining you can still sit outside and watch the world go by. A whole new room for you to enjoy. Proper tidy. Put your table and chairs out under this and, trust me, you'll never eat indoors ever again.'

'Can't you just imagine it? Us all sitting under the stars in front of an open fire,' Olly says, that dreamy look back again.

'Can we have s'mores, Dad?' Jamie asks him.

'You don't even know what a s'mores is,' Evie yawns theatrically. Yep, I hear you. I'm bored of all this Nomad-talk too.

'They always have them in movies, stupid. I've been

71

wanting to try one for ages,' Jamie states, sticking his tongue out at his sister.

'Son, you can have anything you like,' Olly states, ruffling his hair and I sigh. When was it decided that we are going to go anywhere in this rust bucket?

'Why don't you all have a good look around and let me know if you have any more questions? Then who wants to go for a drive? I reckon it's time to take Nomad on your maiden voyage. Edith and I are staying in the Riverbank House Hotel tonight. A real treat. We don't normally stay in hotels, but we thought we'd celebrate selling Nomad. If you could drop me there, I'd be proper grateful.'

'Yes!' Jamie exclaims, 'I call shotgun!' And he races to the driver's cabin.

Olly laughs and tells him that he'll be sitting in the back with me and Evie when we leave. 'I better have Aled beside me for the first spin, just in case.'

And so, before I have a chance to proffer an opinion, I find myself buckled into one of the dinette seats. Jamie and Evie are sitting alongside me, their faces both alight with excitement.

'Can we watch TV while we drive, do you think?' Jamie asks. 'Aled, can we watch TV?'

'You can watch DVDs, Jamie,' Aled tells him.

'Cool,' Jamie says.

Olly turns to me from the driver's seat and the last of the evening light shines through the window. It hits his face, lighting him up in a golden glow. It changes him. He looks young – like he did when we first met. His face has seemed contorted into a continuous frown these past few months, with worry and stress for Pops and the kids. And about me too, I suppose. Well, now it's alive with excitement and I feel guilty once again for not sharing his obvious joy. I want to. I do. I want Olly to be happy.

One problem, though – I'm not going on a crazy-assed mystery tour for eight weeks in a van. Not even for Olly.

Chapter Seven

EVIE

AnnMurphy: Heard about your granddad. Soz. Hope you are ok and not too sad.

My first reaction is, yeah, right, like you care, Ann Murphy.

I re-read the instant message on Facebook for the third time, puzzled and suspicious. Genuine or fake? She's never really spoken to me before, so why, all of a sudden, get in touch?

She's not part of the whole bitch-parade in school. But she stood by and watched Martina and Deirdre make my life hell for the past year and did nothing. I decide to ignore it. Just like I've been ignoring all of the bullshit that's been shared on Facebook about 'E' from so-called friends.

I rub my temples. I still have a nagging headache. I might have been given a clean bill of health from the doctors, but I don't feel back to normal yet. It's all a bit fuzzy still.

Pathetic. Nerd. Weirdo. Loser. That's the usual tone of the messages I get on Facebook.

I shouldn't care what they think. For the longest time I didn't. Then all of a sudden it mattered what everyone thought. I suppose everyone has their limit and I reached mine.

I suppose I could just delete my accounts. But everyone is on Facebook, Snapchat and Instagram. The stubborn part of me thinks that it's not fair that I should stop using them, when I've done nothing wrong. And if I do, surely that means they've won.

Maybe they have already won. Maybe when I let them talk me into that stupid dare I made myself into the very thing they called me – a loser. I feel so stupid and shamed whenever I think about that. I can't tell Mam and Dad what really happened, they'd only freak. And they wouldn't understand anyhow. Better that they think I was experimenting with alcohol and made a mistake. I've not told them about the bullying, I can't just land all of this on them now too.

I wish Pops were here. I could talk to him, tell him about the message. I try to imagine what he'd say, but I can't come up with anything. He's only been gone a few days, but already it's like his face and his voice is beginning to fade at the edges. I'm not ready to lose him. I just don't know what to do.

Jamie peeps in the door. I've no privacy since Dad banned me from closing my door. It's a joke, this house. My whole life is a freaking sideshow.

'Get lost, Jamie,' I shout and he backs away, but he

looks relieved. I know what he's doing. He keeps checking up on me to make sure I'm alive. He thought I was dead when he found me. And now he's worried that I'll die too – like Pops. I hope he knows I'm sorry. I hate that I've upset him. He's just a kid.

He might run around like a Duracell bunny all day and I suppose you could be fooled into thinking he was fine. But at night I know he's scared. That's why he's wetting the bed again. That's when I get scared too. That's when I can't switch off. That's when I think that my brain is about to explode.

I wish I could cry. But I just feel numb most of the time. Is that normal? Everyone else seems to be crying on and off every day since Pops died. But the tears won't come for me.

Mam keeps asking me how I'm doing. But she doesn't really want to know the answer. She just wants me to say, fine, then she can sigh with relief and move on. I wonder sometimes what she'd say if I answered her truthfully. What if I just said, hey Mam, there's this pressure in my brain, in my stomach, in my hands and fingers that is building up so much that I think I'm going to explode. It hurts so much. Any minute now, boom, I'm gonna blow like a grenade.

I can feel their eyes on me all the time, watching me. I know they are worried. But I can't cope. I just want to pretend it never happened. Problem is, I can't get away from it. My mind has it all on loop and keeps going back over and over it all. That moment when I realised I was in hospital, I'll never forget.

They think I'm asleep. I'm afraid to speak, afraid of

what they will say to me. I've been so stupid. The doctor has a clipboard in his hand, all official-like. He looks tired. Like he's not slept in days. I sympathise because I feel exhausted too. And I'm sore all over. What's that about?

They all look super-serious standing side by side, facing the doctor. I know I must be sick, because I'm in hospital, I certainly feel crap, but their faces, all kind of grey and pinched, scare me. At least Jamie is asleep on a chair in the corner. I don't want him to see me like this.

The doc sounds really cross, it makes the hairs on my arms stand upright. 'Your daughter has more than five times the legal limit of alcohol in her system. Enough to kill a grown man. She's lucky to be alive.'

His words hang in the air like an accusation and nobody speaks for the longest time. I close my eyes tight and for a moment wish that I'd died earlier on. I don't want to hear any more about the mess I've made of everything. But the urge to look is too strong and I peep out through my eyelashes at the drama that is unfolding. Drama that I caused. Shit, shit, shit. I'm in so much trouble.

The shock has rendered them speechless. Mam has this weird look, like she is about to speak, but she can't get the words out. I look at the doctor, trying to get a lead on what he's about to say. Does his countenance have the look of one about to bear bad news? Maybe. What if I'm going to die? What if I've done serious damage to myself? Now that the thought takes root, I realise that I don't want to die, I want to be back home in my bedroom, reading a book. I look at the door and for a second consider bolting for it. But I'm hooked up to drips. I'm not going anywhere.

'She's going to be okay, though?' Mam pleads and I'm shocked by her tone. She sounds desperate. I think Dad is half holding her up.

The doc looks at his clipboard once more but doesn't answer her straight away. I don't like him very much. I think he's enjoying the power of it all.

'Give me another chance. Please give me another chance. Please don't take our baby away,' Mam mutters. I don't think she realises that she's speaking out loud.

Oh Mam, don't cry. I'm sorry.

The doctor's face softens a bit and he clears his throat, 'She's stable.'

I'm okay. Oh. My. God. I'm okay.

'When will she wake up?' Mam asks.

'Any time now.' He gives a brief smile, but as quick as it appears, the frown returns.

I realise I haven't taken a breath for a long time because I feel a bit faint. I exhale, just in time to hear the doctor sharing, 'Her alcohol blood level was 0.40. Do you know how many drinks that means Evie must have consumed?'

Oh boy, that doesn't sound too good. They shake their heads in unison, their mouths lolling open. They look ridiculous and I feel awful, 'cos I know this is all my bad.

'I *was* only gone for two hours. I don't understand how she could have gotten into such a state in such a short space of time,' Dad tells him.

Mam throws a look of disgust at him. My bad once again.

'Evie said she wanted to stay at home and finish her homework, she didn't want to come with us to the cinema.

I'd promised to bring Jamie as a treat because he nailed that Irish test,' he explains, looking like he could cry any minute.

Pops murmurs something to him. I can't catch what it is. But it seems to help because he doesn't start blubbering.

'Will you shut up for a minute and let the doctor talk?' Mam snaps. Shit, shit, shit. They're going to start fighting again. I don't know what to do. Maybe I should tell them I'm awake, to divert a row.

'Mae,' Pops snaps.

'I'm sorry, we are all under a bit of strain right now.' Mam does look sorry to be fair. 'We had no idea that Evie drank. As far as we both know, she's never had so much as an alcopop before in her life. How much alcohol are you talking about?'

'Our best estimation is that your daughter had at least thirteen units in quick succession,' he states.

Did I have that many? I can't really remember how many I put into the glass. They kept telling me to put more in.

'How the hell is that possible?' Mam says to Dad.

I remember putting the gin and whiskey into the glass. Oh damn, I put some wine from the fridge in too. It tasted horrible. Like petrol. Only I've never tasted petrol, but I bet it tastes exactly like my stupid cocktail did.

'As I said, she's lucky to be alive. We'll talk again tomorrow.' He walks out, but not before I catch the look of reproach on his face. Thing is, I don't feel so lucky right now.

'I was only gone for two hours,' Dad repeats and he walks towards me.

79

*I'm so sorry, Dad. Don't be upset. It's not your fault.
It was all mine.*

'We've gathered that!' *Mam says. Here we go again.
Ding dong! Round nine hundred and nighty-nine between
my folks.*

I jump when Pops speaks, his voice raised in anger.
'What the hell is wrong with you? This is not the time
to throw punches at each other. You and Olly need to
pull together. For Evie and Jamie, if you can't do it for
each other.'

*I close my eyes quickly, before anyone notices that I
am awake. Sleep, I need to sleep some more, I can't deal
with this. With them.*

I still can't deal with it all. It's not fair. I hear people
talking about getting 'black-outs' after they have drunk
too much. Why can't I black out that whole nightmare,
then? I jump off the bed. I need to get out of this house.
Damn it. I sit back down on the end of the bed. What's
the point? I've nowhere to go anyhow. No one to talk
to. I'm all on my own and the loneliness hits me smack
across my face.

Ping – another Facebook message.

**AnnMurphy: You there? School was so boring for the
last week. You didn't miss anything. Mrs Byrne actually
dozed off on the last day in class. Lol.**

I grin, picturing the scene, and before I can psychoan-
alyse any further, I answer.

**EvieGuinness: Lol! What about Kent, was she still in
that foul mood?**

**AnnMurphy: Yep. She had a go at Shauna, proper lost
it.**

EvieGuinness: She's gonna blow any minute.

AnnMurphy: Like a grenade.

EvieGuinness: Pow!

AnnMurphy: LMAO hey what you at?

EvieGuinness: Nothing.

AnnMurphy: Are you feeling better?

EvieGuinness: I'm fine.

AnnMurphy: I wanted to talk to you about what happened. I feel really bad about it.

EvieGuinness: I'd rather not discuss it.

AnnMurphy: K. But I'm sorry.

EvieGuinness: K.

AnnMurphy: I better go peel the spuds. Mam has been shouting for me to help get dinner ready for ages. Chat later?

EvieGuinness: I'd like that. Laterz.

'It's nice to see you smiling,' Dad's voice takes me by surprise. He's standing in the doorway, watching. Damn it, I need to get them to let me close my door again. 'You want something to eat?'

I shake my head and feel my smile slip away. Dad looks like he's going to try persuade me to eat, but changes his mind and walks out. I'm so irritated with him and Mam right now. I don't buy the whole happy families gig that they have been on for the past few weeks. For months it's been obvious that they can't stand each other. The truce since Pops died is about to end any day now. I can feel it.

As for Nomad, part of me thinks, well played, Pops. Nothing suits me better than to get away from all of this drama for the summer. What have I got to stay around for? I sneak a look at the list of 'friends' who are online on Facebook. Are any of them really friends? Did any of them stand up for me when I was getting bullied? I don't think so.

I look for Luke. Nope, he's not there. The only person I want to see, but it appears that's not the case for him. One perfect evening with him, and then he disappears off the face of the earth. Have Martina and Deirdre been spreading rumours to him about me? I thought he was different. I thought he really liked me.

Yes, we should go on this trip. It's what Pops wants and I've nothing to stay here for. Although, how the hell I'll cope living so close with my crazy family, I don't know. At least here I can disappear to my room. Sometimes I wonder how we're even related. I've always felt a little different to them. I'm not saying that to be dramatic and I don't mean it in a bad way. We all kind of look alike, but we don't like the same things. Dad calls me the family's resident geek.

Pops used to say, 'The people who make fun of geeks, usually end up calling those same geeks "boss" one day.' Pops always knew what to say to make me feel good. I picture being Martina or Deirdre's boss one day. I'd make their lives hell. See how they like it having someone on their case morning, noon and night. Ha!

Pops was a geek too. That's why we got on so well. But now he's gone and I'm all on my own. Who'll buy me the *Guinness Book of Records Annual* now? I can't remember a year when he didn't buy it for me and we'd spend hours poring over it, checking out the new entries. A pain stabs me with the realisation that we will never do that again.

'Time to check out the family annual,' Pops would joke every time. Pops had me convinced for the longest time that the whole thing was named after us. We swore we'd do a record attempt one day together.

Another pain of regret. My bad, Pops. I should have made us do something when you got sick. I should have thought about you instead of all of the stuff going on in school and online.

I should have . . . damn it . . .

I pick up the 2015 album and flick through it to try and stop the should-haves driving me demented. I love reading about the crazy things people do to break records. At a guess, I would say that for almost every day of my life since I was seven I've read about at least one new record. Some are much cooler than others. Some are downright weird.

'There's nowt so queer as folk,' Pops always says. Said. It's past tense now. I bite my lip till I taste metallic blood. It works and I hold my own record for being the non-crying Guinness family member.

I come to the bookmarked page, the last thing I ever read to Pops. The day he died, I told him all about this guy from the Czech Republic. A dude called Fakir something or other. Anyhow, he only decided to break the record for the most days being buried alive. Why anyone would want to do that baffled us, but I was fascinated by the actual doing of the feat. Yep, Pops, you're right. Nowt so queer as folk.

Chapter Eight

EVIE

I take a peek at my phone to see if Ann's been on again. We've been chatting on and off for hours and while it's just chit-chat, it's fun. I like her.

AnnMurphy: Your folks still at it?

EvieGuinness: Yep. Whisper-fighting now. Like, yeah right, we can't hear you.

AnnMurphy: Scarlet for them. When Mam and Dad fight, they go at it like hammer and tongs. All shouters in our house.

EvieGuinness: Mine use silence like a weapon of mass destruction. And the looks they are throwing at each other, all the time. Can't cope.

AnnMurphy: Talking of weapons, Martina had something that looked like a nuclear explosion on the end of her chin today.

EvieGuinness: Wtf?

AnnMurphy: Seriously, it should be paying her rent, the size of that spot.

EvieGuinness: Stop, you're killing me!

AnnMurphy: That zit was killing me. You didn't have to look at it! Btw, just put your earphones on, then you don't have to listen to them fighting.

And just like that, I feel better. I never realised that Ann was so funny before. I get up and put headphones on, and drown out Mam's voice shushing Dad. Who do they think they are kidding? I'm not stupid. I can read the subtext. It's actually insulting the way they try to cover up their impending explosion of a marriage.

'Just a little disagreement, nothing to worry about,' Mam said last night, her voice all stretched like a rubber band about to snap. WTF? Hello, I've an IQ of 131 and she expects me to believe that! And I did that stupid IQ test on a day when I had a cold and my head was all mushed up. I'm not making excuses, I'm just stating facts. I could get at least 140 if I took the test again today.

Mind you, there's also a strong chance that the other week's stupidity could have melted quite a few of my brain cells. So maybe I should be grateful for the 131 score.

I flick through the books on my bedside locker, with no real interest. I normally go through at least three a week, but I've not managed to keep concentration long enough on anything for ages now. Even though I read on my Kindle and get loads from the library, whenever I love a book, I always buy it. Mam says I need to cull some of my books, give them to charity, but I can't part with any of them. I always say to her that having too many books is not a problem. Not having enough shelving is what I struggle with. Not sure Mam gets my sense of humour, though.

Ping. I scrabble for my phone.

AnnMurphy: Don't forget new episode of OUAT on Netflix today. That will cheer you up. Serious crushing on Hook.

EvieGuinness: I'll take him <u>any</u> day over Charming.

Last night I discovered that Ann watches *Once Upon a Time* too. Not sure she obsesses about it as much as me, though. I can't get enough of it. I think about the storyline all the time, trying to work out what's going to happen next.

And I met Luke because of the show. Just thinking about that first encounter at the Valentine's Day disco makes me want to cry. It will never happen again and it was the best moment of my entire life.

I hadn't wanted to go. In fact, I refused to go, but my parents insisted. Talk about irony, there were girls whose parents wouldn't let them go out and mine were horrified that I'd rather stay at home. To be fair, they didn't realise that I was terrified that Martina and Deirdre would start something at school. And I knew that I'd be on my own. Because everyone else in my class seemed to take two steps away from me, the more they ramped up their bullying. I think they were worried that by being my friend, they'd be in the firing line too. Thank goodness Mam and Dad insisted I go. Because I wasn't alone, in fact I had the best night of my entire life. There were posters up on the walls of the school hall advertising a new musical – *Peter Pan* – that was coming to the Dun Mhuire. And as I looked at the poster, at the picture of a smiling, benevolent, happy Peter Pan, I laughed. Because in *Once Upon a Time*, he's the personification of evil.

He's also the Pied Piper – two bad-assed fairytale characters rolled into one. I didn't mean to speak out loud, standing there, looking at that poster, but I did. I can't help myself, like a well read book, I allow the memory of that night to flitter out.

'If only people knew that you are Rumpelstiltskin's father, Peter Pan.'

'Now that was a plot twist,' a voice says from behind me. I turn around, surprised, and come face to face with a guy who looks like he could be the sixth member of One Direction. Masses of dark, curly hair, which should make him look girly, but made him just look beautiful. He's got a red-check shirt on, buttoned up to the collar, with skinny blue denims. I can't stop staring at his hair. I actually feel my hand rise up, involuntarily making its way towards the mop. Scarlet for me and I pull it back to my side. What the hell is wrong with me?

'I'm loving all the underworld stuff now,' he says.

'Me too. It's so clever how they keep changing the story, introducing new characters.' I blush, sure I sound way too excited about a TV show. I'm a little surprised at how much I want to be cool for a guy that I have just met. But he smiles and asks me, 'Want to grab a Coke and swap theories?'

In what feels like two minutes, but in fact is two hours, we chat and laugh about all sorts of things, not just a mutually loved TV show. Is this what true happiness feels like? Is this love? I look at Luke's lips and wonder what it would be like to feel them on mine.

And then, as if he'd taken the thought from my mind, Luke leans in and kisses me. My first kiss. I've dreamt about such an event, had no idea who might actually do the kissing, but I've often thought about it.

There is a bit of a false start at first. Noses bang and we both giggle self-consciously as we realign our necks. It feels like an out-of-body experience. And even though my stomach is flipping and my heart is beating like a runaway train, the rest of the world fades to the background, save for the smell, the feel, the touch of him.

When his lips touch mine, soft, he tastes sweet, like Coca-Cola. It lasts only a few seconds, but it is everything and more than I ever dreamed a kiss could be.

We pull apart and I feel a bit light-headed. Partly because the lights have just come on, signalling the end of the disco. Partly, from the kiss.

Luke whispers to me, 'We've an audience.' I follow his gaze and see Martina and Deirdre watching me. Before I can process why they look so annoyed, he grabs me by my hand and pulls me to my feet.

The best moment of my life that night. Evie, the geek, only went and got the boy.

I sigh as I look down at the yellow t-shirt I'm wearing, with 'Never Trust an Atom . . . They Make Up Everything!' blazoned on its front in bold black writing. Geek humour at its best, there. Luke would get the joke. I know he would. But I don't suppose I'll get the chance to show him this now.

Because it appears that the geek lost the boy just as quick as she got him. I don't know what I've done to make him disappear, but it hurts. Like the time I fell off the tree at the end of our garden. It felt like an eternity till I hit the cold, hard ground. But when I did, every bone in my body rattled and screamed out in protest at the pain inflicted.

Ann then appears to read my mind, sending me another message with uncanny timing.

AnnMurphy: Are you like, going out with Luke?

EvieGuinness: No.

AnnMurphy: Oh. Do you like him though? You looked like you did at the disco.

EvieGuinness: Dunno. Maybe. A bit. Yeah. I do.

AnnMurphy: He's like Harry from 1D.

EvieGuinness: Don't say that! You'll put me off him.

AnnMurphy: You're funny.

EvieGuinness: We kissed at the Valentine's Disco.

AnnMurphy: That's not news. Sure was the talk of the class. Martina was green. Sick as a small hospital. She's been mad about him for ages.

EvieGuinness: I didn't know that . . .

AnnMurphy: That's why she's been gunning for you. She's jealous. The big green nuclear explosive spotty wagon.

Crying with laughter here. I love this girl.

EvieGuinness: As much as you are making me feel better, she's got nothing to be jealous of. Luke disappeared off the face of the earth a few weeks back.

AnnMurphy: That sucks. And Evie, I know you said you didn't want to talk about it, but I need to tell you, that I know I should have stuck up for you before. I wanted to. I don't know why I didn't. I don't even like those two. You didn't deserve what happened.

I don't know what to say.

AnnMurphy: You still there?

EvieGuinness: Yeah.

AnnMurphy: I had nothing to do with the dare. I thought it was all kinds of wrong. But I should have stepped in. I'm sorry.

EvieGuinness: It's k.

AnnMurphy: k.

But before I can answer her, Jamie bursts in and jumps onto my bed.

'Get out.' I don't even look up. If I ignore him, he might go away.

'I'm bored,' he replies. 'What you doing?'

'None of your business. Go on, get out.' I try to twist myself away from him as he tries to use me as a climbing frame. 'I swear if Mam and Dad don't let me lock my door again soon . . . '

How can I persuade them that if I lock myself in I won't get locked again? Ha, that's funny. Must tell Ann that one.

'What you laughing at?' Jamie asks.

'None of your business.' But I'm still smiling. Feels weird, my facial muscles haven't done it in so long, they're all out of shape. 'Go on, get out of here, squirt.'

He sticks his tongue out at me as he slides off my bed. Loser.

AnnMurphy: I promise that it will be different next term.

AnnMurphy: Evie?

EvieGuinness: Soz, little brother came in. Wasn't ignoring you. Thanx. I can't think about school right now. With everything going on . . .

AnnMurphy: I know. Hugz.

EvieGuinness: Hugz.

I can't shift this horrible, heavy feeling of shame. I can't move with it sometimes. I feel guilty about so much in my life right now. The thought of going back to school again fills me with dread. Even with Ann on my side this time. I don't think I'm strong enough.

I stretch out and am relieved to note that physically, at least, I'm beginning to feel better. The body part, at least. It doesn't hurt so much now when I move or walk about. My splitting headache has reduced to a low throb and, when I look in the mirror, the old me stares back.

But I don't suppose I am the old me any more. I'm not sure who I am. I used to think that I didn't care what people thought about me. I used to think that I was confident enough to stand apart and be myself.

That was before I let a bunch of people define me and get inside my head and now I can't get them out. Maybe there is something wrong with me. Maybe I need to change, to fit in with the others. Be less geek-like.

I know that accepting their dare to drink a cocktail is the stupidest thing I've ever done. And the worst thing is, I KNEW that as I downed the poisoned chalice.

Mam said yesterday that we need a big talk. She said that she's giving me a little space because of Pops dying, but that the subject of my drinking is not closed. Someone shoot me now. Part of me feels that I should just tell her everything. But the bigger part of me, the part that answers to the name 'coward', wants to just go 'la la la la' and not think about it at all.

I know she's confused and I know that at some point I have to explain myself to them both. But I don't know what to say. When Mam showed Jamie and me YouTube clips and online articles about alcohol-related deaths a few months back, I felt so sorry for those people. And a bit superior too. I just couldn't fathom the recklessness of the people involved. I kept questioning what on earth would make them do something so ridiculous? But now I know.

Desperation. Fear. Loneliness. And a good dose of stupidity.

I hate myself for letting Martina and Deirdre get to me. I hate myself for being a victim. I hate that Luke seems to have disappeared off the face of the earth. I hate that I can't stop thinking about him and that kiss. I hate that my parents seem to loathe each other now. I hate that Pops is dead.

I hate my life.

Chapter Nine

MAE

I'm not in the door five minutes and Olly is already having a go. This time I'm in trouble because I dared to kick my shoes off in the hall. My right little toe has a blister on it and it's been killing me all day. Every chance I could I'd kicked my shoe off and laid my poor little toe on the cold office floor to try and numb the pain. I'd been dreaming of getting home so I could get into my soft slippers.

Okay, Olly may have just tidied the hall. I get that. But how have we got to a place where we are now arguing about shoes in the hall. There was a time when we couldn't wait to see each other, to find out how the other's day had been.

But now he shows no interest in my work whatsoever. If I bring it up, he gets all fidgety and changes the subject. It's as if he's blaming me that I didn't lose my job and he lost his. Like yesterday when I said I'd had a tough day, he sighed one of his long, God-awful, mind-numbing sighs and muttered something about how it's well for some to have a job.

He's just thrown in another sigh, worthy of my mother, and that's saying a lot, because she's one of life's non-stop whingers. One of those types who think that they've been given a raw deal all their lives. Truth be told, people like that enjoy being martyrs, whilst making the rest of us miserable too.

I can't help myself and snap back, 'For God's sake, you're turning into my mother!'

The look of hurt and horror on his face makes me regret the insult instantly. Because, in fairness, I can't imagine anything worse than being compared to my mother. I apologise and, like a chastened child, pick up my shoes. I then apologise for being sharp and hobble my tired feet to our bedroom, careful to put my shoes in their rightful place in our wardrobe. The temptation to sink into the soft mattress of our super-king is too much for me, so I lie down and close my eyes. But the sound of Olly sighing up a storm again puts paid to that respite. Now what have I done?

'Are you not even going to ask me about how Evie was today?' he complains.

I feel shame flood me, rising from my chest up to my face. I redden, 'I'm sorry, of course I want to know.'

And the most annoying thing is that Evie has been on my mind all day. I wish that I could be the one here, to worry and fret for her. But with exams on and end of year admin to take care of, I can't take any more time off. I already missed several days, because of Pops' funeral.

Oh, for feck's sake, now I'm sighing. It must be catching.

I heave my aching body upright and look at my husband, apologising all the while and urging him to tell me how Evie is.

'She's been in her room most of the day, didn't want any company. Won't eat. Throws daggers at me, whenever I go to check in on her. I don't know whether to force her to eat or not. She looks so unhappy, I'm at a loss as to what to do.'

I put my daydream of a long soak in a hot tub out of my head. I walk back to the kitchen with Olly, just so we could pretend for another evening that we were not disappointing each other more and more with every passing moment.

'We need a holiday,' Olly declares. This is the real reason for his need to talk. He wants to discuss the Nomad trip again. I just cannot believe how set on this crazy idea he is. It's all he's talked about, over and over, around and around like a broken record. My head is melting by the minute as he tries to wear me down. He does this all the time. If he wants something and I don't, he'll keep asking and asking because normally I'll give in just for an easy life. But I'm not giving in this time.

'Camping is not a holiday,' I hiss back. 'A holiday is somewhere where I'm lying on a sun lounger with a piña colada in my hand. A holiday is somewhere I can feel the sun on my bones, as I relax. We are NOT driving to God knows where in a rust box on wheels!'

'She's not a box!' Olly shouts in horror.

I am so irritated with him right now, I could belt him. But of course I can't because his father just died and that trumps all my irritation at his annoying camper-van

95

excitement. I have to play nice, but the more I think about it, how the hell does Olly think we can survive being in such close proximity to each other in Nomad for eight weeks, twenty-four-seven? One of us will go down for murder.

I mean, this whole idea of Pops' is beyond crazy. We don't even know where our first stop on the crazy mystery tour is. And I'm supposed to agree to it all, without even having all the facts?

'Have you any idea how much pressure I'm under in work at the moment?' I say. 'I can't do anything to jeopardise my position. One of us has to . . . ' I stop.

'One of us has to what? Bring in a wage?' Olly shouts. 'Because your no-good-for-nothing husband doesn't?'

'Oh, for God's sake, Olly. I'm worn out from this merry-go-round. For the last time, I know it wasn't your fault that you were made redundant. The current market out there is not your fault. No one blames you. But YES, goddammit, I have to protect my job, because one of us DOES need to bring in a wage!'

I need a gin and tonic. My mouth dries up and I glance at the clock, wondering if it's too early to start drinking.

Silence thunders around the room, with our annoyance at each other crackling like lightning between us.

Am I justified in my annoyance here? I mean, who in their right mind would contemplate just taking off for eight weeks? It's okay for Olly, he has no commitments, other than the children and home. And speaking of the children, is this the right time to bring Evie off to the great unknown? She needs stability and support – at home. Not gallivanting around the world on a mystery tour.

I'm right and I intend to make sure that Olly knows that too. But arguing is getting us nowhere. I smile at him and decide to try the charm offensive. It used to work all the time back in the day.

'Who likes camping anyhow?' I say brightly.

'Lots of people do,' Olly answers, looking a little bit startled by my abrupt change of demeanour. He thinks I'm beginning to change my mind. Think on, boyo, I've not even started yet.

'But do they? Really?' I say. 'I mean, people pretend to like camping all the time. In the same way that people pretend to like reading *Ulysses* or listening to jazz.'

Olly starts to laugh, then stops. 'But you like *Ulysses*!'

'No, as it happens, I don't, and that's my whole point, Olly. When I was young and pretentious and wanted to impress people, I thought it was a cool thing to say that *Ulysses* was my favourite book. But be careful of the lies you spin. Because I've had to spend twenty years pretending to like a book. When the truth of the matter is, I've never even read beyond the first one hundred pages!'

Olly's eyes look like they are about to jump out of his surprised face and then he breaks into laughter at my confession.

'You old fraud!'

I hold my hands up. 'We all do it to some extent. All because we want to impress someone. You do it too, if you're honest,' I add.

'I do not!' Olly defends himself.

'Yes you do. Don't pretend that when you are watching primetime every week, you'd not rather be switching channels to watch *Top Gear*!' I accuse.

In fairness, he acknowledges that I am right.

'Well, just like you pretending to enjoy political debate, it's a fact that people pretend to like camping. It's become one of those trendy things to enjoy right now. But most people, after about two hours of roughing it, would all agree that it's time to retreat home to a warm house and soft bed!'

I'm on a roll now and gain momentum as I continue, 'I mean, come on, look at us. Our definition of roughing it is having beans on toast for dinner.'

When Olly laughs, I find myself smiling back. But this time a genuine smile, not one trying to make him agree with me. There was a time that we used to make each other laugh all the time. When did we stop doing that?

No time to start pondering the state of our mirthless marriage. Not right now, anyhow. 'Remember when that storm happened last year, we'd no electricity?'

'Yes I do! And we had the best night ever. You said that too, don't deny it. We lit the fire, ate peanut-butter sandwiches with candles flickering in the background and we turned on the radio! You and Pops taught Evie and Jamie how to waltz!'

'Yes, it was a great night. I think it was the last night of true fun we all had before Pops was diagnosed, wasn't it?'

Olly nods. 'I can remember thinking how beautiful you looked in the candlelight. And later that night, you know . . . '

I do know. I remember us slowly undressing, kissing and making love, tenderly. I felt overwhelmed with love for my man and so lucky to have him by my side, in my life. I told him that we were lucky, that after ten years, we still wanted and needed each other. That we loved each other more now than ever before. And I meant every word.

Now, I don't recognise that couple . . . I'm not sure we even exist any more.

The air crackles with tension as Olly waits for me to say something. He walks towards me and I want to tell him that I remember it all. But instead, like picking at a scab, I can't stop myself and continue arguing my case against Nomad.

'It was fun, but for one night only. Do you not remember how much of a pain it was on day two with no electricity? And then by day three you wanted to pack us into the car and book into a hotel for the night.'

Olly's face falls as he acknowledges the truth in my words. He's furiously trying to find a rebuttal argument for me. I know he is.

'But, we wouldn't be roughing it without electricity or soft beds. Nomad has both – ha!' He is triumphant in his revelation.

'And if you said that we were going to head off for a long weekend in Nomad, I'd be a good sport and go along with you. I'd pretend that I don't care if I have to shower and wash in a room that is smaller than our downstairs loo. And I'd even go along with the fact that we'd be driving and living in the same tiny space, but this isn't a long weekend we're talking about. It's eight weeks, for God's sake!'

'But Mae, it could be fun. Just think about it. The four of us against the world once again.'

'We can do that from here, Olly,' I remind him, thinking to myself that it would be more likely the four of us against each other than the world.

'It's what Pops wanted,' Olly says.

The ace up his sleeve. The dying wish of Pops. Shit. I feel petulant and want to stamp my feet and I wish I had a wittier riposte, but the best I can come up with is, 'You can do it alone, then, Olly. I'm not going, and that's that.'

The thing is, if he goes on his own, I know that will be the end of our marriage. Philip called me at work yesterday. I didn't take the call, but he left a message saying he wants to meet. Part of me, if I'm honest, wants Olly to just go away. I'm sick of the fights, sick of trying to make him feel better about himself, sick of feeling unloved, unwanted. I'm bruised from the dozens of rejections I've suffered when I tried to initiate sex. Not that I bother any more. It doesn't take Freud to tell me that Olly's lack of sex drive is linked with him losing his job. I know that. I just don't know how to fix all of this. And I'm tired from trying.

I want to go back to that shady corner of a bar and feel wanted, desired for the first time in months, as I did when Philip caressed the back of my neck.

'And that's your final word?' Olly asks and I flush scarlet, putting my hands to my face, afraid he can read something that would betray my thoughts. 'You won't go?' He frowns.

'No.' Stay firm, Mae, stay firm.

He looks crestfallen and I see him work through my words and decide what his next move should be.

Go on, Olly, I dare you. Just go.

'You win, Mae,' he says, as he walks towards the door.

'Don't be like that, Olly. It's not about winning or losing, it's about what makes sense and what's right for our family!'

I feel guilty and in turn feel annoyed with him for making me feel that way. After all, all I'm doing is being responsible.

'What's right for you or the rest of us?' he asks.

I look at Olly and I have no answer. My family matter more to me than anything else in life. But lately, I feel like a stranger to them. I don't know how I have come to be in this situation, nor do I know how to make it right. I ask myself often, do I even love Olly any more? With all my heart I believed on the day we married that he was the man I'd love forever. But now the only thing I'm sure of is that I don't like my husband any more. He's changed so much over these past few months into this new, indifferent model.

'What about Pops' ashes?' Olly asks and I flush once more. I take a steadying breath and compose myself.

I'd already thought about that. 'Why don't we wait for his instructions on where he wants them scattered and we can head off in Nomad for a weekend to do that. That way we do the camping thing, but only for a few days. Everyone is happy.'

Olly nods, but he looks anything but happy. He closes the door softly behind him as he exits the room.

It appears I've gotten my own way. The trip is off. Why then do I feel so bad? A voice a lot like Pops' jumps into my head. Mae Guinness, sometimes being right is lonely.

Chapter Ten

EVIE

Watching Jamie perched on top of the canopy bed in Nomad, swinging his legs back and forth, can only end one way. Before I get the word 'Don't!' out of my mouth, he shouts, 'Robo Jamie!' and jumps.

I hold my breath, sure the daft eejit will break his legs, but he lands on his feet and laughs, delighted with himself.

'Mam will go mad if she sees you throwing yourself off that,' I say, but I'm grinning. That was kinda cool.

He ignores me. But I'm glad to see him having fun. He's been miserable for ages over Pops. And as if he can read my mind, he walks over and sits down beside me on the sofa.

'I miss Pops,' he sighs dramatically, just to really punch home how much. I move a little closer to him on the sofa and nudge his shoulder with mine. He nudges back.

'Me too, dude,' I say.

We sit for ages, both lost in memories of Pops, I suppose. At least, that's where I am.

'Will you help me get Pops' urn down from the shelf? I want to see what the ashes look like,' Jamie asks.

'Ewww. That's gross, and no I will not,' I say. Besides, I've already had a sneaky peek and I'm sorry I did. It's so far removed from Pops that it is a head- wreck. I don't want that for Jamie.

'Paddy Moher says that the ashes look like cigarette ash,' Jamie says.

'Don't mind Paddy Moher, they do not,' I reply.

'Well, I didn't believe him, because he also said that our teacher, Mr Holt, was a werewolf,' he sighs again. 'He is really hairy, but I don't think that's true either.'

An image of Mr Holt howling at the moon pops into my head and won't go away. Thanks Jamie.

'Mam is being a meanie saying no to the trip,' he complains. 'And you know something I've noticed? They always fight when they go into their bedroom. I'd stay out of there if I was them.'

'Funny guy,' I say, and nudge his shoulder again.

'Nothing is fun any more.' Jamie's eyes are locked firmly on his feet, which are kicking the floor over and over.

I place my hand on his legs to quieten them. 'They miss Pops too. Mam's busy with work . . . ' I think she gets a bad rap around here sometimes, working ridiculous hours most days. And she's not been uncool these past few weeks with me too.

But that doesn't excuse what's going on right now. She needs to be more understanding with Dad. I mean, his Pops is dead. If we are in bits, he must be falling apart inside.

'Do you want to go on this trip?' Jamie asks.

'I think so,' I say. 'I know I want to get away from here.'

'Why?'

'Because here sucks right now.'

'Yeah. It sucks,' Jamie agrees, making me laugh again.

It feels like the walls around here are closing in on me. Both Mam and Dad keep suggesting a 'talk'. I don't want to 'thrash it out to move forward' as they keep saying, I just want to forget about the whole thing. And maybe if we head off on this crazy trip, it will take the heat off me.

'We have to find a way to change Mam's mind,' I say.

'What are you guys up to?' Dad's voice calls in.

'We demand a family meeting,' Jamie declares. He's such a drama queen.

Dad looks kind of amused by this. 'Go on.'

'We heard you and Mam fighting – again – about Nomad,' Jamie says. 'We know that Mam doesn't want to go.'

Dad now looks a bit emotional. Oh God, don't let him start to cry again. I can't cope with his boohooing.

'I'm sorry you heard us having a heated discussion,' he informs us.

Yeah, right!

'Okay . . . well it's like this, we er think, like that as Pops went to a lot of trouble to organise the trip, it would be disrespectful not to go ahead and follow his wishes, wouldn't it?' I say.

'I don't think Pops would want us to go ahead if it meant that your mam was unhappy,' Dad tells us.

'But we could go ourselves,' Jamie says.

'Without your mam?' Dad asks and Jamie nods.

I can feel hives beginning to pop up all over my arms now. I must look them up in my records annual. I must be breaking records as quick as I'm breaking skin here.

'It doesn't work that way, guys. I wouldn't do it without your mam or you guys, for that matter. We're a family and we stick together. If your mam doesn't want to go, then we must respect that.' His face is set.

'I think you're wrong,' I tell him. 'Pops had a dying wish and he said that he wants us to go to Europe and scatter his ashes and stuff. We owe him that much. You have to tell Mam, change her mind.'

'A family meeting and nobody thought to invite me?' Mam says, walking into the room. She looks pissed. Awkward.

I itch my legs now, wondering how soon before all the red bumps blend into one and I turn into a strawberry blob.

'No, nothing like that,' Dad reassures her. 'The kids are just talking about Nomad and the trip, that's all.'

'I heard. You all want to go to Europe and would be happy to leave me behind.' Mam looks upset. Oh for God's sake, now she's going to cry. What is it with my blubbing parents?

'I've told the children we don't go without you,' Dad says. 'We are not splitting the family up! We'll go for a long weekend to wherever Pops wants his ashes scattered. That way we'll still get to have a small trip in Nomad, Jamie.'

'You're a big meanie and I hate you!' Jamie screams at Mam. I feel a bit of vomit hit the back of my throat again.

'Nice. Turn the pressure up with emotional blackmail from the kids,' Mam hisses at Dad.

'I didn't say a word,' he hisses back.

I've had enough of this shit, I'm out of here. But the ragged breath of Jamie beside me as his body heaves with tears makes me pause.

'It's n-n-not f-f-fair,' he stammers out.

No it isn't. 'Would you both stop!' I scream. 'Look what you're doing to Jamie with all your fighting! I can't take any more of it either. I wish Pops was here. He was the only one who really cared about us two. All you both care about is yourselves and scoring points off each other. We can't take any more!'

Silence.

Jamie clasps my arm and I pull him into me. My heart is hammering so hard, my face is flushed and I hold my breath when Mam stands up. 'Don't say a word,' she says to Dad and then walks out, leaving the three of us alone, with just the sound of Jamie's tears breaking the silence. None of us move, we just stand there like statues. But then Mam walks back in, with a bundle of rucksacks in her hands. She tosses them towards our feet and they land with a dull thud and the statues jump in fright.

'I've seen the storage in here and no matter how much yer man Aled dresses it up, it's miniscule. So if we are going to last eight weeks cooped up in this thing, you get one small bag each. If it doesn't fit in that bag, it's not coming. Got it?' Mam states.

Jamie stops crying. Dad looks confused. I don't blame him, so am I. Is she saying we're going now? Jamie jumps up and runs over to her, flinging himself into her arms, shouting, 'We're going? For real?'

'Yes, for real,' Mam says, kissing his hair.

He mutters something that sounds a bit like Robo Jamie. That boy gets weirder and weirder.

'You want to go? You're not just saying it?' Dad asks.

'I won't lie to you. I don't want to go. But as Evie says, Pops wants us to go. And my family all want to go. So we should go. But I reserve the right to come home at any stage if it doesn't work out. Without any complaint from you, Olly. That's my condition. Non-negotiable,' Mam says.

'Agreed,' Dad says. Ah shit, he's gone all emosh again.

Mam disentangles herself from Jamie's embrace and walks over to me, kissing me on my cheek. 'I'm so sorry for everything, Evie.'

She grabs Jamie's hand and says, 'Your dad and I owe you both an apology. We shouldn't be letting our silly arguments creep into our family. We're under a lot of stress and sometimes that makes us do things that we're not proud of. Maybe Pops is right. Maybe we do need to simplify our lives.'

'I'm so sorry that we made you feel that way,' Dad says.

'S'alright,' I mumble.

'This is important. Know this, we love you. More than anything else in the world. Never ever doubt that,' Mam says, holding our hands so tight she's hurting me.

'Are we really going on a super, epic adventure?' Jamie cries, wriggling away from her.

'Yes, I think we are,' Dad replies looking at Mam, smiling.

I can't quite believe the turn-around. I'm still shaking from my outburst, I thought Mam would go ballistic. But she changed her mind because of something *I* said. And now we're going off around Europe in this camper van! Wait till I tell Ann.

I pick up the rucksack and realise that my summer reading alone will fill it. 'There's no way that I can fit everything into that one little bag, Mam,' I say.

'We get two, just don't tell the boys,' she says with a wink. 'Right, how about we all go inside, pick a movie and order a pizza?'

She's smiling really, really brightly, more manic than happy. Maybe we're wrong to force her to come. But Jamie is running around in circles, delirious with delight, so to hell with it, I'm going to shelve my niggling doubts. Watch out world, the Guinnesses are going on a trip.

Chapter Eleven

My dearest Olly and Mae

How are you both? How many times does that question just trip off our tongues without us really wanting to know the answer? Well I have to tell you that I'm fretting about you both all morning. I hazard a guess that you are both in a world of pain. When Beth died, I thought I'd never recover from it. It's physical pain too, not just emotional. I felt like my insides had been ripped out through my throat. And I'm heart sorry that you might be feeling a fraction of that. But I learnt that my hurt was worth bearing, because it was physical proof that I had experienced love.

Love hurts, but it's the most exquisite gift we can receive and give in life. Try to keep that to the fore-front of your minds and you'll get through anything that life tosses at you. Olly, it was my love for you and the love that I got back in return that made me get out of bed in those early days after Beth died.

So do me a favour and work hard to be the reason that your family get up every day.

You know, as I plan this trip using the atlas as my guide, with every page I turn forgotten memories echo around in my brain. I keep smelling stewed apples. Isn't that funny? Sugary with a kick of cloves. And brown bread, fresh from the oven, earthy and sweet. I fancy that these smells of Beth are infused into the very fabric of the atlas. It makes me happy to imagine you all, heads bent close, looking at a world as yet unexplored.

Arra, enough of my ramblings. You want to know where you're off to, don't you? Get to the point, Pops, I can hear you scream. Well, I thought about sending you around Ireland for a week to ease you into the world of camping, but, sure, you can do that yourselves some other time. It's time to brush up on your bonjours and au revoirs because you're going to France!

Tickets are in the envelope, along with all the details of where you are staying. All you have to do is get yourself to Rosslare and then you are on the overnight ferry to Cherbourg.

Don't be tearing around those French roads, now, Olly. Take it easy and enjoy the drive. This trip should be fun, so no sweating buckets about it all. I know what you're like. Oh, by the way, remember, they drive on the other side of the road over there, haha!

Your first stop is Bayeux, Normandy. By my reckoning, it's only an hour's journey, or thereabouts. I've booked you into Les Castels Chateau De

Martragny. It's an actual chateau. Thought Mae would like that. You will be staying three nights there. Will you both do me a favour and try to kick back a bit? Remember that life doesn't have to be a race. It's okay to stop and smell the roses, or the smelly cheese, sometimes. I'm looking at you here Mae. You never seem to relax lately.

I thought it might be fun to set you a challenge for each part of your trip. For this first destination I want you to bring the children to the D-Day landing sites. I'm worried that Evie and Jamie don't realise that there is more to life than their iPads and X Factor. You both have to show them that life can be so much more. I went there with your mother before you were born and it stayed with me. When you get there, talk to them about what happened on the beaches. Will you do that for me?

It's crossed my mind that maybe you could all decide NOT to go on this trip. Maybe as you read this, Nomad is already sold. Oh, I hope that's not the case. I won't lie, I'll be heart sorry if you don't do as I have planned. Don't ask me why, but in my very core, I know it's the right thing for you all. Please trust me on this. Life is not meant to be lived in one place, you must travel.

I'll be in touch, but au revoir for now,

Pops x

Chapter Twelve

OLLY

English was my first exam during my leaving cert. I can remember walking into the test hall with great trepidation. My usual strut and swagger gone and it felt like the green mile, making that walk to my little wooden desk. I placed my pencil case and a bottle of water in front of me, feeling awkward, my knees kept banging under the table no matter how I sat. And then I began to panic. Because I knew I was ill prepared. I had done feck-all studying for it and I'd be lucky to scrape a pass.

Well, as I walk around Nomad for the third time in the last five minutes, I have the same feeling. I am ill prepared for Pops' adventure. I'm about to head off for eight weeks in a camper van with the most precious people in my life. And I haven't a clue what I'm doing. Nomad seems to have grown overnight. I'm going to be playing chicken with the oncoming traffic as it will fill the roads we live on around here. I wonder if it's too late to back out.

'Come on, Dad!' Jamie shouts, impatient to start this 'epic' adventure. Everything is 'epic' right now with Jamie. I hope I don't 'epic fail' and hit the ditch before we even get out of Wexford. Nomad is almost unrecognisable now. Mae stated that if she was going to spend eight weeks in it, she needed colour. So bright cushions and curtains are now welcome additions in what she's told me are 'jewel' colours. It looks great, I do know that.

The kitchen is also stocked with cutlery and cooking equipment, the larder presses jam-filled with non-perishable foods. We won't go short on baked beans or spaghetti hoops is all I'm saying.

Our neighbours have agreed to call into home every week and make sure it stays in one piece while we are gone. It's locked up now and we are ready to leave.

So why am I standing here like a gobshite, staring at the back of the van, looking for goodness knows what?

Mae, Evie and Jamie are all in their seats, buckled in, ready for the off. The kids are charmed with the idea of travelling 'in a sitting room'. Mae is up front beside me – my somewhat reluctant co-pilot.

I don't know what is going on with us. We seem to take two steps forward, then three back. Like yesterday, one minute she's asking me about dinner, the next minute she's storming out of the room. I asked her what I did wrong and she said, 'nothing'. Of course that 'nothing' was loaded and meant I'd fucked up royally again. The ironic thing is that just before that we'd shared a moment. Sitting side by side, Googling France, chatting, laughing, with no passive-aggressive bullshit from either of us. It was easy. Like it used to be in our marriage.

Back before it all went wrong. I go over it in my head, trying to understand the unfathomable destruction of our marriage.

'*I miss this.*'

'*Miss what?*' *Mae answers, twisting her body towards me.*

How do I answer that? The warmth of her body next to mine makes me ache with loneliness. Do I tell her that I miss the intimacy of long chats late in the night about everything and nothing as we lay naked in each other's arms? That I miss her smell, her touch, being her best friend, her ally. Us against the world, we used to say. I miss watching her undress, I miss being the one to make her smile.

'*I miss us.*'

She doesn't answer at first. Then, 'I know.' What does she mean by that? Does she miss us too? I feel like an unsure teenage version of myself, trying to get the nerve up to tell a girl that I like her.

'*What happened to us?*' *Mae asks.*

Like a slideshow, images that shame me crawl out of the recesses of my mind and I feel humiliation and guilt. Telling Mae that I'd been fired. Rejection letter after rejection letter from accountancy firms. Mae's face when she realised I'd gone soft while I was inside her, and then the ongoing horror of the next few weeks as we both tried to get past my impotency. And failed. Yep, my bad. Staying up late, my head in the iPad, avoiding eye contact so that I don't have to go to bed at the same time as her, because I can't bear to lie beside her, knowing that my stupid fucking body has let me down in every way possible.

'I don't know,' I lie and whisper I'm sorry, which I am. She leans in close to me and we stay like that for a long time, not saying a word, but thinking about a time when we had to lock our bedroom door to stop the kids bursting in while we were naked, having sex.

Yes, what happened to us Mae.

Will we find the answers in this new home, over the next few weeks? Now that it's time to leave, I'm afraid to. What if the answers are ones that neither of us can live with? What if we can't go back and find us and instead are left with this shell of a marriage that makes us both bleed inside?

'You coming?' Mae sticks her head out her window.

'One minute.' I dive inside Nomad's garage to compose myself. It's crammed tight with not an inch spare. The amount of stuff Evie and Jamie have tried to sneak into the camper every time Mae and I turn our backs, sniggering when we admonish them. In fact, there's been a lot of laughing and chatting these past couple of weeks, about unknown destinations and unopened letters. Mae and I have managed to have more than single-sentence conversations albeit about the humdrum banality of kids, school, household chores and of course Nomad. Just don't ask us to talk about our marriage, because it all goes pear shaped then.

Life is short. Don't spend a lifetime regretting what you should have said to someone you love. That's what Pops said. Problem is I'm not sure that Mae likes me much, never mind loves me. But I know one thing for sure, I can't go on like this. I'm going to have to find my balls and ask Mae how she feels about our marriage. I've been avoiding the conversation because I don't want to hear the answer, but I need to know.

But right now I've got to get inside this vehicle that is the size of a bus. It's time to see what awaits us on this adventure. Shit, it feels like I'm on the precipice of something big. I'm standing on a cliff about to jump off into an unknown world. What do I know about camper vans? Feck all!

I pull out Pops' letter again. We all had fun guessing where he might send us to first of all. These ranged from various parts of Ireland, to the UK, to France. There was even a wildly optimistic guess from Jamie that we might be going to America. Evie got it right in the end. *Félicitations Evie! Viva la France.*

Don't be sweating buckets, Pops said. I can feel a river running down the small of my back. Ha!

Speaking of Pops, 'We have Pops, right?' I say as I jump in beside Mae. Imagine if we left without the urn on board . . .

'Relax, he's is in our bedroom, wedged into one of the cupboards tight.'

Sighing, I stuff the letter back into my jeans pocket and put my seat belt on, turning the engine on. This is it, no more stalling. 'Oh for fuck's sake!' Of course Nomad shudders to a halt. Only fecking stalled it.

'Dad said fuck,' Jamie shouts, causing Mae to throw a withering look my way and Evie to snort laughter.

'Language,' Mae reprimands us both and I resist the urge to tell her to fuck off too. I look at Obi-Wan Kenobi, our resident Nomad mascot, now glued to the dash. I can almost hear Pops saying, 'Relax, lad.' So I take a deep breath and refrain from cursing at my wife.

I check my mirrors again – all five of them. Then realise how stupid that is, because I'm in my driveway still and there's not much traffic behind me.

I look at Mae to see if she's taking the piss at my faffing around, but she isn't laughing. She looks more concerned as opposed to enjoying my discomfort.

'You know what you're doing. You can do this,' Mae says.

'Of course. Piece of cake,' I reply with a confidence that I don't feel. 'I must be getting old, there was a time I'd not have even blinked at this.'

'You are not old. Your confidence has taken a battering these past few months. But just take your time. You've got this,' Mae says.

Her kindness, her understanding is nearly my undoing. She's been saying that phrase to me ever since we met. *You've got this.* The day I met her parents. The day I bathed Evie for the first time. As I walked up to the top of the church to say my eulogy for my beloved Pops.

'You've got this,' Mae repeats and there's so much that I want to say to her, but it's all jumbled up tight in a knot in my throat. If I speak now and it unravels, I might cry and we'll never get away. So I straighten my back, stick my chin up and move the gearstick to first and inch off at a snail's pace. I try to ignore the whoops from Jamie ringing in my ear.

'You're right, as always,' I say and then turn left out of the driveway, clipping the kerb as I go.

'Not a word!' I say to Mae, who pretends to zip her mouth shut whilst throwing her eyes up to the heavens at the same time.

Glancing at the clock on the large dashboard I'm relieved to see that we have over an hour to make the thirty-minute drive. By the way I'm going, I'll need every second of that.

Obi-Wan, the big plastic joker, says, 'You'd swear you were driving a bus the way you're carrying on.'

Ha ha, very funny, get lost, Pops.

Somehow or other, the rest of the journey passes by without any incident. I won't let Mae have the radio on, or the kids play a DVD in the back, which goes down as if I've just announced that Santa has cancelled Christmas. I'd like to see how they'd cope driving the equal of a bus for the first time in their lives. Irritated, I swipe away another drop of sweat, trickling down my face. I've been driving for over twenty years, never had an accident. Nor have I ever felt a moment's stress over it. So why on earth I'm near having a cardiac over driving Nomad I don't know.

Focusing only on the road ahead I manage to arrive at Rosslare Harbour without further incident. I enlist the help of my co-pilot as we try to work out where we should be going. Thank goodness we left early, because we are one of the first to arrive and that means driving into my lane is simple enough.

'You can turn on the DVD now if you like,' I say to the kids, feeling guilty about my earlier narkiness with them. They have already unbuckled their belts and are up and out of their seats, wandering around. Mae takes her belt off too and swivels her seat 180 degrees so she is now facing the cabin.

'This is, as Jamie would say, cool!' she remarks and I have to agree, as I do the same.

I put on my best Captain Kirk accent – William Shatner, of course, the original and the best as far as I'm concerned and say, 'Europe . . . the final frontier. These are the voyages of the Nomad Enterprise. Her eight-week mission: to explore strange new worlds; to seek out new life and new civilisations; to boldly go where no man has gone before.'

I take a bow as the kids whoop and laugh in response to my show. And Mae is smiling too, looking at me in that way she does sometimes, as if I'm surprising her in some way.

'What?'

'I've forgotten how much fun you can be, Olly Guinness. It's good to see you goofing around.'

'I think I've forgotten that side of me too,' I say.

Half an hour passes by in a flash as we listen to Jamie tell us all about what is likely to happen over the next eight weeks. It's what I like to call Jamie TV. When he was a baby, Mae, Evie and I would sit around watching him for hours. As he got older, he seemed to become aware of his fans and would put on a show for us all. Chattering, laughing, singing.

The more we respond, the more he shows off. But it's nice. It's easy and it's fun. Then a flurry of beeps from car horns makes us all jump and we realise that it's our turn to board the ferry. I swivel round and look in my rear-view mirror to see an irritated driver waving me on.

'Relax dude!' Jamie shouts and we all giggle. Yeah, relax dude.

I hold my hand up in what I hope he sees as an apology and, without having time to worry about it, manage to take off without stalling. And then Nomad begins her climb up a ramp, heading into the ship.

'The belly of the ferry,' Mae says and we all repeat it, laughing, not knowing that for many years to come, one of us will only need to say that phrase to set the rest of us off into peals of laughter. An inside family joke that only we will ever get and understand.

I look in my side mirrors again, at the convoy of caravans and trailers and camper vans all following me. I wonder if my insurance will cover us if I roll backwards and take them all out in one big dominos-like hit.

Gritting my teeth, I inch forward, holding the clutch, with my hand hovering over the handbrake. At last I am guided into my parking spot for the journey by a smiling man wearing a high-vis jacket. I exhale and lean back into the seat. Well, I've gotten us onto the boat. It can only get easier.

'Don't forget your overnight bags,' Mae reminds us all. We are staying in a family cabin for the seventeen-hour journey across the ocean, the plan being that we sleep for most of it.

The oily smell of exhausts fills the parking bays. We all squeeze our way between the jam-packed cars and vans, edging towards the entry doors to the ferry. We climb the steel steps and make our way to the reception area to get our cabin keys. There is a buzz amongst the passengers, lots of them with children like ourselves. Excitement bubbles up inside my stomach.

We do a whirlwind tour of the boat, find our cabin and dump our bags. Our first row of the trip erupts when Evie realises that we are in a family cabin and all sharing. She's not one bit happy and tells us she might as well be in a prison. It feels like only yesterday that Mae and I thought Evie would never sleep the night through in her own bed. She was forever sneaking into us in the middle of the night. I miss those days.

We grab a spot in the lounge and while away a few hours having a meal in the restaurant and watching the on-board cabaret show. I've seen worse. Under duress, Evie takes Jamie to the kiddies' disco. And then it's just the two of us and as I look around at our surroundings, I can't quite believe that we are here. 'Thank you.'

'For what?' Mae asks.

'For changing your mind. For throwing yourself into all the preparations. I know there was a lot to do,' I say.

She nods, acknowledging my words.

She doesn't answer me at first. Continues to stare at the stage, where a magician is currently doing card tricks with a kid. Then, without turning to face me, without taking her eyes off the stage for even a moment, she says, 'Pops said, say you love each other every day.'

The muscles in my cheeks are taut as I bite my teeth down hard together. So she has been thinking about his letter as much as I have. Should I tell her I love her? Because I do. I've never stopped loving her. But before I open my mouth to tell her this, she says, 'I suppose I came to see if we do really love each other any more, if we have a marriage worth fighting for.'

Sometimes things are better left unsaid.

'Mae . . . ' I begin, but cannot find words. What is wrong with me? So much I should say to my wife, yet I am rendered speechless continuously.

'It's okay,' she replies. 'I don't want to fight. I'm not

121

trying to hurt you. But Pops is right. Life is short and I don't want to continue living a half-life any more. And that's what we've been doing, Olly.'

'Yes,' I reply and hate myself for not having anything useful to say. Before I have the chance to come up with something, anything, that will let my wife know that I do love her, the kids come back, declaring the disco to be full of toddlers and 'lame'.

Maybe it's the sea air, but I suddenly feel bone-tired.

Our cabin is small but comfortable and despite ten minutes of chit chat from Jamie, we all fall asleep quickly. I think it must be the roll of the boat, but that sleep in the bunk bed is one of the best I've had in years.

Another outburst from Evie threatens to negate my good night's sleep. 'I'm not getting dressed until you all leave,' Evie declares, sitting cross-legged on her bunk and her face is truculent.

Mae whispers to me, 'I told you that her privacy, or lack thereof, was going to be an issue. She's not a little girl any more.'

That I've worked out for myself. I miss the little girl who used to sit on my lap asking me to sing songs to her. Life was a lot easier back then. For the first time since Pops' letters, I worry that Mae is right. Maybe our family will never get into the whole spirit of camping and if so, oh boy, it's going to be one long trip.

'Go into the bathroom to get dressed, Evie. It's a tight squeeze, but manageable,' Mae says.

'I'm starving,' Jamie shouts pulling his PJ top over his head. 'Come on, let's go.'

'We better get breakfast so, but maybe we'll put some pants on first, dude,' I say and we all head to the canteen.

'Our last full Irish for eight weeks,' Mae remarks, picking up a pack of Kerrygold butter and smearing it onto her toast. Jamie declares that the sausages are the best he's ever eaten. As I look out the large windows and take in the approaching Normandy coastline, I can't help but agree. I feel energised and relaxed and ready to take on the world – or at least this French part of it.

When the announcement comes over the Tannoy that we should return to our vehicles, I look at each of my family, one by one.

'Let the adventure begin. I know there will be some adjustments to make, as we get used to living in Nomad, but are we up for it?' I say. They nod one by one.

'Come on, Captain Kirk. Boldly go and all that,' Mae says.

And we're off.

Chapter Thirteen

OLLY

When I wind down the window, a warm breeze tickles my skin. A weird bouquet of fish and oil assault my nostrils. It shouldn't surprise me, considering our location. Mae pushes buttons on Captain Kirk, our recently named sat nav, and we are all set to go. Captain Kirk tells us that we are 'one hour thirteen minutes away' from our destination.

'Are we going straight to the campsite?' I ask her.

'I think so,' Mae says. 'I'm a bit nervous about connecting Nomad to all the services. I'd rather get it done in the daylight.'

'It's not even ten a.m.!' I say, laughing. 'I think even I can manage to do this in the next eight hours.'

But I'm not sorry. I've visions of connecting the water to the electricity and frying us all. Pretty soon, I've navigated my way onto the motorway and signs for Bayeux are in sight. Driving on the wrong side of the road feels alien, but I can't help but feel chuffed with myself as I soon get the hang of the roads over here. I'm on a big road going in a straight line. This I can do.

'Do you notice how many services they have? I've counted three already and we've only been on the motorway for ten minutes,' Mae says.

'I know. Not like us in Ireland, where the only toilet you can find on long trips is the ditch!' I say.

'We don't need a toilet, we have one here,' Jamie shouts to us. 'Can I go now?'

'No!' both Mae and I reply in unison.

He doesn't need to go; we both know that. He just wants the novelty of being able to go to a bathroom whilst in transit. It's the third time he has asked in ten minutes.

I glance in the mirror and see Evie has her head stuck in a book. She's got her iPod on too, lost in her own world. I try not to worry about the amount of time she spends like that. Mae says it's normal, she's just doing what teenagers do all over the world.

I'm not so sure. Every time I think about her in hospital, attached to all those tubes, my chest tightens in panic, so much that I think I'm going to have a heart attack. I thought she'd never wake up and the manic relief that coursed through my veins when she did was almost over-whelming. In that moment, I looked at Mae and our eyes told each other, gleefully, joyfully, we haven't lost her. She's alive. She's here. We have that second chance we prayed for.

By some silent mutual agreement, we both avoided asking any difficult questions straight away. Maybe we were being chicken, putting off hearing answers that we were not ready to accept. Or maybe we just wanted to enjoy the moment for what it was, a joyous celebration of a loved life saved. In truth it was a bit of both. So we held Evie and murmured words of reassurance to her. We smiled in grateful relief at the nurses as they came in and did their early-morning round of check-ups.

But that was then and this is now. She's recovered, physically at least. And I can't help think that she's gotten off this whole drink episode lightly. She's been quiet and uncommunicative pretty much since then. We can put a lot of that down to Pops' death and normal teenager hormones, but bollocks to that. I want to see Evie smile again. She's hiding something, I know it. I can't put my finger on what, but I need to get it sorted on this trip. Whatever it is she's not telling us, we need to get her to open up.

In unison Captain Kirk and Mae alert me to the fact that we are approaching our destination. As we drive up the long, straight driveway lined with green, high trees on either side, we all gasp at the view in front of us. It's an impressive sight.

The sun is shining bright and strong and the chateau ahead of us is like a picture from a French postcard. Shutters frame paned windows and yellow buttercups add splashes of colour on the green grass.

It is picture-perfect. Only nothing is ever really perfect. I glance at Mae and peek at the kids at the back. To the outside eye, *we* are pretty much the perfect family. We look good, as long as you don't get up too close and examine the cracks.

'Wow,' Mae remarks. 'It's perfect.'

Ha! If she could read my mind now. 'I was just thinking the same thing,' I reply.

'Cool,' Jamie adds.

I wind down my window, 'Hear that?' I ask them all.

'I can't hear anything,' Mae says, sticking her head out the window.

'Exactly!' I reply and I can't explain it, but the silence is energising. I feel alert and ready to take on the day. To hell with perfect! Real families never are. I just need to find a way to bring us all back together. With a little help from Pops and this trip, I can do it. I WILL do it!

Birds are chirping amongst the faint rustling of leaves, as if they are singing in agreement with me.

I have heard people talk about the French countryside being all that and a bag of chips. Well, people are right. Whenever I thought about where we would be camping on this trip, I always pictured an earplug-noisy caravan park. This is beyond my imagination. A rural idyll and the quiet stillness is breathtaking.

'It's as if we are the only guests staying in the chateau,' Mae murmurs.

Then the road forks to the right, veering away from the chateau. I figure that unless Pops has something else up his sleeve, then it's to the right we must go. Following the road around, I spot someone with a clipboard waving us over.

'Hope he speaks English,' I say. 'Evie, we might need you for this!' My pidgin French won't get us far.

'I'm not speaking to him,' Evie states and puts her iPod headphones back on quickly to reiterate her point.

I bite back my irritation with her and luck is on our

side as Henri has excellent English. He directs us to the orchard, which will be our new home for the next couple of days. We can choose whichever unused pitch we desire. This feels like a momentous responsibility and I feel panicked again. I mean, we know nothing about camping and I haven't got a clue about what makes a good or bad pitch. I try to remember the recommended checklist that I found on a camping website last week.

'How about there?' Mae points to a spot under trees. 'In the shade.'

'Those trees are full of birds, look,' I say. 'Good chance we'll wake up in the morning with bird poop everywhere.'

Mae nods and says, 'We don't want poop.'

'Speaking of which, we should park close to the toilets,' I say.

'I'm not sure I'd like that,' Mae replies, wrinkling her nose. She doesn't appreciate my humour.

'Okay, not too close to the toilets either.'

'There, Dad!' Jamie shouts, pointing to a spot that's on a slope.

'We need a flat pitch,' I tell him. Visions of Nomad rolling back in the middle of the night and taking out a whole family in a tent sends shivers down my back.

Then I spot an area that looks suitable. It's close to the swimming pool, with the toilet and shower blocks within our eyelines, but with any luck not our noses! I point to it and Mae nods in agreement.

'It's pretty with all the apple trees behind it,' Mae says.

I won't lie, turning that engine off feels good. While I couldn't wait to head off on this trip, the whole driving of a large vehicle thing hasn't been good for my blood pressure. The worry that I'll clip someone or misjudge the size of the van weighs heavily.

'Can we go explore?' Jamie asks.

'Don't go far,' Mae tells him, as she nods her consent.

'I'm staying here,' Evie says.

'Hold up there, dude. You're not going anywhere on your own, Jamie,' I say. 'Either Evie goes with you, or you don't go.'

'Evie, please,' Jamie begs and pulls at her arm.

'I don't want to go,' she snaps at him and swats at his hand.

'Go on with your brother. Don't be like that,' I say and I'm rewarded with a scathing look from her.

'Fine!' she snaps and Jamie runs off chattering away about what they might find on their 'adventure'.

Mae's eyes follow them both as they walk away from Nomad.

'They'll be fine,' I say. 'They're not babies any more.'

Mae gives me a look of irritation again. I can see her biting her tongue in an effort not to speak her mind. For a moment I think it would be great to be inside her head, know what she's thinking. I've a funny feeling I wouldn't be too happy about what I'd find.

'What? Go on, hit me with it, I can take it,' I try to sound lighthearted.

She sighs; not a good sign. 'I've no doubt that Jamie will be fine. But Evie is fragile, she's not been herself for some time. We've both acknowledged that she's hiding something. It was only Pops getting so ill and dying that stopped us from really finding out what the hell is going on. What if she was trying to harm herself? What if it was a cry for help? It's partly why I'm so worried about this trip. It could be a distraction from what's really important.'

So much for my plan to help Evie. 'Shit, shit shit.'

Mae shrugs, with a 'you've fucked up' written all over her face.

'I'm out of my depth here,' I say.

Her face softens and she replies, 'You're not the only one. I don't have the answers, I've no manual for stroppy teenage daughters. Nobody does. But it's our job to work our way through it all. All I'm suggesting, is that we both need to try listening a little harder. Watch her a little closer.'

'I just thought she spends so much of her time on her own, I didn't want her to be cooped up here in Nomad too,' I say.

'I agree with you, but we should give her a moment to settle in, get her bearings,' Mae reiterates.

'All I want to do is find a way to get rid of that frown she habitually wears.'

'Me too. I've thought of little else but seeing her smile again.'

'Should I go after her?'

'Leave her, now she's gone. But if she comes back, not a word. Don't force her to go "mix" with anyone.'

I nod my agreement and then we sit in silent awkwardness. We're back to avoiding eye contact again. I spy a sign that has a bottle of beer on the front and my throat dries up at the thought of a cold lager. Sometimes I wish I had no responsibilities and could just head to the pub and get locked. Instead I say, 'I suppose we should set up.'

I jump out of Nomad and stretch, Mae close behind

me. My earlier excitement at our arrival has gone and it all feels a bit anti-climatic.

'We should have put sun factor on the kids,' Mae worries, looking up to the sun, which is already toasting our pale Irish skin.

'They'll be back soon enough. We'll get it on them then,' I say. Then, in a fit of bravery, I throw in, 'You worry too much. Relax.'

This bravado falters as fast as it arrives and I look away to avoid seeing Mae's sharp look of annoyance.

I decide to scope out the other motor homes all scattered around the grounds, to see how they are all set up. Mae falls into step beside me. It's quiet enough, not too many people out and about, so we are uninterrupted having a nose. Most pitches seem to have a groundsheet laid beside the caravans or campers, with tables and chairs arranged on top. Some have awnings up and others have tents beside their vans, which intrigues us both.

'Maybe it's the camping equivalent of the dog house,' I say. 'Piss off the wife and into the tent you go.'

'Not a bad idea. You better behave yourself, Olly, or into it you'll go,' Mae says and then, thank God, she laughs.

'You look your most prettiest when you laugh,' I say. It appears some of that bravado is still around.

She doesn't answer me, though, just looks at me again as if pondering that same silent question. It hangs in the air between us. Then the moment is gone and she changes the subject and points to the groundsheets.

'We need one of those. Do we have one?'

I shrug and walk back to Nomad's garage to have a

root around. Aled did mention that there were some 'extras' that he'd left for us, but I can't remember if a groundsheet is one amongst them.

Pulling out our garden folding table and chairs, I'm grateful that I did think to bring them. I can see how useful they will be already. The heat in Nomad is stifling. I also grab our new portable barbecue that Mae bought in Woodies before we left too. And when I rummage towards the back, where the tools are, I find a long thin bag. Bingo – yes! – that, I believe, is a groundsheet. And, yep, right beside it a tent.

'Woof woof!' I joke, when I throw them at Mae's feet, who looks at me blankly. 'The dog house!'

She rewards my terrible humour with another laugh and the air feels lighter, as tensions ebb away. For now, anyhow.

'Imagine the shame had we not brought a groundsheet,' Mae remarks and I laugh, once we've got it all set up. We take a seat for a second to toast ourselves, with an imaginary glass.

''Twould be a disaster,' I say. 'Shunned by the campers, one and all, for breach of the motor-home code.'

'What do we have to do next?' Mae asks.

I try to sound informed as I tell her that we have to plug in the electricity and fill the water tanks.

'Don't forget the satellite dish.'

'Will I pull the awning down too?'

'I think so,' Mae says. 'Do you know how to do all that?'

'Of course,' I say, with more confidence than I feel. As it happens, it is easier than I thought it would be. The connecting of electricity, the thing that had caused me the most panic, was quick and seamless too.

I'm feeling a bit cocky by the time I head off to fill our water tanks. Mae leaves me to it. At first it all goes rather well. I find the fresh-water taps easy enough. Not a bother to me. King of the hill. I fill the tank and the beat of the splashing water as it hits the plastic drum is oddly relaxing. Once it's full, I stick the cap on and that's when the fun begins. The drum is not so easy to manoeuvre when full and I struggle to lift it.

I decide that maybe it would be best to hoist it up onto my shoulder. Easier said than done. Five minutes later, sweat dripping, muscles aching, the drum is in my arms. But my hands are now damp with sweat and so the drum begins to slip. Fecked if I'm letting it go now, after all the effort it took to lift up in the first place. I grapple with it and somehow manage to keep a hold of it. But in my fight with it, it's now upside down.

And that's when Houston has a problem. The cap loosens under the weight of the water and in cartoon, slapstick fashion, the shagging thing comes off. Net result, an unwarranted shower.

Peals of laughter alerts me to the fact that I have an audience. Damn it. 'We've all been there!' a good-natured voice says. The voice belongs to a tanned man in his sixties wearing a bright-yellow t-shirt over khaki shorts. 'First-timer?'

As I wipe the water from my face, I nod and say, 'That obvious?'

He laughs again and a few minutes later he returns with a two-wheeled trolley. 'You'll be needing one of these. Or maybe the next time you could just do what most of us do. Pull up beside the taps to fill up, before you pitch.'

Why didn't I think of that! 'Now I feel stupid,' I say.

'Ah, sure, if you've not done this before, you wouldn't know the lie of the land. Rookie error.'

'Cheers for this,' I say to him. 'I won't say no to the lend.'

He helps me load the tank on the trolley and then I fill it again.

'Where you from?' he asks.

'Wexford. This is our first time camping, you'll be stunned to hear that I've not a clue what I'm doing.'

Laughing, he says, 'I remember the first time we camped. I was that nervous I went into reverse instead of drive and hit the flower pots outside our house.'

I smiled back and said, 'It was the kerb for me on the way out of our drive.'

'Give it time and before long you will feel like you've been doing this all your life. I'm Billy, if you need anything else. You can drop the trolley back to me when you finish with it. The Winnebago over there.' He points to an impressive beige motor home.

'Nice.' I nod in its direction. I need to work on my motor-home appreciative lingo.

He wanders off with a wave and I shout after him, 'I'm Olly. And thanks. I owe you.'

'What happened to you?' Mae asks when I arrive back with the water.

As I relay my tale of woe, she giggles, then reminds me, 'I'm not doing the water tanks. Ever.'

She's been busy while I've been gone. There's now a green-and-pink-checked oilcloth on our camping table. Pretty coloured lanterns are on either side of the table and there are several more hanging off the awning on hooks.

'That looks great!' She always has this knack of making everything look like it should be gracing a magazine cover.

'I thought we could have a glass of wine later on, with the lanterns lit. It could be pretty,' she says. She looks almost shy at the suggestion.

'I'd love that.' I can't think of anything that sounds more tempting than a glass of pinot noir right now. 'We used to sit out the back when the kids were small, drinking cheap wine.'

'On those horrible white-plastic chairs,' Mae replies.

I take a seat beside Mae and we sit, this time in companionable silence, both thinking of those early days together. I wish we could go back to then.

'Do we have any wine?' I ask her. 'I can go to *la supermarché*.' I say this in my best French accent. I'm a funny guy when I want to be.

'I have a bottle, but only the one. Seemed a bit silly bringing wine into France,' Mae tells me.

'True. I'll pick some up later on,' I promise.

I take a look around me and I feel overwhelmed as a sense of achievement hits me. We have travelled from our home in Wexford to this eight-by-eight patch of grass, our temporary home, in less than thirty-six hours. It seems incredible.

I wish Pops were here. I can picture him sitting in a chair under the shade, reading a paper, his glasses perched at the end of his nose.

Are you watching, Pops? Is that Wi-Fi switched on over there? Is this how you imagined it, when you were at home planning it all?

If you'd have said to me a month ago that I'd be here, in this very spot, the words 'pigs' and 'fly' would have been said. But here we are.

I hope I don't let you down, Pops. I hope I can make a difference, find a way to get things back on track with Mae and the kids.

Before I have a chance to get too maudlin, Jamie bounds up to us, shouting, 'Can I go swimming with Simon?' He's panting and looks a bit red. Time for sun factor pronto.

'Simon?' Mae asks, looking around.

'He's my friend,' Jamie explains to us slowly, as if we are imbeciles.

D'oh, of course he's his friend. Don't ever lose that ability to make friends, Jamie. It will take you a long way in life. He's a good kid and seems happy. One out of four of us ain't bad, I suppose!

'The pool is huge, Dad!' Jamie continues. 'I'm going to dive into it and do two somersaults before I hit the water. Simon says he can do that.'

'Where's Evie?' Mae asks.

'She's on her way. She's in a bad mood,' Jamie says, throwing his eyes up to the heavens.

'Well, why don't we all check out the pool?' I say, looking down at myself. 'I'm wet already anyhow.'

Another smile from Mae makes me vow to continue my funny-guy routine.

When we first met, I made it my priority to make her

smile on every date. I used to do this thing where I spoke to her in a funny accent when we were out in public. She used to crack up at that. When did I stop doing that? How much of the stuff we loved to do as us have we forgotten about?

Evie shuffles back a moment later and we persuade her to come with us, but her enthusiasm isn't overwhelming. I might need more than lame jokes and fake accents with her.

'Come here, kiddo,' I say and pull her in for a hug, feeling guilty about pushing her earlier. She keeps her arms glued to her side and her body is rigid in my arms. I resist the urge to pull away and keep holding her, kissing her forehead.

'Dad, I'm not a baby any more,' she says, looking around to make sure nobody is watching us.

'Au contraire, you'll always be my little girl,' I say, and stick my tongue out at her, which makes the ghost of a smile appear on her face.

Twenty minutes later, we are all lying on beach towels on sun loungers around the large pool. Jamie is, as he promised, dive-bombing into the water. He's not quite mastered the somersaults yet, but I've no doubt that by the time we leave he will have. He introduces us to Simon, his new bestie, who seems like a good kid.

I have a book beside me, but I can't concentrate on the text. Just lying in the warm sun, letting the rays revive my body, is enough for now.

'I could get used to this,' Mae murmurs, as if reading my mind. I can't see her eyes, obscured behind huge saucer-like sunglasses that take up half her face. She's in a black swimming suit that caresses her curves and, taking me by surprise, I feel desire bubbling up inside me. I've not felt anything stirring for months.

Hello, old friend.

'You look like a movie star,' I whisper to her. My throat feels dry and I reach for some water.

'Would you stop!' she responds, putting her hand to her hair to straighten it down.

'It's true,' I say.

'Thank you,' she replies, and she looks like she's about to say something else, but then changes her mind. But she seems happy with my compliment.

Keep making her laugh. Keep telling her how beautiful she is. I can almost hear Pops' voice whispering to me. I've got this, Pops, promise.

'I'd like to just stay here today,' she tells me. 'We should relax and enjoy the sun. Recharge.'

'I think that sounds like perfect.' The idea of doing nothing appeals to me. The beaches of Normandy can wait. So, for the next couple of hours, we all just lounge by the pool. I even doze off once or twice, a loud snore waking me up with a start. I don't know what it is about the sun, but it always makes me drowsy.

Jamie eventually runs over to us and declares he's starving. 'We can't have that,' I say with a smile. And I'm pretty hungry myself.

So in a very French-like manner, we buy crusty baguettes from the supermarket. Slices of thick, home-cooked ham, gooey Brie and large, juicy ripe tomatoes, water and a glass of wine complete our veritable picnic feast. The simple fare tastes like a Michelin meal.

I pick up a chunk of Brie and start to sing the cheese song, making my family giggle, as I hoped it would. '*Sweet dreams are made of cheese, who am I to diss a Brie? I Cheddar the world and Feta cheese, Everybody's looking for Stilton.*'

'Good one Dad,' Jamie says.

'Funny guy, your dad,' Mae says and even though Evie doesn't say anything, she's grinning. What I didn't know then, was that my silly ditty I'd read on a blackboard years before outside a restaurant, would become an anthem for us all. Over the next couple of months, I would lose count of the number of times we all sang it.

'I think we have to celebrate our first night in France tonight. And I've been thinking about something I'd like us all to do. A challenge, if you like,' Mae declares.

'I'm up for a challenge!' Jamie shouts, excited by Mae's statement. I can't help grinning in response to his enthusiasm. I hope he never loses that too.

'Wait till you hear what it is first,' Mae teases, with a wry grin. 'I want us to try some local dishes every day for dinner. When in France and all that . . .'

'Will we have to eat snails?' Evie asks, looking aghast. 'I'm not eating slugs.'

'Not necessarily, but would it be fun to try the local cuisine?' Mae says. 'Pops has given us such a gift here. The opportunity to visit different cultures doesn't happen for many. I think it's a shame if we don't embrace all aspects of that.'

'Dad could eat the snails. He always says he'd eat the cockroaches on *I'm a Celebrity*,' Jamie throws in helpfully. 'Not me though.'

'Er, less of the cockroaches-talk while we're eating,' I say with a laugh. 'What do we get if we accept your challenge?'

'You get ice-cream for dessert, of course!' Mae declares to the delight of all.

Chapter Fourteen

OLLY

After only one day in the French sunshine, I feel like a different person. I can't remember the last time I did nothing other than just lie flat on my back.

Mae insisted we get a taxi tonight and I'm grateful. I had it in my head that I needed to drive Nomad, but as she said, that would be silly, dismantling all the connections, just to drive a few miles into town.

Green fields with abundant sunflowers dance in the breeze, as we fly along narrow roads. Rustic shutter-clad houses in small villages provide picture-postcard scenery. Our driver drops us on the outskirts of Bayeux and we walk through cobblestoned streets with pretty grey buildings on the hunt for a restaurant.

Mae fills us in on some local history as we go. Bayeux is one of the only towns to survive intact after the destruction of World War II. It was far enough inland not to be considered a threat.

One of the things that strikes me as we wander through

the streets is how quiet it is. For a sizeable-enough town, a tourist attraction at that, you would imagine that it would be buzzing.

As we walk, Mae stops and peers in the windows of restaurants and bars, looking for the right one. She tells us that we should do our best to avoid the usual tourist spots. Finally, at the end of a small cobbled lane-way, she finds a bistro that looks perfect.

'It's full of locals and it's not got overpriced tourist prices,' Mae says.

I'm so hungry that I'll happily eat anywhere. So we file inside and chorus *bonsoirs* back to our waiter, who takes us to a small table in the corner. His name is Jean and he seems friendly enough, despite our poor French.

'We would like to try some of the local dishes. Can you make some recommendations?' Mae asks him.

'Ah, *d'accord*. I can bring some *queues de langoustines rôties* for you all to share. Perhaps to follow *joue de bœuf*. It is one of our local specialities. *Très magnifique!*'

'Come again,' I say. I wish I had paid more attention in French classes now. I didn't get one bit of that. He repeats the dishes, speaking slowly. This time Evie nods in recognition.

'Langoustine tails,' Evie translates for Jamie. 'And cows' cheeks.'

'I don't think I like langoustines,' Jamie mutters with a frown. 'Can I just have a burger?'

Mae shushes him and tells Jean, '*Merci*, Jean, that would be great. And let me see, can we also have some salad and vegetables too?'

'Can you send some chips,' I throw in before he goes.

I know that there is no way that Jamie will eat any of the food ordered. Time for a back-up.

'But of course.' The waiter smiles at us all.

Mae puts her hand up and says to the waiter, 'No chips. *Merci*.'

'Ah we're on holidays, a few chips won't do any harm,' I say.

Mae flashes a look of annoyance at me, but then smiles and says, firmly, 'We are eating the local cuisine tonight, remember? If there are chips on offer the kids won't try the food.'

I hold my hands up in mock surrender and say to a bemused-looking Jean, 'No chips!'

'Aw,' Jamie grumbles and I shrug at him. 'I did my best, buddy. But your mam says no.'

Evie grabs his cheeks and teases him, 'Cows' cheeks for our little baby cheeks.'

'Get off me,' Jamie says, but he's laughing.

Mae isn't laughing, though, she's frowning and says to Jean, 'I'd like a glass of red wine.'

She's pissed at me again. Maybe I should order a bottle. I take a look at the wine menu, but am out of my depth. But I'm fecked if I'm going to admit that. I point to a Bordeaux that won't break the bank and hope for the best.

'An excellent choice, *Monsieur*,' Jean tells us and then, with a little bow, he's off.

'If I don't like this, can I have some Weetabix when we get home?' Jamie asks.

'You haven't even tasted it, Jamie. You might surprise yourself and enjoy it,' Mae says. 'I want us to have courageous palates.'

'Courageous palates,' we all repeat after her.

'Cool,' Evie says.

Jamie doesn't look convinced. I'm not sure I am either. Since he mentioned the word 'burger', I can't stop thinking about a dirty big cheeseburger with chips on the side. I wonder if I call them *frites*, would Mae be okay with them?

I decide to take matters into my own hands. Under the pretence of going to the toilets, I find Jean and tell him to add two lots of chips to our order. I tell myself that it's for the kids, not for me. Mae will thank me in the end. One of these days I'll remember that I should never listen to myself.

When I get back to the table, a platter of crusty bread with oils and garlic salts is awaiting. There's also a bowl of plump green olives. Jamie and Evie dive on the bread like a plague of locusts.

The wine arrives and I taste it. It's good, strong and oaky.

Evie and Mae are full of chat about our tour tomorrow to see the American war cemetery and the beaches too, as Pops requested. Then, on our last day here, we'll do some more relaxing by the pool.

I smell the garlic before the food arrives and my stomach responds by growling in appreciation. A steaming plate of langoustines lies resplendent in the middle of our table.

'Oh, it's prawns!' Jamie says. 'Why didn't you just say so?'

He dives in and grabs one, then hands his plate to me and asks me to cut it for him.

The langoustines are juicy and bursting with flavour.

Pretty soon we all have garlic butter dribbling down our chins.

Mae laughs as she dips her bread into the sauce and we all join in, mopping up butter with doughy bread.

I look at my wife – sitting opposite me – and I wish that she were sitting closer so that I could reach and hold her hand. Her auburn hair falls in soft waves over her face, hiding her eyes. It's gotten long and I'm surprised by the fact. When did that happen? For years she'd been wearing it in a short bob. Echoes of the woman I first fell hook, line and sinker for, all those years ago, in every wave of that hair.

I want to tell her that I'm sorry I haven't noticed, but I see her now. I will her to look at me so I can try to convey some of what I'm feeling.

I yearn for those days, when we were in sync. We used to know what the other was thinking all the time. But Mae's head stays down low. She is apparently on a different telepathic channel to me right now.

We have a chance, though, on this trip, I'm sure of it. We've left all the stresses at home. We can just concentrate on having fun, relaxing. I look around the table and the kids look happier than they've done for months. I feel like I've a coat hanger shoved in my face, I'm smiling so much. It feels good. The Guinness family has arrived in Bayeux and are having a good time.

'It's good, *non?*' the waiter asks when he removes the now-empty plate ten minutes later.

Nods and smiles all round from us and he clicks his fingers to alert another waiter to bring our main course.

Mae asks him to talk us through what the dish is and

he explains that the *joue de boeuf* is meat from the cow's cheek.

He then points to Jamie's face and says, 'From the face, *non*? Not the bum.'

That would have been comical enough, but this French accent saying 'bum' is enough to set anyone off.

'The cheek is marinated in red wine for three days with a selection of *légumes*. Then our chef has braised it for ten hours. It is *très bien*.' He steps back, but doesn't leave and I realise he's waiting for us to taste the dish.

I spoon some of the meat onto my plate and add the vegetables and sauce. Mae serves both the children, but I notice that they have yet to raise a fork to their mouths.

I gingerly take a bite, after all the boasts about how I'd do *I'm a Celebrity* food challenges no bother, I've no option but to suck it up.

But talk about explosion of taste in my mouth! It is the most wonderful thing I've ever tasted. The meat is tender and the sauce rich.

I turn to Jean and say truthfully, 'It's perfect. Kids, you have got to try this. It's delicious.'

Jamie and Evie both scoop up a forkful, just as the evening is about to go all wrong.

I'd forgotten about the chips. I wish Jean had too. But with bloody awful timing, he adds two bowls of golden *frites* to the table, alongside the green salad and green beans.

'Yes!' Jamie whoops, dropping the beef whilst scooping a large handful of chips onto his plate. 'Thanks, Dad.'

Evie looks almost apologetic at Mae, but grabs some chips too.

Mae glowers at me. 'You had to be the hero. You went ahead and ordered chips. Of course you did.'

Shit. She lifts her glass to her mouth and takes a large slug, then refills it.

I try to redeem myself, 'Jamie, Evie, try the beef. It's really good.'

Jamie whines. 'I don't want to.'

'Just try a mouthful,' I coax, but his mouth is jam-packed full of fries. I can feel the heat of Mae's eyes and I do my best to avoid looking at her.

Yep, I'm a fecking eejit.

Evie looks at Mae and then at me. She pushes her chips to one side and starts to eat the beef. All at once, the happy, fun atmosphere at our table is gone and we're back to the status quo of a dispirited family.

'You don't have to if you don't want to,' Mae says and squeezes Evie's hand.

'Hey, this is quite good, Mam.' Evie stuffs a bigger mouthful in to prove her point.

'Jamie, you going to try some of the beef?' Mae tries one last time.

I hold my breath. Go on my, son, help your dad out. 'No way,' he replies.

Feck.

Thick, ugly tension hangs over us once more and this time I know that there's no one to blame but me.

Class-A gobshite. 'I'm sorry.' I mean it.

'It doesn't matter,' she replies and looks down at her plate.

But of course it does. Our mutual dissatisfaction with each other has been simmering like this pot of stew for many months and now it's about to boil over.

Mae pushes back her hair and looks at me, straight in the eyes. I chance a smile of apology, but it freezes when I cop the look of contempt that passes over her face. I don't need any telepathy to understand what's going on in her mind. At first I hold her gaze, thrusting my chin out in a gesture of defiance, but she's better at this game than me and I'm the first to look away.

Chapter Fifteen

EVIE

EvieGuinness: You awake?

   AnnMurphy: Whasup?

   EvieGuinness: So much for this holiday putting everyone in a better mood.

   AnnMurphy: What happened?

   EvieGuinness: ChipGate. That's what happened. They are only fighting over a bag of chips now. That's how lame my parents are.

   AnnMurphy: For real? Scarlet for them.

   EvieGuinness: I hate them.

   AnnMurphy: Hugz

   EvieGuinness: Hugz

I thought Mam and Dad were getting on better. But the tension during dinner tonight was off the scale. Bet Dad will never look at a chip in the same way again.

If Jamie had just tasted the cheeks then we wouldn't be in this mess. Mam wouldn't have minded Dad ordering the chips. But when Jamie says no to something, he is so stubborn, he'll never change his mind. I felt sorry for our waiter. He knew that something had gone down, but had no clue what ChipGate was all about.

The taxi drive home was horrendous. Mam looked out the window in silence the whole way. Dad kept blathering on about sleeping arrangements, setting up beds. He always does that. Banging on about rubbish when he's nervous.

Even my iPod couldn't drown him out. One minute it looks like they are back to being friends again. Then, bam, something silly happens and they're firing dirty looks at each other.

AnnMurphy: Do you think they'll get a divorce?
EvieGuinness: Yep.
AnnMurphy: That sucks.

Yes it does. I just want it to go back to how it used to be. I've been trying to work out when it was that they last seemed happy and relaxed with each other. It was definitely before Dad lost his job and Pops got cancer. Last summer. I keep remembering this one perfect night when we had a barbecue out in the back garden. Dad was chef, natch. What is it about barbecues that means men have to wear a stupid apron and do all the cooking? Anyhow, after the food, we were all just sitting and relaxing. It was so warm. Dad was half asleep on his chair.

Mam had gestured to me and Jamie to go with her. Pops was laughing, he could see we were up to something and Mam put her fingers to her lips, shushing him.

We went into the kitchen and filled saucepans and mixing bowls with water. Then, with Mam leading us to battle, we snuck up on Dad and let him have it.

Mam was screaming, 'Water fight!' and then Dad was up like a scalded cat with the cold of the water when it hit him. Mam and us two were laughing so much, we had to cling to each other to stay standing.

Then Dad said, 'Right, this is war!' And he ran for the hose and turned it on us.

I don't think I've ever laughed so much. They were happy then. Genuine happiness, I mean, not the 'let's pretend for the sake of the kids'.

If I close my eyes I can still see Dad catching Mam around her waist and pulling her into him close while they kissed.

I shouted, 'Eewwww, get a room!' And they laughed, ignored me and kissed again.

They were always PDA'ing all over the shop back then. It used to do my head in. But now I wouldn't care less if they both snogged for hours in the middle of the road, if it meant that they were happy again. I feel tears prick my eyes. I don't want to start crying, I might wake up Jamie.

I think Dad still loves Mam. He has this look on his face sometimes when he looks at her, all goofy-like. It's not a good look for him. I'm not so sure about Mam, though. She looks pissed off with him a lot of the time, like he irritates her. She never used to look at him like that. At Pops' funeral she looked worried for him a lot of the time. I keep holding onto that. If she worries about him, then maybe she does love him. Maybe.

My head feels like it's going to break with it all. I don't want them to get divorced, but they don't seem to like each other much any more. So maybe they should go their separate ways. Because they sure aren't happy the way things are. It's just I know exactly what will happen if they split up. Jamie will want to go with Dad. Come to think of it, Dad wouldn't be the one to leave, would he? It would be Mam. Because it's Dad's family home from his childhood. That would give him first dibs, I reckon.

I'll have to go too, then. I can't have Mam leave on her own. Good job they have two kids, makes the divvying up easier.

The thing is, I don't want to leave Dad or Jamie. I mean Jamie's okay for a pain-in-the-arse kid brother. I've gotten used to having him bug me every day.

My head is going to break with it all.

I peer at my watch and can just about make out in the dark that it's about midnight. Mam and Dad are asleep, or, at least, there is no light on in their room.

Tonight should have been fun. Our first night sleeping in Nomad. But it ended up as much fun as root-canal treatment. They sucked all the fun out of it with ChipGate. Jamie feels it too, which is why I agreed to sleep in his stupid canopy bed with him. He looked so vulnerable when he asked me if I wanted to have a sleepover. I couldn't say no. He better not pee on me.

All the earlier talk of a drink under the stars was forgotten. By the time we got back from the restaurant, nobody felt much like star-gazing. So, instead, we all sat in silence watching TV, pretending all was okay. I would have gone to my bedroom, had I one to go to. And they wonder why I put my headphones on all the time. It's better than listening to the deafening sound of their hatred.

And of course as I can hear pretty much everything in Nomad, I heard them whisper-fighting in their room earlier. I couldn't work out what they said to each other, but I got the gist. And with every word, my stomach churned a bit more, so much so that I thought I'd vomit. I'm so sick of feeling like this – worried and stressed about everything.

AnnMurphy: You going to be k?

Will I be okay? My mind is stuck on the same things over and over, as I keep thinking about what is going to happen when we get home from this trip. My parents. School. Luke. It's like a battle zone in my head, as each thing fights for my attention and an answer I can't give.

I'm thirteen and I think my head is about to break.

EvieGuinness: Yeah, I'm kk. xxx

I close my eyes and try to sleep.

Chapter Sixteen

MAE

'This bloody bed,' I mutter as another spring digs into my back. No matter which way I turn, it's like sleeping on a breadboard. With spikes. What time is it? For pity's sake it's not even two a.m. This night just seems to go on forever.

Looking at Olly fast asleep beside me, with not a care in the world, makes me want to throw a pillow at him. I only agreed to this trip under duress and now I can't for the life of me work out why I concurred.

I know I'll toss and turn for hours before I finally succumb to rest, our row bouncing around my head, making it impossible for me to sleep.

Why is it, when I did nothing wrong, that I feel so bloody guilty? I ended up looking like a killjoy, stopping everyone from eating chips. But it wasn't about the chips. It was about the fact that, once again, Olly took away my voice, chipped away at my parental role.

I look at him over on his side of the double bed and

me on mine. It's funny, in a non-hilarious way, really, how two people can sleep in such a small space but still feel like there are thousands of miles between them. At home we have a super-king-size bed and yet we always seem to sleep at opposite sides of it. Disadvantage of such a big bed, I suppose. The years of kids sneaking into our bed, too, has just made us accustomed to sleeping with a void between us.

But in Nomad our bed is a double and the room is what you would call, at best, cosy. Most would call it miniscule. No room to swing a cat, kind of thing. Maybe we will wake up tomorrow morning in a tangle of legs and arms as we have no choice but to roll towards each other.

On that thought, I begin to feel a bit drowsy and close my eyes and try hard to close my mind so that I can sleep.

Thump.

What the hell was that? A loud bang just rattled Nomad.

'Olly,' I hiss. 'Did you hear that?'

He groans something that sounds like, 'Cornflakes', turns his back to me and lets out a loud snore.

Thump.

A second bang, this time louder.

'Olly,' I hiss a little louder and give him a dig, for goodness sake, we're under attack!

'What, what . . . ' he says, opening one eye.

'There's someone out there. Did you hear that?' I point to the ceiling.

'Your imagination is playing tricks.' He closes his eyes again and, I swear to God, I'm about two seconds away from grabbing my pillow and letting him have it.

Thump.

'Okay, I heard that.' Olly sits up, at last.

'What is it?' I whisper. My mind is going into overdrive, right bang into the area of escaped prisoners or mad axe-men.

'I'll go outside and take a look. Probably just kids messing from the campsite.' Olly pulls on his runners.

'Wait,' I whisper, grabbing his arm. 'Don't go out there. That's what they want!'

'What who wants?' Olly asks, looking a bit puzzled.

'Whoever is out there!' I say. 'Look, they want you to go out, and goodness knows what kind of a trap it is.'

Olly starts to laugh. I don't get the feeling he's taking this seriously.

'Remember that story from years ago about that couple in the car?' I say to him.

He looks blank.

'A couple were making out in the car,' I tell him.

'Lucky feckers,' he says.

I decide to ignore that. 'They hear a noise, so he goes out to investigate. Then a few minutes later, she hears a . . . '

Thump.

We both jump and I'm practically on top of Olly with the fright.

'Oh Jesus,' I say. 'It's just like in the story.'

Olly lifts me off his lap and says, 'What story?'

Sometimes my husband is really dense. 'The one I'm telling you about. The couple! The husband goes out and doesn't come back. Then the wife hears a kerdump on the roof of the car.'

'A kerdump?'

'Yes, a kerdump.'

'What's a kerdump when it's at home?' Olly asks, grinning.

'A bang,' I say. 'It's another word for a bang.'

'Right,' Olly laughs. 'I've not heard that one before.'

'Okay smartarse, so she hears a BANG and goes outside to check what happened. And sweet Jesus, Olly, she only sees a mad axeman on the roof and he's got her husband's beheaded head in his hands!'

'Oh the husband's head is going kerdump, kerdump, kerdump,' Olly snorts and he can't contain his laughter any more.

Thump. Thump. Thump.

'That was three in a row,' I say and feel some satisfaction to see Olly looking a bit more worried.

'Look, relax. There are no mad axeman on the loose outside in the campsite. But I'm sure there are a few kids messing, trying to frighten us. I'll chase them off,' Olly says.

'And leave me and the children here, all defenceless. No way,' I say to him, horrified.

'Okay, so what do you suggest?' Olly says.

'We ring the police. The *gendarme*. Get them to come investigate.'

Thump. Thump. Thumpity thump. 'Oh feck, it's getting louder,' I say.

'Whoever is up there, it sounds like they're doing riverdance on the roof now,' Olly says. 'Look, I'm going outside. If not, the kids will wake up. We don't want that. Stay here and I'll be back in a second.'

He grabs a torch from the kitchen cupboard and goes outside. I look around for a weapon and pick up a small kitchen knife and hold it out in front of me. If a mad axeman is out there, I'm not going down without a fight. I take a peek up at the canopy and see both kids are still fast asleep. That's good.

Despite my annoyance with him, I feel kind of proud of Olly. It is brave going out there. He could be facing anything. I pick up the knife, ready to do battle. I can be brave too. Then, less than a minute later I see the door handle of Nomad turn. I get ready to attack, knife outstretched.

'Oh good, that will come in handy. To pare these!' Olly laughs, throwing something at me.

'Ow!' I'm confused when an apple hits me on the leg.

'This is an orchard. Orchards have apples and right now they are falling on top of Nomad. That's your *kerdump*,' Olly says smiling. 'Not a sign of a mad axeman, I promise.'

'Apples,' I say, feeling a bit foolish.

'Apples,' Olly replies laughing.

'Sssh, you'll wake the kids,' I tell him and turn with as much dignity as I can muster, back to our room.

'Tomorrow I'll climb up and make sure that there are no more loose apples, so no more kerdumps,' Olly says and despite myself, I start to giggle.

'Thank you for going out to check,' I say.

'Sure that's my job. To protect you from kerdumps,' Olly says and turns over to go to sleep.

His job.

I think about all of the ways he made me feel protected

over the years. The countless times he's told me to stay put while he investigates a creak in the house that has woken us both up, just like tonight. The way he will never let me lift anything that's heavy. All of our walks and his insistence that I stay on the inside of the path so that if a car was to clip anyone, it would be him. The feel of his hand on my arm, keeping me steady, when the road is icy. Always getting up early to de-ice the car window for me, before I head to work, checking my tyres are okay, because he knows I'll never think to do it myself.

Oh, Olly. So many small ways you have made it your job to make me feel safe and I've taken it for granted. Have I thanked you enough?

I reach over and touch his cheek, but he's fast asleep already. I lie down close to him, feeling the heat of his body warming mine, and whisper my thanks.

The next morning I awake early. It's strange hearing noises from our next-door neighbours as they begin making moves to start their day, because at home we live so remotely. Olly is still asleep and I envy him, that ability to sleep through noise. And I note we have done an admirable job at keeping our distance from each other as we slept too. Somewhere between the kerdumps and now, my annoyance with him over the chips has softened. I'm determined to avoid another row today. I swore to myself I'd cut out the rows with Olly, when Evie told us how she felt a few weeks back.

In the old days, if Olly and I fought we'd have spent the whole night making up. 'Never go to sleep on a row', we'd always pledged. Oh the innocence of those days.

Back then, even if we hadn't sorted out our differences,

we'd still lie in each other's arms, in silent mutiny. And, of course, the longer I would lie with Olly's strong arms around my body, the more my annoyance with him would disappear. It's impossible to be cross with someone who is giving you comfort. I'd feel his warm breath on my neck, tickling it and then, whether I wanted it or not, desire would follow. He always seemed to be in sync with my body. Because at exactly the right moment, his hand would move down to my breast and he'd flip and tease my nipple till it ached for more. And then that would be it, all thoughts of arguments lost in my need for him.

The bed rocks from side to side as Olly wakes and jumps up, walking out the door in less than sixty seconds flat. I don't know how he does that either. Awake and ready to attack the day in seconds. It takes me at least two cups of tea before I'm able to even speak.

I can hear him rousing the kids and the water splashing into the kettle. I must doze off again, because a while later I awake to muffled voices from the kitchen. Olly and the children. My first thought is, once again, our fight. The fact that we didn't even manage to last forty-eight hours on our holiday without incident weighs heavily. The next eight weeks feel like an exhausting prospect. Oh Pops, I know you don't want this, but the likelihood of me buying a Ryanair ticket home seems stronger by the minute.

I sigh and close my eyes. It's been a long time since I felt my husband's hands on my body. Six months? Yes, about that, I realise, with dismay, since our last failed attempt. I know it must be killing him, this impotency. But I've done everything I can to understand, to listen, to be patient. It's his lack of enthusiasm to do anything about it that irks me. I'm not sure he even misses our intimacy any more. And it's not just sex. I mean, yes, I miss that, but more than that, I miss being in his arms.

On the day of Pops' funeral, we embraced and it shook me. The first time in months I'd felt his arms around me. That's not the kind of marriage I want. Maybe if he had showed any remote sign of affection towards me these past few months, I wouldn't have kissed Philip. The dull throb of an impending headache starts me thinking about that problem that needs to be sorted.

'Breakfast is ready,' Olly calls in.

I wonder what he would think if I called to him, told him to lock the door to Nomad while the kids ate breakfast outside. What if I asked him to make me forget why I am annoyed with him, in the way he used to?

I feel reckless, I feel lonely, damn it, I feel horny, so I call out, 'Olly, can you come here for a minute?'

I rub under my eyes and quickly throw my head upside down, to fluff out my hair.

'Can it wait? I'm kind of busy right now.' Curt, clipped tones. Foolishness replaces my recklessness and any thought of sex disappears. It appears that our bodies are not in sync any more.

'It wasn't important. I'll be there in a minute.' I blink furiously to stop tears from spilling.

I look in the tiny mirror glued to one of the cupboards and wonder what is it that Olly sees when he looks at me. He used to tell me all the time. Declarations of love and admiration were thick and fast. I grew accustomed to them.

I don't think I can now become inured to a life that doesn't include them. So what's the alternative? A fling with Philip? The truth is that while my body was tempted, I don't want him. I have no feelings towards him whatsoever. Later today, I'm going to text him and tell him that whatever we almost started is over. This isn't who I am, getting thrills from a cheap flirtation. Even if my marriage is over, Olly deserves more than that. Damn it, I deserve more than that.

Because however I look at it, right now, I'm alone, no matter what happens. I can stay in a marriage that no longer makes me happy, or walk.

I stand up, put a smile on my face and do what I do a lot lately – pretend that everything is fanbloodytastic. Will they notice what a big fat fraud I am? No, it appears not, because they all smile at me in return.

'We made breakfast for you,' Jamie declares. 'Me and Evie did it.'

I look at the table in our dining room and it has croissants, a smorgasbord of fruit, cheeses and pastries on it, plus a steaming pot of coffee.

'Wow, you guys! It looks wonderful,' I say to them.

'Dad suggested that we make a local breakfast this morning,' Jamie says.

'We thought we'd make the ultimate sacrifice and forgo Weetabix for some *pain au chocolat*,' Olly says, winking at the kids.

'I chose the *pain au chocolat*, Mam, for us all,' Jamie says. His face looks solemn as he says this. 'Not because they are chocolate, but because they are French. I want to be courageous, like you said.'

I feel laughter begin to bubble up inside me and I'm

filled with love for my family. 'Oh I'd say these are good for a courageous palate alright.' I pick one up and take a bite. 'Yep, I'm feeling positively Spiderman-brave right now, after just one little mouthful!'

Olly is standing by the stove looking awkward. I move further in on the bench and say to him, 'You better sit down and grab one of these quick, before our "courageous" children scoff them all!'

He smiles, relief written all over his face, and sits down beside me. 'What did you want back then? I was making the coffee, sorry.'

'Nothing that can't wait,' I answer, looking at the children, who look both happy and relieved that our fight seems to be over. We are long overdue an honest talk about us, but what's another day?

'I got you some mango, Mam, I know it's your favourite.' Jamie is determined to take credit for every choice on the table.

'And I got you the apples,' Olly pipes in, totally deadpan, causing me to snort with laughter.

'What's so funny?' Jamie asks.

Olly and I tell them our 'Kerdump' story and our little van is filled with laughter and fun and teasing that makes me remember years of similar moments.

As Olly and Jamie fight over the last croissant, I watch Evie closely and feel a stab of shame when I notice frown lines in her forehead. She stifles a yawn and somehow or other I know her tiredness is down to us and our stupid row about chips.

'You okay?' I whisper to her. She shrugs, but won't look me in the eye.

163

I'm supposed to be finding a way to make this better for her. We need to do better. It's just . . . well, it's so fecking hard. I can't seem to get anything right at the moment.

Then before I lose myself in a fit of self-pity, Jamie leans in and throws his arms around my neck. As he half-strangles me with his hug, I am consumed with joy. A cuddle, initiated by Jamie. I lift my arms up behind me to pull him over my shoulder and into my lap. I breathe in his chocolaty scent and realise that it's not all bad. Oh, Pops, maybe you are right. Maybe we do just need time. For this moment alone, this embrace, I'll put up with every inconvenience. And as I hold my son close to me, my body rejoices in the memory of how much one of his snuggles can change my mood, my day. My life.

Reluctantly we make a move to get ready. It's tempting to just stay put, but we've a tour to get to. We all head to the dreaded communal showers. When it comes to shower rooms, I'm pants. I've never been one of those exhibitionists who feels compelled to wander around the shower room butt-naked.

But yesterday's ten-minute shower in Nomad has only proven that Aled does talk a load of bollocks! The water might have been hot, but the trickle that came out of the shower head wouldn't rinse shampoo off a bald man, never mind me and my mop! I had to keep changing positions in an effort to get wet all over. It didn't help that Olly was at the door shouting that we were gonna run out of water if I didn't get out. Nope. Nomad's shower isn't going to be a runner.

Peeking at Evie's face, who looks like she's about to

get shot in front of a firing squad, makes me giggle. Like mother, like daughter, she's always hated this communal malarkey too. But when we arrive at automatic doors that whoosh open wide to the shower room, my expectations begin to grow. The facility is pristinely clean, modern and looks spacious. We scope the area and high-five each other when we see individual showers with doors on them.

Evie does a quick 'Yes!' and punches the air. 'No offence, Mam, but I didn't want to see your bits,' she says.

No offence taken. I quite agree.

Chapter Seventeen

MAE

Our tour for the Normandy beach trip collects us from reception at the chateau. We're an intimate group, just four others on the mini-bus plus ourselves. Our driver, Michel, greets us like long-lost family. Double kisses are doled out freely, much to Jamie's glee and Evie's mortification. She quickly puts on her earphones to her iPod and tunes out the chatter in the bus. I can see irritation on Olly's face as she rudely does this and, while I feel the same, I touch his arm and whisper to him to leave her be.

Michel introduces us to our fellow explorers, two American couples – Mabel, Fred, Joan and Don. They are also touring Europe in motorhomes and arrived in the chateau campsite the previous evening.

'Aren't you the cutest little thing?' Mabel says to Jamie, who gives her the benefit of his biggest smile. This elicits an 'aw' from the whole group.

'We're been touring Europe for six weeks now,' Mabel

says. She's the chatty one, it seems. The others seem happy to let her speak on their behalf.

'My, what a wonderful place it is. We've been to Ireland, you know. We just loved it there. Fred's family are Irish. Tell them, Fred.'

But before Fred could get a word out, she continued, 'His great grandmother was a O'Brien from Cork.' Fred looks like he's used to not being heard. I feel his pain.

She fills us all in on their various stops and it's enjoyable to sit back and listen to her. I'm not in a chatty mood, so having someone do it all for me is good. And she's fun company. I like her.

Michel interrupts her flow to tell us that our first stop will be Pointe du Hoc. I know that this is the German battery that was attacked by US Rangers on D-Day. We are all particularly interested in this, because of the film *Saving Private Ryan*, which Olly and I have watched many times. Michel is wearing one of those head microphones and combines being our driver and tour guide seamlessly. I've not always been a fan of organised tours, but this feels less so. Maybe because there are only eight of us, or maybe it's his easygoing manner.

'We approach Pointe du Hoc, where the Rangers, commanded by Lt Col James Rudder, scaled the cliffs to get to the German gun position. This scene you see in the movie *Saving Private Ryan*, *non*?' Michel tells us.

'The site was blown to pieces in the bombings, but little has changed since the US Rangers left it,' Michel continues.

'Take off your earphones,' Olly gives Evie a dig.

'*Saving Private Ryan* was filmed on beaches near where

we live,' Olly turns around to tell everyone with pride. 'And Brooklyn too.'

More 'aw's and 'wow's from the group.

'My cousin was an extra in *Saving Private Ryan*,' he adds. 'He said that Tom Hanks was a real gentleman.'

The Americans all look impressed. 'I liked him in *Forrest Gump*,' Mabel says.

'Life is like a box of chocolates,' Fred says in a pretty decent Forrest impression.

'I like to run,' Olly throws in his own attempt and there is a general air of merriment on the little bus.

Then Joan speaks, for the first time, 'I couldn't watch it. The movie.'

'War movies are not for everyone,' Olly says to her.

Michel parks the mini-van and we all walk towards Pointe du Hoc. I've seen photographs of this site many times, but nothing can prepare you for it in 3-D glory.

'This is the place that looks like an eerie lunar landscape,' I tell the kids and unsuccessfully attempt to link arms with Evie. She pulls away from me and moves to one side of us, on her own.

'I don't think she likes us very much right now,' Olly whispers to me.

I'm not sure I like us either, but I'm wise enough to keep that to myself.

Jamie runs on ahead and then comes back, saying as he skips, 'It's like the moon. It looks like the moon does. Look!'

And he is right. The landscape, or moonscape, as it's often called, is a piece of land filled with a series of holes and cavities or craters. All caused by the devastation from the bombings of that day.

'The Allied warplanes were trying to deliver a killing blow to the four large guns located here,' Michel tells us.

'Cool!' Jamie says.

'I'm not so sure it was cool for the people who were here at the time,' I say to him, but he's already moved away and is trying to jump from one crater to another. How he's gotten to this age without a broken bone I'll never know.

'We'll have to watch *Saving Private Ryan* again when we get home,' Olly says. 'It will take on a greater significance, I think, now that we've seen all this in the flesh.'

'I brought it with me. The DVD,' I tell him. 'I guessed we might like to look at it again, while in Normandy.'

'You always think of everything,' Olly says. 'We'd be lost without you.'

I wonder if he is being smart, but he seems to mean it. To say I'm taken aback is an understatement. I mean, all I've seemed to be good for is my pay cheque and little else. Have I gotten it wrong? It's like the ground below me keeps shifting.

'Do you really mean that?' I ask and Olly stops and looks at me aghast.

'You must know that's true.'

'No, actually I don't,' I reply. I feel my body tremble with the admission, but nothing to be left unsaid, isn't that right, Pops?

'You're the glue that holds us all together. We'd fall apart without you, Mae,' Olly says.

It feels like time freezes and I'm only aware of Olly looking at me, the noises of our surroundings melting into the air. So many questions jumble around my head,

169

things that I should be saying but I can't because, once again, it's neither the time nor the place.

It's never the right time or the right place, though. Children, work, life always in the way of us admitting what is bothering us, being honest, telling it like it is. Maybe it's easier to use them all as excuses. I'm distracted and so I almost stumble on the uneven ground. My stomach lurches and I steel myself to hit the dirt. But then I feel Olly, his two hands steadying me, firm, sure.

I stop and pull him back from getting onto the bus. They can wait. 'You've always kept me from falling,' I say. To hell with where we are, I need to tell him that much. I need to let him know that I acknowledge, I see, I feel his protection all these years.

He looks at me, a little dazed by my words, so I continue in a rush to tell him my thanks. 'You always catch me. You make sure I've petrol in my car and that the tyres are not bald. I don't think I thank you enough for all the little things you do for me.'

And his smile, his obvious delight in my words, disarms me so much that I almost stumble a second time. We laugh so hard, we clutch our stomachs and I know that everyone on the bus thinks we're mad. But it feels good, as if our laughter is an antidote to the pain and stress that's been bubbling up inside of us.

We continue to drive along the coast to Omaha Beach, our next stop.

'Will Jamie and Evie get the true significance of what happened here?' I ask Olly. 'It's known to have been the bloodiest of the beaches on D-Day, but to them it might just be blue skies and sandy beaches.'

'In many ways, that's not a bad thing. I'm not sure I want them to know about the atrocities of war yet,' Olly answers.

Michel tells us, 'We'll stop in two points on either end of the six-kilometre beach. Then you can see the scale of the operations.'

As I step onto the warm sand, with my sandals in my hands, the sea air whips my hair around my face. I look up and down the beach, left to right and then, finally, my eyes rest on the blue ocean. I wonder how the soldiers felt when they landed here. Were they scared? Were they hopeful? Did they know that this would be the last place they would see before a bloody death? I feel humbled.

I look at Olly and wonder if he is as affected as me. He is still, arms folded across his chest, almost hugging himself. He seems thoughtful, but it's hard to read him. Jamie and Evie's eyes are on the water, where water skiers and windsurfers dot the skyline. It is holiday season, after all, and we are on a beach, so it is, of course, to be expected. But it unnerves me because I expected the beach to be a memorial, a grave, I suppose, to the lost soldiers.

I think of Pops and how he said he wanted the kids to realise that there is more to life than our small spot at home in Wexford.

'We need to talk to the kids,' Olly says. 'Try to explain the significance of here. For Pops.'

I'm taken aback. It's as if Olly is in my head. 'That's just what I was thinking.'

'Kids,' Olly calls and when they walk over to us he continues, 'Can you do something for us? Think about this. You are standing on the exact same sand that thousands of US soldiers landed on and died on seventy years ago.'

Their eyes are wide as they take in his words and their eyes drop to the golden sand as the words sink in.

'I know it doesn't look like a battlefield now. But here, along this very shore, men died for a cause. Thousands of them,' I continue.

We are all still as we take this in. 'That's not nice,' Jamie eventually says.

'No it's not,' I say, ruffling his hair.

'What's that over there?' Evie asks, startling us. She's so quiet lately, I've given up expecting much interaction from her. I look over in the direction she's pointing in and see a huge metal sculpture in the middle of the beach.

'Ah, that's the Anilore Banon monument *Les Braves*,' Michel says. 'Tell me, what do you think it looks like?'

'I don't know,' Jamie shrugs. 'Maybe a Transformer.'

Michel laughs, 'Ah *bon*. *Et vous*, Mademoiselle Evie, what do you think of it?' Evie is scarlet.

'Good luck getting an answer,' Olly murmurs under his breath.

She looks like she wants the sand to open up and take her away. But Michel continues, 'I'd like to hear what you think, Mademoiselle Evie.'

Her blush deepens to beetroot red, but she gives the monument her full attention. I think she's going to speak, but she stays silent, taking a few steps to the left, away from the rest of the group. I mouth 'sorry' to Michel at her rudeness.

'It looks like sand exploding into the air as gunfire hits

the ground,' Fred says, stepping forward. He glances sympathetically at Olly and me.

'Ah, *très bon*, Fred. It is symbolic of the chaos of that battle.'

'I love how the artist used metal because you can see the sea and sky reflected in it,' I say.

The murmur of consensus within the group bounces into the air. And standing here in the breeze, as the sun beats down, looking at the sculpture before me, I realise that I'm enjoying myself. How long since I felt like that? How long since I stopped and looked at something beautiful and thought about how it makes me feel?

A cloud floats on by through the blue sky reflected on the sculpture and I can't take my eyes off it.

Then Evie surprises us all by saying, 'It's hopeful.' She turns around to face us all. 'The blue sea and sky that you can see in the metal, I think the artist is telling us that the soldiers who died are free now. Free because they are scattered in the sky and sea.'

Did my daughter just say that? Was that our truculent teen, speaking so eloquently? Olly looks as gobsmacked as I do. 'How wonderfully perceptive,' I say.

'*Très bien*,' Michel says. 'You have the eyes of an artist, *non*?'

'Clever girl,' Olly says. She looks mortified by the attention, though, and steps further away from us once more, turning her back on us.

Michel smiles as he says, '*La Liberté* is in that reflection of an endless skyline,' he tells us, 'and without doubt, as Mademoiselle Evie says, hope is there too. Now, take some time to enjoy the beach. We leave in thirty minutes.'

Barefoot, we sit on the warm sand, our toes digging into the grains while we watch Jamie chase the waves, his Spiderman toy in hand.

'I wonder if the echoes of children laughing reach the heavens, to the ears of the men who died,' I say.

'I hope so. Because when I die that's the last thing I want to hear before I go. Our children laughing.'

I smile in agreement and we look out at the endless blue skyline.

'It was nice just then,' I say.

'What?'

'Talking to the children together. Oh, I'm sure it sounds silly, but it felt good, like we were on the same page.'

'That's not silly at all and I felt it too. It's all I want, Mae. To get back on the same page again.' His face breaks into a huge grin. 'Don't move, I'll be back in a minute.'

I watch him run off with his long strides and he's back a few minutes later with ice-creams. And for a few minutes, as we sit in companionable silence, licking our sugary treats, the Guinness family feels strong and united again. For now, at least, there is no hurt or ugly jealousies. No misunderstandings. Just us, on a beach, looking at the blue sky meet the blue sea.

Our next stop is the Normandy American War Cemetery and while the beach did not look at first glance like a memorial, this next stop leaves us in no doubt as to where we are.

Michel tells us all, 'This cemetery is the largest American cemetery in Europe. It holds the bodies of 9,387 soldiers, who fought to liberate Western Europe from the Germans.'

'That's a lot isn't it, Dad?' Jamie says in wonder, his nose scrunched up as he tries to imagine that large number.

'Yes. It is a lot,' Olly says.

'There are also 307 unknown soldiers buried here too,' Michel tells us, 'Sad, *non?*'

'Those poor men, not even a name to remember them by,' Mabel says.

'And our most famous figure is General Theodore Roosevelt Jr,' Michel informs us, pride in his voice. 'You will see his grave.'

'Who is that?' Jamie asks.

'He's a hero. They all are, but he was their leader,' I tell him.

'Like Spiderman?' Jamie asks.

'Yes, exactly like Spiderman,' I answer. It's as good an accolade as any. 'There's a lot of superheroes buried in here, Jamie.'

I've taught history for years. I've spoken about D-Day at length and marked essays on the subject. But I am quite unprepared for the emotional impact those white headstones have on me. Row after row, pristine, in perfect lines, on a green blanket of grass.

'The caretakers take great pride in keeping the cemetery clean,' Michel says. 'We have an hour and half here. Make sure to leave plenty of time for the visitor centre.'

Michel then turns to our American contingent and addresses Joan, who I notice looks rather pale. Her friends and husband rally around her, looking apprehensive.

'If you follow me, I can bring you to your brother's grave.' Michel does a little bow to her.

So that's why she's been so quiet. God love her. What

this must be like for her, I can't imagine. I am about to usher the children on, to give her some privacy, when she speaks.

Her husband, Don, holds her hand and Joan turns to us to say, 'I've never been before. I've wanted to come for years but it was never the right time. Children, grand-children, jobs – you know how it can be.'

I nod in sympathy. I do know. 'Life has a funny way of keeping us busy.'

'We're here now,' Don says, patting her hand.

'I'm not sure I'm brave enough,' Joan confesses. 'Now that I'm here, I'm not sure I can face it. It's been a long time.'

Jamie walks up to her and cranes his neck back as he looks up. 'What was his name?' he asks with wonderful childlike curiosity.

'Don't be nosey,' Olly reprimands him, and then mouths 'Sorry' to Joan and Don.

'Oh, don't be sorry. Jamie, my brother was called Johnny. He was my little brother, just like you are to Evie here. You know, when I watched you play on the beach it reminded me of him. He liked the water too. He was always chasing waves when we were kids, just like you were.'

Her eyes are now red and watery and her voice quavers. I want to cry for this unknown man called Johnny. I want to cry for his sister, Joan, who is all bent up with age and grief for a lost brother. I want to cry for every brother, son, father, man who lies cold in these graves.

I try to think of the right thing to say to her, to convey my feelings. Then Jamie, in true Jamie style, knows what to say instinctively. 'If you're scared, I'll go with you.'

I see many emotions flash across Joan's face at my son's offer. She seems to tremble as she pulls my son close into her for a hug. 'I'd like that, if it's okay with your folks.'

'If you don't mind, we'll all go. I'd like to pay my respects to Johnny too,' I tell her and my heart swells with pride for the second time today, this time for my warm-hearted son. So, in almost funeral-like procession, we follow Michel through the white headstones. He must have led many others like Joan over the years to see the final resting place of their loved ones. Some of the graves have rosettes on them and that makes me smile. I read earlier the significance of that; the soldier buried there is now found and named. They all deserve to be recognised for their heroic sacrifice.

Some of the gravestones are crosses and others have Stars of David on them. I don't suppose religion matters in the end, when they were all brothers-in-arms, fighting the same senseless war. We could learn a lot from that now.

Finally, Michel pauses and moves to one side, to point to a grave. Joan walks over to it and, with great grace, kneels before it. She takes her glasses out of her bag and reads out loud the inscription, 'Johnny Robinson, 16th Infantry, 1st Division. Killed 15th June 1944.'

We stand in silence and watch this lady mourn her dead brother. Her husband hovers behind her, one hand on her shoulder, supporting her. Mabel is silent for the first time today and is weeping into her hankie. Joan opens her handbag and takes out a small model aeroplane, kisses it, then places it atop the white cross.

'There you go, Johnny. I kept this for you, like you

asked me to when you left, all those years ago. It's time to give it back now to its rightful owner.'

I hear Evie make a squeaky noise and check she is okay. She has her arms folded across her chest, hugging herself tight. Jamie is looking at his Spiderman toy. Don helps Joan to stand up and he holds his arms open to hold her.

'I feel like I should say something, mark the occasion somehow,' Joan says, looking around her, her face tight with emotion. 'This doesn't feel enough. I'm letting him down.'

I wish there was something I could say, something I could do to help her. She's right, there should be more. I look at the rest of the group and they all look the same, helpless in our sympathy to this nice woman, who is mourning the loss of a beloved brother. I look at Olly and he says, 'I can't believe I'm going to offer this.'

Before I can ask him what, he walks towards Joan, clearing his throat. 'There's a song I know, "The Green Fields of France". My father used to sing it a lot when I was a kid. I keep thinking about it, have done from the moment I saw the graves all in a line. Well . . . ' He looks embarrassed and pauses for a moment before blurting out quickly, 'I could sing it for Johnny, for you – only if you want, now.'

'Oh, Olly, I'd like that very much. Johnny loved to sing himself,' Joan says.

After fifteen years of marriage, my husband surprises me once again. He used to sing a lot back when we were doing the pub scene, before the kids. He had a few party pieces that he'd belt out. But that feels like a lifetime ago.

Olly's deep and raspy voice starts to sing the ballad

about a young man called Willie McBride and we all fall silent. Every word, every note, hangs in the air and suddenly the men who have died and are buried here become real to us. They are all Willie McBride. They are all Joan's brother, Johnny Robinson. I've heard the lyrics so many times before, but never really understood them, till now.

Evie nudges me and I look around. We've gathered a respectful audience, as others pause by the graveside to listen to the beautiful ballad. Olly's eyes are closed and his voice rings out in the gentle breeze. I can't take my eyes off him.

> Now *the sun shines down on the green fields of France,*
> *A warm summer wind makes the red poppies dance,*
> *The trenches have vanished under the glows,*
> *There's no gas, no barbed wire, there's no guns firing*
>   *now.*
> *But here in this graveyard, it's still no man's land,*
> *The countless white crosses stand mute in the sand*
> *For man's blind indifference to his fellow man,*
> *To a whole generation that was butchered and damned.*

The words hit every one of us hard and I hear sobs from around the group. Mabel taps my arm and she motions me to link arms with her. I look around and see that everyone else is doing the same. When Olly stops singing the final note, nobody moves, nobody speaks. The sound of silence bounces off the white headstones around us. Then slowly, Fred starts to clap – and one by one everyone joins in.

Joan walks over to Olly and says, 'That was the most beautiful song I've ever heard. I'll never forget that.'

People walk over to Olly and slap him on the shoulder, shake his hand and I have never been so proud of my husband as I am this minute. How have I forgotten that he is a good man? Somehow or other, over the past few months, this Olly here has been hidden from me. In his place, a shadow of his former self: difficult, prickly, uncommunicative, ambivalent. But as he sang, I saw the passion in his words and remembered the man that I fell in love with.

The last of the well-wishers has moved away, so I walk up to him and stand on my tiptoes to kiss him. I mean it to be a peck, but neither of us pulls apart. I lean into him and feel his hand on the small of my back. His lips feel soft and new, almost as if it's the first time we've kissed. When we pull apart, our eyes are locked on each other. I feel lightheaded and powerful all at once and take his face in my hands.

'That was a good thing you did,' I say. He looks a bit stunned and I'm not sure if it's by the whole situation we've found ourselves in or our kiss.

Michel clears his throat to regain our attention and the moment, whatever it was, ends.

He tells us that it is sand from the beaches that darkens the faded inscriptions on the headstones. This helps family members get better pictures of the graves. It is only a temporary staining of the letters, the sand washing away again with the next rainfall.

I'm not sure why this fact gets to me so much, but it does. The sand where these brave men lost their lives, once again, touches them in the sleep of death.

I walk over to Joan and hug her close. 'I'm so sorry for your loss.' Such a trite statement, but it's true. I am heart sorry. 'We'll give you some privacy, but thank you for letting us share this moment with you. It was an honour.'

Olly is standing close to Evie, who is struggling hard not to cry. Jamie's face is all scrunched up in the way he does when he is deep in thought. He walks back to the grave, rummaging in his pocket as he goes. He tugs until his Spiderman toy is free. He looks at it, his best pal, and then he places it beside the aeroplane.

'He can have this. Johnny was a superhero just like Spiderman,' he says.

'I think it's you who is a superhero,' Joan's voice is strangled with sorrow.

'I'm so proud of you,' I whisper to him and pull him in close for a hug. 'That was a kind thing to do.'

The next hour passes by in an emotional blur as we explore the rest of the cemetery. We find Theodore Roosevelt's grave and also the two Niland brothers, who inspired the *Saving Private Ryan* movie. The mood in our little group is sombre, but not morose. The tears we've shed feel cathartic.

I notice that Evie has disappeared and find her sitting in front of a twenty-two-foot-tall memorial. The bronze statue is entitled 'The Spirit of American Youth Rising from the Waves'. Her earphones are back on again and she's staring at the statue. She looks so sad, I want to take her in my arms and not let go till she smiles again. Instead, I walk over and sit beside her, nudging her with my shoulder lightly.

I fully expect to be ignored, but she takes her earphones out and, without taking her eyes off the statue, says, 'I nearly died because of a stupid dare.'

My heart starts to hammer loudly. Where has this come from? I've tried many times to get her to talk about her near-death experience but she has remained tight-lipped about it all. What the hell does she mean, a dare?

'Most of these soldiers were only a few years older than me. They died fighting for a cause, for their countries. And I nearly threw my life away because of a dare.'

'Can you tell me about it?' And when her face floods with pain, it feels like I've been doused in ice-cold water. I want to get Olly, but I'm afraid if I move, if I make the wrong sound, she'll clam up again and I need to know what is going on in her head.

'You won't understand.'

'I'd like to try,' I whisper.

Her eyes don't leave the statue for a moment and then, 'You and Dad have no idea how unhappy I've been.'

'That's not . . . ' Before I can finish defending myself, she turns to me, eyes full of accusations and disappointment.

'If you stopped fighting for five minutes, you might notice how unhappy I am!'

'You've got my full attention, Evie. We're not fighting now,' I say. 'Please. Please tell me.'

'I don't have any friends.' She keeps her head down low and avoids eye contact. I move towards her, to touch her, but she bats me away as if my touch burns her.

'I'm not like the rest of the Guinnesses – Pops, Dad,

Jamie, you. Everyone loves you guys. Everyone wants to be your friends. It's not like that for me.'

My head spins with her admission. She's got lots of friends. Of course she does.

'Martina and Deirdre,' I say. She went through primary school with them. Countless play-dates and sleepovers flash through my mind. But now that I think of it, how long since they were over? What have we missed while we've been so caught up in our own stupid neuroses?

'They have made my life hell for months now.' She answers in a voice that seems stripped of all emotion. It makes me want to weep.

And slowly she opens up and tells me about the months of name-calling, practical jokes, being ignored – both on social media and in school – that she's endured. Martina and Deirdre, the leaders of the mean girls, who seem to have made a sport out of making my daughter's life a living hell. With every confession, I feel more despair and panic beginning to overtake my earlier resolve to be calm and only listen. I have a thousand questions I want to fire at Evie. They are bloody lucky I'm on another continent now, because the urge to run to their houses, drag them back here by their bloody hair extensions and demand answers is overpowering. I want them to feel my daughter's pain. I want them to see the result of their nasty, cowardly, goddamn bullying.

'You've been dealing with all of this on your own?'

She nods. 'I was going to talk to Pops about it, but he got sick . . . '

So many things conspired against our lovely daughter.

'I'm so sorry you didn't feel you could talk to us,' I

say. 'But you have to tell me everything now. You said it was a dare?'

'I begged them to leave me alone. I said that I would do anything if they would just stop taunting me. Martina said she would think about it.'

She's a piece of work. When I think of her smiling at me at the school gates only two weeks ago, asking me sweetly how Evie was. The little bitch.

'She said I had to show them that I wasn't such a weirdo nerd after all, by drinking a pint of spirits mixed together. They watched me drink it on FaceTime.'

'Oh my darling,' I say, and feel tears splash down my cheeks.

'It was the only way I could think of to make them leave me alone, Mam, don't you see?'

'Yes, I see, Evie. I see it all now.' And she allows me to take her into my arms at last and hug her, hold her, and try my best to shush away her pain.

'I n . . . near . . . ly threw my l . . . l . . . life away, Mam,' Evie stutters out as her sobs begin to stop.

I search for the right words. 'Yes. That's true, but you are still here, Evie. I think that what matters now is what you do next. If you don't learn from that mistake, well that's something to be ashamed of. But never be ashamed of making a mistake in the first place.'

'How can I move on from it when I don't know what to do next? I don't know who I am any more. My head hurts, Mam. I'm so tired of feeling like this. I want it to stop.'

I'm scared. I pull her into my arms and whisper, 'It's okay. You don't need to have all the answers right now. We'll help you figure them out, together. I promise you.'

'Together?' Evie says. 'Are you sure about that? It doesn't feel like that much any more.'

'No, you're right. Things have been pretty pants around here lately. And your father and I have allowed our own stresses to colour how we've been at home. That's our bad. But one thing I know for sure is this. We are the Guinnesses and we stick together no matter what. Whatever happens in the future, we'll always have each other's back.'

I don't want to make promises to my daughter that we can't keep. But I know that Olly and I both love the children more than anything else. So we have to start putting their needs first.

I grab my soggy tissue and blow my nose, which at least makes her giggle.

'Attractive,' she says with sarcasm.

I stick my tongue out at her and say, 'Come on, let's go find the boys. I don't know about you, but I need a coffee. And chocolate. Lots of it! We've earned some mindless emotional eating!'

By the time the tour ends and Michel drops us back at the chateau campsite, we are all exhausted.

'Will we go to Bayeux to see the tapestry now or later?' Olly asks. His voice tells me that he'd rather pull his nails out one by one than go anywhere.

'Do any of you want to see it?' I ask them. A chorus of resounding 'no's come in quick succession.

'Then why don't we just hang out by the pool for the afternoon and have a barbecue tonight? Burgers, hotdogs and chips,' I suggest.

'Yes!' Jamie shouts, answering for all.

Evie opts for some time to herself in Nomad. She wants

to finish her book. While Jamie splashes in the pool, I fill Olly in on what's really been going on with her.

I can see the same horror, disbelief and fear that I felt earlier – still feel – flash across his face.

'The little wagons,' he finally says.

'Yes, kind of what flashed through my head too. We'll have to talk to their parents when we get home and the school too. But for now, our priority has to be Evie. Look, we got a second chance with her; she's physically okay again now. But we are not out of the woods yet. We still have to watch her.'

'Lots of things are making sense now. Conversations I've had with her about school and stuff.'

'We've screwed up here, Olly. We've let our own issues get in the way of what's important.'

He nods and we sit in silence for a long time. I've no idea what's going on in his head, but can only assume he's running through scenarios like me, where we missed the obvious with Evie.

'I'm glad she's talking to you,' Olly says.

'Me too,' I reply. 'Tonight, no matter what, we have a nice evening. No squabbles. She needs to relax, feel like she's got a safe place to fall with us both.'

'Agreed. I think we all need to relax,' Olly says.

He's not wrong. 'Maybe we can have that glass of wine under the moonlight,' I say.

'Done. You stay here with Jamie and read your book. I'll go be a hunter-gatherer, get food and wine from the shop for the barbecue,' Olly says. 'I'll check in on Evie, too, make sure she's okay.'

Chapter Eighteen

Dearest Olly and Mae

Are you enjoying Nomad? Is the chateau nice?
Did you go to the Normandy beaches? Have you
killed each other yet? Haha . . .

I so wish I was there to hear all your answers.
But know this, if I can, I'm watching you all from
wherever I am. I don't mind telling you that just the
very thought of this trip is taking my mind off the
pain.

Today is your mam's birthday, Olly. You've been
like a coiled spring all day, in and out of my room,
fussing. That's your way, though. Don't suppose that
will change any time soon. You know, I fancy I can
smell her perfume lately. The doc says it's all the
medication. It messes with your senses. You smelt it
though, the other week in the hospital, didn't you,
Olly?

Arra, enough of that. You want to know where
you are going next. Head south, you are going to

the Loire Valley for three days. Then I have a surprise for Jamie and Evie too, because before you leave France, you'll be overnighting in Disneyland Paris.

I've found the most amazing campsite for you in the Loire Valley – in the grounds of an actual vineyard. I like to think of you both, under the stars, sipping a glass of red. Talking. Listening. Sharing. I've not seen much of that lately.

There's lots for the children to do too. I know that the area is famous for its chateaus, but I don't want the kids to get bored. So here's my challenge for this leg of the trip. You have to go horse riding. Not just for half an hour, either. I've organised it all, the leaflet is in the envelope.

It's important that the kids, and you both, take some risks. Remember to always try something new and, you never know, you might find yourself growing wings and flying.

I'm thinking a lot about Evie today too. She's young and she's always followed the beat of her own drum, hasn't she? Always been a little bit different and she used to be okay with that. But she's forgotten that it's okay to be different. You need to remind her that she's got more to fear being the same as everyone else, following the herd, than of standing out.

But that's not such a bad thing is it? She just hasn't realised, yet, that she's strong, just like both of you. She'll get through all of this, I'm sure of it.

Help Evie believe that she can walk her own path once again, with confidence.

Have fun and you can read my next letter before you leave Paris.

Love to all,

Pops x

Chapter Nineteen

OLLY

Pops is dead. I know that. But somehow or other, he's managed to stay with us, on this adventure he's sent us on. And my relief is enormous, because I am not ready to say goodbye yet. I'm not sure I ever will be. My hands tremble as I pick up his latest letter once again. Not from worry, but from excitement and anticipation. I hold the envelope close to my nose and see if I can smell him. Then I feel foolish when, of course, I smell nothing but paper.

It's as if he knew that yesterday would be the day that Evie would tell us about the bullying. I glance down at his words again and scan for the bit about her.

'*You need to remind her that she's got more to fear being the same as everyone else, following the herd, than of standing out.*' Jesus, Pops, how do you do that? It's his fecking Wi-Fi again.

My attempt to discuss it all with Evie didn't go too well. She claimed tiredness and was reluctant to open up.

I just feel so much anger dancing its way through my body, threatening to get in the way of the job at hand right now. I can do anger some other time. Right now, I need to be a dad.

It's so weird, but it's as if her face has changed since I heard about the bullying. She looks younger. It feels like only yesterday that she was six years old and believed that her daddy could save her from all the bad stuff in the world.

She is still opening up to Mae, though, talking a little more about the isolation she's felt. And at least she agreed to go with Mae and Jamie to the pool when we got back from Bayeaux this morning. I stayed behind because I wanted to read Pops' letter on my own. Some days, the pain of my loss, of his absence, feels so acute that I want to howl in pain. And the only thing that makes it bearable is these letters. I put off opening it for ages. Procrastinating – I know I do that too much. It's just, once it's opened, I can't have that moment again. With only eight letters in total and three read already, I want to make sure I savour every single word.

I keep trying to work out how he was feeling when he wrote each one. What was going through his head. How did he come up with the route? We'll never know that, I suppose. I was full sure he was going to send us west into Germany next. But France is not done with us yet. I know that Mae is hoping for the Loire Valley and the kids for Disneyland Paris, so they'll be happy. I tip my head in salute to Pops because he's no doubt secured a touchdown with this next leg of our journey.

It might even elicit a smile from Evie, who is back to

saying little or nothing, with that blasted iPod and earphones glued to her. Maybe the Bayeux Tapestry finished her off earlier, I think with a wry laugh. Won't lie, wasn't my thing. I mean, I can appreciate the hours of work that went into it, the intricate detail. The kids weren't too impressed either, but Mae seemed to enjoy it. In fairness, we were in and out in a few hours, so nobody grumbled too much.

Last night we all ate too much barbecue food, drank some wine – okay a lot of wine – under the stars and it was the perfect end to what turned into an emotionally charged day. Some of the tension around Mae and I seems to have dispersed itself amongst those white gravestones in Normandy, and for that I'm grateful.

The kids went to bed early, but Mae and I stayed up a little later. The brevity of our time in the cemetery and Evie's confession made us both reluctant to touch on any serious subjects and giddiness set in. So we poked fun at our neighbours or passersby from the comfort of our garden chairs.

I look at Pops' urn, which I've placed on the table beside me. Ringside seat. I know it probably sounds macabre, but it doesn't feel like that to me. I take it out and look at it a lot. Speak to it too sometimes when I'm alone. I don't know – it just makes me feel close to him. Taking a swig from my bottle of beer, I carefully edge my forefinger under the envelope flap and read my father's words once again.

Vanilla and apples, sandalwood. Oh I remember, Pops. Burberry perfume; I'd recognise it anywhere.

I look at the urn and shake my head. For fuck's sake, Pops. Horse riding! Are you off your head? I swig another gulp of my beer and wish my father were here so I could give him hell about organising that for us.

'Here's to you, Pops,' I say, turning to toast his urn. I drink, never taking my eyes off him. I finish the rest of my beer in one long, satisfying gulp. The cold, bitter lager tastes like elixir as it hits my throat, my tongue. I've not had a sneaky beer in the afternoon in the longest time. I might just have another.

I don't remember dozing off, but I must have after that second beer, because a cold hand is prodding my side, rudely interrupting my slumber. 'Dad, wake up!'

I can't believe I did that. What a lightweight. Two mid-afternoon beers and I'm dozing off.

'Hey, Jamie. All okay?' I say, sitting up.

'What's Pops doing here? Did you open a letter without me?' Jamie demands.

'Where's the gals?' I ask, dodging his question.

'On their way. They walk too slow for me. I can beat them in a race even if I hop on one foot,' Jamie brags.

I laugh at this and stick the kettle on for a cuppa. My mouth feels like sandpaper. A few minutes later, we sit down around the small Formica table and I read most of the letter to them.

'I've always wanted to go to the Loire Valley,' Evie says. 'There's a chateau there, the Chateau d'Usee, which is said to have inspired Sleeping Beauty's castle. Can we go there?'

'Course we can,' I tell her.

She starts to Google the Loire Valley straight away. I nudge Mae, nodding towards Evie. She's not frowning, that's an improvement on the past twenty-four hours.

I look at the urn. Back of the net, Pops.

'I want a black horse. One that goes super-fast,' Jamie declares.

Mae looks at me with a dirty big grin on her face. 'Bet you do too.'

I pick up Pops' letter and read out his words, 'Try something new and, you never know, you might find yourself growing wings and flying. Yeah, flying alright, landing with a big fat kerdump right onto my big arse!'

And even though she throws a cushion at my head, with surprising accuracy, Mae is laughing.

We decide to try the restaurant at the chateau for our last meal. Both Mae and I feel lethargic. Her from the sun, me from my sneaky beers. All reports from fellow campers are in its favour. And the fact that we can just stroll there, with no faffing about with a taxi, is a plus too.

'Are we eating local food only tonight?' Jamie asks. Oh, don't mention the war, son.

'But with my chips.' I feel brave and decide to make a joke. I peek at Mae and am elated that she's smiling.

'The whole point of the courageous palates was to have fun. Alright?' Mae says to us. 'How about that, in each new place we go to, we eat local once? Then the rest of the time we can eat whatever we want. As long as the odd vegetable is included.'

'We could try to be a little more adventurous, though,' I say. 'We'll be back home eating the usual stuff soon enough. I think I might see how courageous that palate of mine is tonight. Maybe try some frogs' legs or something!'

'Gross,' 'Cool,' Evie and Jamie say at the same time.

Mae is giving me one of her unfathomable looks again.

Like she can't quite work me out. I feel the urge to grab her and pull her in close, to leave her in no doubt about how I feel. I look at Pops' urn and think of the advice he gave me before he died.

'Stop being so goddamn careless with the woman you love. You need to start paying more attention to her.'

Pops was right. Time to stop being so careless. 'I think I'll go take a shower. Jamie, come on, buddy, you too.'

But before I stand up, I lean in towards my wife and kiss her, right on her lips. While the kiss lasts only seconds, I make sure it counts. It's strong and I put in as much passion as one can while leaning over two kids and a small plastic table.

I can hear Jamie giggling, but I ignore him. This is serious and no time for messing or children. I pull away and look into her eyes. I whisper to her, 'Your hair, it's gotten long. I like it, Mae. You look like you did when we met. I've been meaning to say it for a long time. I should have told you before, but I'm saying it now.'

It was kind of awkward and had I planned my speech, I would have made it perfect. But at least I said it. As I stand up, I feel a mix of giddy relief that she didn't pull away and bravado for being spontaneous.

'Thank you,' she says, putting her hand to her hair again in that way she does when she is unsure of herself. She never could take a compliment. She looks startled. I know I've surprised her.

I walk away with speed. The moment seems perfect and I'm nervous that if I stick around something will happen to make it less so.

Jamie and I grab our wash bags and a change of clothes

for this evening and head over to the showers. When we get back, Mae and Evie have left to get ready too. I look down at my attire – my uniform of late, blue jeans and Converse, with a t-shirt. Feck it! I run into our bedroom and root through my cupboard stuffed with clothes and pull out my faded denim shirt. It's at least twenty years old. But it's got history for Mae and me. I've always called it my 'lucky' shirt and I could do with some of its magic tonight.

If this shirt could talk! Ha! I wore it the night that Mae and I had sex for the first time. The back of my car. Romantic, eh? I've not thought of that night for a long time, but now it feels like it happened but a moment ago. Sitting in the back row of the cinema, how cliché, but we did. We snogged all the way through. God, it was good. By the time we got to the car, we were both at the point where we couldn't just kiss each other goodnight and leave it at that. I'd all sorts of plans to whisk her away to a posh hotel for our first time. But instead, we drove to the beach, parked up and pulled the levers on our seats, so that they were horizontal. And in that unconventional, less-than-perfect setting, we had the most mind-blowing sex I've ever had.

Fuck. I've got to stop thinking about that night. I squirm as my jeans start to feel uncomfortable. But I'm jubilant with the feeling. It's as if the further we go from home, the more I start to feel like me again.

Changed, Jamie and I sit outside Nomad waiting for the girls to return. The summer sun is getting low, but it's warm, with a slight breeze. I'm tempted to grab another beer, but hold off.

Soon enough Mae and Evie arrive back. I try to look nonchalant, but despite good intentions, a goofy smile drops onto my face when I notice that Mae is wearing a dress. And heels. And lipgloss. She's made an effort.

Get in!

'Nice shirt,' she says to me.

'Nice dress,' I reply.

I lock Nomad up and we head over to the restaurant. It's busy, but there are lots of familiar faces there, including our friends the Americans. Jamie runs over to them and hugs them all, like they are family. They ask us to join them, which elicits whoops from our son. He's really taken a shine to them and the feeling appears mutual. Food and drinks ordered, all without a mention from anyone of palates, courageous or otherwise. And for the first time since we arrived in France, it feels like we are on holiday. You know that feeling when you start to feel relaxed and you've left all your cares at home? Everyone, even Evie, is sporting a hallmark grin.

The restaurant sports benches as opposed to chairs and Mae and I sit beside each other – close. I can feel her thigh against mine. She feels close to me, but just outside my reach. I feel like I'm twenty again.

I join in the conversation, laugh at Fred's jokes, chat about Ireland and where we live, but all the time all I can think about are Mae's thighs. After dinner, we all wander into the bar and there is music on. Mabel pulls out a box of the game Jenga from her handbag, like Mary Poppins. 'We're addicted to it,' Mabel tells us. 'It's really quite compelling.' Nods from Fred, Joan and Don confirm this.

The kids are soon coerced into a game with them, albeit Evie being a bit more reluctant. She has her head fixed onto her phone, which is beeping continuously.

'Turn that off!' I say to her. 'It's rude.'

'I'm just chatting to Ann. She wants to know where we're going to next,' Evie moans.

'Five minutes, then put the phone down,' Mae says and Evie nods, giving us both a dirty look.

Bloody teenagers. Where did my lovely daughter disappear to, who was always throwing herself into my arms? These days I'm lucky to get a word out of her, never mind a hug.

'I'm good at this, aren't I, Dad?' Jamie boasts, giving me another dig.

'Oh, we've got a cocky one here!' Fred jokes. 'You'll not find a steadier hand than mine, though. Jenga champion right here.'

'You joining in?' Mabel asks us, then gets distracted. 'Oh would you look at that move from Evie!' Mabel says with approval. 'Nicely done, dear.'

I see an opportunity here and it's that kind of day, so I seize it. 'You know, I've eaten so much tonight, I wouldn't mind a walk. If I can persuade my wife to join me, we might leave you to your Jenga battles for a few minutes?'

Mabel looks at us both and leans in to whisper, 'Oh I remember what it's like always having kids around. You both go have your walk, but don't be in any rush to get back. I think this Jenga game could go on for at least an hour. We'll take good care of the children, you have my word.'

'Mae?' I ask, and hold my breath. What if I've misread

the signals and she says no? If she chooses a pile of wooden blocks over me, I give up.

Her hand moves up to her hair again, 'I don't think I can think of a single thing that I'd like more.' She glances at the kids, 'Be good, you two.'

The children don't even look up from their game, concentration at a premium, and mutter with a distracted, 'Bye.'

We make our way through the busy bar and I wonder how soon I can pull her into my arms and kiss her. As we leave the building, I reach for her hand and I try not to whoop when she takes it. We walk in silence, holding hands, and I wonder if she feels like I do now.

As in a horny teenager.

'I remember the first time you wore that shirt,' Mae says.

'You said I looked sexy,' I say.

She stops, turns to me and says three words that undo me, 'You still do.'

I pull her into my arms and I kiss her, slowly at first, in some attempt at tenderness. But she pushes her body in tight to me and our kiss changes. She bites my lip, lightly, and our tongues collide.

In that kiss, the world around us stands still. I know that in real life, Hollywood moments rarely happen. Things are a lot messier than the images we see on the big screen. But this kiss, well, it is the real deal. We pull apart and wordlessly walk towards Nomad. I fumble for the keys and somehow manage to open the door without dropping them.

I wonder, should I say something? Mae is silent, but I

don't want to mess this up. 'I know things have been weird between us lately . . . ' I begin.

Mae silences me with another kiss. 'Don't speak. Not now. There's time for that later.'

My wife, my heart, walks towards our bedroom, pulling her dress over her head in one fluid moment that takes my breath away.

Chapter Twenty

MAE

'That was unexpected,' I say, stretching lazily. I'd forgotten what sex felt like.

'That was amazing,' Olly replies, nuzzling my neck. He looks jubilant, like he's climbed Everest. And I suppose, for him, he has.

It was quick, messy, but nevertheless very good. Even so, it feels strange to be lying naked beside my husband. Shyly, I sit up and reach for my clothes. I freshen up in the small bathroom, then get dressed.

'We don't have to go back yet, do we?' Olly asks. 'We've only been gone half an hour.'

'Let's have a drink outside,' I say, and grab two beers from the fridge. A few minutes later Olly is beside me and we sit in silence.

'I miss that,' Olly says.

'Me too.'

'We're good at it too,' Olly says in such total seriousness that it makes me giggle.

I want to say to him that just because we had sex doesn't mean that we are okay. It was sex, nothing more. But he looks so goddamn pleased with himself, I am loath to spoil the mood.

'I'm sorry things have been so strained between us,' Olly says.

I should tell him how I feel. I should tell him how miserable I've been for nearly a year now. I should tell him about the kiss with Philip. I should tell him that I'm not sure who we are any more. I should tell him that I'm scared, that we are not going to make it. So many things I should tell him.

'Tell me about the perfume,' I say instead. Should have, could have, would have. To hell with it, there's lots of time to talk about us.

Olly looks at me, puzzled by my change in conversation.

'I really want to know. Pops said you both smelt the perfume?'

Olly sighs and closes his eyes for a moment. 'A nurse was wearing Burberry perfume that day in the hospital. It reminded Pops and I of Mam. I bought her a bottle of it on the day she died. For her birthday.'

'I know that there's never a good day to die, but on your birthday, that's particularly cruel,' I murmur.

'I'd recognise the scent anywhere,' he says and looks down into the neck of his beer bottle. 'When . . . when it happened, that smell kind of infused its way into my brain. I used to spray it every day in the house. Made me feel close to her.'

I say nothing. I want to give him the chance to talk. He rarely shares anything about the day his mother died.

I know it's such a painful time for him that he prefers to avoid it. Of course he talks about her, about all she did for him, God knows he does that a lot. But he rarely mentions the actual events around her death.

'You know, there aren't many things that you know for sure in life. But one thing I knew for sure back then was that my mam's main ambition in life was to make me and Pops happy.'

'And that's how it should be,' I say. I decide to ignore the question in my head. Do Evie and Jamie feel that surety of love?

'I'd noticed her lingering over an advert for a new perfume in her magazine – called Burberry. Her hand caressed the page and her face looked – well it looked yearning. Yes, that's a good word for it. I ripped the page out of the magazine when she was finished. I decided there and then that I was going to get her that perfume for her birthday. I enlisted Pops' help and he agreed it was a fine plan. He said he would give me extra pocket money for doing odd jobs around the house to help pay for it. "This kind of perfume don't come cheap, lad. It's the good stuff."'

I laugh at Olly's near-perfect impression of his father.

'Pops made me work hard for my wages. I cleaned windows. I washed his car. I weeded the garden. I mowed the lawn. Then finally, when I emptied my piggy bank and handed over my savings to him, he declared that I had saved just the right amount. A plan was hatched that when he was next up in the "big smoke" – he would buy the perfume.'

Oh, Olly. I reach over and place my hand over his and squeeze it.

'Pops came home one night and winked at me. We snuck into my bedroom and he presented me with a little bag from Clery's. I can still remember the weight of it in my little hands. I didn't sleep all night, I was so excited waiting for her birthday. Had I known what fate had planned for us all that day . . . '

He stops and stands up.

'I bet she loved it.'

His face breaks into a smile as he remembers, 'Pops often said to me that on that birthday, her last one, I made Mam happier than he'd ever seen her before. I'm sure that's not true. But even so, I'm grateful to be up there amongst her best moments. I do know that when she opened the pink wrapping paper she gasped. A proper exclamation of surprise, not the fake ones that parents do to please their children. I thought my face would break from the smile that took root there. I couldn't take my eyes off her as she kept looking at the bottle, then at me and then at the bottle again. I wanted to tell her that I'd bought the perfume all by myself, from my own money, but that seemed awkward and boastful. Pops had that covered, of course, and threw in before I could say a word, "He's been saving up for months. Every penny came from his hard work doing jobs for me. He's a good lad."'

Mae smiles at this. 'Pops always did the right thing. He never got it wrong, did he?'

'I remember feeling like I was ten foot tall under his praise and my mam's smile. And the look of awe and gratitude on her face made me feel so proud. It was such a perfect moment. You know how sometimes when you are so happy you feel like crying? Well, it was one of those moments, but she hugged me so tight, she stemmed my tears. She could always do that. Little did I know that, later that day, I would cry a river, with no more Mam to dam the flow.'

I want to try to take away the pain that is etched on his face. 'You were a good son. She was lucky to have one so thoughtful as you.'

'I loved her,' he shrugs.

'And she loved you. That's obvious with every story you've ever told me about her.'

'We better go back.' Olly looks at his watch, ending the conversation. 'Pesky kids. Tell you what, why don't you sit here, enjoy your drink and I'll go get them?'

I sit back and watch the stars in the black sky. It's quiet, peaceful here. Too bloody quiet, because now I have free rein to feel all weird about what happened earlier.

How can we go from not liking each other to that? I mean, I've actually felt violent on a few occasions. That's not good. But since we took off on this madcap adventure I've seen echoes of the man I married. And it felt right to just let caution fly into the French wind. I wanted to be spontaneous and have sex, for no other reason than I felt like it. To hell with it! I'll worry about it tomorrow.

Chapter Twenty-One

OLLY

We've been in the Loire Valley now for two days.

I think we all felt regret as we said goodbye to the chateau. Mae said, 'We'll be back,' as we drove down the long avenue. This sentiment was echoed by the whoops from Jamie and even a smile from Evie. Me? Well, I'm just glad that Mae is thinking about a future that includes the word 'we' in it. I'll take all the victories, even the small ones.

The drive down south was uneventful. We took our time, stopping off at the services for a coffee. Door to door it took us just over four hours. And with some relief, somewhere over the past few days I've gotten used to Nomad's intricacies. Here's a top tip though, don't leave it to the last minute to hit the brake when driving downhill. Especially when the lights turn red and you have no choice but to sail on through them. Whilst you pray that you're not about to kill your family in a spectacular moment of idiocy. Just saying.

Top tip two, if you are planning a bank robbery, you wouldn't choose Nomad as your getaway vehicle. Zero to sixty mph in about ten minutes, I'd say, is a fair assessment.

It is tiring, driving a camper van. Far more so than, say, our car at home would be for the same distance. It's just heavier, I suppose. Mae has offered to drive, but I know she's not keen.

Pops found us another gem of a campsite. Domaine de l'Etang is in the Anjou wine-growing region of France. Surrounded by vineyards, our site even produces its own wine, which we've happily bought from the campsite shop. As Mae said last night as we sipped a glass under the stars, 'We're a long way from home, Toto.'

Jamie is having a ball because there is a water park next to the campsite, with slides, toboggans and rafts and we seem to be spending most of our day there. We've been walking along the river to the local town each evening for dinner. I like Brissac-Quincé. It's small enough, but has a majestic feel, with its own castle. We even stumbled across a fantastic market on Thursday and managed to buy lots for only a few euro.

Taking aside the unmerciful amounts of cheese we are eating every day, Mae and I are in better shape than we've been for a long time. Since that night – which is now up there with the best I've ever had – it seems we haven't lost our inner teenager. We can't stop touching each other. And I don't even mean that in a sexual way. I mean the small, fleeting touches during the day as we pass by each other. I'd forgotten how much a touch can sustain me until an opportunity for some time away from the kids.

Mae will touch my shoulder as she walks by me. Or walk up behind me and hug me from behind, resting her chin on my shoulder, as we watch Jamie or Evie splashing in the water.

I can't get enough of her. I feel like a man freed from captivity. I don't need a psychologist to tell me that my impotence was all to do with losing my job. I'm self-aware enough to know that I resent Mae's employment and pay cheque every month. And I hate myself for that. But now, here, it's like none of that matters. And starved of intimacy for so long, now I'm reacquainted with it, I am insatiable. Well, that's maybe the wrong choice of word, because that would make you think that we are at it like rabbits. Which, of course, we're not, because we are in a camper van with two children sleeping a few feet from us. But now I feel that with every touch, however fleeting, there's a promise of more to come.

I also know that no matter how much I hate 'talking' we're going to have to do it at some point. I'm not stupid. I know that all we've done is place a plaster on a deep wound that needs stitches. I'm not sure when surgical intervention will happen, but for now Mae seems happy with the plaster too.

'You ready for this?' Mae asks, interrupting my thoughts.

'No. Not even remotely. Last time I was on a horse I almost broke my neck. Cannot believe that Pops is insisting on this!' I say.

Mae starts to laugh. She thinks it's hilarious. It's okay for her, though. She grew up horse riding, galloping around fields in Wexford for years as a child. We've found a local trekking company who will collect us from our campsite and take us to the stables. I have done everything in my power to avoid this day, but none of them will hear of me missing it.

We get a warm welcome from our instructor when we arrive at the stables. The day kicks off with a talk about what to expect, what not to do during the day. For me it's quite simple. Do not fall off the horse, Olly Guinness. That's the only thing I need to remember.

'So now we go meet ze horses for ze day. *Alors*,' the bubbly instructor says. Her name is Elizabeth and she is of indeterminate age with weathered, tanned skin. I'm guessing in her fifties.

The children meet their ponies first of all, excitement oozing from them. Jamie gets a jet-black pony, which pleases him, called Paris.

'Paris is, how you say, *très doux*? Gentle, *non*? He'll take care of you,' Elizabeth tells Jamie, who impresses us by jumping up on his back with little help from anyone.

Elizabeth adjusts his stirrups and declares him all set. Evie, then, is handed a white horse, called, you guessed it, Snow White.

'You need to be firm with Snow, because she can be *très* lazy. But once you show her you are ze boss, you will be fine,' Elizabeth tells Evie, who clambers up, albeit a little less gracefully than Jamie.

Mae is next and her horse – grey, tall and majestic-looking – answers to Lumière. Without any help, she puts her foot in the stirrup and heaves herself up into the saddle, in seconds.

'Ah *bien*, you 'ave done this before,' Elizabeth says,

with approval. Wait till she gets a load of me, I think.

My horse arrives, chocolate-brown, shiny coat, rippling muscles, black eyes and white socks. '*La* majestic Beau. He will take good care of you,' Elizabeth says to me and indicates to me to jump up. Considering the fact that Beau seems only average height, I have a hard time swinging my leg over his back. He turns his head and looks at me with his piercing eyes. I swear that bloody horse is laughing at me.

'Hold onto the saddle to help pull yourself up,' Mae says cheerfully.

I bite my tongue. Our new truce could come to an abrupt end any second if I respond to her advice with the two words that have sprung to my head. I try again, giving it all my strength, and once more fail, falling back on my feet. Damn all those French baguettes and chunks of Brie. My stomach seems to be spilling out over my jeans.

'Look, I can stay here while you guys go on yourselves,' I say in a vain last-ditch attempt at dodging the equine bullet. 'I'm not that pushed.'

But, of course they won't hear of it. Nonsense about sticking together and all that malarkey thrown at me by one and all.

'Do not worry, Monsieur Olly. We have ze step for ze less-abled riders,' Elizabeth says with a patronising smile. Herself and the majestic Beau are taking the piss.

A step appears *toute suite* and I feel like a right fecking eejit. It's third time lucky thankfully and I'm up. For a horse that seems quite small from the ground, now I feel like I'm at a dizzying height.

Pops, you are pushing me this time.

Elizabeth jumps up on her horse and we are off – a convoy, of sorts. Mae first, then Evie, Jamie and last of all me. At first it seems okay, the horses seem to know their way well enough. At a guess they've done this route quite a few times. I'm just beginning to relax when Beau decides that he wants to go up front. This horse is strong! He starts moving up, overtaking the children and then Mae, one by one.

'Go, Dad!' Jamie shouts, thinking I'm getting brave and speeding up on purpose.

'Ah, Beau is quite ze character. You must show him who is ze boss,' Elizabeth says.

Just exactly how am I meant to do that? I think, with irritation.

But the gods are kind. He seems happy enough now he's up front and he slows down to a gentle walk.

'Zat is good,' Elizabeth praises me.

As if I had anything to do with it! I'm at Beau's mercy. And I swear to God, he is playing with me.

'How you doing?' Mae trots up beside me, her hair bouncing like she's in an advert for shampoo or something. Is she mad? Trotting up like that could send Beau into a complete panic.

'Isn't it just the most wonderful feeling? Look at that view,' Mae declares, throwing her arm around her like a lunatic.

'View? I can't look at anything but Beau's neck and my hands clasping on for dear life!' I say.

Mae laughs, thinking I'm joking.

My fingers keep fumbling on the reins. They feel strange

in my hands and awkward. Beau has this thing he does where he half-turns his head and peers at me and it's freaking me out.

'How are the kids getting on?' I ask, feeling a bit guilty that I've not been doing the father thing. I can't risk turning to look – I reckon I'd fall.

'They are both pros, like they've done it their whole life,' Mae says.

'I don't think I'm naturally coordinated for horse riding,' I admit.

'You are trying too hard,' Mae says. 'Try to relax, then Beau will too. Sit deeper into the saddle, use your knees to keep balance and look up. I promise you that you will feel more secure in the saddle by looking ahead as opposed to looking down.'

I'm not sure I believe her but nothing can be worse than how I feel, so I look up and see that we're rambling through an orchard.

'How does that feel?' Mae asks. 'Just try to move with Beau. Don't fight his natural rhythm, mimic it.'

I nod and attempt to do as she says.

'Aahhh . . . ' I scream for dear life. Beau has ducked down with no warning and I'm face down on his neck.

'Oh, naughty Beau,' Elizabeth laughs. ''E 'as stopped for ze apples!'

'Aw,' Evie says, 'He's hungry.'

'What are you doing down there for, Daddy?' Jamie asks.

'Pull yourself back up into the saddle,' Mae says, being helpful again.

One more word from them and I'll . . . damn it, Beau!

I'm not sure how, but I manage to pull myself upright again. I think I may have pulled a muscle in my groin. I need a drink.

We continue on and Beau, the little shit, behaves himself – more or less. The approach to the chateau elicits gasps from everyone. I chance having a look around me and have to admit that it's stunning. Stone turrets adorn either side of the chateau, giving it a fairytale appearance. Manicured gardens are resplendent in front of it and framing it from behind are rolling hills of vines.

'It's beautiful,' I hear Evie say. 'Just like the Beauty and the Beast castle.'

We follow Elizabeth to the stables, where two young boys are awaiting us. I jump down from Beau far quicker than I mounted him. I feel like I should kiss the ground, such is my relief that I've gotten this far with no broken bones. Just a shattered dignity, I suppose. I got off lightly. The horses, now tethered, are slurping water in the shade.

'Now we eat,' Elizabeth says, and we all follow her towards the chateau. 'We will go to ze secret garden. *Très jolie!*'

Now that I'm on firm ground my humour begins to return and I realise that I've worked up quite an appetite. The garden is, as advised, beautiful, and a table is laden with the usual French luncheon. We feast on crusty baguettes and cold meats, cheeses, olives and tomatoes. Wine appears too, which I decide to accept. I've earned a glass.

Once lunch is finished, we explore the grounds for thirty minutes before heading back to our steeds.

'Would it be awful if I got a taxi home?' I whisper to Mae.

Her face explodes into laughter. 'You are that scared?'

'I'm telling you, that horse has it in for me. Did you see how he tried to bite me earlier?' I say.

'He was nuzzling you! Honestly, Olly, you are being a baby. The kids will be so upset if you don't come back with us. Remember what your dad said. Take a risk!'

No escape. Right, shoulders back, Guinness, time to slay this dragon. Or, at least this horse. But the second I walk over to Beau, he turns around and bares his teeth at me.

'See that?' I shout to Mae, but she's got her back to me, helping Jamie up onto his horse.

I'm not sure how, maybe it's the help of two large glasses of red wine, but I manage to jump up in the saddle without too much trouble.

'Look at you!' Mae says, with approval. 'No stopping you now.'

I can do this. I just need to show Beau that I'm the boss. I am master of all equine-related skills, I tell myself.

'We might try ze slow trot on ze way home, *non*?' Elizabeth says to us all, and everyone nods with enthusiasm.

'Why not,' I say to her.

So we head away from the chateau towards the orchard again and I start to feel more confident. My balance has definitely improved. I'm even checking out the rolling French countryside as we go along.

'Now we trot,' Elizabeth shouts and she takes off. Evie and Jamie are bobbing up and down on their horses like they've done it for years and Mae, of course, looks like a pro.

I feel like my bollocks are about to break in two.

Beau has started to pick up speed and I have no option but to grit my teeth. The thought crosses my mind that now that I've finally got a sex life again, this 'ride' is going to kill it forever more.

Then Beau jumps to the left – something's spooked him and he takes off in a gallop. I hang on and try my best to pull on the reins to slow him down, but the fecker is ignoring all my efforts and stubbornly moves faster, passing Mae, Evie, then Jamie.

'Look at Dad go!' I hear Evie say.

'Help!' I shout.

'What did he say?' Mae asks.

I keep pulling on the reins, but it makes no difference whatsoever.

'Slow down, Olly. Pull on ze reins firmly,' Elizabeth shouts behind me.

'I'm trying!' I shout back, but on Beau goes, at breakneck speeds.

I run through my options. Cling on as I'm doing and take my chances that he'll slow down. Or bail out at this speed and hope that I land in one piece. I try to stay calm, but it's not working. The faster he goes, the more I panic.

For feck's sake, Pops, this better not be how it all ends up. I can finally see a chink of light, that maybe we can find our way back out of this godforsaken black tunnel we've been in for months. Don't tell me that after all we've been through, I'm going to break my fecking neck on this horse.

'Don't move forward in ze saddle,' Elizabeth shouts beside me, her face a blur. 'You must pull Beau's head up to slow him down.'

Right, you little bastard, no more Mr Nice Guy. I've got way too much living to do yet. I lean back and use all my might to pull on the reins and he begins to ease up. Little by little, he's slowing down. I keep the pressure on the reins and then finally we are at a standstill.

'Well done, Monsieur Olly. You 'ave done *très bien*,' Elizabeth praises me.

'I 'ave just had ze fecking heart attack,' I say back to her, mimicking her accent.

'Are you okay?' Mae asks. I swear, if she's laughing at me now I'll explode, but she's only got concern on her face.

'Wow, Dad, that was so cool. You were like a super-hero,' Jamie says and I start to feel mollified.

'Well, it was nothing,' I say, shrugging.

'It was super-fast, Dad,' Jamie says. 'I want to go that fast.'

'We vill just walk back. No more super-fast,' Elizabeth says.

Thank goodness for that!

Chapter Twenty-Two

EVIE

The happiest place in the world. Disneyland. And we're here.

I don't think I've ever seen Jamie so excited in my whole life – and that's saying something, because he spends his life bouncing about like a puppy. But when we walk through the entrance and see Sleeping Beauty's castle at the end of Main Street USA, I'm not sure whether I'm going to laugh manically or cry. I'm as bad as him.

I am hit with so many emotions at once. Joy, excitement and, at the same time, I feel so overwhelmed. It's such a strange feeling because I've dreamt of going to Disney for years and now, standing here looking down to the castle, it's like I'm going to visit an old friend.

That's the lamest thing ever, I know that, but it's a powerful, emotional hit. I stand for a moment because I want to commit it to memory. Then, I can't help it, I need to start experiencing everything straight away.

'Slow down!' Dad shouts at me and I realise that I'm sprinting towards the castle.

'Stick together, only rule, okay?' he says. 'No running off on your own!'

'I want to go to Space Mountain!' Jamie says, pulling at his arm.

'He's surprisingly strong for a little fella,' Dad says to Mam.

She laughs, pulling Jamie to a standstill, and tells him, 'We've fast passes booked for that later on. We planned all of this last night, remember? Our first one is in five minutes, so we better get going to the Toy Story ride now.'

'We'll come back to the castle on the way to Tomorrowland,' Dad promises.

'It feels like Christmas morning and my birthday all wrapped up into one,' I say and then a realisation hits me. I'm happy. The past couple of days in France have been good. I'm having fun!

'I know, it's great, isn't it?' Mam says. 'Come on, let's all wear Mickey and Minnie ears.'

She runs over to a concession stand and quickly buys said ears and hands them out to Dad and Jamie and me.

'Quick, put them on, then let's get a selfie!' She's laughing and I realise so am I. So the Guinnesses strike a pose and Dad holds his hand aloft to take the shot.

Dad says, 'Look at the head on me!' And Mam looks up at him and giggles. What the hell is going on with them two? They're like newlyweds again with their PDAs. I pretend to be grossed out, but inside I'm smiling. At least we are in France and no one I know can see them.

Scarlet for them if they carry on behaving like this when we get home.

The park is jammers. People everywhere, pushing buggies, wearing Mickey Mouse ears and little kids dressed in their favourite character's costume. I can see Jamie looking at them, his little eyes green with envy. And part of me wishes I was still seven, so I could put on a Snow White costume.

'You know the *Guinness Book of Records* for the most princess costumes in one place was over 57,000 people!' I tell them.

'Wow. Is there one for Spiderman?' Jamie asks me.

'I don't know. I'll check for you later,' I tell him.

'I've missed that,' Mam says to me.

'What?'

'Your *Guinness Book of Records* facts. It's been a while since you shared any with us,' Mam says.

And even though I make a face at her and shrug away her hand as she tries to catch mine, I'm smiling inside. It feels nice that she noticed that. I had been trying to stifle my inner nerd, but every now and then it creeps up before I know it. Like just now. And it felt good. Like I was flexing an underused muscle once more.

I just wish they'd stop freaking me out with their constant worried heads on them. It's like they are on suicide watch or something.

Ann says that I should just sit them down and tell them I'm not going to harm myself. But I reckon if I say that word out loud, they'll think it's in my head and they'll get worse. And my head doesn't feel like it's going to implode any more. Some days I only think about Martina and Deirdre fleetingly. It's at night that I've the most trouble, right before I go to sleep. Ann says I'm over-analysing it all and that I'm already yesterday's news. Everyone is talking about one of the sixth-year girls who snogged Mr Lyons, the fourth-year teacher, at the debs' ball. In front of everyone. She reckons that makes my drinking pale into insignificance.

Even so, I'm toying with the idea of asking Dad to home-school me. Mam has also broached the subject of me transferring to her school as an option. It's tempting. I mean, at least that way I can avoid any more showdowns with my so-called 'friends'. But, would I be jumping from the fire to the frying pan?

We spend the next two hours racing around the park, doing all of the big rides – Space Mountain, Buzz Lightyear, Pirates of the Caribbean, even the baby rides were a laugh. But the moment I've been waiting for all morning is finally here. I'm actually in the castle. We've been to see the animatronic dragon in the dungeon below. Jamie pretended he wasn't scared, but he sure stood close to Mam and Dad all the time we were there. Now, we've moved upstairs to the second-floor walk-through retelling of the Sleeping Beauty story. It's depicted in the stained-glass windows and tapestries. And the whole thing seems even more romantic and magical written in French.

'*Le Château de la Belle au Bois Dormant,*' I whisper, trying the words out for myself.

'Try this for a fairytale. Luke thinks he'll never see the beautiful Evie again. Plot twist, she's standing in front of him in Sleeping Beauty's castle.'

It feels like time is now moving in slow motion and I

turn around to see if I've hallucinated the voice that just spoke to me. But standing behind me – how is this possible? Is Luke. My Luke. *Once Upon a Time* loving, boy-band gorgeous, Luke.

'Hello,' I say, then want to kick myself for such a mundane response to such an epic introduction.

'Hello back,' he replies. 'Every time I've walked by the castle this morning, I've thought of you and as if by magic, here you are.'

'Yes,' I reply. It appears that I have lost all ability to utter more than one word at a go.

'Nice ears,' he says and I die. My Minnie Mouse ears! How could I have forgotten them? I whip them off quickly, stuffing them into my bag.

'Are you okay? I heard about, you know . . . ' he asks and I think I do die for a minute, because everything goes a bit black. I shouldn't be surprised he knows. Sure, there isn't a person in Wexford who missed my humiliation, it nearly made the papers.

'Fine,' I say. There I go with my long lyrical monologues.

'I was worried about you when I heard . . . ' he says.

And before I can answer him, Jamie swaggers up and shouts, 'Who are you?' He sticks his face up close to Luke's.

'I'm Luke. You must be Jamie,' he answers, not skipping a beat.

Oh, kill me now, here's Mam and Dad walking over, curiosity stamped all over their faces.

'I'm sorry,' I say to him, nodding towards my parents. There, I said two words together. That's an improvement at least.

'For what?'

'What's about to happen,' I reply.

'Hello,' my mother says cheerily, but her face doesn't match her voice. She looks a bit manic, like she's trying hard to be all breezy and bright and nonchalant. But the reality is that she is freaking out that I'm talking to a boy. Yawn.

Luke smiles at them both, 'I'm Luke. A friend of Evie's.'

'Oh Luke,' Mam says and I swear her eyes are about to pop out of her head. Why did she have to say it like that? I throw daggers at her and they hit their target because she seems to get that I don't want Luke to know that I've spoken about him.

'I don't think I've heard Evie mention you before,' she says and then, can you believe this, she winks at me. A big, comical, stupid wink.

Oh my God! Shoot me now. Nice save, Mam, NOT!

'That's a bit of a coincidence. You turning up here today,' Dad sounds suspicious, like I'd planned it or something.

'Small world, eh,' Luke mumbles back. 'Have you been on Space Mountain yet?' Luke asks me. 'I'm heading over there now with my sisters, if you wanted to go too?' He nods towards two girls, who are pretending not to watch from the other side of the room. He's told me about his sisters before. They are a lot older than him, both in their early twenties. He's the baby of his family. They look so glamorous and pretty.

'We've already done that ride,' Dad says before I get a chance to speak. 'Never mind, don't let us hold you.'

Mam gives him a dig in his ribs, to which he squeals, 'Oi! What? We have just been there!'

'Didn't you say you wanted to go on Space Mountain again, though, Evie?' Mam says.

'Yes,' I reply. Right, I'm back to single words again.

'I tell you what, why don't you head off with Luke for a few hours? You have your mobile. We'll give you a ring later on.' I want to kiss her. 'Olly, give Evie some money for lunch.'

Dad looks uncomfortable with the turn of events, but he takes out his wallet as requested by Mam. She leans in and pulls out twenty euros and hands it to me, whispering in my ear as she does, 'He's cute! Have fun and smile!'

'Can I go too?' Jamie asks. 'I want to go on Space Mountain again. You said I could.'

Mam, Dad and me all answer at the same time, 'No!'

'Next time you can come too, dude,' Luke says to him and I can tell that Jamie has just awarded him superhero status.

I wave goodbye to a still-pouting Jamie and follow Luke over towards his sisters, who are smiling in welcome.

'Hey, Evie. I'm Melissa and this is Sophie,' Melissa says.

'Luke was right. You are pretty,' Sophie says. 'Love that t-shirt. So retro.'

'Sophie!' Luke moans, but I feel like dancing. He must have spoken about me to them. I feel slightly less mortified now about Mam dropping me in it.

We arrive at the entrance to Space Mountain and are gobsmacked to see that the queue time is only twenty minutes.

'It's lunchtime; best time for the big rides,' Melissa tells me.

As we queue, I tell them about Nomad and Pops and the adventure we are on.

'Seriously, that's so cool,' Luke says. 'And you have no idea where you are heading to next?'

'Nope. We find out today, actually. Dad is going to open the next letter later on.'

'Any room for a few extra?' Melissa asks with a laugh. 'I think I could cope with eight weeks in Europe on a magical mystery tour!'

For a moment, I fantasise about Luke going with us and I blush. Space Mountain was as good second time around as the first and we all laugh as we check out our photographs at the photo pass booth.

When we exit, Sophie turns to us both and says, 'Listen, at a guess, you two would rather head off and do your own thing. So scoot, have fun, keep in touch by text and we'll meet up later on.'

'Thanks, sis,' Luke says with a grin, looking at me to see if I'm happy with that. I quickly nod to confirm yes, yes, yes!

'Are you hungry yet?' he asks.

I shake my head. I don't think I will ever eat again. My stomach is flipping and I feel lightheaded. I'm in Disneyland Paris with Luke, whom I'm pretty sure I've fallen in love with. If this is a dream, I never want to wake up.

As we enter Fantasyland, Prince Charming's Carousel is right in front of us.

'Come on,' Luke says, grabbing me by my hand. 'We can't not do this.'

So we join the queue, which is mostly full of small children.

'Can I ask you something?' Luke says.

Oh shit. Here it comes. I should have known he would want to know the gories. 'Okay. What do you want to know?'

'Why did you do it? I know I don't know you that well, but you just didn't seem the type, that night when we met,' he says.

I can feel embarrassment creep up from my toes right up to the top of my now-prickly scalp, which is on fire.

'You don't have to talk about it if you don't want to,' Luke says. He's letting me off the hook. But I can't hide from this – better to get it out in the open.

'I didn't think I was that type of person either,' I say. 'But things just kind of snowballed into crazy town before I had a chance to exit stage left.'

'I'm sorry to hear that. I'm a good listener, if you want to talk about it,' he says.

'What's that saying "share don't scare"? How much do you want to know?' I answer.

'All of it,' he replies.

'Well, I'm not the most popular girl in school,' I say. 'Which is fine, because I don't want to be. But up until this year, I had friends. A group of us have always hung out. I suppose I thought we'd always do that.' I take a peek at him. He's nodding, encouraging me to continue.

'But last summer my friends all decided that I wasn't cool enough any more. It took me a while to cop on that I was being frozen out by them. It appears that my geek-chic charm doesn't do it for them,' I try to joke.

Luke puts his hand on my arm. 'Don't joke.'

I take a deep breath and decide to tell him all. 'After

225

Christmas break they upped their dissatisfaction with me a notch. They made my life a misery in school, online too. They made stuff up about me. I tried to ignore it, but it's hard not to get sucked into the whole madness.'

'I'm so sorry,' Luke says, reaching for my hand. But I pull away. I can't be distracted if I'm to get this out.

'It got much worse after the Valentine's disco.' I can feel another flush of embarrassment take over my body. I know, without looking, that I've got one of those awful red rashes on my throat now. I always do when I get nervous.

'How so?' he asks, but his face looks harder.

'Apparently Martina has a thing for you. She was pissed that you and I met. So she got crueler.'

'I barely know her and, by the sounds of it, that's not a bad thing,' Luke replies.

'She knows you, though. Anyhow, long story short, she said they would leave me alone if I took their challenge. It seemed worth it at the time,' I say.

'Jesus, Evie, they are such wagons. I'm so sorry you had to go through all of this.'

'It's not your fault,' I whisper. 'It's mine.'

'None of this is your fault,' he says, taking my hand in his. This time I let him.

'But it is, Luke. You see, I knew I was brain dead doing that bloody dare, but I did it anyhow. I'm so annoyed at myself for being so weak, for letting them get to me. I should have been stronger than that,' I say.

'Are you always this hard on yourself?' he asks.

I shrug. I suppose I am.

'I wish I had been strong enough not to care what they

thought. But I was lonely. It's hard being the odd one out every day,' I say.

'I bet. But you're not odd. You're wonderfully unique,' Luke says again. 'Why didn't you tell me you were getting such a hard time?'

'I was embarrassed. I didn't know how to say it to you. Plus we didn't swap numbers or anything,' I say.

'That's my bad,' Luke says. 'I should have made sure I had your number before you left that night. Because I wanted to see you again. I haven't been able to stop thinking about you.'

'You could have found me if you really wanted to,' I accuse. And it's true, he could have.

'Things have been a bit crazy for me too. My folks are splitting up. I found out the day after the disco. It kinda floored me, even though I should have seen it coming.'

'Oh,' I say.

'They were going to split up when my sisters were kids, but then they decided to have me, to see if I could fix them,' Luke looks so sad right now. I realise that there's probably a lot he's not telling me about everything at home.

'The reason I'm here with the girls is that, right now, Mam is packing her stuff and leaving. They thought it would be easier for us all if we weren't there to see the actual moving out,' Luke looks so solemn as he says this, my heart contracts in sympathy.

'Sounds like both of us have been having a rough time of it lately,' I say.

'Today is pretty cool, though,' Luke replies and goes beetroot red. 'I swear, I was thinking about you right at that minute in the castle and then you just appeared. Unreal, Evie.'

'Yes, unreal,' I say.

We're suddenly at the top of the line and next to have our turn on the carousel.

'One each or share?' Luke asks me. 'Please say share.'

'Share,' I say and realise that I'm back to my one-word show again.

So we choose a white horse with a flowing porcelain mane and I climb up front, then Luke hops up behind me. He holds his hands on either side of him at first. Stiffly. Awkwardly.

Then the music starts and we begin our circular motion, around and around. And by our second rotation, Luke's hands find their way to my waist. I twist to look at him and we bump noses. He laughs and apologises, but he doesn't pull away. We are at most an inch apart, nose to nose. Then he leans in and kisses me. Soft, sweet and wondrous and I know that this is the kiss that I will measure all kisses against for the rest of my life.

Chapter Twenty-Three

MAE

'Don't,' I say to Olly, 'Sshh.'

A flash of Evie's red t-shirt catches our eyes as we queue for the carousel. There she is, our daughter on a carousel horse, kissing Luke.

It's the weirdest sensation, seeing your daughter in a grown-up embrace. And I'm not prepared for it. It feels like seconds ago that she was in my arms while I sang lullabies to her. Yes, there she is, on the brink of being a woman.

'They're kissing,' Olly splutters. He's not prepared for it either, it seems. Jamie, on his iPod, is oblivious to the whole thing. Probably just as well.

'It's innocent,' I say to him. 'It's just a kiss.' It'd better be innocent, I think. We're in Disney, for feck's sake; nothing other than snow-white innocence is allowed.

'So do we just pretend we're not here?' he demands. 'Let them snog it out in front of the whole world? I think not, I'm going in there right this minute and telling him to get on his bike.'

'Whoa there, Victorian-dad. You can't embarrass her,' I say.

'But she's kissing him,' he says again.

'And now she's not. Look,' I say. I exhale in relief, seeing them finally end their embrace.

'Will I call out to her?' Olly asks.

'No, if she sees us, she can decide if she wants to come over or not. This is a huge deal for Evie, meeting Luke. Especially after all that happened. She seems to like him. And he seems to like her. You must have seen that in the castle,' I say.

'He was like a bloody lovesick puppy, the way he was looking at her,' Olly says in disgust.

'They're getting off, look,' I say to him. 'Aw, they're holding hands.'

'Will we follow them?' Olly asks, his eyes darting after them.

'Stalk them from a distance, kind of thing?' I say.

'Yes. They don't even have to know we are there,' Olly tells me. 'Come on. We'll lose them if we are not quick!'

'Would you ever relax, Olly? We'll be doing no such thing. You better get your head around the fact that our daughter is growing up. We have to let her have some privacy,' I say.

'Are you mad?' Olly says. 'Did you see that kiss? You forget that I was once a randy fourteen-year-old. I know what he's thinking of right now.'

'Olly Guinness, give your daughter some credit, even if you won't give him any. It's innocent. First crush, that's all. He won't be the last boy she kisses, I daresay, but he'll always be her first. That's special,' I sigh, remembering my own first kiss many years before with a boy called David.

'We don't know anything about this boy,' Olly says.

'I know we don't, but she does. And we'll not leave them together for much longer. It's almost three anyhow. Let's give them one more hour. You can grill him to your heart's content then. Play the over-protective-father role, frighten him senseless and see if he's a suitable suitor!' I joke.

'How can you be so calm about it?' Olly demands.

'I'm not calm at all, Olly. I'm freaking out that we have a daughter old enough to be kissed like that on a carousel. But, I'm also about to burst with happiness too. Did you see her face just then? She's happy. She really is.'

He nods. There was no arguing with that.

'Yeah. Maybe. I'm just worried, because she's so vulnerable at the moment. What if he takes advantage of that?' Olly continues. 'But if you're sure . . . '

I look at the two of them as they get off the carousel, holding hands and giggling. Evie will be fine.

Hang on – is that his hand touching her bum?

'Quick, we'll lose them!' I shout, grabbing Jamie by his arm and yanking him hard.

'But what about the horses?' Jamie asks.

'Boring. Let's go find something else,' Olly declares, delighted that I'm on board his crazy train now too.

Evie and Luke head towards the Snow White ride. We hang back a few minutes, then follow behind them.

'If she catches us, she'll go mental,' I tell Olly.

'If I catch that Luke fella up to any shenanigans, I'll

show them mental,' Olly answers. 'What's so funny? I'm deadly serious.'

'You guys are weird,' Jamie tells us.

The line is moving quickly and ten minutes later we are all squeezed into one seat. Olly is going to do himself a damage, the way he's craning his neck. But at least it's keeping his mind occupied. I've been watching him today and he looks sad, pensive and I reckon I know why. Pops. We're to open another letter tonight. I think if my dad was about to send a message from beyond the grave I might be a bit off sorts too. He's doing great, all things considering.

I've never seen a bond as close as Olly's and Pops ever before. I don't think that there are many who can say that pretty much for their whole childhood and adult life too, they lived with their parent. I know that Olly's mam dying played a huge part of this dynamic for them both, but even so.

We all miss Pops, but for Olly it must be an unimaginable pain. This whole adventure stunt is doing a great job at keeping Olly moving forward. Because I think, if we were at home, he might have flailed by now.

I can't help but worry too that Olly will put Pops' death and his grief in that same box as he has put his mam's. I don't care what he says, it's not natural that he never talks about her actual death. Over the years I've tried to talk to him about it, but he gets so defensive and upset, I end up dropping it.

So I watch my husband closely. Worried that he'll fall apart at any second.

'Quick. They're getting away!' Olly shouts at me, as the

ride comes to an end. I can feel hysterical laughter bubbling up inside me. What are we like, chasing our teenage daughter around a theme park? Jamie and I catch up with Olly, who is standing in the middle of the walkway, scouring the surroundings. 'She's disappeared. We've lost her.'

'Would you relax!' I say. 'Jeepers, you'll never survive her teenage years if you let yourself get so worked up all the time.'

'Is Luke going to have Pops' room when we get home?' Jamie asks.

'Of course not!' Olly says.

'Where will he sleep then when they get married? Can I be the best man?' Jamie asks.

'They're not getting married, you loon.' Olly laughs, 'Luke is just Evie's friend, that's all.'

'I don't get it. I thought if you kissed someone, you married them. Oh look, there they are. Queuing for ice-cream. I want one too.'

Before we can stop him, he's run over to them both.

'What a coincidence bumping into you,' I say. I don't need Evie to tell me how lame I sound.

'We know you've been following us,' Evie says. Oh oh, she doesn't sound very happy with us.

'Er . . . We were just . . . ' Olly mumbles, then he looks away. He's . . . he's laughing, the fecker!

'Whatever,' Evie replies. 'You might as well just stay with us, if it's that important to you. You obviously don't trust me.'

'Er . . . well . . . ' Bloody Olly snorts laughter, not even remotely trying to cover it up. 'Busted. It was your mother's idea. I told her we should just leave you to it.'

'We weren't following you,' I say with as much dignity as I can muster, but damn it, I can feel my face colouring up.

'Well, just so you know which way to go next, when you're not following us, we're heading to Adventureland,' Evie says.

'We're just getting an ice-cream, then we're going back to the carousel, actually,' I say.

Evie throws a dirty look at both of us. 'Whatever.'

'Bye Mr and Mrs G,' Luke says and then they are off.

'Thanks for throwing me under the bus,' I say to Olly, who is clutching his sides now he's laughing so much.

'I couldn't resist. Oh I needed that laugh. Your face. Her face!'

'You are both busted,' Jamie agrees. 'She's mad.'

Olly laughs again. 'Oh give me one of those ice-creams. I'm banjaxed after all that running around. I'm too old for this!'

'Are we going on the carousel for real?' Jamie asks.

'That depends if your dad is ready for another equine adventure,' I say.

'I reckon this is the type of horse riding I can cope with,' Olly replies and his face is full of merriment and laughter.

'It's good to see you so happy,' I say.

'I vote we do happy a lot more around here.' Olly kisses me lightly, then continues eating his ice-cream.

'Do you think she'll forgive us?' I ask.

'Probably not. At least, not for a while, anyhow. But, sure, it's our job to make a show of her. Goes with the territory when you have kids. Thou must make a show of your children at least once a week.'

Then a thought strikes me. We might actually have a chance here. Olly and me. Days like today make me feel like we're going to make it. I'm going to stop over-analysing everything. My whole life I've put minute details under the microscope and dissected them. I can't stop till I've everything pulled apart. I need to just accept that we are in a better place. The sex is amazing; I feel alive again. In fact, the more we are intimate with each other, the more I crave him. I don't think it's been like that since we first got married.

But then doubt jumps back into my head. Can we find our way back to happiness again? I throw my ice-cream stick in the bin and spy a bruised peach, beginning to rot. Please don't let us be the peach.

'Mae? You okay?' Olly's voice interrupts me. 'You were miles away then.'

'Can we be happy again?' I ask him.

'We're happy now, aren't we?' he replies.

I nod.

'Can't that be enough for now?' he asks.

'Yes, I suppose it can,' I say.

We both know that at some point the plaster has to come off, but as we go around and around in circles on the carousel, I allow my doubts to float away in the breeze. We're happy now and that's all that matters.

Chapter Twenty-Four

Dear Olly & Mae

Week two is about to kick off and it's finally au revoir to France and hallo to Germany.

I've pulled together some phrases for you all to remember. Ich kann nicht so gut Deutsch – I don't speak any German. And if that doesn't work, you can say Kann hier jemand Englisch – which means does anyone here speak English? And failing all that, you can just say nothing! Ha ha! Ja?

You'll be spending your first three nights in the Rhine Valley, before setting sail on a cruise. I've found an overnight one that leaves from a port close to Koblenze and brings you to Stuttgart. From there you are going to Tripsdill Park in Cleebonm. I think the kids might like that one.

Have fun!

Love
Pops x

Chapter Twenty-Five

OLLY

Should I be worried about the evil eye that Evie is sending in my direction? She has me second-guessing my every move now, I don't want to upset her. She's been through enough. But I can't be held to ransom by my thirteen-year-old either, who thinks she's in love with the first guy she's kissed.

'Why can't we stay one more day and leave tomorrow?' Evie tries for the fourth time in as many minutes.

'Because Pops has gone to a lot of trouble to organise this trip and like it or lump it, we are leaving – now!' I tell her. She storms out of our room, muttering, whilst typing furiously into her phone.

'She thinks she's in love,' Mae shrugs.

'I don't give a shit, Mae. I preferred her when she was sad. At least she was less vocal.' When I clock Mae's frown, I add, 'I'm joking!'

'Look, I know she's being difficult right now. But that's her job. She's a teenager and she'll always push boundaries, try to change the rules. We wouldn't want her any other way. Being vocal one minute and then being silent comes with the territory too.'

The size of Nomad never bothered me before. I've been enjoying the simplicity of just a couple of rooms. But right now I'm feeling claustrophic.

'There's no fecking place to escape from the wrath of our hormonal teenager here!'

'You should come hang out in my school some day. I've got nearly 1,500 hormonal teenagers under my care. And despite being on several acres, there's no escape there either,' Mae says.

'It would be the end of me,' I say. 'Do we have six more weeks of her mooning over yer man?' I ask.

'At a guess, yes. But look, despite all the moaning this morning, she's happy. And once we get to our next destination she'll be fine. It's just knowing he's here for another day, that bothers her. But you know what? I, for one, am happy to see her mooning over a guy. I'd rather be worried about her being lovesick than worried about her being bullied,' Mae replies.

Fair enough. I know Mae's right. But I'm all aggravated. Everything and everyone is getting on my nerves. 'Ask her to put her bloody phone on silent, will ya? If I hear it buzz one more time with another message from himself, I'll not promise I'll hold my tongue!'

'If you push her, Olly, she'll want to go home to Wexford,' Mae says.

'So what? You'd not leave if she wanted to?' I say, horrified at the thought. I figured that the whole 'we might call it quits at any stage' promise was gone now.

'I don't want to go home. I'm having a great time. But if it was the right thing for any of us to leave, I'd push for it.'

I can't speak I'm so annoyed. She just throws that bombshell at me, like it's no big deal.

'What's really going on with you, Olly? You have been in a foul mood all morning. Last night wasn't much better. This is more than Evie's hormones, I know it is,' Mae says to me. 'Was it something in Pops' letter?'

She hit the nail on the head first time. She knows me well. 'Did you not think Pops' letter was a bit short?'

'Well . . . ' Mae says.

'I mean, it didn't say much other than tell us where we're heading to. It wasn't like the others.' I know I sound petulant, but I can't help it. 'There was no message in this one. I've looked over and over to see if I missed anything. Not a bloody thing.'

'Maybe, when he wrote it, he was having a bad day. Pain-wise,' Mae suggests.

'Maybe,' I say. 'So is that it from now on? All the letters are going to be just a few sentences and nothing more? I feel like I'm losing him all over again, Mae. All I have left of him is a few fecking ashes and those letters.'

And then to my absolute horror, I start to cry. I'm forty years old and have only cried a handful of times in my adult life. When each of the children was born. On our wedding day, when I saw Mae walk up the aisle towards me. God, she was beautiful. The day that Pops died and then at his funeral.

My head is spinning with so many thoughts. I can't believe that this is it. I'll never talk to my father again.

Never sit down and watch the football together again. We'll never drink a pint of Guinness together and make the same joke about saving the family business.

Mae slides in beside me on the bed and puts her head on my shoulder. 'I miss him too.'

'One more time. I'd just like to see him one more time,' I say and the tears start to come thicker, faster.

'Of course you do,' Mae says and I see that her eyes are filled with tears too.

'I'm not ready to say goodbye,' I say.

'And you don't have to. We've still got more letters to come. Who knows what they will hold? But Olly, you've got to be prepared that they might be short. Try to focus instead on this gift – the trip he has given us.'

I grab a towel and wipe my face till it feels raw and red. It stops the tears at least.

'And letters or not, you will always have a warehouse full of memories. What you both had is way more than any letter from him now. Don't forget that.'

It's more than I had with my mam, I know that. But she's part of this too. It feels like I'm mourning her for the second time. Both my parents dead and, while I know I'm not alone, I feel suffocated from the weight of my loneliness. I want my parents. I want Pops.

Mae places her two hands around mine and squeezes hard and once again the tears take over. Finally, spent, the well of tears dries up and in its place I am left with a feeling of embarrassment about my emotional breakdown.

The pain felt inescapable, but now I wish I could take it back. This isn't how I'm supposed to be. I'm supposed to be strong.

'I'm sorry.'

'For what?'

'That. I shouldn't have let it all get to me.'

'Olly, your father was the wisest man I have ever known. He said to us, straight off in his first letter, grief is inevitable. Remember that. You've nothing to apologise about. You earned that cry. It's been a shit year.'

How did I get so lucky to have Mae in my life? I want to thank her, but I think I'll cry again, if I say any more.

'You go freshen up and I'll grab a couple of lattes from the shop. Then we can head off. We're all set to go. Rhine Valley, here we come.'

'We'll be a couple of alcoholics by the time we get home to Wexford with all these wine regions Pops is sending us to,' I joke.

Mae looks relieved to hear me joking and kisses me. I need to get my shit together. I've a long drive ahead of me – at least five hours.

'As we'll be passing through Luxembourg to get to Koblenz, we could stop there for a lunch, stretch our legs. That way we can add another country to our list,' I say.

'Great idea! And once we get to Koblenz, we've got four days in the one spot. I'm making an executive decision that you make tomorrow a day of rest. With wine!' Mae winks at me as she walks out the door.

As we leave France and see the sign signalling our entry into Luxembourg we all cheer and I find my good humour again. Evie seems reconciled to her fate as a lovesick teenager. She has stopped moaning that we have taken her away 'from the only good thing in her life!' and instead we are subjected to lots of conversations that start with 'Luke says . . . '

I must ask Pops if I was that bad when I was her age. Then I stop as another avalanche of pain hits me. Of course I'll do no such thing. I keep thinking of things to tell Pops and then in the realisation that I can't, the pain doubles. I know that it's all part of the grieving process. But . . . but bollocks to that!

I'm grateful for the long drive as it's keeping my mind occupied. Nomad and I do fine in the slow lane, cruising along at a steady ninety.

I exit the motorway when we get to Luxembourg. 'Let's see where the road takes us. We might find a gastro pub somewhere, so we can try eating Luxembourgish food.' Check me out, Mr Spontaneity.

'With chips?' Mae winks at me and I marvel at how far we've come in such a short time.

'Get us, with our in-jokes.' And when she smiles I feel the last of my morose feelings slip away. 'I'm a lucky bastard.'

She raises one pretty eyebrow in question.

'Because you're always there for me. You can sense when I'm down. You get me. I'm sorry that I've been such a grumpy old bollocks.'

'You've had reason.' She lets me off the hook. I cannot lose this woman. I cannot lose us.

'I love you.'

'I know.' She smiles and reaches down to switch on a CD. Soon we are driving through rolling hills and green fields with Ellie Goulding serenading us.

'It looks a lot like France,' Mae murmurs and she's right.

We come across a pretty village after a few km and pull in, to park up Nomad. A quick stroll through the main street and we find a small restaurant. Evie immediately starts looking for Wi-Fi.

'Right, so far we've had cows' cheeks, shellfish and half our body weight in French cheese. What do you think traditional Luxembourg cuisine is going to offer us?' I ask.

Our waitress speaks excellent English and tells us that the local speciality is a potato dish called *Gromperekichelcher.* Easy for her to say. She also recommends a pork dish called *Judd mat Gaardebounen.*

The pork arrives and is in a large casserole with broad beans and a thick creamy sauce. The potato dish appears to be deep-fried shredded potato cakes with onions, shallots and parsley in them. Both are gorgeous and we all tuck in with vigour. The waitress also brings us a dish called *Kachkéis,* which is a soft cheese, melted and served with bread. Jamie starts to sing the cheese song and we all join in, giggling.

'We're all going to turn into cheddar or Brie, the amount of it we've eaten!' Mae says.

We all munch in companionable silence and with no bleeps from lover boy to interrupt us. It's nice.

'You look happier,' Mae says.

'I am. I'm good,' I say. 'Cheese makes me happy.'

'I'll remember that,' Mae laughs.

'I'm good too,' Jamie declares. 'Super-good.'

'And how about you, Evie? Are you super-good?' Mae asks.

Evie's smile is the answer. 'Luke posted a picture of us both on Facebook. Look.'

We look at the picture of them both in front of Sleeping Beauty's castle. They look young and carefree. And indeed, super-happy.

'Check out the couple auditioning for a toothpaste commercial,' I joke.

'You look beautiful,' Mae tells Evie, who looks chuffed with the compliments.

'Should I share it too?' Evie asks Mae. 'I've not posted anything for ages.'

I watch her looking at Mae for guidance, her nose scrunched up as she doubts her next move. Mae takes the phone and looks at the photo again.

'This picture is way too cute not to share,' Mae nods her approval.

'What will I say?' Evie asks, but she is beaming. 'What if Martina or Deirdre makes a smart comment?'

'Just say, had great fun with Luke in Disney,' Mae advises her. 'Keep it simple. And if I may, I have a suggestion to make.'

'What?'

'Remove them as friends from your Facebook page,' Mae states and I cheer my approval.

'But they'll know I did that. What would they think?'

'Who cares what they think?' I say.

'Life is hard enough, pet, without having those kind of toxic "friendships" in your life. They made your life hell for the past year. Remove them. And I bet by doing that, it will make it easier to move on.'

She looks down to her phone and flicks away at the screen for five minutes. 'They're gone. And three others, too, who've been horrible.'

Mae picks up her glass and makes a toast, 'To detoxing negativity from our lives.'

And we all raise our glasses and chink them and I try not to whoop when I see the smile that is lighting up my daughter's face.

I marvel at my wife once again. Every day she proves to me once again how much the children and I need her. She said last week that she didn't feel needed. Well, I better change that.

We go for a quick stroll to work off the plum tart we shared after our meal. Then we fill Nomad up with the cheapest diesel we've yet to buy on this journey and head back to the motorway.

'It says here we've another 221 km to go. We'll be there around four,' Mae says, looking at Captain Kirk.

I check the mirrors and see that Jamie and Evie have both fallen asleep. And when I look at their contented sleep-filled faces, innocent and pure, I feel tears prick my eyes again. It's another lucky bastard moment.

'We make good kids,' I nudge Mae, pointing to the kids.

'Yes we do. Pretty perfect.'

They awake with perfect timing just as we arrive in Koblenz. Pops has booked us into a campsite south of the town. We start to climb a steep hill, where we find the campsite right at the top. A few weeks ago this hill would have bettered me. I feel a sense of achievement that it doesn't even cause me to break out in a sweat. I park Nomad up and we all climb out, glad to stretch our legs after the long drive.

When we walk into reception, there are two elderly

ladies watching us. I smile as I approach the reception desk and say in my best German, '*Sprechen-sie Englisch oder Franzozisch?*'

I'd practised in Nomad with Mae, because I'd read it was rude to launch straight into English. So I half expect a round of applause for my efforts. Instead they throw daggers my way and one of them says, '*Ich spreche Deutsch.*'

I've got nothing.

'*Englisch?*' Mae rescues me and bestows on them one of her dazzling smiles. Why the hell does it work for her? Fräulein Grumpy, who was so terse to me, can suddenly understand and speaks English to Mae. She gives us a map with directions to our allocated pitch, I pay her the deposit and we make our way to our new home.

'Wow look at that,' Mae says as we pull into our pitch. We have an amazing vantage point and can see the whole town twinkling below us. On one bank there is a castle and on the other we can see the reflections of lights on the River Rhine.

'You know what I fancy right now? A cold beer.'

'Then you shall have one,' Mae says. 'Let's get set up, then we'll sip a Kronenbourg as we take in this stunning view.'

'I'm knackered.' I realise I haven't felt this bone-tired in a long time. I think between my emotional breakdown this morning and the drive, I'm fit for nothing.

'Let's stay in the campsite tonight. The kids can explore, I'll cook and we'll have an early night.'

I like that plan and start my ritual of getting Nomad set up. Each time, it seems easier to master. I made sure the tanks were half-full this morning when I left, so I can leave that job till the morning. Awning up, groundsheet down, satellite hoisted and within twenty minutes I'm sitting in a chair relaxing. Mae and the kids have gone off in search of essentials.

Then it starts to rain. It's funny, two weeks of sunshine and I've forgotten what it's like to feel rain on my skin. All four of us are slightly stunned to see its return. Mae cooks pasta for dinner as we hear the rain pelting down on the roof of Nomad. I like the sound of it, like drums, serenading us.

We all tease her about not embracing her courageous palate in Germany, as she plates up our food.

'*Ein sauerkraut bitte*,' I say to her.

To which she responds by throwing a tin of tomatoes at me.

'Your mother has a violent streak in her. You all saw that,' I say to the kids, who start threatening to call the police.

After dinner, we switch on the TV and settle down on our couch to watch *Independence Day*.

'If aliens come here, I'll punch them in the nose too,' Jamie declares as Will Smith heroically knocks out a green being from outer space. 'Hit pause, I'm going to the toilet.'

'Dad, Mam . . . ' Jamie screams from the bathroom. We jump up and find him standing in a pool of water. The toilet is overflowing, flushed water splashing onto the floor.

'I didn't do anything,' Jamie swears.

Mae grabs some towels and starts to mop up the water and I investigate. Fucking blocked. That's all I need.

'Who put something in the toilet?' I feel the remnants of my earlier good mood disappear.

Nobody answers me, but I notice Evie looking shifty. 'I'm gonna have to go check the tank. See what's clogging it all up. I told you all, nothing but pee down here, unless it's an emergency.'

'I hate you. I hate this stupid camper van and I want to go home!' Evie shouts and walks into our bedroom.

'What the . . . ?'

We follow her and her body is heaving with sobs, she's crying so much. I never said a fecking word to her. What the hell is going on?

'I want to go home. Mam. I want to go home.'

'Ssh. Come here. It's okay.' Mae ushers me away.

'Dad . . . '

'Not now Jamie,' I say, trying to hear what's going on behind the door.

'Dad . . . '

'I said not now.'

Then I hear crying and turn around to see Jamie with big fat tears splashing down his face and a puddle of pee at his feet. 'I couldn't hold it any more.'

How did we go from watching a bloody movie to me standing in a pool of piss? I mop up the mess and strip Jamie, getting him into fresh pyjamas, telling him that it's all okay, then head outside to investigate the blockage.

It's pitch dark and the area around Nomad is uneven. As I step down, I land in a hole, full of rainwater. 'Fuck!' I swear as I twist my ankle, go down in a heap. And then a stench hits me, the putrid stench of shit. I look down and realise that my hand is in a pile of dog shit.

That's it. I have fucking well had it! Damn it to hell. Piss and shit all over me now. I try to scramble up, but the ground is wet and I slide back down again. And then I see her, Mae, standing in the doorway, laughing her ass off. I swear to God, I'll kill her.

Then she says in between snorts of laughter, 'Are you quite alright?'

And the red mist disappears and I'm laughing so hard my stomach hurts as I remember Pops and me at the funeral, him on his ass.

'You okay now?' Mae asks.

'The best.' And I stand up and walk to the blocked toilet tank like a boss.

Chapter Twenty-Six

OLLY

A full morning listening to the pelting rain bang on the roof of Nomad and I'll be honest, I'm not hearing drums any more. I've a bloody headache from it. Tension fills our home, corrupting the air around us. We're getting on each other's nerves.

It turns out that a tampon was the cause of the blockage last night. Evie's, hence the tears. She won't even look at me and I can feel her embarrassment and dissatisfaction bouncing off the walls. Mae has been great, whispering soothing words to her. As she said to me, she's mortified. I'm not going to say one word to her. Poor kid.

'I'm bored,' Jamie complains. I feel for the lad, he's been stuck inside for too long now. The rain just won't let up. He needs to burn some energy.

'I'm over this rain now,' Evie says. 'It's sunny at home. Ann is going to the beach today.' She sighs long and loud, just in case we've not cottoned on to the fact that she'd rather be at home.

'We got spoiled in France with that glorious sunshine,' Mae says. 'I think we have to accept that we'll not be doing any go-karting as planned today.'

'Don't make me go see another castle,' Jamie says, pretending to fall asleep at the thought.

'Let's go do some shopping, then check out the recreation room here,' Mae says.

An hour later we are unpacking groceries from a trolley directly into the kitchen of Nomad. 'The true definition of pack and go,' I say.

'There's a lot to be said for it,' Mae agrees.

'I've got Wi-Fi!' Evie shouts, looking more animated than she's done for two days. 'At last! Can we stay here for a minute? I want to check my messages.'

'Oh never let it be said that we came between you and true love! Happiness is . . . free Wi-Fi,' I joke.

'Ha ha, very funny, Dad,' Evie says, in a tone that says I'm anything but.

I spy a coffee shop, so head to get Mae and I lattes, leaving my family with their heads down in their phones and iPads.

Coffee, patisserie and various electronic devices in hand we kill an hour in that car park.

'Read us the letter again, Dad,' Jamie asks, when he eventually looks up from his game.

I reach for the atlas and pull out Pops' most recent missive. The kids, unlike me, loved the letter.

'Pops is funny,' Jamie laughs.

'*Ja*,' Mae replies.

'How early do we have to be up tomorrow for the cruise?' Evie asks.

'Six,' Mae replies. 'By the time we pack up Nomad and get going, we'll need every bit of the time. Boat sails at seven thirty a.m.'

We opt for another quiet night, this time with the movie *Thor*, Evie's choice. After snacking on some hot-buttered toast and mugs of tea, I head to bed early, leaving them to their movie.

Mae follows me into our bedroom, 'You okay?'

I shrug. I feel out of sorts, but I can't put my finger on why. 'I'm still feeling a bit off. Sorry, Mae. I can't shift it. I'm not trying to be a killjoy. Maybe it's this bloody weather. It feels like I'm stuck in this fog and no matter how hard I try, I can't get out of it.'

Mae walks over to me and climbs into my arms, hugging me. 'You're grieving. We all are. It's only been a few weeks since Pops died.'

'I'll snap out of it,' I say.

'You don't have to snap out of anything,' she tells me. 'You are allowed to mourn the death of your father. Truth is, we all have good and bad days. Don't be so hard on yourself.'

I kiss her forehead, grateful for her words. 'I'm glad we're back on track, though,' I say to her, smiling.

Something flashes across her face.

'We are okay?' I ask her and am annoyed with myself at how desperate I sound.

'Yes. Sure,' she replies, but I don't believe her. When she lies, she always looks away from me and she's now fidgeting and her eyes dart from one side of Nomad to the other.

I pull her to face me and make her look me in the eye. 'I thought we were happy.'

'We are. The past week has been wonderful. But you have to admit that it's like a holiday romance, a fun, sexy, happy romance. But we've got to go home again. And all the issues we had back there are waiting for us, that's what worries me,' she says.

'It feels real to me,' I say.

'Let's not do this now,' Mae says. She stands up to walk away, but then stops at the doorway. 'Things were pants at home, Olly. I was unhappy and so were you. We can't ignore that. Because if we do, we'll go home and two weeks later we'll be back in the same trouble. I don't want that.'

I know she's right. But knowing something and accepting it are two different things.

She walks to the door, smiling at me. 'Sleep well, I won't be long. I'll just get the kids settled once the movie is over.'

I feel like a condemned man who has been granted a last-minute reprieve from the governor. Our big talk averted for now. But I'd still rather bury my head in the nice sand and ignore everything that I know a 'talk' will bring.

As for it being like a holiday romance, how bad is that? We're having sex. A lot of it. I think of Mae's face over the past year at home. Sad, lonely, angry, unhappy. I don't want to see that again. I want to bring home the happy, carefree wife that I have now. The old Mae. My Mae. So I've got to find a way to bring our holiday romance home.

I know that I need to work some stuff out. Like what I'm going to do with my life. I'm forty and I've no job and no matter how much I try to make myself into the perfect stay-at-home dad, I miss work.

But my breathing starts to feel shallow whenever I think about starting again. I'm on holiday. Fuck work. It can wait.

I pull open the drawer that holds the urn of Pops' ashes. When and where are we scattering these, Pops? What do you have in store for us next? I feel exhausted; every bone in my body aches and I'm done.

Next thing I know, I hear a noise, shrill and persistent. But I roll over and ignore it. 'Wake up!' Jamie's voice is in my ear, impossible to ignore as is the pain as he shoves my shoulder.

'Would you stop?' I grumble, then register my phone that is beeping away. How on earth are Mae and I sleeping through the alarm? I bolt upwards and shout, 'Quick, get Evie up and get dressed both of you. We need to be out of here in ten minutes!'

Mae is half-dressed when I run outside and get Nomad ready for the off. We've paid in advance, so we can just go. I don't know how we do it, but somehow, within ten minutes, we are driving out of the campsite, bang on time.

'A lot to be said to this lark of living and sleeping in your getaway car!' I say over my shoulder to Mae. She is putting some moisturiser on, sitting in the back with the kids, who are eating cereal at the table.

I'd found the cruise ship departure point the day before and with no issue or drama, within the hour, we are on board, Nomad parked up, and ready to find our cabins.

'We're in the belly of the ferry again, Dad!' Jamie says and we all laugh.

It's an old, small ship, as cruise liners go, but clean and the smiles of the staff put us all in a good mood immediately. I can't wait to get to our cabins, because I have a surprise for Evie. The booking was for two cabins, one for the kids, one for us. But I rang the liner yesterday and managed to get a further cabin for Evie. With its own bathroom. Some much-needed privacy for twenty-four hours, at least for her. And I'm rewarded by the biggest smile on her face. It was worth the exorbitant fee they charged.

Jamie's cabin interconnects with ours; Evie is across the hall. We are all pleasantly surprised at how big they are.

'Maybe, our expectations have changed, because of Nomad,' Mae ponders and she could be right. Had we gone straight from home to here, we would have found them cramped. But now, they look more than adequate.

The captain announces that we will be departing shortly, so we decide to head up to the deck to wave goodbye to Koblenz. It's early still, not quite eight thirty a.m., so the sun hasn't come out yet and a slight mist hovers over the Rhine.

'I'm so glad we didn't miss this,' Mae murmurs and she clasps my hand tight.

As I stand on the deck, I can't help but think about the journey to France only a few weeks before. We stood side by side then, much like now, but we were a thousand miles apart. But we're taking little steps closer to each other every day. I have to believe that it's working, my fight to save our marriage is working.

As the day goes on, I realise that the fog hasn't just

lifted from the day, but also from my head. I feel more like myself. The wine-tasting Mae and I partook in Mannheim may also be playing a contributing factor in my renewed good mood.

Soon it's time to dress for dinner. We've been informed that shorts are not allowed. It feels strange to put trousers and a shirt back on.

'It's nice to get dressed up,' Mae says, smiling as she pulls on a red strappy dress. Her skin is dark and tanned. My breath catches as I look at her.

Don't be careless with her, Pops once said. Never again, Pops, never again.

'All you are missing is a flower behind your ear and you could be a flamenco dancer,' I say, touching her hair lightly.

She spins around and says, 'Olè!' and I pull her in to me and kiss her long and hard.

'We'll be late for dinner,' she says, but she's only half-heartedly protesting. I continue kissing her and trace my hand down her spine to the small of her back.

'We can be quick,' I say and I feel like she is drugging me with every touch of her hand on my body. The sex is quick and for those few moments of desire, I forget everything but the hedonistic feeling of Mae.

'Wow,' Mae says. She looks flushed and I've smudged her makeup. I've never seen her look sexier. 'That was something else, Mr Guinness.'

'Not too shabby for an old married couple, eh?' I say to her.

'No.' She smiles and kisses me, with great tenderness. 'I love you. Know that to be true. No matter what else happens, I love you, Olly.'

I feel tears prick my eyes, in the way that is becoming more and more familiar. She loves me. It's like the first time she said it to me, fifteen years ago.

'I love you too,' I whisper and bury my head in her hair, fighting the urge to cry.

A bang on the door interrupts us. 'Mum, Dad!' It's Jamie. 'I'm starving.'

We giggle. 'Bad parents,' Mae says.

'The worst,' I concur. 'But if you will go around looking all sexy, what's a man to do?'

We both scramble to get ready and tell Jamie we will be there in five minutes. Dinner is excellent; above and beyond our expectations. We even manage to tick off some more local dishes to add to our courageous palates. Then we move to the bar, where the evening entertainment is about to start. Our cruise manager is a middle-aged English man called Terence. He tells us that there will be a musical quiz followed by a pianist and singer.

'Now, let's see, we need a name for our team,' I say.

'The Travelling Nomads,' Evie says straight away.

Not bad Evie, not bad at all.

'Will I write the answers down?' she asks. The difference in her since yesterday is remarkable. The simple thing of giving her her own room. I'll remember that. Maybe we can find a way to do that again.

We nod and then Terence begins the quiz. 'Question one. Former Spice Girl Melanie Chisholm duetted with which Canadian singer-songwriter on the 1998 single "When You're Gone"?'

'I know this one!' Mae says. 'It's Bryan Adams!'

Evie scribbles it down neatly.

'Question two. Elvis Presley's manager, Andreas Cornelis van Kuijk, was better known by what name?' Terence asks us.

'Pops was an Elvis fan,' I say. 'That would be Colonel Tom Parker.'

This is going well.

'Now this usually gets people! Question three. In the song, how many ships came sailing by on Christmas Day?'

'Two,' Mae says.

'Three,' I say.

'Four,' Evie says.

'Twenty?' Jamie shouts, causing the table beside us to laugh.

'We'll have to come back to this,' Mae says.

'Question four. Which member of Take That replaced Simon Cowell as a judge on the British *X Factor*?'

'Gary Barlow,' Evie says, to which Mae and I start to laugh.

'Always knew you were a closet fan of the show!' Mae teases and Evie throws her eyes up to the heavens.

We get quite competitive as a team, especially after round one, when we realise that we got all ten questions correct.

'We can win this.' I've never wanted to win anything so much in my life. I feel like our family needs a win for a change. Eight more rounds fly by and then it's the final round and the last question. We know we're in with a shot. Three teams are hovering at the top of the leader board and we're right in the middle of them.

'Now, a tough one to finish off. Pop band Abba wrote

the song "Chiquitita" to commemorate the 1979 "International Year of the . . . "what"?' Terence asks.

An audible gasp goes around the room as most of us haven't got a barney. 'Anyone?' I look around at my family.

'I've not even a decent guess to give you here,' Mae says.

Jamie has lost interest by now and is busy building houses with the beer mats, but glances up to say 'bananas'.

'The year of the banana?' My son is pure comedy genius.

'Yeah. The advert on TV, it's about Chiquita bananas.'

Mae has tears coming out of her eyes she's laughing that much.

'What?' Jamie asks, no idea why we're laughing at him.

'I might know this,' Evie tells us. 'Chiquitita is Spanish for "little one". Abba did a charity song for UNICEF years ago. I think it could be this one. I remember in my *Guinness Book of Records*, it said that it is one of the most famous charity songs ever made.'

'So what would the international year be of then?' I ask, feeling excitement bubble up inside.

'Maybe International Year of the Child?' Evie says, looking self-conscious. 'It's just a guess.'

'It's a good guess,' I say.

'What if it's wrong and we lose?' Evie asks, looking worried.

'Then we lose,' Mae replies. 'No big deal. But at least we tried. And had fun along the way.'

So Evie writes the answer down, folds the answer sheet up and hands it to Terence.

A few minutes later, Terence is back on the stage, microphone in hand and ready to put us out of our misery. 'Now everyone, I can tell you that after round nine, we have a tie-breaker situation. Both the Travelling Nomads and the Silver Foxes have seventy-six points.'

A cheer from a group of pensioners on the other side of the room erupts, so we give a few whoops out too.

'So it was all down to this final round. Can I have the score sheets for round ten please.'

A drum roll from the band, with perfect timing, makes us all gasp.

'I can tell you that one team got all ten questions right, the other only nine, getting question ten wrong,' Terence proclaims, with a flourish of his hands. The pianist wants to get in on the act. He throws in a dramatic clang on the piano.

'Will it be the Travelling Nomads or the Silver Foxes?' Terence says, enjoying his moment of power.

'Come on!' I shout.

'Oh I feel sick now,' Evie says.

'Question ten, the answer is, The International Year of . . . ' He pauses, of course he does, a salacious grin over his face. 'The Child!'

We realise we have won and jump to our feet and whoop. You'd swear we'd just won the European Cup.

'You star!' Mae says to a charmed Evie, who is bursting with pride.

'Will the winning captain please come up to collect the prize?' Terence says.

'Go on, kids. Do it together,' Mae says. I expect Evie

to say no, but she surprises me by nodding her consent. And then the strangest thing happens. It's as if time slows down. The noise in the room stretches into muffled sounds. I watch Jamie jump up from his seat, punching his arm in the air, and I see his mouth open wide, obviously shouting, but I can't hear a thing.

I turn to look at Mae and watch her reach for her phone in one long, glorious, graceful movement. My heart contracts as I see her joy as she snaps pictures of our children, capturing this Guinness victory. And then I turn to my daughter, my little girl. Her face fades for a moment, or is it a lifetime? And then all at once, my little girl disappears and in her place is a beautiful young woman. And this young woman is laughing.

The kind of laugh that will break and make a man's heart one day. Then she turns to Jamie and they raise their hands up in double high-fives, a gesture old as time for them, yet one we've not seen for a while. I don't think I've ever experienced a more perfect moment. I turn to look around the room and see strangers clapping, smiling and one of the losing members of the Silver Foxes is wagging their fingers at us in jest.

And then I see them. Standing there, it's Pops, holding Mam's hand. And she looks so beautiful, I can't breathe. He nods at me and I cannot take my eyes from him, my father, my teacher, my best friend.

'Olly,' I hear Mae's voice, muffled as if she's miles away and I turn to her and she's pointing to the children, who have started towards the stage.

Then, with one last smile, my parents are both gone. Time speeds up and the room fills with chatter, glasses

261

clinking and the band doing a drum roll for the children's arrival to the stage.

'You're crying,' Mae says, reaching up and brushing away tears from my face.

'Am I?' I reach up and wipe my eyes and blink twice, then look around again, searching, but knowing that they are gone. Wi-Fi.

'You big softie.' She smiles and kisses me on the lips. 'Quick, look at the kids!'

Terence says, 'Congratulations to the winning team and here is your winning prize – a box of luxurious truffles.'

He hands the tiniest box of chocolates I've ever seen to Jamie, who looks down at it, then up at him and then back down to the box again.

'Do you have anything you want to say?' Terence says, pushing the mike under Jamie's chin.

'Is this all we win?' Jamie says and the room breaks into laughter.

A giggling Evie grabs Jamie and they run back to our table.

'Open them up, let's celebrate!' Mae says and Jamie pulls the box open in thirty seconds.

'There's five chocolates in it,' he says.

'One each and I think the extra one should go to Evie, because she got the question right,' Mae says.

I nod in approval.

'We're a good team,' Mae says. 'What would we do without you, Evie.' My daughter blushes and smiles again.

I reach over and grab her hand. 'You are a beautiful young woman, you know that?'

She looks startled at my compliment. 'I'm so proud of you.'

'Thank you,' she squeaks back, but I'm rewarded with one of her amazing smiles. I'm doing it, Pops. I'm not leaving anything unsaid any more.

'You're a good man,' Mae whispers to me and I answer truthfully, 'I'm only what I am because of each of you.'

And then the waitress comes over, saving me from further tears, and we order more drinks and sit back to enjoy the music. We leave the bar at eleven-thirty, with a sleepy Jamie in my arms. Mae and I fall into bed and are both asleep before our heads hit the pillow.

I awake to the sound of banging on our door. Jamie, of course, and he surprises us by telling us that he's 'starving'. But I realise that I'm ravenous too.

'Must be the river air,' I say to Mae. We both have a quick shower and get dressed and we are sitting down to a hearty breakfast from the buffet within half an hour.

'I like cruising,' Mae declares. 'I think I'd like to do one of those big cruise ships one day. Maybe around the Caribbean.'

'Then we'll put it on our wish list,' I say to her. And I think about Pops, Mam and I looking at the atlas every week, planning and plotting our trips together. Maybe it's time that we continue that tradition. How do you like that, Pops? Your legacy: look what you've created.

'We're off to Tripsdill Park once we dock,' Mae says.

'Please can we go to the theme park first? It has a catapult and water rides and roller coasters,' Jamie asks.

'Yes, we can go get your thrill on!' Mae says, laughing.

'Our campsite is about twenty km from the park. As

long as we're there by seven tonight, we're grand. The website says that they only speak German, so I'm leaving that to you, Fräulein Mae,' I tell her.

'Okay. Time to get the phrase book out,' Mae says. 'Actually, Evie, if you can tear yourself away from instant chat, will you get a few likely phrases sorted for us?'

'How is Prince Charming himself?' I tease.

'His name is Luke,' she tells me, sticking her tongue out.

Just the thought of him breaks her face out into a huge smile. Shite! She's got it bad.

'He's so funny, Dad,' she gushes.

Oh Lord, a funny one. All we need.

'I saw you've had lots of comments about your picture you posted,' Mae says to her.

'Seventy-nine people liked it,' she answers, clearly delighted with this number.

'Well, it is a beautiful picture,' Mae says.

'Can I say something here?' They all turn to look at me. 'I've no problem with Facebook as long as it makes you happy. But Evie, don't value yourself based on how many likes you get on a picture you post.'

'Very deep, Dad,' Evie replies and throws her eyes up to the heavens, just in case I'm in any doubt about how lame that comment was.

'Evie, don't do that. Don't be rude to your dad.' Mae's reprimand surprises and delights me.

Evie looks equally surprised and her mouth has formed a rather comical O.

'I agree with your dad. Your life is far too valuable to be wasting it following the crowd, doing whatever everyone else is doing. One of the things we love most about you is your wonderful uniqueness,' Mae says.

Oh, that's good, I think. She's a way with words, my wife.

'Celebrate who you are and live your life, as you want to. Now if you want to be on Facebook, that's great. But do it on your terms.'

'Okay, whatever,' Evie replies.

'Don't you love it when heartfelt words really hit home?' I whisper to Mae and she snorts laughter, making the kids look up at us both.

We're still giggling when we pack up and head back to Nomad to disembark the ferry.

'Did you notice how easily you got on and off that boat?' Mae says to me once we are on our way. 'Remember that morning in Rosslare? I thought you were going to pass out with the stress of it all.'

'That feels like a lifetime ago,' I reply, thinking I almost had a stroke back then.

'We've come a long way,' Mae replies.

'We have,' I look at her, wondering if she is being literal or alluding to the state of our family.

'But we've a way to go yet before we're done,' she continues and when she holds my gaze I know that neither of us is talking literally.

'It's fun, though, right?' I ask.

'Yes. It's fun, Olly. Far more than I ever thought possible.'

It's only forty km to the theme park, so once we get to the motorway, we are there within the hour. The park has lots of rides and Jamie is in heaven. He is big enough for every single ride and is currently on his fourth go of the wooden roller coaster.

'Look, I don't think he's going to leave here without a huge fuss. Why don't we divide up? I'll go with Evie to the wildlife park for an hour. You guys hang here and do some more rides. Meet back in Nomad at five?' Mae suggests.

'Sounds like a good plan. Keep your phones on and see you in a bit,' I say.

'Okay, Jamie, come on, let's go back onto the water raft again!' I shout to him as he runs towards me.

Chapter Twenty-Seven

MAE

'Okay, what do you want to see most of all?' I ask Evie, standing in front of the information desk.

She takes a quick look over the map of all enclosures and says, 'The wolves. They might be cool.'

'Okay, we've only an hour, so let's do that first, then maybe check out something else afterwards,' I reply.

I manoeuvred this split in the group because I want to have another chat with Evie. She seems like she's coping, she's recovering, but I'm still worried. I can remember what it was like to be thirteen, unsure about yourself. And the slightest thing can seem like a big deal.

But now we are on our own, I'm feeling a bit awkward and don't know where to start. I don't want to embarrass her and make her shut down. On one hand, she seems happy, but I also know now that what Evie shows the world is not, in fact, always the truth.

I'm not just concerned about what happens to Olly and me when we get home, but also to our daughter.

There could be other Martinas and Deirdres. Life is full of them. What can we do to ensure she has the strength to stand up for herself?

I feel ill-equipped to deal with teen issues. They don't give you a guidebook on all this stuff. Bullying, self-esteem, alcohol and we're adding in first love and maybe sex into the mix too. Oh yes, burying my head in the sand seems like a safer and more appealing option.

I know that I can't just rattle off questions to her or spout unsolicited advice about what may or may not be a good idea. So I bite my lip to stop myself falling into the trap of doling out clichés. I want Evie to open up to me, so decide my best bet is to just ask the odd question and let her do all the talking.

'You seem to be on Facebook a bit more lately,' I say to her. I try to sound casual, but my voice sounds tight, strange.

'A bit,' she replies. Then looks off to the right at the horses grazing in the paddock.

So much for asking an open question.

'Have you heard anything from your classmates other than Ann?' I throw in again. Get me, all casual like.

'No,' she replies and devotes all her attention now to the birds of prey in the glass cages to our left.

Shite, double shite and shite again! I'm a legend at this mothering lark.

Right, third time lucky, I'll try another approach. The direct one.

'Has there been any more bullying, Evie? On Facebook? Because you need to tell me if they are up to their old tricks again. Are you okay? You can talk to me. I'm here for you.' Right, that was really casual, Mae Guinness. Subtle.

She sighs. Long and loud – and keeps staring at the animals.

'I'm just aware that before all that stuff flew under my radar. I didn't know about it. So I'm worried that you might be dealing with stuff again and I don't know about it,' I blurt out.

She turns to look at me for the first time and decides to put me out of my misery. 'They've gone really quiet. At least online, anyhow,' Evie answers me.

'Hmmm,' I murmur, hoping that she will continue to open up.

'A few of the girls have been more chatty this past few days. I put a picture up of the cruise ship and Ann and Luke were chatting to me about it. Then a few more joined in, asking questions about it all,' Evie says.

'Are they any of the girls who were part of the bullying?' I ask.

'No. They knew it was going on, though,' Evie says. 'One of them, Katie, she sent me a message today.'

'Oh, what did she say?' I ask and I swear to God if she tells me it's a nasty message I'll grab the first flight home and kill her.

'She apologised, Mam,' Evie replies. 'She said that she felt bad that she did nothing, that she didn't stand up for me.'

'Oh,' I reply. I want to find this girl, Katie, and hug her hard. 'What did you say to her?'

'I haven't answered her yet,' she says, shrugging. 'I don't know what to say. I mean, I know she didn't actually say anything to me herself, but she saw me on my own, every day at lunchtime.'

'Well, you forgave Ann for the same thing and look how much of a friend she's turned out to be.'

She doesn't answer me at first. 'Ann said that a few of the girls feel bad about what happened.'

'It takes a strong person to admit when they made a mistake,' I say.

'Yeah. Maybe I'll answer Katie later on.'

I don't give a shit that we're in broad daylight and it's the very opposite of a cool thing for a mum to do with her teenage daughter – I reach down and clasp her hand. She pulls away quickly, but at least she's not scowling.

'Come on, let's find those wolves.' Standing in front of the enclosure, we watch the grey wolves walk around. They are graceful, with a quiet beauty, and their coats glisten in the afternoon sun.

Then one of wolves stops and stares at a lone wolf. It's incredible but his body language changes immediately and it's obvious to all that he's the dominant one. He looks at the cowering wolf right in the eyes, and the subordinate wolf cringes towards him. His tail is low and he has bent legs, ears back and down, in a submissive nature.

'That's me,' Evie whispers, pointing.

'It doesn't have to be,' I whisper back and my heart hammers so hard in my chest I think I'm going to explode. 'And you don't have to be him, either.' I point to the dominant one, who has bared his teeth now.

'It's possible to be strong without being mean,' I continue. 'It doesn't have to be black or white.'

'I don't know how to be strong,' Evie says.

'Are you kidding me? You are the very definition of strong. You faced so much of this all on your own. Most would have crumbled long ago. And all the time it was going on you were amazing at home, supporting Pops, helping with him,' I say.

'I don't know if I'm strong enough to go back to school and face down Martina and Deirdre,' she replies.

'What do you want to do in an ideal world? What would you choose?' I ask.

'I don't know. Luke says I should go back, ignore them, move on. Don't let them win,' she says.

I like this boy.

'But part of me wants to just forget about it all, so maybe I should start school in your place,' Evie replies.

'I've been in email contact with your principal. Several times,' I tell her. 'And the school have assured me that they will not tolerate any more of this behaviour. They've written to the girls and their parents. There will be zero tolerance next term.'

Rather than comforting her with my words, I've made things worse here, because she looks angry again. 'You just don't get it. Have you any idea how humiliated I am right now? I hate that I'm the point of discussion.'

'I understand. It must be horrible,' I say. 'But I'm your parent and sometimes I have to do things that you hate. Not because I'm trying to humiliate you, but because I need to protect you, support you. I can't look the other way, Evie. This is serious. Because of their behaviour, you nearly lost your life. They have to realise that. If we weren't over here, on this trip, I'd be meeting the parents to discuss it all.'

She shrugs. But I think she's at least trying to understand my point of view.

'Look, why don't we just wait a few more weeks before any decisions are set in stone. We can arrange a meeting with Martina and Deirdre outside of school, before you go back. If that would help.'

Nasty wolf is at it again. He's standing in front of lone wolf again. He is staring at him, every facial expression clear. He is telling the wolf to bow down to him.

But then something wonderful happens. Another of the pack moves over to the lone one and stands by his side, and this seems to give the lone wolf courage. This time he doesn't cower. Instead he stares back, unmoving. He looks that wolf in the eye and refuses to budge. And after what feels like an hour, but is in fact only a few moments, the nasty wolf backs away, defeated, with one last growl as he goes.

'Now that's who *you* are. That right there,' I say to Evie. 'You don't have to back down to anyone, not with the right people by your side. This time you have Ann, Luke, your dad and I, by the sounds of it Katie and maybe others.'

She doesn't say anything, but she's not disagreeing with me either.

'It's not easy to stand up to bullies. But I'm confident that you can do it.'

I chance a quick kiss on her forehead. This time she doesn't pull away. 'It won't be long before I can't kiss you like this. You're nearly taller than me now.'

We look at the wolves one more time and I am humbled by nature. I'm not sure that anyone else would understand what just happened. But it feels like a force bigger than us stepped up to send Evie a message.

I shiver and say, 'Come on. Let's go find the boys before they get into any mischief.'

As we walk back to Nomad, I ask her, 'Are you glad you came? On this trip, I mean?'

'I'm not sure, Mam. I'm not having a terrible time, but some days are better than others,' she says. 'I hate having to wait until you and Dad are up, to get dressed. I hate that I can't just disappear on my own for a bit. There's always someone a foot away from me. And we all fart a lot.'

'What?' That last one has stopped me in my tracks.

'You can hear everything in Nomad. And there's a lot of trumping going on.'

In fairness, she's got a point. 'Maybe we should rename Nomad, Trump Towers,' I say and she giggles.

'Or Ninjavan. As in the farts are silent and deadly. I swear Jamie has those ones down pat.'

'So aside from the farts and lack of privacy . . . ?'

'It's more fun than I thought it would be,' she admits. 'And I met Luke in Disneyland Paris because of the trip. That was cool.'

'He's a great guy. I'm happy you've got him in your life,' I say.

'What about you, Mam?' Evie asks. 'Are you happy you came?'

'I can't believe I'm saying it, but, yes, I am. I know I really hated the idea of Nomad, but now I love it. The simplicity of living in such a small space is quite liberating. I've realised I don't need three-quarters of the things I have at home, that I thought were essential to my life!' I tell her, making a shocked face.

'Not sure I'd go that far,' Evie says. 'But it's okay.'

We start to walk back and I feel a sense of achievement. We're talking. I think I've made a difference. I've just got to keep listening and watching out for her.

'Can I ask you something?' Evie asks.

'Anything.'

'Why haven't you added me as a friend on Facebook?'

'That's a good question. Well, it's like this. I'm your mother, not your friend. And I didn't want to spy on you. I suppose I wanted to give you the opportunity to decide if you added me as a friend or not. I want it to be your choice.'

'Oh.'

'I enjoyed this. We should do more of breaking off on our own without the boys. You're great company,' I say.

'I like it too,' she replies. She pulls her phone out of her jeans pocket and starts swiping as she walks. I don't know how she does that. I'd be in a heap on the dirt.

Then I hear my phone beep in my pocket. Olly, I bet, looking for us. But when I look at the screen, I see a Facebook notification.

You have a new friend request from Evie Guinness.

Oh, Evie. I stop and look at her and she shrugs. I hit accept and hear her phone beep in response and that makes us both giggle. And right there, all my insecurities about my place in the family just melt away. I'm necessary. I'd just forgotten that for a while.

When we get back, we find the boys in the back of Nomad, Olly stripping Jamie of his soaked clothes.

'The water raft,' he explains.

With Jamie telling us how hungry he is, we buckle into our seats and Olly drives us to the campsite.

'Allo and velcome,' the receptionist says. He's in his fifties with a round face and even rounder stomach.

'Ah, *sprechen-sie Englisch*?' Olly says, grinning.

'*Nein*,' he replies.

'*Bitte. Ich bin* Guinness,' Olly steps forward, slowly, throwing in a few hand gestures for good measure.

'*Die Taverne ist da*,' he says, pointing to the bar next door and raising a pretend glass to his mouth. 'Guinness, *ja*?'

I feel a fit of the giggles coming on and whisper to Olly, 'He thinks you want a pint!'

'*Nein. Danke. Ich bin* Guinness,' Olly says, pointing to his chest, looking like a chimpanzee.

'*Ja. Die Taverne ist da*,' he says again, pointing to the room next door.

'*Wohnmobil reservierung*,' Evie mutters. 'Try that.'

'*Wohnmobil*,' Olly shouts. '*Reservierung*. Guinness.'

'Ah. *Wohnmobil!*' he answers and opens a book in front of him.

We peek into it and see our name listed towards the end.

'*Das* . . . is us!' Olly says, at the end of his German repertoire.

He smiles and laughs when he sees the name written down. 'Guinness. *Is werden als* Guinness. *Lustig!*'

When he sees our lost faces, he repeats, '*Lustig!*' and starts to laugh. '*Lustig!*'

'Oh *lustig*!' Olly says and starts to laugh. Clear as mud.

He hands us a map with a circle drawn around our pitch and we are off.

'Your German is coming on leaps and bounds,' I say to Olly. '*Das* was brilliant!'

'Ha ha. I love how the rest of you help out in these situations.'

'You know what I have an awful longing on me for,' I say to him. '*Ein* Guinness *bitte*!'

Looking at Olly laughing, his tanned face, hair slightly longer than he normally wears it, with stubble on his cheeks, I feel overwhelmed with love for him. It's like we've just come out of turbulence on a particularly nasty flight. The fights and misunderstandings, the petty annoyances, all seem so insignificant now, when balanced with how I feel for my husband, for my family.

I can't believe I nearly blew what I have with Olly for a quick flirtation with Philip. My stomach starts to flip, anxiety making me sweat.

Should I confess it all to him? I mean, we didn't actually do anything, except for one kiss. Does Olly need to know? Of course he does. I know that in order for us to make it through further turbulent moments, we have to both be honest.

Any further deliberations are postponed as Olly finds our pitch. We all go into set-up mode. The kids go get water, Olly sets up the satellite and electricity, I get the groundsheet out and we're sorted in record time.

'Mam,' Jamie says.

'I think I can guess,' I answer.

'What?' he says, grinning.

'You're starving!' I say and he nods. 'Come on, let's go grab some food and a pint of Guinness for your dad, seeing as he is so desperate for one.'

Our friend from reception also runs the bar and restaurant and he bellows, laughing, when Olly asks for two pints of Guinness.

We grab a table and pick up the menu, which is one hundred percent in German. 'It appears that we'll all have to live a little dangerously tonight!' I say to them.

'You just order for us, Mam,' Evie says.

Olly and Jamie nod and I realise I may have stumbled across some sort of milestone here. The ghost of ChipGate finally laid to rest.

Using the international method of communication hand gestures and pointing to the menu – I manage to place our order. I've chosen a smorgasbord of food and tell them we can pick at it all – sauerkraut and various kinds of sausages, plus dumplings and some potatoes. I even order chips and tell them when they arrive that I made a mistake. You've got to give them the occasional win.

Sated, we saunter back to Nomad and hunker down for the evening. 'You've not complained about your back in a long time,' Olly says to me.

He's right. I haven't. 'Isn't that strange?' I say. 'It's not hurt me for ages now. And goodness knows it should be, with that bloody bed!'

I look around the small cramped living area of Nomad. The dining-room table is strewn with cups and glasses and snacks. Olly and the children are all squished close together watching me. There's the distinct whiff of a sneaky fart from one of the gang and, by the look on Evie's face, my money is on her.

I don't think there's a place in this world I'd rather be right now than right here.

Chapter Twenty-Eight

MAE

'It feels like we're back in Disney again,' I say, craning my neck to take in the magical view in front of me. The castle in front of us towers over rocky crags at the foot of snow-capped German Alps.

'Or on a film set,' Olly adds. 'It doesn't feel real, does it?'

'Walt Disney used this actual castle as the model for the one in the movie *Sleeping Beauty*. And then again for the castle in Disneyland too,' Evie tells us, her face alight with excitement.

'I thought I'd out-castled myself this past two weeks, but I have to admit, this one is pretty spectacular,' Olly says.

'To think I'd never even heard of this place before last week,' I say.

'It's a big world,' Olly answers.

'It's incredible to me that if it wasn't for Pops, we'd more than likely have gone through life never seeing this view,' I say, pointing to Neuschwanstein Castle.

'That's a scary thought,' Evie agrees.

'I used to think that Bavaria was a made-up place,' Olly admits.

'Geography's not your strong point,' I smile at him.

'This is my favourite castle, out of them all,' Evie declares and takes another selfie in front of it, no doubt to send to Luke and Ann.

We continue making our way down the steep downhill walk towards the village of Hohenschwangau. We parked Nomad there earlier when we arrived from Tripsdrill. We decided to take one of the horse-drawn carriages up to the castle rather than drive and that was a good decision. With every clip, clop of the horses' hooves echoing through the Alps, it felt like a fantasy come to life.

'I've loved Germany, but this has been my stand-out moment so far,' I say.

'Mine too,' Evie declares.

'Mine was the water raft. It was super-fast,' Jamie tells us.

'No surprise there,' I smile. 'What about you, Olly?'

'The cruise,' he replies, with a wink. No guesses for what he's thinking about.

'The website says that there isn't much Wi-Fi at our next campsite,' Evie tells us. Her shoulders sag and she looks like the world is about to end.

'How will we ever cope?' Olly jokes. 'But small mercies, it also says that there's a sauna. And that, Evie pet, has my name written all over it.'

'Don't forget we have another letter to open from Pops today too,' I say.

'Thinking about nothing else all morning. Where to tomorrow, do you reckon?' Olly asks me.

'Switzerland or Austria, I reckon. They make the most logical sense – they are closest,' I reply.

An hour later, we pull into our campsite and check in with no problems. We park up and let the kids off to explore.

'Stay together,' I say to them both as they run off. 'Your dad and I are going to the sauna, but you have to be back here again in an hour.'

I watch them walk away and get a bad feeling. I shiver despite the warm sun.

'You look like you saw a ghost just there,' Olly says, taking in my face.

'Oh you know that feeling like someone has walked over your grave?' I say to him. 'Just got a bad feeling for a minute. Are we sure that they are okay on their own?'

'Evie is thirteen. You keep telling me we have to give her some responsibility and independence. Come on, I've been looking forward to this sauna.'

A few minutes later, we are both sitting on wooden seats in the small, hot room and I begin to feel better. The more I sweat in the intense heat, the more tension and stress seem to leave my body.

'It's like we've closed the door on the rest of the world,' Olly sighs. 'If we win the lotto, I'm installing one of these in the garage.'

'Oh, yes please. And a hot tub,' I answer. I close my eyes, all distractions from the world shut off in our little room. The heat is relaxing the muscles in my lower back. I stretch out along the bench and decide that I'll join a gym when I get home and do this again.

'We'll sleep well tonight,' Olly murmurs.

With reluctance we shower and return to Nomad to find the kids.

'No sign of them,' I say to Olly. 'Will we go look for them?'

'Mam, Dad!' Evie's voice screams, and when I turn to follow the sound of her voice, I see her running towards us, obviously distressed.

That feeling of foreboding I felt earlier returns and floods my entire body.

'I can't find Jamie,' she says, tears running down her face.

'When did you last see him?' Olly asks.

'About ten minutes ago,' Evie admits.

'Where?' I scream. 'Quick, Evie, tell us everything.'

'We were down by the lake. He was right in front of me playing. Then I looked up and he was gone,' Evie cries. 'I'm so sorry, Mam. I'm so sorry.'

'Where have you looked?' I ask.

'Everywhere. I can't find him,' she says.

'Go to reception and get help,' I tell Olly, 'I'll go back to the lake and keep looking.'

As I run, I shout his name, 'Jamie! Jamie! Jamie!'

But there's no reply. No shock of blond unruly hair bouncing towards me. No cheeky face saying, 'I superhero robot Jamie.'

I scream louder, 'Jamie!' running all the time towards the lake. I can hear Evie sobbing beside me, but I've not got time to deal with that now.

'Has anyone seen a little blond boy, aged seven, wearing a blue t-shirt?' I shout to the few people who are on the shore.

Everyone shakes their heads. 'Please, if you see him, his name is Jamie, keep him here, don't let him move.'

I run up and down the lake shore and scream his name over and over.

Nothing. Evie and I look at each other.

'Would he go into the water? Did he say he wanted to go into the water?' I scream at her.

'No,' Evie says. But she looks doubtful. If he's in the water . . . Oh God, I can't breathe . . .

I run to the water's edge and start wading in, screaming his name over and over. By now there are people all around me, calling his name too. I see two men in the water with me.

'Mam,' Evie screams, pulling at my arm. 'What are you doing?'

I don't know what I'm doing. I feel like I'm running around a maze, hitting brick walls. I stop and stand in the water to look around me. It's still, bar the wind-surfers, who are skitting along the lake.

'They would have seen a little boy, wouldn't they?' I say to Evie. 'If he came out, they would have seen him if he were in trouble.'

A man shouts to me, 'I've been here for the past hour. I didn't see a little boy near the water. I don't think he could be out there.'

The men beside me tell me that they will stay in the water, to go back and keep looking.

I turn to wade back to the shore and see a path towards a wooded area. Fear returns. Someone's taken him. I know it. He's been abducted while I had a sauna. I want to fall to the ground and close my eyes from my horror but instead I start to run towards that path. I quicken my pace, but I'm hindered by wet trainers. So I throw them off and continue barefoot, screaming for my baby all the time.

I no longer am thinking about him drowning, now I'm imagining a stranger greeting Jamie and leading him by the hand into the woods.

I run faster than I've ever run before in my life, my eyes darting in all directions.

'Mae,' I hear Olly's voice chasing me. He grabs me around my waist and halts me from my frantic search.

'The staff have started a search party. We'll find him,' he says. He sounds reasonable and calm and I slap his hands away from me. Later I will find out that he's vomited a few moments earlier, from the same fear – that our boy is taken.

My head is spinning but I cannot stop until I find my son.

Then without any warning, it starts to pour with rain. The sun disappears and clouds darken the landscape. The once-pretty vista now looks ominous.

'Jamie,' I scream again, 'Baby, where are you?'

Evie and Olly are shouting his name too and I'm aware of others around me, helping in our search.

'What if we don't find him?' I say to Olly. 'It's getting dark.'

'We'll find him,' Olly repeats, but I notice that he's white as snow and sweat has soaked his shirt.

'Sshh . . . did you hear that?' I say, turning towards the sound.

We stand still, the three of us and listen.

'Mammmmy . . .' A child's voice. It's Jamie. He's calling for me.

I start running towards the sound of his voice, calling his name over and over.

'Where is he?' I shout to Olly, frustrated that he has not appeared in front of me.

We stop and look around us, then Evie shouts, 'Look over there. In those bushes. I can see something blue.'

We run towards that flash of colour, all three of us shouting for him. I hear his voice again, weaker now, 'Mammmmy. Daddddddy.'

And then I see my baby and nothing else matters. He's on the ground and crying, 'Mammy, I hurt my leg.'

I crawl over to him and he's soaked to the skin. But he smiles through tears now that we are by his side.

'Sshh. It's okay. You're okay. We're here now,' I tell him and scoop him into my arms.

'Mammy,' he sobs and I begin to cry too, heaving sobs that rack my body. I hear Evie crying too. Olly holds onto her and wipes tears of his own away.

'*Danke. Danke,*' I hear Olly say to the helpers and word begins to spread that we have found him.

'We need to get out of the rain,' Olly says, and picks up his son in his arms.

The manager of the campsite looks like he might cry with relief too when he sees us emerge. He leads us into his office, where he calls a doctor to check out Jamie's leg.

It turns out to be just a sprain and other than a few scratches as he fell down, he's unharmed. An hour later, we go back to Nomad and tuck him up in a makeshift bed on the sofa.

'I just wanted to practise my superhero moves,' he tells us. 'But then I got lost and I couldn't find my way back. I was running super-fast, then I tripped.'

'It's my fault,' Evie says. 'I was looking at my phone. I didn't see you go.'

'We've all learnt a lesson here. We need to be more careful. All of us,' I tell them. 'But you . . . ' I say to our son, 'No more running off.'

'I promise, Mam,' he says.

I walk into our bedroom, Olly follows me.

'What would we have done if we had lost him?' he says.

'We'd have blamed ourselves for the rest of time,' I reply. 'And we would have been right to. That's a warning. We can't leave him alone for a minute. We shouldn't have left him with Evie. It's not her responsibility.'

'Agreed,' he answers.

'For a few moments there, I was convinced he'd been snatched. Or drowned,' I say to Olly.

'Don't,' Olly replies.

'We'll have to stay put this evening. To give his leg a chance to heal. The doctor said keep him off it overnight and he should be fine,' I say.

'What about you?' he asks, looking at my feet, which are scratched and bloody from my barefoot run through the woods. He walks to the bathroom and comes back with a dampened towel and begins cleaning the cuts.

'You need to keep your feet up too,' he says, giving me a hug.

'I'm fine,' I say and I am. I'll never complain about anything ever again. I head back to Jamie and snuggle under the duvet with him. 'Let's see if we can find a movie to watch,' I say to him and Evie.

'Can I sleep with you tonight, Mam?' Jamie asks.

I hug him close and look at Olly, who is nodding at me. 'Yes. You and me can have a sleepover tonight. Dad can sleep on the couch.'

'Nothing like Mammy-hugs after a bad fright,' Olly says and fresh tears threaten to fall. I think of the insecurities I have spent months worrying about and am shamed at how trivial they are. Who cares who Jamie needs more? All that matters is that he is safe and loved by both Olly and me. I hold him tighter.

Jamie looks up to me and says, 'Mam?'

'What, darling?' I say to him, my heart bursting with love for my little man.

'I'm starving,' he announces.

And with that we all start to laugh – uncontrolled, hysterical laughter.

'That's my boy,' I say.

Chapter Twenty-Nine

Dear Olly and Mae

So it's Auf Wiedersehen to Germany. Until we see you again. I much prefer that, than goodbye, which seems so final.

And drum roll here . . . say 'Gruus Got' to Austria for week three. That's hello, to you and me.

You will be making your way to Vienna, via Innsbruck and Salzburg. It looks like a wonderful drive with lots to do along the way. I've made some bookings for campsites that I think you'll enjoy.

I've two events organised for you this week. In Salzburg, get ready to sing 'Edelweiss' because I've arranged for you all to go on a Sound of Music tour. This one is for Mae. She's made us sit through that movie every year at Christmas now for near-on twenty years. I've a feeling that she might like to release her inner Maria.

When you are in Vienna, I want you all to learn

a new skill, one that I think you should enjoy. You'll be learning how to waltz.

What's it the kids do now? Twerking, Evie told me. Nobody waltzes any more. Beth and I did, we were quite good, if I do say so myself. I loved holding her in my arms, whizzing around the floor.

Well in Vienna, the waltz is as popular as ever and you'll be learning it in a palace. I wish I'd have had the chance to bring Beth to Vienna. She'd have loved it there, I think.

There's romance in every turn of the floor, I promise you. It has a sneaking, disarming charm that I think you'll find irresistible.

When I close my eyes now, I imagine what the trip will be like for you all. At first, when I dreamt this adventure up, I just wanted to give you all a distraction from your regular life. But the more I've worked on the itinerary, the more I hope that you are being influenced by everything you are experiencing. With each new destination, I hope that you are being exposed to new diverse cultures. I hope that you are all beginning to look at the world with different eyes.

I suppose you could all be back home in Wexford by now if it's all gone wrong. But I hope not. I'm going to have faith that you are all grabbing the opportunity to learn not just about the places you are visiting, the people you meet, but more importantly, about yourselves.

With love,
Pops x

Chapter Thirty

OLLY

The room is quiet as we all take in Pops' words, digesting this latest missive.

'If you thought my German was pants, wait till you hear my Austrian,' I say.

'German is the official language there,' Mae says, smiling at me. 'We might even get fluent yet.'

'We need to get some basic phrases learnt,' I say. 'I mean, we can't be fluent, but I think it's only good manners that we at least try to have some stock sentences ready that we can use.'

'Good thinking,' Mae says.

'Fancy doing that for us?' I nudge Evie. 'Just prepare a list of phrases that we might use every day and teach us lot as we drive along?'

I'm half expecting her to give me a dirty look, shake her head vehemently and stick it back into the goddamn iPod. But I've noticed that Evie is unsure of herself. And she never used to be like that. She was always fearless, but those stupid girls have knocked her confidence. She just needs to start trusting herself and her abilities. Maybe giving her a few jobs, some responsibility, might help build her up.

'That's a great idea,' Mae says.

Finally, Evie looks up and says one word. 'Okay.'

'That's my girl.'

'I'm not doing any dancing,' Jamie declares. 'Superheroes don't do twirling.'

'How do you know?' Mae asks. 'Remember what Pops said, grab every opportunity.'

'I had to go horseriding, so you have to dance, dude,' I say.

I wait for his retort, but he surprises with, 'When is Pops coming back, do you think?' I think I've misheard him.

'What do you mean?' I ask.

'Pops, when does he come back again? He said that he'd always find a way to come back. I just wish he'd do it soon.' The whole time he speaks, he keeps playing with his toy on the table in front of him. 'I miss him.'

And then he starts to cry. Silent tears at first, spilling in big fat splashes onto the Formica table. Then, as if a dam has burst inside of him, he starts to sob loudly, his skinny little frame shuddering.

I thought he was doing okay. More than okay, as he seemed to be more interested in playing than talking about Pops and his death.

Mae has scooped him into her arms and is gently rocking him.

'I miss him,' Evie says.

'I'm sad too, guys. We all are,' Mae says.

I search through the briefcase and pull out the bundle of letters, untying them. I flick through them, till I locate the first letter. I want to find the exact words, here it is!

But grief is inevitable. So I'll not tell you to stop crying.

'It's okay to cry. It's okay to mourn his absence,' I say, pointing to his words.

'Remember, Pops is here, in our hearts,' Mae says. 'I am in awe at how much he loved all of us. That's what keeps me going.'

I grab some kitchen roll and pass it to Mae, to help mop up Jamie's face. That's the thing about grief and loss. You think you are doing okay, then suddenly you are on your knees, hobbled by it.

'Just think of how much work he put into this trip. How thoughtful he's been,' Mae continues and we all nod.

'Do you think he's going to come back?' Jamie asks.

'I think he'll find a way to let us know he's thinking of us. He always does. I speak to him a lot. In my head, I tell him stuff and sometimes I can hear him, see him,' I say and this seems to mollify him. His breathing regularises and his tears stop.

'Go to Daddy,' Mae says, passing him over to me for a cuddle.

'You okay?' She turns to Evie.

Evie shrugs.

Mae picks up the letter and passes it to Evie. 'I think your first translation should be finding the word for lederhosen!'

'I'm not wearing any lederhosen,' I say. 'Don't be getting any ideas.'

'And don't even think of making dresses out of curtains for me,' Evie says, a smile beginning to come onto her face.

'Oh, you'll all be singing the hills are alive by the time that tour is over. I know you lot,' Mae says.

I pull out the battered atlas and open up Austria. And the four of us huddle over it, heads touching, as we look over our route for the next week. Germany has been a mixed bag for me. Parts of it were incredible, others not so good.

We leave Germany with the anticipation of a new week in a new country at an all-time high. For me, Austria feels like we are venturing into unknown territory. I notice the changing landscape around me and slow Nomad down.

'Kids. Take a look at that,' I say to them and am gratified to hear suitable oohs and aahs from them in response. We are looking at snow-covered mountain tops, with waterfalls and glaciers on either side of us.

The road is quite good, but even so, I drive carefully. Soon, the peaks of the Otzal Alps stand proud and tall in front of us.

'What's that?' Jamie asks as I drive right into the heart of the Tyrolean Arctic.

'It's a glacier region. No wonder it's called the most beautiful spot in Austria,' Mae answers.

We take our time and whenever I find a spot to park up safely, I do, and we take dozens of photographs. I've always felt that Ireland is one of the most beautiful countries in the world, with amazing diverse landscapes. But this here, well, it's competition for my home country.

We find a village that looks like it's straight out of a folk story and eat ice-cream. I think back to our first few days of the trip, licking ice-creams on the beach in Normandy and can hardly credit that we are now here.

It's slightly surreal looking at snow-capped mountains in the sunshine and I promise Jamie that I'll bring him back one day to ski.

After the drama of Jamie going missing, we stick closer together. Evie, to my surprise, is going for several hours at a time without pining for Wi-Fi. When we find our campsite in Otz, a pretty town that lies on a sunny slope at the foot of the Alps, she doesn't even mention it once. We've begun to find our rhythm as a family again. It's as if we suddenly have lost our two left feet and are no longer tripping each other up.

The drive towards Salzburg is another lazy, enjoyable day, enjoying the landscape and beauty around us. There's a quiet beauty to Austria. Mae said last night that she feels like it's almost magical. And while I normally don't go for that kind of stuff, I can see where she's coming from.

We have some fun teasing Evie while she tries to teach us some basic phrases in German. She's taken to my task with surprising vigour and, in fairness, takes our messing on the chin. And despite our proclamations of never wanting to see another castle again, we all vote to go check out a palace en route, the Schloss Ambras. We stop to light a candle in a beautiful church called the Wiltener

Basilica, and I feel a serenity that I've not experienced in a long time. The frantic, at times manic and fast pace, of the previous few weeks, has been replaced by this gentler transition.

And when we spend our second night in Austria in the most basic campsite we've come across so far, everyone seems to find it hilarious. A few short weeks back, this would have sent us into complete panic. With no electricity, we just light candles and a barbecue, chatting about our favourite moments of the trip so far.

'Are you tired from all the driving?' Mae asks me as we set off towards Salzburg early the next morning.

'Best vantage from the driving seat,' I answer. 'It's more fun than I thought it would be. The odd time I'm wrecked from it, but in the main, it's grand. Honest.'

Once I mastered Nomad's little quirks, I've started to enjoy myself.

'The difference in you, this week, is quite remarkable,' Mae says.

'How so?'

'Well, look at you now, drinking coffee as you drive. You wouldn't even let *me* drink a coffee in the first week!' Mae laughs.

I suppose I'm no longer terrified any more. 'I thought I'd never get it up that ramp going into the ferry in Rosslare. Look at this now.' I wave at the steep incline we're slowly making our way up.

'I always had faith in you,' Mae says and I feel like a boss.

'And you? Are you won over by Nomad's charms yet?' I ask.

'Evie and I were only talking about that very same subject. There are moments that I miss our home. But I'm finding that I'm missing the things I thought I would the most, the least.'

'Like what?'

'Shoes, handbags, stuff. All the gadgets in the kitchen. A hair dryer. When I think of the hours every week I spend blow-drying my hair!'

'And you've never looked better,' I say.

'Charmer.'

'I tell it like it is. But are you glad this charmer talked you into this?' I ask this quietly, holding my breath.

'Hell, yes.'

And then we smile at each other and at that moment, a ray of light hits her brown eyes and they change colour. They look like spun gold and her skin translucent in the beam.

'I love you so much,' I whisper.

'I know,' she whispers back. 'I love you too.'

'If this were Hollywood, I'd stop and pull you into my arms right now.'

'Why don't you?' Mae asks.

'Because, if I do, Nomad might just roll back down this hill!' I say.

'I keep forgetting we're basically driving a house,' Mae laughs. 'Drive on.'

We stop for lunch in the Tyrolean city of Lienz, which lies at the junction of three valleys. Another afternoon wandering the cobblestoned streets of Lienz helps to walk off our big lunch.

It starts to get dark early and once we get to our

campsite on the outskirts of Salzburg, it's quite late. The amazing panoramic views make us gasp and excited to explore the following day.

'I've not seen you this excited about anything in years!' I say to Mae. She's trying on her third outfit, trying to work out what to wear for our tour.

'I've loved this musical ever since I was a little girl,' she says, breathless as she pulls a dress over her head.

'Pretty,' I tell her.

'I just can't believe that I'll be following in Julie Andrews' footsteps today!' she tells me. '*The Sound of Music* is one of the most iconic love stories of all time. The steely-eyed Captain von Trapp falling for singing nun Maria. Who can resist that?'

'Nobody,' I agree, joyful to see Mae so happy.

'I used to wish she would come be my governess when I was a little girl. I dreamed of her making me an outfit from my nana's living-room curtains.'

Mae then twirls out of the room, launching into song as she goes, 'I simply remember my favourite things, And then I don't feel . . . so bad!'

'You're going to sing all day today, aren't you?' I ask.

'Yes!' Mae sings back to me.

I check my watch. It's time to go grab our taxi into Salzburg.

Maybe it's Mae's enthusiasm, but we all get swept up in musical mania. We find ourselves singing along with the rest of the nut-job fans that are on the *Sound of Music* bus tour. Some of them *are* wearing lederhosen. And there are several nuns and one Captain von Trapp.

When we find ourselves in a flowery meadow at the foot of the alpine peaks and lakes, it takes no encouragement from our tour guide to make us all spin around with arms outstretched. Soon there are a dozen mismatched voices all belting out 'The hills are alive, with the sound of music!'

Then we stop at the Benedictine convent on Nonnberg and everyone has a go at solving the problem of Maria. In song. And the tour guide insists we all line up in rows to sing 'Do-Re-Mi' in front of the Mirabell Gardens and Palace. One or two of the tourists take it too far, in my opinion, when they start jumping up and down on the railings.

There's great excitement when we arrive at *The Sound of Music* pavilion, which is at Hellbrunn Palace. Mae and I both torture poor Evie by singing to her 'I am sixteen going on seventeen'. Then the rest of the bus starts to join in too. She may never forgive us for that one.

When we reach Leopoldskron Palace, the ladies on the bus all get particularly excited.

'It's the famed balcony where the captain and Maria first dance!' the tour guide shouts, creating even more hysteria.

I take a look at Mae's face and decide, feck it. I grab her and spin her around in a clumsy attempt at a waltz. My moment of romantic spontaneity gets a round of applause from everyone and I get a kiss from Mae. Result!

I will admit to feeling a bit emotional now that we are at the Felsenreitschule. It's where the Von Trapp family performed their farewell song and Captain von Trapp sang 'Edelweiss'. I can't imagine living in a time where the safety of your family and country was so perilous.

The day flies by in a musical flash and, by the end of it, we all have our hallmark cheesy grins back.

We feast on wiener schnitzel, dumplings and apple strudel, washed down with cold frothy beer and home-made lemonade, declaring the day a triumph. Jamie falls asleep in the taxi on the way back to our campsite, so we decide to have an early night once again.

Mae and Evie can't help themselves, they start to sing 'The sun has gone to bed and so must I,' as they climb into their beds. They think they're hilarious. And they're right. I don't think I've laughed so much, continuously, in years.

Me? Well, I'm just grateful for the magic of Austria, because it's putting smiles on both of my girls. And that's priceless.

Our early night pays dividends and we all arise early so we can do some last-minute sightseeing in Salzburg. We fulfill Mae's ambition to follow the Von Trapp family's final path to freedom by huffing and puffing our way up the towering Untersberg peak.

'Climb every mountain, Forge every stream, Follow every rainbow, Till you find your dream,' Mae belts out, insisting that we all hold hands as we get to the top to recreate the movie's final scene.

'Happy now?' I ask her.

'Delirious,' she replies. 'Pops has just succeeded in ticking off one of my life-long ambitions.'

We opt for the route nicknamed the 'Austrian Romantic Road' when we head to Vienna. As we follow the River

Danube I wonder how we will ever go back to our lives in Ireland. Less than three weeks on the road and I can see how addictive this nomadic life must be for many. I allow myself to daydream about not going back. Ever. I wonder what they would all think if I suggested that we stayed in Europe, following the road wherever it takes us. Mae and I are happy. There would be no bullying for Evie. And Jamie, sure, he's happy no matter where he is.

I say all this to Mae. And she looks at me like I've just suggested we fly to the moon.

'What about work? How would we finance it all?'

And just like that, the big fat elephant is back in the room, pissing us all off and stomping all over our lovely, happy day.

But before I have the chance to fester about work, or lack thereof, I have to concentrate on the road. The Danube valley we are now in has small roads that are not unlike the ones back home in rural Ireland. I'm surprised to feel nostalgic at this comparison. We pass through villages crammed with historical old churches, ancient houses and cobblestone streets.

'This part of Europe is fierce fond of their cobblestones,' I say to Mae, determined to break the uneasy silence that's descended between us. Please Mae, let it drop. Don't let's fight.

And she must be getting better at reading my mind, because she replies,

'Well, I can't say I love them!' she says. 'I keep twisting my ankle!'

'How much further?' Jamie asks. 'I'm bored.'

'Stick on a DVD for Jamie, will ya?' I ask Evie. 'We've about another hour to go.'

'I'm glad Pops sent us to Austria,' Mae says.

'And it's a gift doing the journey this way. I hate to think of all we'd have missed out on by just flying into an airport,' I reply.

'Yep. Nomad has a knack of making you see places that are off the beaten track alright. Tonight we're in a campsite right on the outskirts of the city centre,' Mae says. 'There's a bus and train we can get to bring us into Vienna.'

'That's handy,' I say. We've realised, very quickly into this adventure, that campsites close to public transport are the way to go.

'And the city's biggest shopping mall is close by too!' Mae throws in. 'We packed so light, I'm getting a bit bored of wearing the same clothes every day.'

'Is that your way at hinting for a shopping trip?' I laugh.

'I thought that you could drop me in the centre on the way to the park. I could get a taxi, then, to you guys later on, in time to cook the barbecue. I wouldn't mind some time to myself, if I'm honest,' Mae says.

'Why? What's wrong?' I ask.

'Nothing at all,' Mae says. 'It's just we're in each other's pockets constantly. I would like a few hours to myself. Wouldn't you?'

'I hadn't really thought about it,' I say. I feel peeved. Slighted. And petty all at once. I know it's a perfectly reasonable request, her wanting some time out. But I don't like it.

'Is this because of the comment about not wanting to go back to Ireland and me finding a job?' I say and the look on her face immediately tells me that it's not.

'For goodness sake, Olly. If it's that big of a deal, we can all go shopping. Happy now?' Mae says.

'No. It's fine,' I say and even though I try to disguise it, I know that my voice is curt.

I don't even need to look to know that she's frowning and I know that I've killed our mood with my irrational response. We drive in silence for the next thirty minutes and I try to work out why I got so freaked about Mae wandering off on her own.

'We need to take the next exit,' Mae says, breaking the silence.

'I'm sorry,' I say. 'I can't work out what the hell is wrong with me. I just kind of panicked when you said you wanted to go on your own.'

'Why on earth?' she asks.

'I don't know. I genuinely don't,' I say. 'I just feel scared.'

'You've never been clingy before,' she says.

'It's not that. I promise you, I'm not being clingy. A fecking eejit, maybe, but not clingy,' I say.

'I won't argue with that,' she says.

'It's just we're in a strange city we've never been in before. What if something happened to you?' I say.

'Oh, Olly. I'm a big girl. I'm able to take care of myself,' she replies.

'I know. I told you. I'm an eejit. I think I'm still a bit jittery after Jamie getting lost the other day. It shook me,' I say.

She doesn't look convinced and I don't blame her. 'And

we couldn't cope without you. Me and the kids. If something were to happen to you, we'd not cope.'

I keep my eyes fixed on the road ahead all the time. I think if I turn around to look at my wife, I might cry.

I reckon I've cried more than the kids on this trip. That's not good. One thing being a sensitive guy; another being a total sap.

'What's the name of that mall? I just saw a sign for one there,' I ask.

'Shopping City Süd,' Mae replies.

'Right, there it is, just over there. I'll drop you off and you call me if you have any problems getting a taxi back to the campsite. I'll come get you, no problem at all,' I say.

'I've a compromise,' Mae replies. 'Why don't we all go in, but you take the kids off for a drink and snack. Give me an hour to do some shopping by myself and then we'll head back to the campsite together.'

'You don't mind?' I ask.

'It's the perfect solution. Knowing my luck, had I ordered a taxi myself, I would have ended back in Salzburg!' I know she's letting me off the hook, but I'm relieved she does.

When I see that the mall has 250 shops in it, I realise that one hour isn't going to cut it. 'Let's make it two hours to meet back here,' I say.

I look at the Obi-Wan figurine on the dash, when Mae jumps out and practically runs from Nomad. I need some help here, Pops. I'm screwing things up again by acting like a total dickhead. What will I buy her? Some flowers? No, that's stupid. A vase would only fall in transit.

And then a couple walk by pushing a heavily loaded IKEA cart in front of them. Pops, you genius. I know exactly what to do. I turn to the kids and point to the couple, 'Look, I have a plan!'

Chapter Thirty-One

OLLY

'I cannot wait to see Mam's face when she gets back,' Jamie says to me.

'If we're quick, we can have it in place and made before then,' I say. 'Hold on tight to the front, kids.'

Between us we are managing to balance a new memory-foam mattress on our large IKEA trolley. Mae has tossed and turned for almost three weeks now, complaining about the crappy mattress on our double bed. I'd been kicking myself that I'd not changed it before we left Ireland.

'What are you going to do with the old mattress, Dad?' Evie asks.

'I'll have to put it in the garage,' I say. 'Till we find a place to dump it.'

'We can sunbathe on it!' Evie says.

'Can I get a new mattress too?' Jamie asks.

'You never miss a trick, do you, kid?' I say with a laugh. 'Not today, but another day, maybe.'

We get a few surprised looks from passersby, but that

only makes us giggle more. With a little help from the kids, I heave the new mattress onto Nomad. I pull out the old one and stash it in the kitchen.

'Help me take off the plastic cover,' I say to the kids. It fits as if it was made for our bed frame and we all flop back on top of it to try it out.

A communal groan from us all fills the small room as we sink into it.

'What's going on? Why is there a mattress in the kitchen?' Mae asks and we all jump at her voice.

'Ah, damn it, I wanted to have it made before you got back,' I say. 'Get up!' I tell the kids.

Mae walks in and I point to the new mattress saying, 'Ta da!'

She's stunned into silence and I lead her over to the bed so she can sit down on it.

'You bought a mattress?' she says. 'I was only gone for a few hours.'

'I did. You've had to put up with that crappy one for long enough. What with your back and all. This is a memory-foam one,' I say, delighted with myself.

'Olly Guinness, that is the most romantic thing you've ever done for me in my whole life,' Mae says and pulls me into her for a hug.

'We got some sun loungers too,' Evie adds.

'And a hammock for me!' Jamie says.

'My, you've been busy!' Mae laughs. 'Well, we better get to the campsite so, to try them all out!'

'Did you get a dress?' I ask.

'I got something for everyone,' she says. 'But they are a surprise. I'll give them to you later.'

She lies back on the bed again and sighs. 'I also dropped into the supermarket and picked up some stuff for a barbecue. We should come back here again. There's a cinema too!'

And just like that, things seem to be back on track again. The campsite turns out to be only a few minutes' drive away. No matter which way we try to dress it up, it's the most basic and unappealing of all the campsites we've stayed in.

'At least it's got electricity and water, which is the main thing,' Mae says.

'We've just gotten spoiled by the other sites,' I say to the kids, who are not happy.

'I bet there's no Wi-Fi,' Evie grumbles, walking around in circles, trying to find a signal.

'There's no pool or playground,' Jamie chimes in.

'First-world problems, kids,' Mae says. 'Evie, you had Wi-Fi earlier in the shopping centre, don't pretend you weren't FaceTiming Luke then, whilst simultaneously messaging Ann! You can last till tomorrow, when I daresay we'll come across a signal at some point. Jamie, there will be pools again in a few days. You'll cope,' Mae says.

Jamie and I lay out our groundsheet and then I add our new sun loungers onto it, followed by the table and chairs.

We pull down the awning and stick up Mae's lanterns and, between them and the sun-lounger cushions, it looks bright and colourful.

'Sweet,' a voice says and we look up to see two middle-aged women and a teenage girl staring at us. 'Nice set-up.'

'Oh thanks,' I say. 'We just arrived.'

'We got here yesterday,' she replies. 'Watch out for the laundry. The machines eat tokens.'

'Thanks for the warning,' I say.

'There's a nicer site a few miles out. But this is much more convenient for the city,' she says.

'Ah, we've already had complaints from the management about the lack of Wi-Fi,' I joke, pointing to the kids.

'Don't get me started!' she laughs. 'I'm Judith, by the way.' She points to the other lady and says, 'This is Lorna. And this here is our daughter, Lulu.'

I walk over and shake all their hands, introducing each of us.

'That an Irish accent?' Judith asks.

'Guilty as charged,' I say. 'From Wexford. We're on a tour of Europe. What part of America are you from?' There's no mistaking their accents.

'Down south, Kentucky,' she answers. 'That's us over there.' She points to the motor home to our right. 'Nice talking to you.'

We get the barbecue lighted and then, whilst the coals heat up, I open a bottle of beer from the fridge and lie back on the sun lounger. It feels like a slice of heaven.

'Don't drink too many of them tonight,' Mae whispers in my ear, waking me up from my almost-snooze. 'We've got a new bed to christen.'

'Knew that bed was a good decision,' I say with a grin.

'Go back to sleep,' Mae tells me and starts cooking the barbecue whilst Evie lays the table.

'I'll never smell charcoal again without thinking about this trip,' Mae murmurs.

'We don't barbecue enough at home,' I say. 'Why is that?'

'No idea. Seems like too much effort or something, maybe. But it's not, when you think about it. Or at least no more than cooking a meal, anyhow,' Mae says.

And when she puts that first piece of pork onto the hot flames and the fat and meat mix with the sweet aromatic barbecue sauce, the aroma makes my stomach groan in anticipation.

Evie and Jamie are sitting at the table playing cards together.

'Amazing what no Wi-Fi can do!' Mae mouths to me. 'Alleluia!'

After a meal that tastes even nicer than it smelled, we get coerced into a game of gin rummy by Jamie. Drinking beer, playing cards as the sun goes down is up there now as one of my favourite things to do.

'Hello.' We look up and Lulu is standing a few feet from us. She looks expectantly at us and I cotton on after a moment that she is waiting for an invite to come over.

So I oblige and introduce her to Evie and Mae.

'I don't know how to play this game,' she admits.

'I'll show you,' Evie tells her and within a few minutes the two of them are giggling away like best friends.

Mae nudges me and I mouth, 'I know!' Seeing Evie so relaxed with someone new is something we've not seen for a long time. She looks happy.

Then Judith and Lorna join us too and it begins to feel like a party. The coals of the barbecue are still glowing and with the lanterns twinkling in the twilight, the campsite starts to grow on me.

'So how long are you in Europe for?' Mae asks.

'About three months. But we're flexible,' Lorna says.

'Wow. We thought eight weeks was a long trip!' Mae says.

'Well in total we're on a year-long trip,' Lorna replies. 'We decided to quit the rat race and take a year's sabbatical.'

'Okay. Now you've got my attention!' Mae replies. 'What about school for Lulu? Sorry, I'm a teacher, just being nosey here.'

'We're home-schooling,' Lorna says. 'And Lulu is already months ahead of her curriculum, so it's working out for us.'

'That's impressive,' I say. 'What made you decide to take off?'

'For me I'd been feeling restless and frustrated for months. I felt dissatisfied with life, I suppose,' Lorna says. 'Like there had to be more to it than the humdrum days our life had become.'

'It's not that we weren't okay at home,' Judith jumps in. 'Lulu was happy in school and we have a nice house at home. We both had jobs.'

'Are you married to each other?' Jamie squeaks, to which Evie gives him a box on his arm, saying, 'Sshhh . . . '

But luckily they all laugh and Lorna says, 'Yes, Judith is my wife.'

'But you're a woman. And so is she,' Jamie says.

'I am,' she replies. She's smiling and taking his questions in her stride.

'So you have two mammies?' Jamie asks Lulu.

'Yep,' Lulu answers and she looks a bit defensive. I'm about to intervene and tell Jamie to quit his questions, when he just says, 'Cool,' and continues drinking his juice.

'Sorry about that. Seven-year-old inquisitive mind. Please go on,' Mae says.

'No apologies needed. Nice he shows an interest. Well, one day I was online and came across a blog about a Canadian family who were touring the world. I started to read about their experiences and the more I read, the more my heart hungered for a similar experience,' Judith admits.

'So she came home and said to Lulu and me that she wanted us to take a year out. We thought she'd lost it,' Lorna laughs. 'But then the more we talked about it, the more the idea appealed to us. I realised that I still have dreams that are not yet fulfilled. Maybe a year out can help me work out what I want to do.'

'Wow,' Mae says. 'So what happened then?'

'Well, I'm a freelance journalist, so I realised that I could still work, no matter where we lived. I write features about my travels,' Judith says. 'And last month, I started to work on a novel. I've always wanted to do that, but never seemed to find the time.'

'That's fantastic,' Mae tells her. 'You've worked out what you want to do already!'

We all clink our glasses to that.

'And what about you, Judith? Are you more content now?' I ask her.

'Well, yes . . . and no. I'm happy, I love Lorna and Lulu and I'm getting great pleasure in the simple things. But I still haven't worked out what I want to do when this year is up. I do know that I'll never go back to working in an office again,' Judith replies.

We've all stopped playing cards now, caught up in the magic of their story.

'What do you do, Olly?' Lorna asks.

'I'm a stay-at-home dad,' I reply. I knew she was going to ask me this and I hate how crap my answer makes me feel. I shouldn't be ashamed. But I am.

'Good for you,' Lorna says.

'It wasn't by choice,' I admit. 'I've spent years working as an accountant, but was made redundant. So now I need to figure out what to do next. Like you, I know I don't want to go back to that type of role again.'

'I hear you,' Judith says.

'Must have been tough losing your job, though,' Lorna sympathises.

'Yeah, it was at the time. For all of us – Mae in particular. But I've enjoyed the past year all the same, spending time at home.' And it's only as I say this, I realise that I've not really acknowledged that before. I've spent the past year thinking only about how much my redundancy impacted me, but it wasn't just me living through that. Mae was too.

'I bet,' Lorna says. 'You've great kids.'

'I'll drink to that,' I say, so we all clink our glasses together.

I can feel Mae's eyes boring holes into me, but I am resolute in not meeting her eyes. I've just seen something clearly that's been sitting right in front of me and I feel like a right eejit. How did I get so bloody self-centred that I made it all about me this past year?

'Where have you been so far?' Evie asks, saving me from my guilty conscience by changing the subject.

'We started off in Denmark. Lulu wanted to go to Legoland,' Judith says and we all laugh.

'Can we go there?' Jamie asks. 'I want to go to Legoland.'

'That's up to Pops,' I say, delighted to have absolution on this matter.

'We're heading to Italy next, via Slovenia,' Judith says.

'After Europe, we're gonna backpack around South East Asia and India for three or four months,' Lorna tells us.

'That's so cool,' Jamie says. 'I wish we could do that.'

'Maybe one day,' I say with a laugh.

We tell them about our own adventure courtesy of Pops.

'That's an awesome story. A mystery every week,' Lulu says.

'Lots of memories being created, for sure,' Mae says.

'We've found that we are making our best memories when we throw away the guidebook and just see where we end up,' Lorna tells us.

'Do you remember that village festival in Germany?' Judith asks and she throws her head back in a loud guffaw. 'We took a wrong turn and before we knew it, we were driving behind a parade with a marching band. We pulled up and had an awesome time,' Judith says.

'Mom won a prize in a raffle,' Lulu says giggling. 'It was a rabbit!'

'A live rabbit?' I ask.

'No, a dead one! It was for us to eat that night,' Judith replies. 'I mean, I would have been happy with a bottle of wine or a box of chocolates, but a rabbit? No thanks!'

After a while the kids go inside Nomad to watch a DVD, bored with us adults now. We continue chatting, drinking wine and beer and swapping stories about our travels.

'I hate to break up the party, but I need to get the kids to bed,' Mae says. 'Jamie must be about to drop.'

As they turn to leave, Judith says to us, 'You know something, you guys have an awesome family. Thanks for letting us be a part of it tonight.'

'They were nice,' I say to Mae as we clear away the empty bottles and dishes.

'Yeah, I liked them too.'

'Don't think I've ever been called awesome before,' I joke.

'Not often we get to see how others see us,' Mae states. 'I liked their spirit. In particular what they said about throwing away the guidebook. We could learn a lot from that, I think.'

'How do you mean?' I ask.

'Maybe we all need to stop thinking about where we're going and just see where we end up,' Mae replies.

'You, Mae Guinness, are fucking awesome,' I say, truly astounded by her.

'I know,' she answers and I've never loved her more.

Chapter Thirty-Two

JAMIE

Mam and Dad want to have a 'talk'.

They look so serious. I bet they've found out that I broke Dad's radio yesterday. I'll be paying for that out of my pocket money for years.

'I can explain everything,' I start. 'I was just jumping from my bed when . . . '

'We want to talk to you about Judith and Lorna,' Mam says at the same time, stopping me mid-flow.

Phew! It's not about the radio.

'What can you explain?' Dad asks.

'Nothing,' I say, giving them my best 'I didn't do it' smile.

They look at each other and decide to let it pass because Dad says, 'There are all kinds of families in the world.'

'Okay,' I say. I'm not sure where they're going with this.

'Like, for example, there are families like us, with a mam and a dad,' Mam tells me.

'And then there are families with two mams and no dad. Like Judith, Lorna and Lulu. Or sometimes two dads and no mam,' Dad continues.

They are both smiling at me in a really weird way. I figure I should smile back too.

'And in some families, there is only a dad or a mam,' Dad tells me.

'Like Eric,' I say. 'My friend in school. He doesn't have a dad. Or at least not any more. His dad lives with his Aunty Mary now.'

'Yes. Like Eric,' Mam says. She looks sad now.

'Oh, don't be sad for him, Mam. I think he likes his Aunty Mary,' I tell her. 'She buys him chocolate a lot.'

'I'm not so sure his mam is so fond of Mary. But that's another story,' Mam says, making Dad laugh.

She then grabs one of my hands and asks me, 'What do you think makes a family?'

'Hmm,' I think about that for a minute.

Then I picture our own family. 'Easy! Love makes a family.'

Mam gets all weird when I say this. She starts to cry. Dad starts ruffling my hair and coughing and fidgeting. They are so weird.

'Where's Evie, anyhow? How comes she doesn't have to answer these questions? Is it like a quiz? Do I get a prize?'

Now they are both laughing. Told you, weird.

I wonder, does Spiderman have two mams? Or maybe he has two dads. Yes, I bet he does. Maybe Superman and Iron Man are his dads. That's why he's so strong. Or maybe they are superheroes in hiding that we've not even heard of yet. They must have to wear a different-colour costume to Spiderman's.

'Does Spiderman have two dads?' I ask them.

They think this is funny and both start to laugh again. At least Mam isn't crying any more.

'I feel sorry for Lulu,' I tell them.

This makes them stop laughing.

'Why?' Mam asks.

'Well, I'd say it's a right pain every Mother's Day. I never know what to buy you, Mam. Imagine having to buy two presents every year?' I tell them, shaking my head.

Oh good, they're laughing again.

'Can I have something to eat?'

'We know! You're starving!' they both say together. Weird.

Chapter Thirty-Three

EVIE

Even though I have no idea what they are singing, I get it. I can feel the love and despair transcend through the music and drama. My first opera. I didn't think I would like it, but I was wrong. As the last note rings out in the theatre, I am captivated and cannot take my eyes off the stage.

'Thank goodness Judith and Lorna told us about this place,' Mam is breathless and her eyes all shiny.

'My ears hurt,' Jamie complains, pulling a face. 'She sure took a long time to die.'

I can't help myself, I giggle. I mean, she did drag that bit out, in fairness. Ten minutes on the ground, singing that last death song.

'Can we go now? I'm hungry,' Jamie is pulling at Mam and Dad's arms, dragging them towards the exit.

'I take back all my moaning about queuing for tickets. It was worth the wait. Pretty incredible, in fact. And Jamie, well done, buddy, on keeping quiet,' Dad says.

'Where else can you watch a world-class opera for less that ten euros?' Mam remarks. 'The hairs were standing on the back of my neck, it was so electrifying!'

'It was kinda cool to watch it from the back. Didn't feel like the cheap seats at all,' I add.

'Can I have a treat because I was so quiet?' Jamie asks, never missing a trick.

'How about we find a café and some Viennese cake to put a smile back on your face?' Dad says to him.

We find one opposite the theatre and get a table within minutes. 'I just want to check in with Ann and Luke, okay?' I say, hooking up to the free Wi-Fi in the café. I peek through my fringe to see if Mam and Dad are making faces at each other. Yep, there they go again, throwing their eyes up to the heavens.

I wouldn't mind, but I'm hardly ever getting to chat to Ann or Luke any more. I haven't had a chance yet all day because we've done so much sightseeing. I'm banjoed with all the walking. Wrecked. We walked the major tourist attractions along the outer ring road. It's all right for Jamie, he gets to go on Dad's shoulders when he gets tired.

I take a picture of the sweet pastries and cakes that arrive to the table. They look amazing and I ping the picture over to Ann.

AnnMurphy: You've been so quiet!

EvieGuinness: Soz. Been crazy busy, no Wi-Fi!

AnnMurphy: Where are you now? I can't keep up any more.

EvieGuinness: In Vienna. Went to the opera. Pretty cool. Any news?

319

AnnMurphy: Dropped Mam's phone and it managed to break into a million pieces. She went crae crae. Awkward! And speaking of crae crae, did you see Deirdre's Facebook post?

EvieGuinness: No? I'm not friends any more, remember?

AnnMurphy: She's off her head, that one. I only stay as friends for the comedy element. She posted – wait for it – 'all I want this summer is to find a Romeo and Juliet relationship. Is that too much to ask for? #Sigh.'

EvieGuinness: Not sure she has seen that movie! Who wants to be Juliet? Sure she's dead by the end of it!

AnnMurphy: With a dead boyfriend. Nevermind #sigh, #gobshite more like!

EvieGuinness: For sure! Soz, I've gotta go. Mam is giving me the evils. Will try chat later.

AnnMurphy: Hugz

EvieGuinness: Hugz

'What are you smiling about?' Mam asks.

'Ann,' I say.

'What did she say?'

'Nothing.'

'Well, I'm glad that nothing makes you so happy. Eat up while you do that, though,' Mam nags.

I take a big bite just to keep her quiet. It's gorgeous, so I stuff the lot into my mouth quickly so I can get back to writing a message to Luke. He's not online, but there's a message from him earlier.

LukeKavanagh: I've been looking at Google maps, trying to follow your journey through Austria. Looks really cool. Wish I was there with you. Still crap here. I'm going to stay with Mam for a few days, she's settled into her new house now. Dad is still moping. He's not shaved for nearly two weeks and is beginning to look like Colm McGregor's dad. Are you having fun? I miss you.

I can't imagine what it's like for him. He's being passed back and forwards between his parents every couple of days. It's not fair. It's also my worst nightmare. I look up at my parents, who are at this moment feeding bits of their cake to each other. And while it's gross to look at, I can't stop smiling. They've not had a row for ages. No more whisper-fighting.

EvieGuinness: I miss you Luke. So much. But I can't believe I'm saying this, yes, I am having a great time. I hate Nomad and I love Nomad all at once, which I know sounds bonkers. Miss having my own room so bad. Jamie is driving me nuts. But earlier today we saw this guy stop in the middle of the street, open up his suitcase and strip down to his boxers, then change his clothes in front of the world. Not a bother on him. So funny, Dad kept shouting at us to look away and Jamie was shouting that he could see yer man's willy. We're going dancing now. Shoot me now!

'Say goodbye,' Mam says. 'Time to get to Pallavicini Palace for our dance class.'

As we walk along, I keep checking my phone to see if he's back online, but there's no sign of him. I daydream about him surprising me and turning up at the palace and dancing with me, like we're a real prince and princess. And even though I know it's not going to happen, I still feel a little bit disappointed not to see him sitting on the steps when we arrive.

Dad turns to me with a big serious head on him. What

have I done now? I stuff my phone in my jeans pocket quickly, before he starts lecturing me.

'Don't take this for granted, Evie. You're about to have a Viennese waltz lesson, in Vienna, in an actual palace. Do you have any idea how lucky we are?'

'I know, Dad,' I say and he looks like he's about to say something else. But Mam gives him one of her looks and he shuts up. Jeez, relax already. He's so uptight sometimes.

When we enter the lobby, Mam opens her backpack and pulls out two folded shirts, giving them to Dad. 'I bought these for you and Jamie. We are in a palace, after all! See you back here in ten minutes. Come on, Evie, time to beautify ourselves.'

Then she grabs me by my hand and pulls me into the ladies. She's off her head if she thinks I'm taking off my jeans and Converse trainers.

'I don't do dresses, Mam, you know that,' I say, when she hands me a bag.

'You don't have to do dresses every day. But sometimes you have to dress for an occasion. And this is one of them. Remember for one moment what it felt like when you were a little girl, reading your Disney princess books. You wished you could be Cinderella and go to the ball,' Mam is insistent.

I shrug. I suppose she's right. The odd time I did wish I was Cinderella.

'Well, today, we get the chance to learn something new. In a palace. Just like Cinders. So whether you like it or not, we're wearing a dress. And Evie, honest to goodness, would you just enjoy the moment? You might surprise yourself and have a good time.'

'Okay already.' I take the bag and go into one of the cubicles. I'm nearly afraid to look at the monstrosity she's bought me. If it's a pink dress, I'll scream. But it's actually nice – pale blue with tiny grey and white butterflies all over it. I shrug off my jeans and t-shirt and pull it on.

'It fits!' Mam sighs when I walk out. 'You have to take off your Converse. Put the kitten heels on. Please. For me . . . '

This has to be the lamest thing I'll ever do, but I figure I better do it. And, despite myself, I want to see what it all looks like in the end. Mam is wearing a bright-yellow dress, similar in style to mine. And she's got her heels on. She looks really pretty.

'Right, let's sort our hair out and then we are good to go,' Mam comes over and, before I have a chance to complain, she's pulled my hair out of its ponytail and let it fall loose over my shoulders. She grabs a couple of pins and clips back parts of it, leaving some soft tendrils at the side.

When she turns me around to face the mirror, I don't recognise the person staring back at me. I don't look like me. I look . . . pretty.

'Beautiful. I knew that colour would just suit you so much,' Mam says and dabs some lipgloss on. 'You are so lucky, you've got the most beautiful skin. It tans a lovely shade of golden brown. Not a single blemish, either. When I was your age, I was covered in spots!'

'Can I try some of that?' I ask, wondering what it would feel like to wear lipgloss.

And Mam laughs out loud, clearly delighted with that

question, pushing her makeup bag towards me. 'There's a lovely coral gloss in there, try that one.'

'It's a bit like lip balm. Just stickier,' I say. But I like it and I feel already a more glamorous version of myself.

A few minutes later I follow Mam out. She's showing off and does a big twirl for Dad and Jamie. The fifties skirt of her dress whips around her legs as she does.

'Very Grace Kelly,' Dad says and I say a quick prayer that he doesn't grab her and start kissing her again.

'Wait till you see our daughter,' Mam replies, then she grabs me and shoves me in front of Dad and Jamie.

I'm mortified and refuse to look up.

'Hey, you look beautiful, darling,' Dad says. 'When did you get so tall?'

He looks all weird and then they both start staring at me. I'm scarlet.

'I don't know if I can walk in these shoes,' I say.

'You don't need to walk, Evie, just dance,' Dad replies, grinning. 'And at a guess, even with those on, you'll do better than your old man. Two left feet me.'

Jamie walks over to me then, and says, 'Are you my date? Dad made me wear this. I can't breathe,' he tugs at his buttoned collar.

I giggle, he's so overdramatic. 'Yes, I think I am. You look handsome, little bro.'

'You look like a Barbie doll,' Jamie tells me and I giggle again because I think if you'd told me this morning that anyone would ever compare me to one of those, I would have said, yeah right, pigs, flying right now.

'You have to save a dance for me,' Dad says. 'I don't know, one minute you're a little girl climbing on my shoulders looking for a carry and now here you are, standing before me, on the brink of becoming a woman.'

Mam takes out her phone and snaps some pics of us all.

'Wow. Come here Evie, look at this photograph of you and Jamie.'

I'm looking down at Jamie and we're both laughing. Is that really me? I look alright. Pretty, even.

'That right there is your new profile pic,' Mam declares. 'Shall we?' She holds out her hand to Jamie and Dad offers his arm to me. I look around to make sure no one is watching. I mean, it's just mortifying. But at the same time, I kinda like it too. Maybe Mam is right, I need to smile a bit more. I've been spending so long expecting things to be horrible, I've forgotten what it's like to just enjoy the moment.

Plus, it's probably safer if I let him help me walk in. Seriously, how does Mam walk in heels every day in work? I feel like a new-born Bambi standing for the first time on ice.

Madame Stella, our tutor, is a tiny woman, wearing a long black skirt and tight black polo jumper. She holds a cane in her hand and even though it's unlikely, I'm kind of terrified she's going to rap it off the back of my legs.

'I hope she's not planning on using that on us!' I whisper to Dad.

'Good afternoon. Welcome,' she says. Oh, she's English. I wasn't expecting that. And then she smiles and she doesn't look so scary any more.

'Hello,' we all chorus.

'Don't look so scared. We are going to have some fun,

I promise you!' She turns to Jamie. 'First of all, let me tell you a little background. It's over two hundred years since the Viennese Waltz came to international fame. At that time, Strauss melodies filled ballrooms all over Austria and the city danced the night away.'

Madame walks over to me then, 'The city was like a Fred and Ginger movie, with ballgowns and black-tie suits.'

'What's a Fred and Ginger?' Jamie asks.

'I think it's a brand of ice-cream,' I tell him. I'm confused, but I'll look it up later tonight to find out what she meant.

'Sshh,' Mam hisses.

'And today, we will learn the basic pattern of steps,' Madame tells us. 'Come, come.'

We soon learn what the cane is for, as she uses it to stomp the beat on the floor.

1-2-3. Step-side-close. 1-2-3. Step-side-close. 1-2-3. Step-side-close. 1-2-3. Step-side-close. Step-side-close. 1-2-3.

We all swirl round and round, trying to look like we know what we're doing. Jamie proves to have natural rhythm and follows the beat with ease. How does he do that? It takes the rest of us a little bit longer to master the moves to the three-quarter time.

I get the three basic steps quick enough, but fecking hell, putting them together with speed is the tricky part. I keep standing on Dad's toes but he doesn't seem to mind.

'I feel like I'm in a Jane Austen novel,' Mam whispers to us when we stop for a break. Her face is flushed from exertion.

'I'm not sure Mr Darcy was sweating buckets like I am,' Dad jokes.

Then Dad starts to dance with Mam and I'm with Jamie. And we're all moving around the floor, by the end of the hour, with some level of fluidity.

I also realise that I'm enjoying myself because when Madame declares the lesson over, I'm a little disappointed. But then she tells us of the annual formal balls and Dad whispers to me, 'I'm going to surprise your mother and bring her back here for a weekend one day. So she can experience her full Jane Austen experience and go to an actual ball.'

I reach up and give him a hug.

'What's that for?' he asks, clearly bemused. I suppose I don't do that much any more.

'I don't want you and Mam to split up and live in different places, like Luke's parents. So I'm glad you want to take Mam away for a holiday. She'll like that, Dad. And I can take care of Jamie.'

Dad looks at me and places his hands on my shoulders. 'Do you trust me?'

I nod.

'Well, trust me when I tell you this. I've no intention of ever leaving your mam. I promise.'

I've never felt more relieved in my life. Hearing him confirm what I've been hoping for makes me want to run back inside the ballroom and skip around the floor.

We all head back to the campsite and Dad starts to fire up the barbecue.

'Can I go see if Lulu is around?' I ask. 'I told her yesterday I'd show her some of my *Guinness Book of*

Records albums.' I've started to check out the records for each place we visit. And there are some seriously cool ones.

'Tell you what, why don't you ask them if they want to join us for a burger?' Mam says. 'We've loads of food in. Plenty to go around.'

'Are you sure?' Judith asks, walking over to Nomad with me. 'Wow, don't you all look fancy!'

'We've been dancing,' Dad says. 'Just call me Fred.'

'And of course we are sure,' Mam says. 'The more the merrier! We leave here tomorrow; we'd love to spend our last night with you all.'

'Awesome. I'll make some salads,' Lorna tells us. 'And we've got wine!'

'Great! I'm about to open a bottle here. Hate drinking alone, don't we, Olly?' Mam smiles as she places glasses on the table.

I think about that barbecue in Ireland a year ago, just before everything went wrong. I was so scared that I'd have to cling onto that memory as the last happy Guinness family moment. But I was wrong. We've had lots of fun moments since then, but right now I think this is my favourite.

Mam and Dad, standing side by side at the barbecue. He's laughing at something she said and he puts his arm around her shoulder. Jamie is playing with a robot and is running around Nomad in circles. And then Judith, Lorna and Lulu arrive and I realise how lucky I am that I'm here. In Austria. Making new friends. In a camper van with my crazy family, who I love and who love me.

And I realise that the feeling in my head, that buzzing, that tightness, like I was about to explode, has been gone for a while now.

Chapter Thirty-Four

Dear Olly and Mae

Well, were the hills alive with the sound of music? Did you solve all Maria's problems? I was going to add to the challenge by insisting that Olly wear lederhosen, but I figured I might be pushing it with that.

Do you remember how I used to joke with you, Olly, when you first went to university? I'd say that if you ever decided to emigrate, I was coming too. And then, quick as a whip, you'd reply, you'd better believe it, Pops. Who else is gonna carry my cases?

You always made me laugh, lad.

Now, I need to share with you what's going to happen next. I hope you're rested, because you have a bit of driving to do over the next two days. About 900 km in total, which I know is a lot. But you need to travel across Hungary and into Romania.

I've told you a few times that I wanted you all to see a different world. Well, the next couple of weeks

I think will be life-changing for you all. Or, at least, I hope they will. Because your challenge, this time, is a big one.

Olly, do you remember a guy I used to work with, called Andy O'Connor? Well, he's retired now and works for a charity in Romania. He does amazing work with orphanages over there. Rebuilding them for the kids and building homes for families. For two weeks you will all be volunteering with his charity at one of the orphanages. Andy is expecting you and will show you all the ropes.

Your next letter is in two weeks. This will be tough, I daresay. But I have faith in the Guinnesses. I have faith that you will be able to deal with whatever the next few weeks throw at you.

Work hard, learn, teach and make a difference.

Love
Pops x

Chapter Thirty-Five

OLLY
Holy shitballs.

I nearly forgot about this letter. Today has been so busy, I nearly forgot. And this is the mother ship of all letters.

'I can't believe you had to remind me,' I say to Mae. I feel shit, like I've let Pops down, by forgetting about him.

'It's good that you forgot. It shows you are doing exactly what he wanted you to do. Relaxing and enjoying yourself,' Mae tells me.

'So, go on, don't leave me in suspenders. Where are we going to next?' demands Mae.

My chest is hammering like a freight train. 'You are not going to believe what he has planned for us.'

I grab Mae's hand and bring her back to the table. Judith, Lorna and Lulu look delighted to be part of the reveal.

'We're driving 900 km to Romania. Pops has only

organised for us to volunteer at an orphanage for two weeks.'

'What?' Mae shrieks.

'I know!' I say.

'Read it out loud, what did Pops say?' Evie says and I recount Pops' letter.

'I wish I could have met your Pops. He sounds like he was an awesome guy,' Judith says.

'He was. The best,' I say with pride.

'What will we be doing, do you think?' Mae asks.

I pull out some A4 sheets that Pops has printed off and enclosed with the letter, about the orphanage.

'No idea what we'll be doing. But we'll stay there. We can sleep in Nomad or in the dorms, whatever we want,' I say.

'That's a long drive you have ahead of you,' Judith says to me.

I pull out the family atlas and we pore over the map of Europe, looking at the expanse of country we'll be crossing.

'I need a drink!' I say and grab a glass of wine.

'I'm kind of jealous right now,' Lorna says. 'I wish we had thought of doing something like that.'

The evening passes in an excited blur as we chat about the possibilities of the next few weeks. We all swap contact details and promise to stay in touch.

'If you ever head to Ireland, we've a big back garden. You'll always have a place to pitch up,' I say to them.

'And likewise, you have to come visit us in America next year.'

Pops would love this. Us making friends and, I don't know, I have a feeling that we'll see them again.

I'm whistling as I pack up the garage, while Mae and the kids tidy the food and drink away. I hear Mae's mobile phone beep, so I pick it up and then all at once, the bottom falls out of my world.

'When are you coming home Mae? I miss you. Philip x'

Who the fuck is Philip?

Chapter Thirty-Six

MAE

'Right, we've about 500 km to do today. Pops has us booked into Kiskunmajsa for tonight, which is in the Great Southern Plains of Hungary,' I say.

'What's the campsite sound like?' Evie asks.

'I've no idea. I just have an address,' I reply.

'I reckon we should be realistic with our expectations. It could be quite basic,' Olly says. He sounds off.

'You okay?' I ask him.

'Fine.' Clipped, curt tones again. Followed by a dirty look.

He's quite obviously not okay. I can't work out what the hell is wrong with him. One minute we're having a great time, then he's gone all moody and silent again. Maybe the letter from Pops has shaken him.

'From what I can gather on Captain Kirk, our halfway mark today is Budapest. Let's stop there for an hour, get lunch and maybe pick up some Wi-Fi. We can see what we're dealing with then,' Olly suggests.

'That's a good plan. It would be an awful pity to not at least have a quick look around Budapest, when we are driving right through it,' I say.

'Right kids. Buckle up, we're off,' Olly says, ignoring me. Yep, definitely me he's pissed off with.

'Best thing I bought for this trip,' I say, pointing to the AA driving guidebook for Europe. 'It says here that you need to have your headlights dipped at all times. It's compulsory during daylight hours.'

'Fine,' Olly replies.

'And we'll need to stop at a gas station near the border to get our e-vignette stickers for the toll again. And according to this, they really frown on speeding,' I tell him.

'For God's sake, Mae, it's not like Nomad is even capable of breaking any speed limits,' Olly says. 'Would you stop nagging?'

Philip's text flashes into my mind. Shit. There's no way Olly saw that – is there? I replied to him straight away and told him to stop contacting me. I told him I wasn't interested. Then I deleted the message.

Cold sweat dribbles down my back. No. He couldn't know about Philip. I look at Olly again. There's no way he could have seen that text. My stomach flips.

Why do I have such a bad feeling, then? I should have told him about him. I'll tell him tonight.

Within an hour, we cross the border, saying goodbye to Austria.

As it's motorway for at least 140 km, Olly doesn't need me as co-pilot, so I join the kids in the back to watch a DVD, grateful to escape from the oppressive atmosphere.

'How will we go back to driving around in a car after this?' I say to the kids.

An hour and half later, I climb back up front with Olly. We're close to Budapest.

'So we just have a drive around? Then find somewhere for lunch?' Olly asks.

'Yeah, I think so,' I say. 'There's a real East-meets-West vibe here, isn't there?'

'Hmm . . . ' Olly answers, distracted. 'I'm not sure I'm going to get parking.'

'Look, it's not the end of the world if we don't stop here,' I say. 'Let's try and soak up as much as we can from driving around for a bit. Then if we see a good spot to park up, out of the city, great stuff. But it's more important for us that we get to Romania on time.'

We drive over a series of elegant bridges and watch the landscape change from flat to hilly as we go.

'That's the Chain Bridge!' I say. 'I'd hoped we'd see that.'

So Olly drives over it and we start climbing hills that give us stunning views. We pass by many intricate-designed buildings that are magnificent.

I spot a sign to Buda Castle. 'Must be parking there – a tourist attraction,' I say.

So we head that way and Olly parks up Nomad. We climb the stairway and once we get to the top we not only get to see the impressive castle, we get breathtaking views of Budapest below.

'I like those bright-coloured rooftops,' Evie says, snapping some pictures.

'At least we are getting a good bird's-eye view of the city,' I say to Olly.

He ignores me and walks over to Evie, laughing as she takes his picture.

Yep, it's me he's got the hump with. Not the kids.

We find a restaurant within walking distance and all order some traditional Hungarian goulash or *gulyás* as it's called here, except Olly, who insists on getting a burger with chips. I can't help thinking that he's doing that to make a point to me.

The goulash is spicy and aromatic and quite delicious.

'OMG, look at the campsite we're going to,' Evie screams, making me almost choke mid-mouthful. We all take a look at the website that is causing her to squeal so much.

'I was expecting a field with maybe a toilet block,' I say. 'Colour me impressed.'

'It's got a spa, thermal baths, pools, restaurants! It's lush!' Evie says.

'Okay, eat up, we're leaving in five minutes,' I joke. 'I've a date with a hot bath!'

Knowing what awaits us makes us all eager to get there, so we don't delay and take to the road again, towards Kiskunmajsa.

'I don't know what was in that salt bath, but I feel ten years younger,' I say.

'Salt,' Evie says, without looking up from her book.

'See, all that money we've spent on her education, not gone to waste at all,' I joke to Olly, but he ignores me again.

For weeks we have skirted around the issue of our marriage. I know our reluctance to sit and talk is fear-driven.

It's a scary thing taking off a plaster, especially when that plaster seems to be doing an admirable job of keeping us together. But either way, Olly's obvious annoyance with me just shows me that it's time to rip it off.

The kids fall asleep quickly, both exhausted from the aqua park and long drive. So I follow Olly outside and open a bottle of wine.

Before I have the chance to speak, he turns to me, anger and hurt glistening in his eyes and demands, 'Who is Philip?'

I want to die.

'I was going to tell you about him,' I say.

'Yeah, right,' he replies, obviously not believing a word of it.

'I was. You saw his text last night,' I say.

He nods, but won't look me in the eye.

'Well, first of all, you need to know that it's not what you think it is,' I say. I'm surprised my voice sounds so calm. Inside I'm dying.

'I have no idea what I think,' he hisses at me. 'Who is he?'

'I met him at that conference I was at a few weeks ago. The one in Dublin,' I reply. 'He's another teacher.'

'Are you in love with him?' he asks in a quiet voice and I feel like the biggest bitch in the world when I see how every word is slicing him up into little pieces.

'No!' I cry. 'I swear to you, I am not having an affair. I've not slept with him.'

He closes his eyes for a moment. In what? Relief maybe? Disbelief?

'So what exactly is this guy missing about you? Your startling wit? Your thoughts on sixth-year curriculum?'

I take a deep breath. This is harder than I ever thought it would be. When I made our vows I never dreamt that I'd ever even consider cheating on Olly. How did I ever allow it to happen? I can't justify it in my own head. I'm not sure how I'll explain it to Olly. 'We got on well at that conference. He made me laugh. I'd not done much of that for a long time.' Okay, that sounds lame – even to me.

'Because I've been such a drag to live with,' Olly says. Hurt all over his face.

I ignore that. 'We were both in Connolly station waiting for our trains home, he kissed me goodbye. It didn't last long. But longer than it should have.' I don't want to hurt Olly any more, but I know I have to be completely honest.

'And that's it?' Olly asks.

'No. The night that Evie drank too much, when you called me, I was with him.'

'Where?'

'Does it matter?'

'YES!'

'In a bar. Having a drink.'

And now, as I remember his hand caressing my thigh, I don't feel flushed with passion at the memory, I feel flushed with guilt and shame.

'If I hadn't called, what would have happened?' Olly asks.

'I wouldn't have come home that night,' I reveal myself, in all its ugly naked truth, to Olly.

I wait for the shouting, the accusations, the natural fall-out of my confession. But I'm met with silence instead.

Olly refills both our glasses and we drink in silence,

save for the sound of other campers as they go about their evening business.

'I don't think I've been a good husband this past year,' he says.

I'm startled by the admission. My immediate reaction is to start contradicting him, but I hold my tongue and remain still, waiting to hear what he has to say.

'Spending time with you these past few weeks, I've realised something. I took you, I took us, for granted. I was careless with us, Mae. I became so fixated with being the perfect stay-at-home dad, I forgot that I was a husband too. I'm sorry.' Olly puts his glass down.

'Thank you for acknowledging that. I needed to hear that. I'm sorry too,' I answer. 'Because I am not without blame. I was jealous of you and the children. I felt side-lined. And that made me bitter and I'm pretty sure not pleasant to live with.'

We both let the apologies hang for a few minutes. The air feels charged with honesty and the raw open wounds of confession.

'Can you forgive me? The kiss?'

'It's over, whatever it was?'

I nod. 'I give you my word.'

'Then, yes, I forgive it. I think that there are bigger issues we need to sort out. Maybe it's time I stopped running and took a deeper look at my life. I've not been happy, Mae.'

'I know. I felt so helpless watching you this past year. I tried to help, but it was hard. You kept pushing me away.'

'I know. I felt such a fucking failure when I lost that

job. And it clouded everything. I knew things were falling apart at home.'

'Why did you ignore it, then?' I ask.

'I think because I was reeling from the redundancy, I felt useless. A failure.' He stops and looks at me. 'Was it because I couldn't . . . you know . . . because I was impotent, is that why you and Philip had whatever you had?'

'No!' I exclaim. 'No, Olly. Do you think that our marriage is that shallow, that it's only about sex?'

He shrugs.

'It was part of it, of course. But more how you reacted to me when I tried to talk to you. You didn't just push me away in the bedroom, Olly. You pushed me away in every part of our life. In the end, I suppose I gave up trying. It was easier to stay away.'

'I wish I could go back . . . do things differently.'

And that, right there, brings me right to the very question that's been plaguing me for weeks. It can't be avoided any longer. 'How do we know that it will be different when we get home? I can't do this dance any more. I'm not strong enough to go through that again, feel like that again.'

'I don't want to lose what we have here, you and me and the kids. We've got to find a way to bring that home with us,' Olly says.

The fact that we both want the same thing gives me hope that we can find a way out. I feel like we are at a junction in the road. And we can very easily take the wrong turning and then there would be no way back.

'Pops was right. It is easier here, less complicated. But

when we get back to Wexford, all those issues we left behind will still be waiting for us.'

He nods in agreement. 'It was just that with Pops being ill, I was thinking a lot about Mam and him, my childhood. She was such an incredible mother, so selfless and devoted to me. I figured that if I couldn't work, I could at least finally give our children the same childhood I'd had. I could do that much at least.'

I feel like he's turned around and soccer-punched me with that statement. 'Do you know how insulting that is? You make it sound like the children were neglected up until you stepped in.' I try to keep my voice calm, but I'm dangerously close to crying. 'I was a good mother. I am a good mother. I might not bake every day, but the kids are loved and taken care of. It's so hard constantly hearing about your saintly mother and it's impossible for me to compete with a dead woman.'

There, I said it out loud. All the anger and resentment of the past year spills out. All the moments where I felt sidelined explode within me.

'The children have a good childhood, courtesy of both of us, I'll have you know. They have a mother who loves them!' I say.

Damn it, I can't stop the tears. I'm furious that I am getting so emotional.

'I never meant that you were a bad mother!' Olly shouts back. 'Of course you are a good mother. The best.'

'But you did mean that, Olly. Nobody can ever compete with the perfect image you have in your head of your mam. I'll always fall short. You've just said it. You wanted them to have the same as you had with your mother.

Therefore inferring that I don't give them that,' I say, the anger now gone from me.

He looks horrified by my words, but he doesn't deny them and I can see in his eyes that he knows I'm right.

'I am so sorry your mother died when she did. My heart breaks thinking about it. But your ode to your mother this past year was a slap in the face to me. You changed everything at home, constantly telling me how much better it was now that you were in charge. You eliminated all my roles, till I no longer felt that I was needed!' I say.

'I didn't mean to do that,' he says. 'I had no idea, Mae. I'm so sorry.'

'Well you did,' I reply. 'While you were trying to reenact your idyllic childhood, you stomped all over *my* role as a mother. Every day telling me when I came home about the things you'd done with the house, with the kids, that had never been done before. If I heard the phrase, we don't do it like that any more once, I heard it a million times. You made me feel shit as a mother, as a wife, as a woman.'

Olly's eyes are wide with shock. I don't think he had any clue how upsetting it had been for me, to lose my sense of identity at home.

'I had no idea of the extent of your feelings. I guessed some of it, but fuck, Mae. I've been a gobshite,' Olly says.

'The crazy thing is, I would have given anything to meet her. But I can't live in the shadow of a saint; it's too hard. What don't I get here, Olly? What am I missing?' I say.

He is quiet for a long time before he turns to me with such sorrow stamped on his face. 'It's my fault she died.'

'I don't understand.' The hairs on the back of my neck stand up in fear.

'The day she died. It should have been me, Mae. I should be dead and Mam should be alive,' Olly repeats.

'It was an accident. A lorry killed your mother. It was speeding, it couldn't stop. How is that your fault?' I say.

'I turned the bend and she was standing at our gate waiting for me. Just like she did every day. She was smiling and I started to run towards her, because there was going to be cake. She'd promised me cake,' Olly says, his body rocking back and forth. 'I saw a stone in the middle of the road. A big one and I couldn't resist. I ran over to kick it.'

Olly's voice is flat and my heart breaks for him as he remembers that awful day.

'I wasn't expecting the lorry to come around the bend and it was hurtling towards me. I heard Mam shouting my name. But I froze. I couldn't move,' Olly continues. 'The next thing I knew she was pushing me to the ditch, out of the lorry's path.'

'Oh, Olly,' I say, reaching for his hand, wishing with my every fibre that I could find a way to stop this.

'But the lorry couldn't swerve in time and he hit her. So you see, it was my fault she died. I should have been the one, not her,' Olly says, looking at me with such unwarranted shame.

'And you've thought that all these years? You've carried that with you? That you were somehow responsible?'

He nods.

One life lost and another spent feeling a guilt that isn't warranted. I want to cry at the injustice of it.

'She saved you. There's a difference. She chose to save her son's life. You didn't kill her. She died happy knowing you lived.'

I continue, 'Listen to me. If Jamie ran out in front of a lorry, I would die to save his life in a heartbeat. That's what parents do. They sacrifice everything for their children. That's what your mother did. Willingly.'

Olly looks at me and I see in his eyes the child that he was, so much like our Jamie now.

'You were the same age as Jamie when your mam died. A child. You were kicking a stone on the road, as boys do. That's all. You didn't kill your mam. It was a horrific accident,' I say again. 'You have got to let this go, Olly. You cannot carry this burden of guilt around with you any more.'

I walk over and sit in my husband's lap, pulling his head into my breast and we rock together for a long time.

'I've never really spoken about any of this to anyone before, except Pops,' Olly says.

'Well, you've told me now.' And so many things begin to make sense now that I know the full story. Olly's constant guilt at not being a good enough son or father. The times where he looks haunted whenever his mother's name comes up. 'That day, when your mother died, she was happy wasn't she?'

Olly's face is contorted in pain as he recalls that last day. 'Every day, even when it was raining, she'd stand there with an umbrella over her head, unfaltering, watching for me to saunter up the road. No doubt with me kicking a stone as I went, imagining I was Ian Rush, striking gold.'

I smile at this and gently stroke his cheek, as he remembers. 'She was a beautiful woman, I recognise that now. She was wearing a blue tea dress and I can still see it rustling against her legs in the early-morning breeze. She loved that dress. Just before I turned the bend, I looked back and she was blowing kisses at me. Her face was alight with humour as she did so, thinking I'd be all embarrassed. I knew that I might have been seen by one of the Murphys who lived next door to us. They were awful slaggers. But I didn't mind and I chanced blowing a few kisses back to her. It was almost as if she danced in mid air as she caught them in her hands, pulling them in close to her heart.'

'Oh, Olly.'

'I'm so glad I blew those kisses to her now,' Olly says and my heart splinters into a million pieces for his pain.

The air now changed, tension gone and in its place a sense of peace.

We talk for hours, about our marriage, our hopes and dreams for the future, our love for each other and the children.

'I need you to know that I never thought you were a bad mother. The kids adore you. You've earned their love, because you have given them nothing but love since the moment they were born. And Evie, well, the reason she's doing so great now is because of you,' Olly says.

'Because of both of us. We're a good team,' I say. 'Most of the time, anyhow. It's so good seeing Evie smile again. Even if it's just at her phone, rather than at us! She's making new friends, getting back her spark again.'

'I know. And Jamie is . . . '

'Starving most likely,' I say, making Olly laugh. 'Jamie is just joy. Simple as.'

With our second bottle of wine we excavate deeper, maybe feeling brave because of the wine, maybe because we are on this road to truth and now that we are baring all, there's nothing that can remain hidden.

'So what's going to happen when we get home?'

'I wasn't happy in that job. I don't even know how I ended up working there for so long. I mean, the plan was that when I studied accountancy I'd open my own firm. Instead, I spent twenty years working for a company that tossed me out without even a backward glance,' Olly says. 'Not that I'm bitter!' He raises his glass in a mock salute.

'At least you got some redundancy. That will help put the kids through college,' I say. 'Plus we paid off some debt and the car loan. But it's clearly not working as it is at home. You need to figure out what you want to do. If you want to be a stay-at-home dad, that's fine. But I can't go back to the way it was. I mean, I was afraid to bring up the subject of money for fear of you going into a meltdown.'

'Every time you said how tight things were, how we needed to work on a household budget, I felt like you were giving me a dig.'

'I'm sorry I made you feel like that. It wasn't my intention.' I hope he realises that now.

'I thought that I wanted to be a stay-at-home dad. I'd convinced myself that it was the right thing to do. Up until this trip, I had it all figured out,' Olly sighs.

'And now?' I say to him.

'Now I think that I've wasted a lot of years playing it

safe. I feel different now. These past few weeks, this trip, embracing the unknown, spending so much time with you and the children. It's changed me.'

'In what way?' I ask.

'Well, I want more from life, Mae,' he states. 'I want to do bigger and better things. See more of the world. Make a bigger contribution than I am right now. I don't think I can truly be the real authentic Olly Guinness, whatever or whoever the fuck that is, until I am true to myself. So I've got to find a way to be who I really am.'

He looks at me with such intensity the hairs on the back of my neck rise once more.

'Wow. So who do you want to be?'

'I want to be your husband. I want to be the children's father. I want to work, have a new career. I just haven't worked out what that is going to be yet.'

'I want to be your wife too,' I whisper and he kisses me. 'What don't you want?'

'I don't want to go back to sitting in a cubicle again. I know that much. And I know that I've made mistakes with the kids, but I've loved spending so much time with them. I don't want to lose that,' he answers.

'Okay, well that's a start,' I reply. 'We can work on the rest – together.'

We go to bed, emotionally and physically drained from our talk. But I don't think I've ever felt so close to him in all our years together. I swing my legs over him and with my lips trace every inch of his face, his torso. We make love and, in every touch and kiss, I think we are on the right road to finding our way back home to each other.

Chapter Thirty-Seven

MAE

'I know the motorways are handy for clocking up the miles, but we could have been driving anywhere in the world this morning. It was like one long grey carpet stretched empty for miles in front of us,' I say, then point to the view in front of us. 'But this – look at the landscape now!'

We are driving through a small village. A mix of white-washed and pastel-painted cottages sit prettily on the road's edge. Residents look up with interest as Olly drives Nomad at a snail's pace past their houses. I wave and smile and in return see only grinning, warm faces waving back at me.

We pass a cart, pulled by strong draught horses, driven by a woman with a brown, leathered face, wearing a heavy sheepskin coat. She shouts something to us over the clip clop of the horses, but of course we don't understand.

'Hello,' we all roar back through the opened windows.

I feel like I have stepped into a new, exciting world, straight from the pages of a Grimms' fairytale.

'Imagine the heat of that coat she was wearing,' Olly says, wiping his forehead with his hand. He's sweating in the hot Romanian summer air.

We turn a bend in the road and Olly brakes hard because the road is filled with a caramel-coloured herd of cows.

'She was warning us about the cows, not saying hello,' I realise.

A farmer dressed in blue overalls and wellies chews a blade of straw, as he ushers the cows towards an open gate ahead. He's totally unfazed by us in our motorhome.

The farmer looks up then and smiles a toothy grin at us. He says something, followed by a bellowed laugh. While we don't understand him, we get that he finds the whole situation hilarious. We can't help but laugh in response.

'I love it here,' I say. 'It's like a town that time forgot.'

'What's that smell?' Evie asks.

Nomad is now filled with the aroma of cow dung and hay.

'That, my dear Evie, is the smell of the country,' Olly tells her. 'It's the complete opposite of what I thought it would be.'

'What did you expect?' I ask.

'I got it into my head that we'd be passing by tanks on the road, not horse-and-carts and cows wearing blue bells around their necks!'

'I would think the big cities of Romania look different to the sleepy villages,' I say.

I turn around to face the children. 'It's not that long ago that the Romanians united in uprising and ousted communism. When you learn about this in school, remember that you were here. You're lucky.'

They look at me without much enthusiasm.

'Only another 10 km or so and we arrive in Valea Screzii,' Captain Kirk tells us. 'I'm excited, but also nervous. I just hope that whatever they throw at us, we're up for the challenge.'

'We'll be grand,' Olly says. 'We're a good team, us Guinnesses.'

'My name is Evie. *Mă numesc Evie*,' Evie says suddenly.

I turn to look at her and she shrugs. 'I've pulled together some phrases for us. You've got to learn how to introduce yourself to the kids at least.'

'My numbers is Jamie,' Jamie attempts.

'*Mă numesc Jamie*,' Evie corrects him.

'That's what I said, silly,' he replies, making us all laugh.

The village is in the foothills of the Carpathian mountains and once again we pass by several horse-and-carts along the way. We spot a local farmer pitching hay in a field as we enter the village, so we stop and Olly asks him where the orphanage is.

And although neither of them can understand a word the other is saying, somehow or other, he realises what we want. He gestures with his pitchfork, straight on and left.

He doesn't steer us wrong and we arrive in the orphanage compound a few minutes later. We are all silent as we drive in, taking in the large building in front of us. I think we are all awed by the challenge we are about to undertake.

'Let's try find this volunteers' farmhouse at the back,' Olly says. He follows the road around and parks up as we enter a yard. The sound of Nomad's engine alerts the people inside a large whitewashed farmhouse and the door opens and several walk out to greet us.

'That's Andy,' Olly says, waving at a man with a shock of white hair. He jumps out to greet him.

'Olly Guinness,' he says, pumping Olly's hand up and down. 'What's it been? At least ten years since I've seen you, I reckon.'

'That sounds about right. Good to see you, Andy. This is Mae, my wife. And the kids, Evie and Jamie.'

'You made good time. We thought it would be much later before you arrived,' Andy says. 'That's some vehicle you've got there.' He walks around Nomad, admiring it as he goes.

'A gift from Pops. But you probably know all that?' Olly says to him.

Andy walks over to Olly and puts his two hands on his shoulders. 'I'm so sorry about your dad. He was a good man. A true friend to me when we worked together.'

We stand for a moment in silence, awkward and unsure what to do next.

'Come on, let's get you inside to meet everyone. It's teatime, so we've a full house,' Andy says.

He leads us into a large kitchen and dining room. There's a long rectangular table in the centre, with about a dozen people sitting around it.

The table is laden with pots of steaming food and bowls of salads.

'Everyone. This is the Guinness family. Olly, Mae, Evie

and Jamie. They are with us for two weeks,' Andy says. 'I'll let you meet everyone yourself, bit by bit. Don't expect you'd remember all the names if I throw them at you at once!'

A chorus of hellos and warm smiles descends upon us and seats materialise at the table, squeezing us in. Then plates appear and a glass of wine for Olly and me, juice for the kids.

From first glance, it appears that every age group is amongst the volunteers, from late teens right up to Andy in his seventies. And they are all speaking English, so we don't have to rely on sign language as we did with the farmer earlier on.

Jamie is the youngest by the looks of it, though. But within minutes he is chatting to a pleasant-faced woman in her forties from Germany, who seems to have taken a shine to him.

I sit beside Gloria, a woman who boasts that she is almost sixty-seven and is from the Lake District in England. She's a retired nurse and is on a long-term volunteer programme.

'You'll soon get used to everyone,' she tells me. 'It can be a bit daunting at first, but by tomorrow you'll know the lie of the land.'

Evie is quiet. I can sense how overwhelmed she is with it all. I give her hand a little squeeze of reassurance.

'Can you tell us a bit about the orphanage?' I ask Andy.

'Well, there's several parts to Ripples Orphanage. There's about a hundred children of varying ages. Plus a larger community that includes families in difficulty, abused mothers. We've also got adults who grew up in state institutions and pregnant women who have nowhere else to go,' Andy replies.

'What will we be doing?'

'Well, as you are a teacher, Mae, we plan on taking full advantage of that. We want you to help out in the baby and toddler room and then do some classes with the older kids. Maybe work on their English, which is sporadic at best, do arts and crafts, that kind of thing. Evie and Jamie can help you.'

He turns to Olly then and says, 'Hope you're feeling fit and able, young man, because we're after your muscle. We've a project we're working on that we need every strong pair of hands we can get. We're building houses for some families.'

'Muscle I can do,' Olly says.

'That all sounds brilliant,' I say. My mind starts to buzz with ideas of what I might teach these kids. I can't wait to start.

'I have muscles too,' Jamie declares with a pout. 'I'm super-strong.'

'Well, maybe, young sir, you can come help your dad out a bit too. Super-powers are important over here,' Andy says.

'I'm glad I'll be with you,' Evie whispers to me, with obvious relief.

'Me too,' I tell her.

After dinner, Andy takes us on a tour of the house. There's a large family room with a huge TV in it. Plus a games room, with a snooker table and a dartboard, plus lots of board games stacked in the corner. There are four dormitories, which Andy tells us are pretty much always full.

We decide to sleep in Nomad each evening, but to eat with the group every day. Andy has a generator for us that we can hook up to Nomad for electricity and we're sorted.

'I don't think I'll sleep tonight,' I say to the children as I tuck them into bed.

Andy has told us that the volunteers do either a morning or an afternoon shift each. We are all on mornings for our first week, then we'll switch for our second week.

We also get free time to do some sightseeing or relax outside of our shifts, with one day off each week. I set the alarm on my phone, to make sure that we don't oversleep. But I needn't have worried. We are all awake an hour before it goes off.

After breakfast, the children and I walk with Gloria to the orphanage and Olly heads off with Andy to the construction site.

'I'll be your go-to person while you're here, Mae. So don't be shy, ask me anything.' She's got a kind face, round with few lines that defy her years.

'How long have you been here?' I'm curious about how she ended up here.

'Since 2007. I watched a programme one night about the abandoned babies in Romania. 350,000 of them, left alone after the revolution. It broke my heart. I couldn't get the images of them tied up in cots like animals out of my head,' she tells us.

I remembered seeing those same images and the horror at the conditions they were living in. But I didn't pack up and give up my life like Gloria did. I'm in awe.

'I was widowed, never had kids of my own and had retired. I thought: what have I got to lose? So I came over here and I've never left. Turns out I had everything to gain,' she said.

'You're incredible,' I say to her.

'Wait till you meet the kids – they are the ones who are incredible,' she says.

'Are there any other long-term volunteers?' I ask.

'Yep, we have six long-timers. And lots that are here for a year at a time. We get a lot of volunteers who are on a gap year in university or on a career break. And sometimes we have families who come here as part of their extended vacation, like you guys,' she tells us.

'Well, we are glad to be here and will do anything you need us to,' I say to her. 'Won't we kids?'

Evie and Jamie both nod in silence. They are clearly overwhelmed by it all and I don't blame them. It's a lot to take in. Pops, you've really set us a challenge here.

'We're lucky to have you,' Gloria says, with kindness to the kids. 'Although Romania joined the EU early in 2007, it's still one of the poorest countries in Europe. There's widespread poverty, unemployment, and corruption. That's a tough cocktail for a country to move through.'

'We see some of it at home, on the news, but I think this could be an eye-opener for us,' I say.

'I've learnt that we can't save all the kids, but the ones who end up in our orphanage get a shot at a better life,' she says.

I hold each of the children's hands as we enter the orphanage. It's a large impersonal white building, with grey concrete paths around it and red metal fencing on the surrounds.

It's still early and the only sound is birds chirping and

the leaves rustling in the breeze. It looks deserted it's so eerily quiet.

'The morning shift starts at seven a.m., so volunteers will all start to arrive any time now. Some will go to get breakfast ready for the kids, others will go to the infirmary to do the meds,' Gloria says. 'Don't be taken in by the quiet now. It's going to get noisy any time now. I've put you on baby and toddler duty for a couple of days. We'll help get the children dressed and washed, ready for breakfast,' Gloria says. 'And the babies have to be changed and fed. We need every pair of hands we can get. It's quite chaotic for the first hour!'

The tiled floors are white, walls are all spotless and a faint smell of bleach lingers in the air. Glass windows gleam. I'm impressed with the cleanliness.

'Let's start with the baby room,' Gloria says. 'Always makes me smile, this place.'

She walks into a room filled with cribs, lining either side of a large room.

'*Salut*,' she addresses the staff, who are already there. 'Meet Mae, Evie and Jamie.'

Three women greet us in return and we are given our jobs.

'Jamie, you will be in charge of the diapers. You can hand them out to each of us as we change the nappies. Right, let's get going,' Gloria tells us.

She walks to the first crib, where a baby who looks no more than a month old is fast asleep.

'*Salut*, my little Nicolae.' She picks him up and kisses his forehead, smoothing away his dark hair. He's wearing a simple white babygro and is adorable.

'Here you go.' She hands him to me and I hold him in my arms, close to my chest. I've forgotten how small babies are.

'You were this size once,' I tell the children, who are mesmerised with the baby in my arms.

'You got this?' Gloria asks me. I look her in the eye and I tell her, 'Yes, I've got this. Babies I can do, especially ones that are as beautiful as this little one.'

I breathe in that smell – that only a baby exudes – and make a vow that while I'm here, I'll work so hard to make a difference. Just like Pops wanted.

'Evie, watch how I do this and in no time you'll be changing nappies too,' I say to them.

Nicolae opens his eyes and looks at me with interest.

'He's awake!' Jamie says with excitement.

'That he is. Let's see what he's got for us.' I set him down on the changing table and open his babygro.

I show Evie how to clean him properly, then add Sudocrem and a clean nappy.

'You made that look easy,' Evie says.

'Years of experience with you two,' I say to her, smiling.

'Ewwww,' Evie says. And while she thinks it's gross to think of me changing her and Jamie, she has no idea how many memories this single act evokes for me.

In hospital, sore from birth, but jubilant and feeling more like a woman than I've felt before in my whole life. Holding Evie, my firstborn, in my arms, breathing in her special new smell. And looking at Olly's face every single time he holds his daughter in his arms.

I look around at the room full of babies and my heart aches in sympathy for all the women who never got the chance to do any of those things. I try to imagine a world where my children are not in it and I can't. It's unfathomable to me.

'Penny for them?' Gloria asks.

'Just realising how lucky I am. How different my life has been to the parents of these children.'

'Gets you in the gut, doesn't it?' Gloria sympathises, as I place Nicolae down with care and kiss him one more time, before moving to the next crib.

'Who do we have here?' I say, and read the name above the crib. 'Stefan. Another boy!'

I pick him up and cuddle him for a moment before changing his nappy and replacing him in the cot.

'Can I try?' Evie asks when we get to Lucia's cot next. A beautiful three-month-old little girl is awake and smiling, waiting to be scooped up into someone's arms.

So Evie, for the first time in her life, changes a nappy.

'Good girl. That's it. Don't forget the Sudocrem. Perfect.' I smile at her, my daughter, who is getting stuck in without any prompting from me.

There are fifteen babies in the room, under the age of two, and between us we change each of them in thirty minutes. Jamie is a star, running between each of us with his kit of nappies and bags.

'Right, before we do their bottles, we'll go next door and get the toddlers dressed for breakfast,' Gloria tells us.

The toddler room is lined with camp beds, low on the ground, with mismatched blankets on top. I count nineteen beds and Gloria tells us that the children in this room are aged between two and four.

'Each child has a locker with their clothes and shoes.

Their names are above their beds, as in the baby room. Right, we better crack on, breakfast will be ready in no time.' Gloria walks to the first cot and rouses a little girl.

I walk to the bed opposite, where a little boy, about three, is lying face down on his cot, bum up in the air.

'You used to sleep like that,' I whisper to Evie and the innocence of his position and the stark difference of his location to that of Evie's when she was a baby makes me shake with the injustice of it all. This perfect little boy – how did he end up here with no parents?

'We can do this,' Evie says to me, sensing that I am faltering. I repeat that again. 'Yes, we can do this.' Little do I know that this will become our mantra for the next two weeks.

'*Salut*, Robert,' I say, gently stroking his face to wake him. '*Salut*.'

He opens his eyes and looks at me, wary at the new voice.

'*Mă numesc Mae*,' I say to him, pointing to my chest. 'Mae.'

He smiles and says, '*Salut*.'

As I pull out a pair of shorts, a t-shirt and some trainers, I look at Evie and smile. She's beaming because she knows she taught me that phrase. She did that.

Robert is a little star, obviously used to the early-morning routine, because he lets me get him dressed without any issue. Evie wanders over to the next bed and I hear her waking a little girl. Jamie is shyer in here than the baby room, without a job to do, so I ask him to fold the pyjamas for each child and put them in their lockers.

'They are all so good,' I say to Gloria.

'Yes, they are. Most have been here since they were babies, so they know the drill well,' she replies.

I think of all the firsts these children have experienced here in this orphanage. First roll, first words, first steps. I think about Olly and I teaching our children 'Mama', 'Dada' – wondering which word would be their first. Do these children say 'Mama' and 'Dada'? Do they miss what they don't have? And I falter, once more, not sure I can continue, as the sadness of the situation becomes too much.

'Mam?' Jamie tugs at my arm, worry on his little face.

'I'm okay, my darling. I'm just feeling a little sad.'

'Because these children have no mam and dad?'

'Yes. Exactly that.'

'Where are they?' he asks. 'Are they at work? Did they forget to come home and get them?'

'I'm sure they haven't forgotten them at all, my love. Because a mother never, ever forgets her child. Even if life makes it impossible for them to be together.'

'Oh.'

Then he grabs my hand again, 'You won't leave me here, will you?'

'No, my darling. I'd never leave you – here or anywhere.'

He seems satisfied with this and we move to the next child.

Once the children are all dressed, we lead them to the dining room, where a long table with benches awaits them. I recognise one of the young girls from dinner last night, handing out bowls of steaming porridge to them all. Another girl, about twenty, hands them glasses of milk.

Gloria ushers us back to the kitchen, where bottles of formula are awaiting us for the babies. We head back to the baby room and hand the older of the babies their own bottles, who guzzle them back. I show Evie how to hold a bottle and she once again takes to it with ease. Jamie lies on the floor mats with some of the older babies and plays with them, making faces.

We hold and feed the babies for an hour and then place them back in their cots for their naps and I know that right now, right here, is exactly where we should be.

'Well done,' Gloria says to us all with approval. 'You just got stuck in. I like that.'

'My jaws ache from smiling. Those babies are adorable,' I say to her.

'Well, we'll have a coffee now. Then we'll go to the play-room with the toddlers. You'll enjoy that,' Gloria tells us.

'Where are the children's parents?' I ask Gloria. 'Are they all dead?'

'You hear the phrase "home alone" a lot over here. It comes from a time when many parents had no choice but to leave their children behind, when they left for Western Europe to find work. Some of the kids were lucky and taken care of by relatives or even neighbours, but some ended up on the streets,' Gloria tells me.

I'm horrified at the thought. But I don't live in this world and I know I can't judge. All I do know is that I'm heartbroken for those children.

'The babies, now, a lot of them are from unmarried mothers who were once those "home alone" children,' Gloria adds. 'Others are from parents who just can't cope, so they leave. We take as many children as we can fit in.'

'Can they stay here indefinitely?' I ask.

'Yes. We'll love them, feed them, teach them until they are old enough to go out into the world themselves. And then the houses that Olly is working on today come into play. They are to help some of the single mothers who have nowhere to live. If we can, we want to reunite some of the children with their parents,' Gloria says.

After our coffees we go into a large bright-yellow playroom. We take out toys, walkers, play mats and high chairs and sit and play with the children. Jamie and Evie, once again, astound me by their eagerness to just jump right in and help.

The bell rings for lunchtime and we bring the children to the dining room again, where pots of pasta and fruit await them.

And then, just like that, our day has ended. Our working day, that is. Gloria says, 'Can you find your way back okay?'

'Yes, of course. And thank you for today. You've been great,' I say to her.

'Can we come back here tomorrow?' Evie asks.

'Just try stopping us.'

'Let's go home, see if Dad is finished yet,' I say.

'You called Nomad home!' Evie says.

Jeepers, I did. When did that happen? 'You know something I've just this second worked out? Home is where we are. As long as we're together, the four of us, that's our home.'

'Can we live in a cave like Batman?' Jamie asks.

'Probably Pops' next trick for us,' Evie jokes.

Chapter Thirty-Eight

OLLY

The heat is the worst part of this. It creeps up to thirty degrees most days by noon. We start early each morning, levelling the road to the site for the thirty houses that we will be building. There are ten of us: eight men and two women, and we all work hard, for the first two days, digging a trench for the water and utility pipes.

We're captained by an Australian called David, who answers to the name 'Skippy'. He's a builder by trade and while he doesn't say much, he seems to get an awful lot done. We are all eager to impress him.

When Skippy tells us that we're done for the day, I can't believe that I've put in a full shift. It flew by.

'You know, I've spent years watching the clock in work, wishing away my life,' I say to Mae when I get back to Nomad. 'The shift here just disappeared in an instant. I didn't want to finish up.'

'I was the same. When Gloria said it was time to go, I could have stayed there for hours more. Olly, those little children. You've got to get up there to spend time with them. See it for yourself,' Mae says to me.

'How are our kids getting on?' I ask her.

'I've never been more proud of them. Jamie already knows every single baby's name. I still have to read their name badges above the bed! And Evie is a natural. She's so gentle with the children, they love her,' Mae tells me. 'I'm moving into the classroom tomorrow, with the older kids, but Evie is going to stay in the baby and toddler room.'

'What about Jamie?' I ask. 'He wants to come with me tomorrow. What do you reckon?'

'How about you bring him for a few hours, then if he gets tired send him back to me,' Mae says. 'I've been thinking about this, to be honest, a way to make it easier on Jamie. I don't want it to be too long a day for him. He's only seven. We could do different shifts – me mornings, you afternoons. Then he can dip in and out of the volunteer work, just do as much as he's able. Evie is grand, she can cope with a full shift, no bother,' Mae suggests.

'That's a great compromise. I'll talk to Andy about that in a bit,' I say. I put my feet up and lie back on the sofa. 'Jesus, I'm knackered though,' I say. 'That heat is gruelling. I don't think I've done that much manual work . . . well ever!'

'It's a different kind of tiredness for me. More emotional. Every time I hold one of those little babies in my arms, I want to cry. I don't know how Gloria does it. For eight years now, Olly. She's like a mother to them,' Mae says.

'Andy was telling me that they have a lot of long-term volunteers. They try to discourage short-termers like us. It's not fair on the kids having too many people dipping in and out of their lives,' I say.

'I can see that. Those little toddlers only met us yesterday and today when we walked in they ran over kissing and hugging us like we were family. They are so affectionate. I'm already worrying about saying goodbye to them,' Mae sighs and I reckon I've got the easier job, digging trenches.

A mark on Mae's arm catches my eye. 'Hey, what's that?' I peer closer and see teeth marks.

'A gift from a little girl called Magda. She's feisty. And scared and so she lashed out. Doesn't hurt in the least.'

'What's her story, do you know?' I ask.

'She's had a miserable life, her mother was killed in a car accident and her father left years ago to get work in Italy. No one can find him. Her aunt couldn't look after her any more, so she ended up on the streets fending for herself. She's still used to fighting to defend herself, and while she's been here a month now, she still doesn't trust anyone. Who can blame her?' Mae says.

'Jesus, the poor kid.'

'She's just one of many. But there's something about her. I don't have much time to help her, but I'd like to try.'

'Anything I can do?'

'Right now, no. But maybe go have a hot shower. You're a bit ripe there, Mr Guinness! I'll make lunch for us all,' Mae tells me.

We fall into a pattern quick enough over the next few days. Mae and Evie head off to the orphanage for the early shift, with Jamie. I'll follow over mid-morning and spend some time in the playroom, with the kids, before taking Jamie home with me.

Mae seems to be getting on great in the classroom. The older kids already have a basic grasp of English, so she is working to improve on that. Then, after lunch, I head off for the afternoon shift at the construction site, leaving Mae and the kids behind.

In only a few days, this life here has become our new normal. Having spent weeks being only in each other's company, it feels a bit strange to be away from them all. But, more than that, it feels bloody good. I'd forgotten what it was like to head off to do a day's work away from home. I adore those children, but it's good to have some time away, on my own. We almost trip over ourselves every day as we share all the things that we've done on our shifts. It's like it was before, only better, with more understanding and respect.

And while Mae and I needed this time together, now I find myself looking forward to seeing her more, after a few hours apart. When we get home, it's time to dust off that CV and start looking again for work. What, I'm not sure, but there must be something out there for me.

Today, we're mixing things up a bit. Mae and Evie joined Jamie and I for a couple of hours. The houses are simple four-walled timber constructions, so there's a lot of hammering of nails. But the results are quick and it's satisfying seeing one of our houses go up to roof level by the end of week one.

And I don't mind admitting that the beers we had to celebrate were the sweetest I've ever had.

While the work is strenuous, my body is already beginning to get used to this new normal. Muscles feel less strained. More than that, I feel useful.

The days are short and the evenings filled with laughter as we get to know our fellow volunteers. The kids spend most nights in the games room and all of us fall into our beds exhausted by nine p.m.

'So what have you planned for us today?' I ask Andy. It's our day off and he's taken us sightseeing.

'Fancy going to check out Dracula's home?' he asks the kids, who seem excited by the prospect.

We spend the day visiting local spots that have laid a claim to the Prince of Darkness, Count Dracula. There's even a hotel named after him, which we stop to have a cold drink in.

'I think a lot of locals find the whole fascination with Dracula quite strange,' Andy says. 'I think for a lot of people around here, there's a much more frightening monster from these parts: Dictator Nicolae Ceausescu. He pretty much obliterated everything of beauty in this land, during his twenty-five-year reign.'

'It's hard to imagine what it was like for everyone back then,' Mae says.

'What was the catalyst to make you move here, Andy?' I ask.

'I never married, never had kids. And the older I got, the more dissatisfied with life I became. I had nothing to complain about – on the surface all was good. Great friends and family, job I liked. But I couldn't shake the feeling that something was missing,' he said.

While I have Mae and the kids, unlike Andy's bachelor status, I can identify with every word he's saying.

'A friend talked me into joining him out here on a short-term volunteer programme in 2006. And while I loved that month here, there was a huge amount about it that I hated. We weren't allowed to be too affectionate with the kids and that drove me nuts,' Andy says.

'Why ever not?' Mae asks. 'That doesn't make any sense. Surely the children need every bit of human touch we can give them?'

'The thought was that as volunteers who were on a short-term placement, it would be unfair to let the children form emotional bonds with them,' he says.

'That seems cruel, though. If a child needs a hug, they need a hug. End of,' Mae says. She's getting upset.

'Yep, that's how I felt. I went home and couldn't settle back into work. I couldn't get the faces of the children from my head. I started researching all the charities that were out here. At that time, not so many. And one night, I was at my brother's house for dinner. I was on my soap box, giving out about the system. And he said to me, "Why don't you go back? Change the things you don't like?" And I thought to myself, why not? I'd no commitments. So I decided to retire early from the civil service and I came over here and started up Ripples,' he says.

'You say that, like it's nothing,' Mae says. 'It's incredible, Andy. You're incredible.'

'I do what I can,' Andy says, shrugging. 'I got lucky, because Gloria, Skippy, Donal and Martha were all amongst my early volunteers. And they all wanted to stay here long term. While we have lots of short-term volunteers, having that core team consistently – it makes all the difference. The children get to form healthy bonds with their carers.'

'And the children blossom under this system. I've seen

it myself and I'm only here a week,' Mae tells him. 'Gloria, by the way, is a force of nature.'

'She sure is. Not sure what we'd do if she left. She loves it here, so with a bit of luck she'll stick around. I own the farmhouse, but it's in the charity's name. And we get by. We're not in the best shape financially. But thanks to volunteers and donations, we're keeping our heads above water.'

'You're a good man,' I say. I'm filled with nothing but respect for this guy. I know now why Pops had so much time for him.

He shrugs the praise off again. 'I can't change the world here, but the ripple effect of everything we do combined might do. The way I see it, everything we do, no matter how small or seemingly ineffectual, creates a ripple.'

'That's why the charity is called Ripples!' I say. 'D'oh!'

'Give that man a medal,' Andy laughs. 'It's not just about the ripple effect this orphanage has on the children in it. Yes, of course we are making a difference in their lives. They have shelter, food, love and an education. We can keep them safe. But the ripples are more far-reaching than that.'

He looks out the window of the bar, at the children who are playing in the garden. 'These few weeks – who is to say that it won't change your children? Evie and Jamie may leave here with a renewed sense of purpose because of the time helping here. And maybe they will do something incredible with their lives – all because they were changed by Ripples. So that's what makes this place special. Yes, we can help the children here, but we can help ourselves too.'

the receipts. Mae supplies me with endless cups of tea and biscuits and then heads over to Nomad with the kids, blowing a kiss at me. By midnight, I've gotten them into at least a manageable state, ready for filing later this year.

'So that's pretty much the system you need to continue working with,' I say to Andy. 'I'm not sure you're getting all the correct tax exemptions, so I'll work on that when I get home to Ireland for you. Only if you like, of course.'

'I do like. Jesus, Olly, I didn't expect you to do all this tonight!' he exclaims. 'I see the apple didn't fall far with you. You've got your pops' work ethic. He was just like you when he had a bit between his teeth.'

'I wouldn't have been able to sleep until I got it done,' I say and feel inordinately pleased with the comparison to Pops. 'And don't think I'm weird, but I enjoyed it. Good to get back to it again. But I better get some sleep or I'll be nailing my hand to one of those walls tomorrow!'

The next morning I'm awoken by my alarm and someone banging on the door of Nomad.

'Hey Andy,' I say when I see him standing at the door, two cups of coffee in hand.

'Sorry. I woke you up,' he apologises. 'But I brought coffee. And a proposition.'

'You saved me from sleeping in!' I laugh, taking a slurp of the coffee. 'Thanks for the coffee, but sorry, mate, you're not my type.'

'Ha! Not that kind of proposition. I wanted a chat with you, if you've got a few minutes,' he says.

'Sure.' We take a seat at the table in Nomad.

'The board of management have a vacancy at the moment. For a fundraiser/administration manager. I'll cut to the chase. I think you'd be perfect for the role. Are you interested?' Andy says.

'Whoa! You don't hang around! Say that again?' I ask. I'm dumbfounded.

'We need someone primarily to increase the contributions of individuals and groups. Someone who can go out and build relationships with corporate Ireland. Explore new fundraising opportunities from various sources. And as you saw last night, we are in dire need of an accountant. With you, I think we could get both. Kill two birds and all that,' Andy says.

I start to laugh, because I reckon he's pulling my leg. 'For serious?'

'For serious. Pay won't change your life, but it's a salary and you can work from home. Choose your own hours. You'd have to spend some time over here, but not anything that would interfere with home too much. Maybe Mae and the kids would like to come back with you the odd time, in school holidays,' Andy continues.

'You've taken me by surprise here.' I take another sip of the coffee. But I feel excitement bubbling up inside of me.

'You can make a difference,' Andy says.

I stop and look at him, taken aback. 'That's what Pops said.'

'He was right. You can make a difference,' Andy states again. 'Help us make a few ripples over in Ireland.'

'I need to talk to Mae,' I say to him.

'Of course. But are you interested?' he asks again.

I start to laugh again, 'Hell, yes!'

I head to the orphanage to see Mae and find myself

running, so eager I am to get to her. She's in the break room making a coffee when I go in.

'I had such a breakthrough today!' she exclaims. 'Remember that kid I told you about, Magda, the five-year-old?'

'The one that bites you every day?' I say. Mae has managed to accumulate quite a few bruises courtesy of that little girl. But she's not complained about it, even once.

'Yep, well, she's been a tough one to crack. Gloria says that no one has managed to get close to her. Every time I went near her this week, she lashed out at me. She's got some kick on her! But today, just now, she smiled at me. A big, toothless, beautiful smile,' Mae tells me.

'That's brilliant,' I say to her. Mae is jubilant.

'We have to come back here, Olly. Two weeks is not long enough. There is so much more I'd like to do with the school. It needs a library in the worse way. I know the very place we could put it. And we could get the older kids to run it, on a rota. Give them some responsibility. I'm sure I can get the books donated in Ireland, if I get on to some of the schools.'

Mae is buzzing with ideas, her words tumbling out in a rush.

'I could talk to the local libraries too! Bet they have some books spare they could donate.'

'You could talk to the fundraising manager here about all those ideas. See if he can help you,' I say to her.

'Good idea. Who is that?' she asks. 'Have we met him?'

'You happen to know him very well,' I say and fill her in on Andy's suggestion.

'Did you say yes?' she demands.

'No, of course not. Not without speaking to you,' I say. 'But Mae, I want this so bad. I know it's the right job for me, for us. It won't interfere with home. I can still help out with the kids, I'm sure I can work my trips here around school holidays.'

'What on earth are you doing standing here for? Get your ass back there right now and say yes. This is perfect for you. For us!' she says, eyes alight with excitement.

'You don't mind if I have to travel a bit? Be away from home?' I say.

'That's just details. We'll work them out later. Together. Now go accept that offer!'

Together. That word has never sounded so good. Every single misunderstanding, hurt feeling, lonely moment that led us to here, in this orphanage, has been worth it.

'Together,' I repeat.

'Yes.' She looks at me and smiles and I realise that the unanswered, unfathomable questions I've seen glisten in her eyes have disappeared.

'I'd turn this down in a heartbeat, if I thought it would do anything to jeopardise us, the family,' I say.

'I know you would.'

Everything seems clear to me now. All the bullshit has been stripped away and I know what's important. 'You and the children, our life together means more to me . . . '

'Sssh,' Mae stands up on her tippy-toes and kisses me. 'Olly Guinness, listen to your wife. You've got this.'

Chapter Thirty-Nine

EVIE

It's our last day here in the orphanage and I don't know how I'm going to say goodbye to everyone. Not just the volunteers, but the children.

Dad says we'll be back next summer and that helps a bit, I suppose. He's taken a job with the orphanage and I don't think I've seen him this excited. Except maybe when Liverpool win a game. I look down at Stefan, sleeping in my arms and sing a lullaby to him.

'He's going to miss you,' Gloria says. 'You're a natural with the small ones.'

'I'll miss him,' I say. 'But I'll come back again, Gloria. I promise.'

I'm going to help Dad do some fundraising. I have an idea about a *Guinness Book of Records* attempt we could do to raise funds. A convoy of caravans and motorhomes across Ireland, or something like that. I emailed Luke, Ann and Lulu last night and they all said they'd help me.

Martina and Deirdre pop into my head. I'm sure they'll

have loads to say about how lame that idea is. But I realise I don't care what they think any more.

'To hell with them,' I whisper to Stefan. I'm one of the lucky ones. I've had a privileged childhood – more than all these kids in here.

'I'm going to help you have a brighter future,' I vow to Stefan.

I spent so long at the beginning of this trip, counting down the days, wishing I could get home again. And now that we are down to our last two weeks, I want time to slow down. I can't wait to see Ann. It's weird, but I feel like we've been best friends our whole lives. And Luke has already planned an ice-cream date with me, when I get home. I know he's been having a rubbish summer.

'It's time to say goodbye. We've got to go up to the site now.' Dad pops his head into the baby room.

I give Stefan one more kiss and place him in his crib. Gloria walks with me to the playroom, where Jamie is playing with all his friends.

'He's a real-life superhero,' Gloria says to Mam and Dad, as Jamie swoops around the room like Spiderman. Mam is crying and I realise I'm only a nano-second from joining in too.

'Did you say goodbye to Magda?' I ask her. I know she must be finding that one the hardest. She's spent so much time with her this week.

'Yes,' she replies. 'She bit me again, as I hugged her. But then, when I walked away, she said my name and then ran over to me and hugged me one more time.'

'You worked hard with her. And you've done a great job. I know it's awful saying goodbye. But Magda will be fine, I promise you. We'll keep working with her. And she'll soon realise that she doesn't need to attack everyone that comes near her,' Gloria tells Mam.

'We'll be back next summer,' Mae promises, hugging Gloria.

'I know,' Gloria says. 'I always get a sense about the ones who'll come back. Romania isn't done with the Guinnesses yet.'

We leave the orphanage holding hands and we walk up to the construction site. The first of the houses is ready and we get to see the new owners move in before we leave.

It feels like Christmas Day. The air is heavy with excitement and anticipation of a sackful of great gifts about to arrive. Skippy has tied a big red ribbon around the front of the lodge, resplendent against the brown woody frame. The construction volunteers are all lined up on either side of the house and Dad joins them, with Jamie.

They call me and Mam to join them too, because Skippy says we hammered a few nails in.

'Even if they were crooked!' he teases.

Then a woman and two children arrive with Andy. They have a rucksack each on their backs.

'At a guess, that's all they own in the world,' Dad says.

'They have each other, they don't need anything else,' Mam replies and I nod. I get that now.

As they get closer to the house, the woman starts to cry and the children follow soon with tears of their own. It must be overwhelming to walk up and see us all lined up, watching them. The woman keeps repeating something over and over.

Andy shakes her hand and hugs the children. 'This is Liliana and her two children, Razvan and Nicole. And what she is saying is: You don't live, but you don't die either. Maybe now we can live.'

You don't live, but you don't die, I repeat the words to myself over and over.

I wonder what horrors they have all faced in their lives to warrant such a statement. And what strength they have to be here still. Fighting to live their lives.

Flashes of the girls in school taunting me, making fun of me, bound around in my head. I repeat Liliana's words again: You don't live, but you don't die either. Maybe now we can live.

'I'm not going to let Martina or Deirdre get to me ever again,' I say to Mam. 'I'm going to live, stop being scared.'

She looks surprised at me bringing this up. But she turns to me and says, 'You already are living. You're stronger than you can ever know. The way you've handled yourself this summer, but these two weeks in particular, is incredible. I am so proud of you, but you should be proud of yourself. You can do anything.'

'Like go back to school, to hell with the lot of them?' I say.

'Yes, exactly. Why should you leave when you've done nothing wrong? Because it's their bad. The best way to defeat a bully? Ignore them. And live your best life,' Mam tells me.

Dad picks up Jamie in his arms and Mam puts her arms around me and we all watch Liliana cut the ribbon to her new life. The children run and open the door.

'*Mulţumesc mulţumesc!*' Liliana sobs when she walks

through the door. We don't need a translation for those words. Thank you, thank you, she is saying.

As I look around at everyone clapping and cheering, some wiping away tears, I know that right now, in this moment, I'm changed.

Chapter Forty

JAMIE

Maybe I'll be a superhero builder when I get bigger, instead of a superhero robot.

Kind of like Bob the Builder only with superhero powers.

And a cape.

Chapter Forty-One

Dear Olly and Mac

My head is full of you all. What it's been like these past few weeks? Would you believe I've just put down the phone to Andy? More than any other part of this trip, I'm most excited about this one. I've told him all about you all. He's a good guy, but you know that by now.

From what he's shared with me, there's magic in Ripples. I hope you all got to experience that.

While I don't know what has happened these past two weeks, I'm so proud right now. Because I know that you will have all been amazing, in whatever role you played out there.

I've been thinking about us, Olly. A lot. Dangerous thing to do, I know. Many men go through life feeling regret for the relationship or lack of relationship they have with their sons. It can be a precarious, complex dynamic. I've listened to colleagues over the years confess that they don't know who their sons are. That they don't understand them and have such different interests that the gulf between them feels as big as the Grand Canyon. But that's not how it is with us two. Maybe it's because of Beth's death, but I don't think we could be any closer. It's always been us two against the world.

There's not a single person I like more than you, Olly. My son.

And I say the word 'like' on purpose. I know that most parents automatically love their children. But here's the thing. A lot don't like them.

And that goes for you too, Mae. People give lip service to the phrase that you gain a daughter when your son marries. But that's exactly what happened to me. I know how lucky I am that I have you, Mae. Thank you for letting me be such an integral part of your family. A lot wouldn't have put up with the intrusion.

So, I reckon you'll be tired though now. Fancy a little treat? Your penultimate week involves a drive through Serbia to Croatia. I've booked you into a five-star hotel in Belgrade for two nights. What do you think about that? I hear the spa is pretty good there, so that might help revive you all! Park up Nomad for a couple of days and have some much-deserved luxury.

Then, when you leave Belgrade, you are to make your way to the coast in Croatia. I've found a gem of a campsite right on the beach.

My challenge for this week is that you learn how to snorkel. I've always wanted to do that, but never got a chance. Be my eyes. Do it for me, will you?

Olly, you remarked to me earlier today that I'm looking better. And I am feeling better. And I think I know why. Doing this for you all. For my family that I love with all my heart.

I know I keep saying this, but I wish I could be there with you. But know this, I'm watching this adventure, every second of it.

Much love
Pops x

Chapter Forty-Two

MAE

'Oh. My. God, Wi-Fi again!' Evie shrieks with delight, eyes glued to her phone.

'Oh. My. God, never mind Wi-Fi, look at the size of this bathroom!' I respond with an even bigger shriek.

I start to run the bath immediately, looking in the basket of toiletries for some bubble bath. It's hard to believe that we are in Serbia. Just thinking about our journey, where we've been, is a mind-trip. The past two weeks in Romania are already beginning to feel like a dream now.

I can't get Liliana's words from my head. You don't live, but you don't die either. And I feel humbled that something we had a small part in changed that outlook for her. I hope she is living now. She deserves that chance.

I wonder, does she know that she has changed us too? I'm going to write to her when we get home. Tell her that. Because I feel like we're living our best lives now. We're finally becoming the very best version of our family that we can be. The time spent at Ripples was so good for us, working apart, working together for a common goal. I could imagine how we'll be when we get home. I can go back to work and we can co-parent the children together. Because they need both of us. It doesn't matter who makes the dinner, just that it's made.

We don't stray far from the hotel much over the next few days. We all need some downtime to do nothing but eat lots of food, lie by the hotel pool and sleep. Pops booked us a suite, with three bedrooms. It's nearly the size of our house at home! And despite the fact that we've all been bemoaning the lack of space we have in Nomad, we find ourselves all congregating in one of the rooms, staying close to each other.

Our few excursions to the city are uninspiring, if I'm honest. The wars of the 1990s have stained the pedestrianised streets, colouring the landscape.

It's funny, but at first I feel guilty using the spa at the hotel. It's as if I'm cheating my friends back at Ripples. It takes me twenty-four hours to switch off, relax and accept that it's okay to have a treat. By the time we leave, to start our four-hour drive to the campsite in Porec, I feel rejuvenated.

I find myself thinking about how different our lives are to those of the children and their absent parents in Ripples. Olly says that we shouldn't forget. We need to remember how lucky we are, how privileged our lives are. And he's right, of course. Pops told us right at the start that he wanted the children to see that there was a much bigger world out there than at home. I wonder, did he have any idea of the impact this journey would have on Olly and

I? Because we are all changed. With every mile we've driven, we've taken another step towards each other.

Our campsite in Croatia is pretty impressive. We're on a pitch right next to the beach, and the water changes from green to blue depending on the time of the day.

It has multiple swimming pools and lots of games and activities, so Jamie is really happy with that. We divide our time between the beach and the pool.

Jamie has, of course, already made several new friends in the kids' mini club. Evie acclimatises to having Wi-Fi in her life again and is back chatting to Luke and Ann daily. But we don't mind. She's smiling and does join in on some of the tournaments the campsite runs for volleyball and table tennis. And she turns out to be quite good at table tennis, winning several games in a row. I'm going to look into a local club in Wexford when we get home. It might give her a new avenue for meeting like-minded friends.

We have a glorious day learning to snorkel along the Croatian coast. Because it's rocky, our instructor tells us it makes this kind of seabed perfect for snorkelling, with excellent underwater visibility.

Then our guide throws in that in the Adriatic Sea we won't find dangerous sea creatures like sharks or barracudas. I hadn't even thought of that until he said the word 'shark', but now that's all I can think of. The water is crystal-clear and warm. At first I just can't find the nerve to place my head under water. Even though I have my little tank and snorkel and am completely safe, I don't trust I will be able to breathe. Olly is so patient with me. While the children take to it like ducks to water, he stays by my side, urging me to give it a go. And once I manage to try it and find out that I can breathe under water, I'm hooked. There's a whole new world underneath the crystal-blue seas.

At our orientation, we were all told about some shipwrecks. Of course Jamie is hell-bent on finding buried treasure. I can see him swimming around in circles looking for a splash of gold, with Olly chasing after him, keeping him close.

I am spellbound by the colours I see underwater. The reef is coated with green, brown and red algae. Yellow coral dazzles me, like buttercups in an aqua-blue meadow. I see lots of small fish darting in and out of the rocks, as if playing hide and seek with me. Then a bright-red sea urchin, its spikes ready to pierce a stray foot, illuminates the rocky floor.

Then I feel a hand on my arm and swim around to face Olly. He holds his hand out to me and I take it and we swim together, kicking our flipper feet hard towards Evie and Jamie, who are swimming side by side. He beckons them and points to the far right. He wants us to follow him. So we all swim side by side, eyes wide as we look around us. We circle around a large reef and he points to the rocky seabed. We all see it at the same time and are overjoyed for Jamie, as he reaches down. A small gold pot, about four inches in size, lies on its coral bed.

Jamie has found his sunken treasure.

Once we go back to the shore, Jamie throws off his snorkel and jumps up and down, delighted with himself. 'I found the treasure. Look, I really did!'

'Pretty cool, little bro,' Evie says.

'You did good,' I whisper to Olly.

'What?' he replies with a wink. He planted the gold pot. I know he did. He made one of our son's dreams come true. And I love him for that.

We are all hungry after our swim and head to the restaurant, sitting outside under a canopy, with blue seas and skies as our canvas.

'Lots of courageous dishes here, Mam,' Evie says, pointing to the menu.

I order black-squid risotto and Olly a dish called *brudet*, which turns out to be a spicy fish stew. Jamie tries the local sausages, but they turn out to be way too spicy. Thank goodness for chips! Evie tucks into a tuna-fish salad, which is her new favourite thing to eat. I call to the waiter and ask him to take a photograph of us, with the sea as our backdrop. I don't think I'll ever forget this moment, but in case I do, I want a snapshot.

'Look at us,' I say to them all, showing them the digital image. 'Have you ever seen a happier, more good-looking bunch?'

We all laugh at this, congratulating ourselves. I flick back to the first picture taken of us in Bayeux, on our first week. We're on the beach and Fred took it for us. We are unrecognisable as the same family.

White faces and limbs are now brown and glowing. Scowls and frowns are replaced with smiles and laughter. Hunched shoulders are now relaxed. And hurt and fear now banished, with only love and strength in the faces of us all.

The Guinness family.

Chapter Forty-Three

Dear Olly and Mae

Here's a little song to set the mood for today's letter. Do you know it?

When the moon hits your eye
Like a big pizza pie, that's amore
When the world seems to shine
Like you've had too much wine, that's amore

You've guessed it from the clue, right? Week eight. Who would have thought it? Your final week and it's goodbye to sunny Croatia and hello to . . .

Dean Martin gave it away didn't he? You're off to Italy. Lake Como, to be precise.

Apart from George-Clooney-watching and taking in the beauty of the lakes, there's an important job I need you to do for me there. Your last challenge and I know it's going to be tough. But you guys are strong now, right?

Beth and I had our honeymoon at Lake Como. The week we had there together was one of the most perfect weeks of my life. There's something about the lakes that has an old-world elegance. You'll see it yourself soon, but it looks like a film set, with the fancy villas and hotels on the hilltops above the lake.

I remember telling Beth that Lake Como was the perfect destination for her. Because she was like a film star to me. Elegant, beautiful, breathtaking. She wore a pretty dress every day of our honeymoon and would have given Grace Kelly a run for her money.

Beth joked that we were in Italy's romantic Ring of Kerry. And that made me smile. We were a million miles away from Ireland, or so it felt. Then one day, Beth wanted to go for a picnic, so we asked our hotel for help. They packed a fabulous hamper for us and sent us to Punta Spartivento, which literally means 'the point that divides the wind'. Isn't that wonderful?

Sitting on a blanket, our picnic laid out between us, I felt like we'd stepped into a Renoir painting. There we were in the shadow of the Swiss Alps, gazing out at the still lake. I can remember saying to Beth that if this was as good as it gets, I'd die happy.

I told her that day that she was my world. And she was at that time, until you came along, Olly, making my world a bigger and more beautiful place.

As I get closer to dying, I am getting more reflective on my life. Memories keep coming back, like a tag team, replacing one another, over and over. Happy and sad times.

But that day on that picnic was pretty much one of the happiest in my life. So I want to go back to that spot one more time. Beth and I are part of its story, part of the fabric that makes it so special. We planned to go back with you one day, Olly. But we never did. I regret that.

So will you do one more thing for your old Pops? Will you bring me back to that spot and say your goodbyes to me there? Scatter my ashes in the point that divides the wind. Try not to be sad, try to be happy for me. Because I know I'll reconnect with my Beth there. I have faith.

Before I go, I want you all to know that each and every one of you has given me so many happy memories. I've lived a good life, the best life, because I've had you with me. So thank you.

I hope this adventure has been a good experience for you. I hope you realise that you have something special. All that matters is family, each other. Hold that tight when everything else gets crazy in life.

Olly, my son, my heart. I'll see you again one day. You can bank on that. Be happy, lad.

Mae, Evie, Jamie, be happy, love one another, okay?

For the last time,

Goodbye,
Pops x

Chapter Forty-Four

OLLY

It took a while for me to find the perfect spot at Punta Spartivento. I left Mae and the kids at our campsite enjoying the sunshine. I walked for hours along the shores of the alpine lake, searching. As Pops said, it was a breathtaking location, a cascading ribbon of blue lakes, surrounded by the Swiss mountains.

I felt the weight of responsibility to find the right place to release Pops' ashes to the wind. I tried to put myself in Pops' and Mam's shoes all those years ago. Where would they have laid out their picnic? I tried to look at likely spots through their eyes. With their hearts full of love and romance, I'm quite certain they would have wanted somewhere private, away from prying eyes. Because my mam was not the type for public displays of affection.

So I avoid the main picnic spots along the lake. Instead I trek up small walkways, towards a lighthouse until, finally, I see it.

On our last day in Lake Como, we walk up to fulfill

Pops' last challenge. We're a sombre group, silent the whole way.

'This is it,' Mae says. 'Wow, it's breathtaking. You've chosen well.'

The view from this vantage point is dazzling. The distant Alps are softly silhouetted against the early-morning sky. It's early, as I want to take no chances of any interruptions from passersby. I feel it's unlikely that there are any trekkers out and about at six a.m.

Jamie is holding Evie's hand, both with eyes wide. I know that this is incredibly hard for them, but I also know that they need to be here. Because I am clutching Pops' urn and I'm not sure if I have the strength to let it go. With them by my side, I'll find the strength to do it.

Mae says, 'Look at the rainbow colours of all those rooftops.'

Vividly painted walls of sunshine yellow and ochre reflect on the deep-blue lake before us. Is this your heaven, Pops?

'It's time,' Mae says. 'Let's share our memories of Pops. Who'd like to start?'

We'd agreed the night before that we should do something to make the scattering more ceremonial. We came up with the idea that each of us would say a few words about our own special 'Pops' memories. But now, it appears we are all dumbstruck.

'I'll go first,' Mae says. 'I've got so many happy memories, it's hard to choose. But the one that sticks out for me is back when we first married. I'd just moved into our house. But it didn't feel like my home, it felt like yours and Pops' house, I suppose.'

She looks to the children and smiles, 'And the decor left a lot to be desired! The kitchen was an explosion of terracotta and burnt orange. I used to get a headache looking at it with my morning cuppa. But I didn't know how to say I didn't like it. It didn't seem right to come in and start throwing my weight around.'

I smile, remembering that kitchen. Pops and I thought we were designers of the year when we painted it.

Mae continues, 'But Pops always seemed to read minds, didn't he? One morning, after you'd gone to work, Olly, I was having breakfast and he asked me what my favourite colour was. I told him it was green. Olive-green. I'd no idea what he was up to. I thought he was just curious. But when I came home from work that day, I found him in the kitchen knee-deep in olive-green paint.'

Mae sighs as she holds back a sob. 'He said, "It's all yours, Mae. I'm just the lodger. You paint it any colour you want." I loved him before that, but in that moment, I adored him.'

Funny how things get lost in time, but when they are recalled it's as if they were yesterday. 'I came home and you two were giggling like kids. Covered in paint, but the kitchen did look much better.'

Evie then takes her turn. 'My memory of Pops is when I was about five. We were walking down north main street in Wexford and I was holding his hand, skipping along. I loved holding Pops' hand.'

'He loved holding yours,' I say to her.

'He'd promised he was going to buy me a present. We passed by a hairdresser's. And in the window was one of those doll's heads they use sometimes to show hairstyles off. A hairdressing doll, I suppose. I took a shine to it and asked Pops for it. He tried to talk me out of it, saying it wasn't a real toy, it wasn't for sale. But I couldn't be swayed. I was adamant I wanted that doll. So in we went and he started pleading for it. The owner of the salon kept saying, "It's not for sale." And Pops kept repeating, "But my granddaughter has her heart set on it." I don't know how much he paid for it, but he made sure I went home with that doll.'

'He would have done anything for you, Evie,' I tell her.

'I know. I miss him so much,' Evie starts to cry a river and Mae hugs her close.

Then she turns to Jamie, who is still silent. 'Do you want to speak, darling?' she asks him. He nods without speaking, so she kneels down beside him, pulling him in close to her.

'I miss playing superheroes with Pops. He always let me be the superhero. He was a great baddie. He roared like a dragon more better than anyone else,' Jamie stammers out. Tears follow within an instant.

I look at Mae and the children, all with faces awash with tears, but I remain dry-eyed. I look down at the urn and see white knuckles that are clenching the urn so tight.

Mae looks at me and then hugs the children before walking over to me.

'It's time to say your goodbyes.' She kisses me, a soft caress on my cheek. And when I remain silent, she whispers, 'You've got this.'

'Pops was the last link I had to Mam,' I whisper.

'I know,' Mae says and I'm grateful that she doesn't try to mollify me with a platitude.

I was the only child of two parents who both adored not just me but each other too. I wonder sometimes did I imagine how good it was back then? Was there as much love in that house as I remember now as an adult? But I know I've not created an idolised version of history for myself. Even after Mam died, Pops never faltered or changed in his love and support of me, his only son. So no rose-tinted glasses for me, because I had a good childhood. All because of Pops.

I look at the urn and run my fingers on the engraved plate that says his name. 'I don't have any one memory of Pops, just a lifetime of moments. Him teaching me how to ride my bike. Drive my car. Kick a football. Watching Liverpool together. He bought me my first pint. I felt so proud that day, sitting on a bar stool, two cold pints of Guinness in front of us, toasting the family business. Walking out of the delivery room, each time you guys were born, and him sitting there, waiting for me. He was always there, waiting for me, no matter what I was doing. He wasn't just my dad, you know. He was my best friend,' I say.

'But you were his best friend too,' Mae tells me. 'That's something that most parents don't get to experience. What you both had was special.'

I nod. I know that. 'Pops, this isn't goodbye. It's just farewell for now, because guess what? I've got faith now that one day I'll see you again. This journey has taught me that,' I say. 'Tell Mam I love her. I want you to know that this epic adventure you created for us, it's changed us all.'

I look to my family and they all nod at my words.

'You've given us a gift that we will never be able to say thank you enough for. So what we'll do instead is keep loving each other. And we'll live our best lives. And we'll not leave anything unsaid. I promise you that,' I say.

I open the top of the urn and kiss the top of the ashes, closing my eyes for a moment in silent goodbye to a great man.

And then I scatter Pops' ashes into the point where the wind divides, tears finally falling in tribute of my pops.

Once the urn is empty, we sit down, shoulder to shoulder, looking out to the beautiful landscape. Silent, except for tears of grief and loss. But despite my pain, my unbearable pain, I am at peace. I'm not sure how long we sit like that, in perfect silence and harmony, but finally our tears dry up and we feel strong enough to move.

I stand up and look at my family.

I remember Pops' words in his final letter to us. He told us that we had made his world a bigger and more beautiful place. I understand that now. Because Mae, Evie and Jamie have done that for me too. Yes, Pops, you are right, I think. If this is as good as it gets, that's fine by me.

I pull Mae to her feet and say to my family, 'Come on, you lot. It's time to find our way back home.'

Epilogue

May 2016

OLLY

It's Jamie's communion in three days' time. Mae is fussing over his hair, wondering does it need another trim? Evie is teasing him about his shoes, which are too shiny and new and not in the least bit cool. He takes the comments from two of the women in his life in his stride. There's little in life that worries him. And that's as it should be.

Back in 1981, when I was his age, my biggest worry was whether Liverpool was going to win the league for the thirteenth time. Hours were spent with Pops discussing the worth of Ian Rush, whether he would be worthy of his transfer fee.

I've watched Jamie's face change in the last few months. The baby roundness is gone and I can see glimpses of the young man he's going to become. And sometimes he looks at me and I can see Pops. I never used to think he looked like him, but he does. And that makes me happy.

'What time is your flight on Monday again?' Mae shouts over the whistle of the kettle she's boiling.

'Early. I'll be gone by four a.m.,' I reply. I'm itching to get back to Ripples. We've finally succeeded in getting a new government grant. I've not told them yet. I want to see Andy's face in person when I break the news. We can make a real impact and build housing for many more families.

'And you'll tell them about the books I've gotten?' Mae says, placing a cup of coffee in front of me.

'Yes. I promise I will. Gloria will be thrilled to hear about the new donation of books. That library of yours will need its own building yet by the time you're done!' I say and pull her into my lap for a quick squeeze.

'I want a school house and a library. You know that,' she replies, not missing a beat. But then leans down and kisses me.

'We'll do it,' I promise and know that between us we can do anything we put our minds to. And living proof of that just ambles into the room.

'Mama, may I juice please?'

MAE

'Oh my goodness, that was just beautiful manners, Magda!' I say to the little girl tugging my arm. 'Did you hear that, Dada?'

'I sure did. That's my clever girl.'

She beams in response to the praise and holds her arms up to me saying, 'Carry.'

She's small for her age, only weighing three stone, but we'll build her up in time. I feel her bones sticking into my ribcage as she squeezes me tight.

401

'Snuggles,' she sighs and I stroke her hair gently.

'Yes. Snuggles. Mama Mae loves them.' I look over her head and nod once, as Olly looks at me. I know what he's thinking. That's the third time in a row she's looked for snuggles herself. We're making real progress here.

We thought we'd never swing it. Endless paperwork to become foster parents and we've got mountains more to plough through so that we can achieve our ultimate goal of adopting her. I thought we'd never be allowed to bring her home, but she's here now and settled into her life as a Guinness.

Finally, she seems to believe us, to trust us that she's here to stay as part of our family.

EVIE

'So we are really going to do this?' Ann says.

'Yep. It's all in place. On June first we start the convoy from here. We've got nearly four hundred motor homes lined up.'

'Four hundred and one, because Sophie and Melissa hired a motor home for the day too!' Luke says, grinning.

'That's fantastic.'

'And I've contacted all the local papers and also the radio stations. They've all promised to come along,' Luke adds.

'Most importantly, the *Guinness Book of Records* official confirmed he'd be here too!' I say. It's been a lot of work, but I don't care. I'm elated to pull it off. We've got local sponsors from a number of big businesses. As it stands, we've cleared nearly three thousand euros, after any costs are paid.

'Luke, time for you to say goodnight. It's getting late. Olly said he'll run you home, it's no night to be cycling,' Mam pops her head into the family room.

'Okay, Mrs G. That would be great.'

'I can't be doing looking at you two getting all smoochy smoochy together. I'm off to torment Jamie,' Ann declares, winking at me as she goes out. She's staying for a sleepover tonight. We're planning on watching the *Hunger Games* trilogy back to back.

'You did it,' Luke says to me. 'I knew you would.'

'We did it, Luke. You, me and Ann. We did it together.'

'And even though my sisters have a caravan for the convoy, I still want to ride in Nomad with you.'

'I was hoping you'd say that. You have to be up there at the front with me and Ann.'

'Luke. Are you right, come on!' Dad shouts in.

'I better go before your old fella loses it. I'll call you later, okay?' He leans in and kisses me and I wrap my arms up around his neck, leaning in close.

I walk with him to the front door and even though Dad is watching, I don't stop holding his hand. I love him. We've not said that to each other, but we will one day soon. Because I know he feels the same way too.

Mam said yesterday that she worries that we are both too young to be so serious about each other. But she's wrong and I told her so.

Love knows no age. *Love just is.*

I wish Pops were here to see the record-breaking attempt with me. But I feel his presence all the time. Little things that happen, that we all call Wi-Fi now, that make us remember his words, his letters, his love.

OLLY

I pretend to scowl at Evie and Luke as they kiss goodbye. It's in my job description to be the over-protective dad. But in truth, I don't mind in the least. I like the kid. Luke is a good guy and has proved himself over and over this past year or so. Not least of which in his enthusiasm to help Evie and Ann organise the record-breaking attempt.

I'm so proud of Evie. It's been a work in progress, teaching her to be confident, to walk with her head held high. We had to be careful not to make her too reliant on us. In the end she went back to her own school and looked Martina and Deirdre in the eye, telling them that she forgave them. And I think that killed them both more than anything else. They wanted a row, they wanted the drama, but they didn't get it. Evie just got on with her life and eliminated the toxic parts of it.

That's what we've all done, really. There's days when Mae and I barely see each other because of work. But every night, no matter what has gone on that day, we go to bed together. When I'm in Romania, we Skype every day and I can honestly say that I never leave anything unsaid.

I don't think even my wise Pops could have predicted how life-changing his surprise adventure would be for us all. Our lives are unrecognisable, yet exactly as they were and how they should be now. None of us want to take this for granted. We don't want to forget. So between us all, we came up with our Guinness Family House Rules, which we've had printed, framed and hung in our hallway. These rules are mostly based on the wisdom Pops imparted to us. But we came up with a few of our own lessons too.

The Guinness Family found their way back home.

The Guinness Family House Rules

Once you are with family, you are home.

Leave nothing unsaid.

Grief is inevitable. It's okay to cry.

Keep your eyes open for 'Wi-Fi'.

Take risks.

Life can be as complicated or as simple as you want it to be.

Raising your voice doesn't make what you say any truer.

When kerdumps happen, look for the apples, not the axe murderer.

Sometimes the only way to a happy ending is to find a new beginning.

Talk. Listen. Share. Laugh.

Life is not meant to be lived in one place. Boldly go!

If you love someone, tell them.

Have courageous palates.

It's okay to be different.

Never dis a Brie.

Work hard, learn, teach and make a difference.

Remember how lucky you are, how privileged your life is.

Live your best life.

All that matters is family

Acknowledgements

Dear Reader

My first thanks go to you all! Whether you've been with me since the beginning or this is your first Mrs H read, I'm so very grateful that you chose The Things I Should Have Told You. *I love our chats on Facebook and Twitter. One of the nicest parts of this writing malarkey is the wonderful fun I have with you all, talking books! Know that every message of support, every review, every shout-out is cherished.*

I hope you enjoyed the Guinness Family and their story about how they made their way home to each other. Over the years, like them, I've also boldly gone and travelled the world. I've backpacked around the Greek Islands, whale-watched in Fremantle Harbour in the Australian sunshine, flown around South Africa in a two-seater Cessna, survived an earthquake in the Philippines and snorkelled in the Caribbean seas whilst holding hands with my husband. I've wept in the Garden of Remembrance in Berlin and joyfully watched my children do the hot-dog dance with Mickey Mouse in Disney World. These travels have given me some of the best adventures of my life. And there's no doubt that these experiences have helped to shape me into the woman I am today.

Like the Guinnesses, I want to teach my children that the world is both a big and a small place. That abject poverty can sit side by side with lavish wealth and kindness can be found in the most remote and unusual of places.

As a child, I was a book nerd, just like Evie. And like her, I was bullied too. So to all the Evies out there, young or old, remember that being different is kinda cool. Don't let the bullies win, don't change, you are perfect just as you are.

Thank you to Tracy Brennan, my fabulous agent, for all your hard work on my behalf and for your friendship. I'd also like to thank the amazing team at HarperCollins Ireland – Tony Purdue, Mary Byrne and Ann-Marie Dolan for welcoming me into your little family and taking such good care of me. We've had a lot of fun over this past year and I can't wait to see what the next twelve months bring.

Thank you to everyone at HarperCollins UK who played a part to help bring The Things I Should Have Told You to life – Kimberley Young, Jaime Frost, Cait Davies, Elizabeth Dawson, Lucy Vanderbilt, Charlie Redmayne and so many more. Thank you to Heike Schüssler for the amazing cover art. Special thanks to Charlotte Ledger, friend and warrior queen, the first to see something in my

The Things I Should Have Told You

writing, who made my dream a reality. And to Emily Ruston, my editor, for her wonderful suggestions that helped make the Guinness family sparkle, I will be forever grateful. You pushed me hard, but the story is so much better for it.

The life of an author could be solitary, but for me, I'm lucky to have a huge gang of writerly friends, who find ways to hold me up when I'm under pressure and who also make life a whole lot more fun. In no particular order, thank you to Claudia Carroll, Hazel Gaynor, Cat Hogan, Sharon Thompson, Maria Nolan, Alex Browne, Margaret Madden, Louise Hall, Ciara Murphy, Caroline Busher, Catherine Evans, Damian Byrne, Lynn Marie Hulsman, the team behind Wexford Literary Festival, the IWI'ers and the amazing supportive book blogger community, too many to mention. Thank you also to Elaine Crowley of TV3's Midday show for letting me be part of your fantastic show, it's always great fun.

Special thanks to Sophie Hedley, of 'Reviewed the Book', who has, for each of my books, done a Twitter daily countdown to publication day and to Melissa Puli, commissioning editor of ChickLit Club, all-round legend who came up with the genius Guinness surname for my family! I hope that you like that I named Luke's sisters after you both.

My supportive family and friends, I love and thank you. Mam and Dad – Tina and Michael O'Grady; my siblings and their other halves – Fiona and Michael Gainfort, John and Fiona O'Grady, Michelle and Anthony Mernagh; my in-laws – Mrs Evelyn

409

Harrington, Adrienne Harrington and George Lawlor, Evelyn and Seamus Moher and Leah Harrington; nieces and nephews – Sheryl, Amy, Louis, Paddy and Matilda; aunt and uncle – Ann and Nigel Payne; and my person, Ann Murphy. Evie's best friend is pretty special so I couldn't think of a better name for her than yours, my best friend.

I'm going to reach out to my own 'Wi-Fi' now and thank my grandparents. (This will only make sense if you've read the book!) While they are not here any more, they kind of are, because they are part of the wonderful and wise Pops. Margaret and John O'Grady, John Farrelly and Corinne Syms taught me so much about family, love and life. I miss them and wish that they were still here with us all.

I'm lucky to have lots of friends who help keep me sane! The dinners, drinks, chats and laughs but also the support you give me with the children when I'm under pressure with a deadline are incredible. Catherine and Graham, Sarah and John, Rosaleen and Chris, Davnet and Kevin, Fiona and Philip (keep moving those books around P!), my childhood pals Maria, Siobhan and Elizabeth.

I know that if this were the Oscars, the music has started and it's time for me to exit stage left. Nearly done, I promise! Huge thanks to Crossabeg Childcare Centre. Nate will join Amelia in school this September (sob!!!) and the H's say goodbye to all at the centre. Every single member of staff there, past and present, took such good care of my children. Knowing that they were safe and loved made it easy for me to switch off and write. That has been a gift.

The last words must go to my H's. As Pops said, all that matters is family. We know that's true, right? Roger, Amelia, Nate and Eva, you are the loves of my life. As I always say, I couldn't do this without you all, wouldn't want to.

Thank you all for reading,

Carmel

Q&A with
Carmel Harrington

What was your inspiration for this story and why did you decide to write about the Guinness family?

I've always wanted to write about a family who travel and how seeing the world from a new vantage point, can change you. If a family were fractured, what impact would their travels have on them? Throwing them into a small space like Nomad seemed like the perfect way to explore the complex dynamics of family life. I particularly wanted to look at the relationships between husband and wife, parent and child, and how lies and half-truths can tear people apart. Ultimately I wanted to write a story that explored the true meaning of home, of family, of love. I hope I have created a moving portrait of family life for my readers.

Do you see yourself or anyone close to you in the characters you have created?

Actually yes, I do. My grandparents are all wrapped up in Pops character. Their wisdom, fun, and love for family is in his every word and action. In fact, the story that Evie shares about Pops buying her the hairdresser doll, is mine. My step grandfather, John-dad, did that for me. I've never forgotten it. And there's bits of me in Evie's character too. Like her, I was a book nerd as a kid (still am!) and unfortunately I was bullied. Jamie's character was inspired by my son Nate. A fellow Spider-Man fan with a vivid imagination and thirst for adventure and fun.

This book is dedicated to your brother and sisters, how important are they to you?

One of the last things that Pops tells his family, is 'all that matters is family' and I couldn't agree more. I have an extremely close relationship with my brother and sisters. We're in steps, only a year between each of us, and as a result all of our childhood memories include each other. That's pretty special.

We all love *The Guinness Family House Rules!* Which are the most important ones to you and your family?

Oh, that's such a tough question! Because I love all of them! *All that matters is family* is at the heart of who I am and what I believe to be true. Taking risks is a big one for me. Had I not taken a leap of faith and changed careers five years ago, I wouldn't be doing this right now! I never leave anything unsaid either, good or bad. And those I love, know it, because I tell them often. Rog and I regularly ask ourselves, are we living our best lives? I can thank Oprah for that little gem! Oh and of course, I never ever dis a brie.

Who are your favourite authors or books and have they had an influence on your writing?

To Kill a Mockingbird had a huge impact on me when I read it as a young teen. It was the first time that I realised that the world could be cruel and unjust. It made me think long after I closed the final page and I loved that. Any author who can leave me with a book hangover is golden as far as I'm concerned. Maeve Binchy, is one of those. She was an early influence, I fell in love with her conversational style of storytelling when I borrowed *To Light a Penny Candle* from Wexford Library as a young woman. I've read it since many times! Other authors I love include JoJo Moyes, Cecelia Ahern, Marian Keyes, Sheila O'Flanagan, Claudia Carroll, Danielle Paige, Dean Koontz, Harlan Coben and Liane Moriarty. All incredible storytellers.

Have you ever taken a similar trip to the adventure the Guinness family go on?

Before I got married, I travelled a lot. I found the travel bug when I worked for Aer Lingus, our national airline. Let's just say, that my friends and I used the staff concessions a lot! I've never done an eight week campervan epic adventure, but it is on my bucket list of things to do! I have backpacked in parts of Europe and also holidayed with family in a small caravan! So many of my experiences are shared through the eyes of the Guinness family. Pops is right. Life is not meant to be lived in one place. Boldly go folks, boldly go!

Laugh, cry and be *inspired*

with more from

CARMEL HARRINGTON

'Will make you see life in a different way'
Woman's Way

'Heartwrenching and heartwarming'
Evening Herald

Read on for an exclusive look at Carmel's stunning Christmas novel, based on the timeless movie *It's a Wonderful Life*.

Every Time a Bell Rings

'Beautiful and uplifting . . . Written with such heart it warms the soul' – Claudia Carroll

'Embraces the spirit and the message of the movie . . . A must read' – Karolyn Grimes, actress, 'ZuZu' in *It's a Wonderful Life*

Prologue

Blessed is the season which engages the whole world in a conspiracy of love.

Hamilton Wright Mabie

Christmas Eve, 2005

'Happiness is ...' I exhale a long, deep, satisfied sigh, and the cold breath of winter floats out of my mouth up into the air.

'*This* is the best Christmas street lighting yet.'

I know I say the same thing every year, in this very same spot, at this very same time. I'll probably say it again next year too.

In this moment, I've never seen anything more perfect. The Victorian-inspired decorations are from a bygone era that shine with goodwill to all men. I know, I know, that sounds all cheese on toast, but when it comes to Christmas, that's allowed. With extra parmesan on top, as far as I'm concerned.

My city, my beloved Dublin, is sparkling in a festive glow. And its inhabitants are collectively holding their breaths, because Christmas is almost here.

And this year, I've been delivered an early Christmas present. The fact that it's the same one I received when I was eight years old isn't lost on me. Coincidence, fate, magic, I don't know what forces are at play to make this happen, but I'm grateful.

Just two weeks ago, I was single, happily so too, living my best life, teaching kids in St Colmcille's. I honest to goodness didn't wake up each day lamenting the lack of love in my life. Because I had a *good* life, boyfriends coming and going. I figured that one day I would meet Mr Right. But now that he is here, I cannot believe that I ever got through each day without him by my side.

Here I am, at the foot of Grafton Street with Jim Looney of all people. If you would have suggested such a thing to me a mere few weeks ago, the words 'look up' and 'flying pigs' would have been uttered.

Jim Looney.

I sigh again as I take him in, standing beside the statue of Molly Malone, laughing at the tinsel that someone has draped over her cleavage.

An image of Jim strutting down a runway pops into my head and I giggle at the thought. He could give any male model a run for their money, but I think he'd rather pull his nails out one by one than do that.

I grab my phone and take a photo of him. I've already taken at least a dozen this evening. He could be modelling a new line in men's winter clothing, he looks so good. I mean, not many could get away with that multi-coloured Dr Who-inspired scarf wrapped around his neck over and over. But on him it looks quirky and cool.

And, this is the bit that I still can't quite believe.

He's my boyfriend. All mine.

Don't go getting too used to this, Belle. It never lasts.

I quickly banish the little voice inside my head. Go away nasty mean voice.

I know full well that I'm punching above my weight. I mean, for goodness sake, he's even got a chiselled jawline. Seriously, I'm telling you, he's fecking gorgeous. I can't find ways to describe him to you without sounding like a big sap. But trust me when I say this. He's, as we are want to say in Dublin about a good-looking man, a 'ride'.

When I look into his big blue eyes, I'm done for. I keep forgetting what I'm about to say when he directs those baby blues at me.

And don't get me started on his hair. That's always been my Achilles heel. It makes me feel all protective and full of love. You see, it has this habit of just flopping over his right eye. I'm sure most would say it's red or ginger, maybe even auburn. But I like to call it foxy.

Jim McFoxy Looney.

When it does that flopping thing, it's as if my hands have a mind of their own and they involuntarily reach up to brush it back off his forehead. But there again, I'm not complaining about that, because I don't need any excuse to touch Jim. And I've realised that when I do touch him, it seems to have a delicious knock-on effect. One minute I'm lightly touching his forearm, then the next we're kissing.

A shiver ripples through me as I remember what happened only this morning when I brushed past him on my way into the bathroom.

Twice.

Who would have thought that Jim Looney had *that* in him? I'm telling you, it's ridiculous how sexy he is.

He is, no other word for it, but a fecking ride.

You'll notice that I'll find any excuse to say that.

Jim Looney, the big ride, my boyfriend.

I feel a bit giddy with it all, to be honest. It's like it's five o'clock all the time and I'm half drunk. The mad thing is, I've not had much to drink in weeks. Jim's not a big drinker and that in itself is charming, because all the guys I've dated recently seem to be more in love with a pint of lager than me. Kind of refreshing to be with a guy who gets that there are more things to do in life than prop up a bar.

'What are you thinking about?' Jim asks, with a raised eyebrow.

'Ah, that would be telling,' I say with a grin.

Thank goodness he can't read thoughts. If I tell him what I've just been thinking, we'll be in a taxi and on our way back to my apartment before the words are out of my mouth. And as tempting as that thought is, it will have to wait.

Because it's Christmas Eve and we're on Grafton Street, where its festive delights await us.

'So, tell me about this tradition of yours, the one you do every Christmas Eve?' Jim asks.

'This is my tenth year. Started because of Joyce O'Connor,' I say.

4

'Why do I get the feeling there's a story there?' Jim remarks.

'Oh yes, there's a story alright. She asked me to go into the city with her one Christmas Eve, when I was fifteen,' I say.

I wonder what Joyce is up to now. We lost touch a long time ago. But she's wrapped up in this particular tradition and standing here usually sparks a memory of her.

She wasn't even a close friend. In fact, if I'm calling a spade a spade, she was a bit of a bitch. I don't know why I said yes in the first place when she asked me to go with her. I mean, she'd been one of those passive aggressive wagons for years. The queen of making snide comments behind my back, giving inverted compliments that everyone knows is really an insult.

I spent half my childhood trying to dodge Joyce and her cronies in the hallways at school. Anything to avoid one of her 'chats'.

'I remember her. At least I think I'm remembering the right one. Blonde, small girl? Touch of the mean girls about her? She was one of the gang who used to give you a hard time,' Jim says.

I laugh, yep, he's got her number. 'Good memory. She had her moments, for sure. And the only reason she asked me to go with her on that day was because she had no other options. Her usual cronies were busy and she needed a decoy. Her parents would never have let her go off to meet a boy on her own. But a nice innocent trip into town with a friend, well, that was different.'

'Oh, I get it. You got to be a big, fat, green, hairy gooseberry,' Jim says.

I nod. 'I'd nothing better to do, so thought, why not? And it made Tess happy when I told her I was off gallivanting. She was always worrying about me being such a loner.'

'Did you have fun in the end?' Jim says. 'Maybe she wasn't as bad as you thought?'

'No, we didn't bond over hot chocolate or anything. She was true to form and remained a wagon. But despite that, I did have fun,' I say.

The 16B bus had been jammers with lots of people with the same idea, to head into the city to soak up the festive atmosphere.

'Joyce didn't even bother keeping up a pretence that we were together for more than a few minutes. Once we jumped on board the bus she ran upstairs to the upper deck and within seconds was doing a round of tonsil hockey with a pimply, horny boy called Billy Doyle. I swear her arse hadn't even hit the seat he'd saved for her before his tongue was down her throat,' I say.

'You can't buy class.' Jim says shaking his head.

'A right dirt bird.' I say and he laughs with me. 'You know, they hadn't even bothered to save a seat for me. As the upper deck was so full, I had no choice but to retreat back downstairs, tail between my legs and stand. Joyce didn't give me a backwards glance, the cheeky mare,' I say.

I marvel that I ever allowed myself to be treated like that.

'Once we arrived at O'Connell Street, the two love birds headed to McDonalds to share a strawberry shake. It was clear I wasn't included in their romantic date, so I left them to it. I suppose I should have been annoyed with her, but I didn't mind in the slightest.'

Jim throws a sympathetic glance my way, but I'm quick to reassure him, 'I was used to my own company back then, preferred it a lot of the time.'

It baffled me as to why they wanted to sit on plastic seats in a noisy fast-food restaurant, when they could be out, soaking up the Christmassy atmosphere in the city.

'It was their loss. I got to explore Dublin, on my own. It was almost dusk and the city changes in that light. Everything seemed so magical.'

I pause, feeling embarrassed, 'This probably sounds silly but, to me, it felt like I was looking at my city with new eyes.'

'Not silly at all.' Jim replies. 'You know what I thought when we got to O'Connell Street? There's a touch of Bedford Falls about it all now. You know, the town in *It's a Wonderful Life.*'

I smile and nod in agreement. I've always thought the same. 'I love that movie.'

I jump as a badly dressed Santa roars in our direction. 'Merry Christmas. Ho ho ho.' He rings his bell and rattles a box loudly, collecting change for charity. He seems intent on frightening passers-by and is clearly delighted with himself when everyone jumps in shock.

I throw a few euro into his box and then Jim says, 'So fill me in on how this tradition of yours works.'

'Well, ever since that year, I've come back each Christmas Eve. I start off in O'Connell Street, then walk over the

Liffey, past Trinity College, say hello to the Molly Malone statue in all her glory, stroll up Grafton Street, then head over to the Ha'penny Bridge, before going home,' I say.

'You ever mix it up and change the route?' Jim asks.

'Oh, God no. Has to be in that order,' I say. 'Oh, I nearly forgot to say, I do have a quick pit stop in Captain America's for hot chocolate and a slice of their, quite frankly, decadent Mississippi Mud Pie. Just to keep the energy levels up.' I grin like a four-year-old.

'Sounds like quite a nice tradition to keep.' Jim says. 'I'm glad I'm here to share it with you this year.'

'I'm glad you're here too. You know, I've had years of strolling up and down this cobbled street with boyfriends, girlfriends, school friends and, yes, I'll even admit it — the shame – on my own a few times.' I look at him, feeling a little shy. 'But this feels special, more than any other year. That's because of you, Jim.'

He grabs my hand and laughs, 'I'm honoured. Come on then, Ms Bailey, show me what this great city of ours has to offer.'

My eyes greedily take in the view ahead of us, down Grafton Street. Red, flickering lights coil around luscious green garlands, which drape from one side of the street to the other. In the centre of each garland is a large red Victorian lantern and the light casts a warm glow over the busy cobbled street. Each shop window is alight with Christmas lights and resplendent baubles in rich jewel colours.

There's something about the energy here … well, it is breathtaking.